THE CUBE
IS COMING

Books are great for—

Reading pleasure

Information

Inspiration

And make **good <u>Gifts</u>**!

If you've enjoyed this one, <u>bless others</u> by sharing it.

<u>Additional copies may be obtained by ordering</u>:

* From the author's e-mail, **gettheword@comcast.net**
* Through the author's web site, **JERRYISMITHMINISTRIES. COM**
* Author's address: Jerry Smith, P.O. Box **591594**, Houston, TX **77259**
* Download as an **e-book** through Xlibris Publishing House, from Amazon, B&N, BoB, Kindle, Nook, Scrib, Sony, Google Search.
* Xlibris online bookstore, **Xlibiris.com**
* From your local book store by using the **ISBN** (International Standard Book Number) below for the order.

Hard cover book	978-1-4771-1847-4
Soft cover book	978-1-4771-1846-7
Ebook	978-1-4771-1848-1

These numbers are like a license plate for each issue of the publication. The number for *this* book is also found on the back cover and on the copyright page.

Thank you for helping make this story known.

THE CUBE IS COMING

A Teaching Novel

Jerry Irvan Smith

Unless otherwise noted, all Scripture quotations have been taken from:

The Berkley Version (TBV), New Testament Copyright ©1945, by Gerrit
Verkuyl; assigned to Zondervan Publishing House 1958; Old Testament
Copyright © 1959 by Zondervan Publishing House. Used by permission.

Holman Christian Standard Bible (HCSB), Copyright © 1999,
2000, 2002, 2003 by Holman Bible Publishers. Used by permission

To order additional copies of this book, contact:
Xlibris Corporation
1-888-795-4274
www.Xlibris.com
Orders@Xlibris.com
116865

CONTENTS

With grateful appreciation to **John Clayton** of Santa Fe, Texas, a beloved long-time friend and faithful deacon who planted the seed for this story

With thanks to **Steven Carpenter**, an exceptionally talented high school computer graphics student and grandson of **John Clayton**, for the excellent cover art

Cast of Characters

Main Characters*

God—The unseen, main character of this book. All persons and events are His means of revealing Himself to mankind and showing His good will for the nations.

Jim Waltham—Physicist, Astronomer; Astronomy professor at Quad State Astronomical University in Odessa, TX; Head of Space Telescope Science Association at Ft. Davis, TX, involving 18 universities; Home of Orion Observatory Complex and the Lippershey Telescope site

Laura Drake Waltham—Jim's wife, mother of Keith & Scott
Marcus Loshan—Associate to Jim and American history buff
Rex Fleming—Pastor, Skyview Church, Odessa, TX
Samuel Stone—Pastor, Faith Church on the Rock
Kenneth Snow—President of the United States of America

David Harris—Head of Dept. of Astronomy at Quad State University and Dean of Faculty

Margaret Thames—TV reporter who is hostile toward Jim

WHY A TEACHNG NOVEL?

The CUBE is Coming deals with issues that have long been a plague to pastors, educators, and people in general: evolution, and understanding the relationship of America's government with Christianity. In this novel, God uses Jim Waltham to address these two difficult matters as a scientist, astronomer, and educator in a university setting. America has a unique relationship with God because its governing principles were based clearly upon the Word of God. It parallels Israel who is both our good and bad example.

America's founding principles were opposed every step of the way and still are today. It's essential for this country to understand its roots and God's requirements if it expects to be blessed. Standing against these issues are atheists, evolutionists, secular humanists, immoral libertines, a prejudiced media, political forces, influential institutions, and heavily funded sympathizers. It appears that all hope is gone—except for God to intervene. And He does.

The coming of the Cube, the New Jerusalem, brings what humanity longs for: peace, prosperity, justice, safety, health, righteousness, and joy. But these are all temporary unless one receives Christ as Lord and Savior.

When the Messiah Jesus Christ returns, the government will be upon His shoulders (Isa. 9:6). After that, the actual New Jerusalem will be the dwelling place of the saints forever. It is hoped that this book will be a whetting of the appetite for that glorious day.

Jerry I. Smith

1

WHAT IS IT?

"Jim, did you catch the news about the new object in the area of the Little Dipper?" Marcus Loshan asked, wide-eyed and brow wrinkled, as he entered Jim Waltham's Quad State Astronomical University office.

"What object?" Jim answered, as he sat down his cup of coffee, turned from his computer and his desk piled with books and papers, giving Marcus his full attention.

Marcus was sharp-minded, and wore stylish clothes to match his quick wit. He chose a chair close to Jim and leaned forward as he spoke. "An amateur astronomer named Jay Smith in Evansville, Indiana, spotted it three days ago. There's a new speck in the area of Polaris. Its size is unknown, but its light is unbelievably bright. Evidently appeared out of nowhere, and it's a wonder the whole world of astronomy hasn't seen it before now. It's been reported in a couple of news articles and will likely catch the eye of major media soon. No one knows what it is."

"A new object in space, too bright to miss, and yet no one knows what it is?" Jim said, with his eyebrows raised, emitting a slight irritation and doubt.

"It's anybody's guess at this point. Don't know how fast it is moving, but early tracking from Los Alamos shows it's moving in our direction."

The professor stood up, raised his hand and dropped it, saying as he grinned, "I haven't heard any news for several days, you know; besides, that's what I've got you for—to keep me informed!" He picked up the remote and clicked on the small office TV. "Let's see if we can find out anything about it."

The TV news reporter was saying, ". . . it hasn't been charted long enough to tell exactly how fast it's traveling. This is definitely not a fireball, but its illumination surpasses imagination. There is no word on where it came from. There's conjecture that it may be a break-off from a comet. Sam Goldberg, a professor of astronomy at the University of Chicago theorizes that it could be a dangerous chunk from a meteor."

The reporter continued, "Here's what some people on the street are thinking." He put a clip on the screen of a man saying, "If it's real, God made it. And it's probably coming to judge the world."

The reporter followed with, "It's too early to know much at this point. These things have a tendency to produce fear simply because of the unknown."

Jim punched off the TV with the remote, sat down and stroked his chin, "Well, obviously they don't know anything yet. Let's meet at dark-thirty and check it out at the LT, Lippershey Telescope."

"I'll be there!" Marcus replied, as he hurried out the door.

Jim Waltham had spent years studying physics, held two positions in the area of astronomy, and was a frequent contributor of scientific articles concerning space and its exploration. He was looked upon as an authority in all matters concerning space. His contribution to both the institutions in which he participated had resulted in numerous discoveries and awards of high acclaim throughout the world of astronomy. He'd received many accolades from his peers who saw him as a focused individual, committed to exploring the universe through the telescope. All who knew him were certain no one ever enjoyed their vocation more than he. If he had any fear, it was that he'd fail to fulfill God's plan for his life. And, surprising for someone who spent considerable time looking at slow moving objects in space, he also tended to be impatient.

Marcus Loshan, an associate to Dr. Waltham at the Orion Observatory Complex of five observatories, was an energetic, alert and practical man—and the ideal guy for a busy, overloaded person to have around. He was a little shorter than Jim, not fat, but just a little plump and wore glasses. His dark hair was cut short, and he tended to walk fast. And he was also an astute American history buff. Jim knew he was fortunate to have him. At dark thirty, Jim and Marcus drove the short distance from his home to the Orion complex area where the large Lippershey Telescope was located. Nothing could compare with its ability to see and to magnify space objects.

That evening, curiosity was gnawing at the minds of these two astronomers. Before long, they were able to turn the large lens upon the Little Dipper. Coming down from Polaris, the North Star, Jim focused on the unusual object. It was not near Polaris, but could have come from that direction and apparently was moving in a straight line toward the Earth. But how could it have not been reported before now? At first, he was shocked at what he saw. He wondered if it was an apparition, a phantom. The brightness of the light made it difficult to guess its accurate distance from Earth. With that much light, it would have to be huge. Yet for anything that large to go unnoticed before now would be impossible. After all, this was near the Little Dipper, an area that the whole world looked at every night. To say he was puzzled would be an understatement. The Little Dipper was about four hundred light years away. That is to say, if you were traveling from the Earth to Polaris, the North Star, at one hundred eighty-six thousand miles per second, it would take four hundred years to get there. This star, comet, or whatever it was appeared to be about three hundred light years away. But that would have to be confirmed after a day-by-day computation. About all he could say was that it was definitely bright and traveling from the north.

Marcus waited impatiently as Jim took his time staring through the lens. Jim's mind was racing, questioning, and trying his best to come to a conclusion or explanation that made sense as to what this object was before he quit. Finally, and without saying a word, he relinquished the lens to Marcus, who went through the same mind-twisting consternation that Jim had endured. Together they looked at each other with a confounded expression on their faces and concluded with the three most used words in every human language: "I don't know."

> *Lord, my heart is not haughty, nor mine eyes lofty: neither do I exercise myself in great matters, or in things too high for me.*
>
> *(Psalm 131:1 KJV)*

"This object is the most unusual thing I've ever seen," Jim said. "It's not that far away for our modern telescopes, but the light is different and impossible to penetrate."

"I know," responded Marcus. "What do we make of it?"

"All we can say at this time is 'wait and see.' Until we can establish its speed—assuming it's not traveling faster than the speed of light—we still have about three hundred years before it could arrive at or near Earth—if indeed that's its true direction. But I'm sure it will create lots of speculation."

The "Smith object" caused quite a stir among the world of astronomers. Soon numerous theories were postulated. The usual number of sensationalists jumped up with new, far-out ideas, hoping to gain funding for their projects, honorable doctorates, faculty positions, and promotions for their new books. However Jim, who was firmly anchored in science, knew that there had to be a logical, understandable explanation for this object, and there was something beginning to stir inside him to get to the bottom—or the top—of it.

For the next several days, some of the staff of all five observatories were involved in trying to determine what the newest object in space was. Where did it come from? Why wasn't it spotted long ago? It remained a mystery—primarily because of its unusual brightness. Jim explained to the inquiring public, "The brilliance is like no other in space. It's comparable to looking into a spotlight aimed at your face and trying to tell what's going on. You want to turn it away, get to the side of it, and hold up your hand to shield your eyes, so you can get your bearings. I don't know how we're going to overcome its piercing illumination. The difference between this object and the sun is that the sun illuminates in all directions out around it. This object appears to have its total light directed toward us like a searchlight. I've never seen anything like it before. It's very interesting, arresting . . . and makes us admittedly somewhat apprehensive."

During the first thirty days after the announcement of the unusual space phenomenon, everybody took potshots at the unknown object. It was the subject of talk shows, astronomical and philosophical articles, comedy routines, and political hog-wash. Numerous statements were made by authorities who pretended they knew something, but there was a general uneasiness about it everywhere. What everyone wanted to know was, "Is this good or bad?" and "Can it hurt us?" And no one with certainty had the answer.

Jim was friendly, easygoing, intellectually alert, and goal-motivated. He never lost the sense of awe about the vastness of space since he was a child. It all began at the age of six when he wondered what the moon was doing shining in the daytime. From then on, his father and Uncle Tue began giving him lessons about the stars and space.

In spite of extensive, frustrating work and observation, for thirty days little else was discovered about the unusual space object. However, on the thirty-first night after its sighting—it took a giant step! It suddenly appeared closer to Earth—much closer than it could've possibly traveled since the night before. Reports from observatories confirmed its distance to be approximately one third closer to the Earth, an unprecedented travel distance in the history of space. Dr. Sammy Whitfield at Los Alamos National Laboratory in New Mexico said, "It's certainly not moving that fast now. It appears to be standing still compared to that move! How unusual to have an object move at different speeds in such a short span of time. Incredible!"

All available telescopes were trained toward the area in space one third closer down from the Little Dipper. Jay Smith's discovery had turned the world of astronomy upside down. It was astounding how much was being said and how little was actually known. Doubtless no other matter had so gripped the heart and imagination in academia. Practically every branch had something to say, to suggest, or to offer as a possibility. Because of the object's sudden appearance over a distance impossible to travel at any known rate of speed, some observatories concluded that the object was daring the world to figure it out. Compared to the Sun, Polaris, and other stars, the "object" was small, yet its brightness, which baffled everyone, prevented details from being distinguished. But it had had plenty of attention. The newness of the object and its unknown identity was an obstacle to all astronomers. None of the observatories had any helpful answers. All efforts to calculate its speed were confusing. Some observatories even reported it had a current erratic behavior—to be stationary for a while and then to have moved a few minutes later. Certainly, it was unique from all other space objects and beyond classifying.

The move had also exposed some details of the object. Up to now the brilliant light of the unusual object had been too much for anything but speculation. However, Jim gave some startling information to the Odessa Post: "The object is in the form of a square—or more precisely a cube. The size of the cube is approximately fifteen hundred miles in all three directions. That's as far as the border of Canada to Brownsville, Texas, near the border of Mexico, and as far as the Atlantic Ocean at South Carolina to the middle of New Mexico! In other words, it would cover most of the entire United States—New York to San Francisco being approximately twenty-five hundred miles apart. Its height is also fifteen hundred miles."

Marcus was munching on donuts as he and Jim took turns viewing the cube at the Lippershey Observatory, LT, late into the night. They were dressed casually, having come from a bowling tournament earlier at the Satellite Bowling Alley. "Isn't that still the strangest thing you've have seen?" Marcus asked.

For my thoughts are not your thoughts, neither are your ways my ways, says the Lord . . .

(Isaiah 55:8 KJV)

"It's more than strange," Jim replied, as he looked away from the telescope, scratching his head. "It's not very large as space objects go, however the most gripping thing about it is its shape. It's definitely a cube—something totally different from everything else in space. We've looked at it by gamma ray, infrared, and radio telescopes, and no one has a clue about what it is. Even our newest and largest telescope using our hyper-generation of interferometers can't get beyond that penetrating light! We know nothing about its internal or surface structure. It's beyond mere physical calculation and reason." After taking a long sigh, he said, carefully and deliberately, "Material objects in space do not and cannot behave like this. What we're seeing is a miracle. I believe it has to be spiritual. Ever since it took that impossible move closer to Earth, it's actually performed maneuvers that no object is space can do. It's defied every physical law. Science will never be able to explain what's happening. It's as if whoever controls it wants to make certain that we know we've never faced anything like it before! It's treating us like it wants us to acknowledge that there is no use trying to figure it out—because we can't."

Marcus stopped as he was about to take another bite of a donut and with raised eyebrows said, "So . . . you're actually thinking there's a supernatural being in charge, and this object is supernatural too?"

"That's entirely another realm, but there's nothing about this object that fits in with any scientific knowledge of objects in space. It defies all known laws of travel and movement. It beats all I've ever seen. It seems impossible that we're even looking at it! Classification is out of the question. The scariest thing is that it suddenly jumped so much closer than it was in merely one day. How can anything be in one place in distant space and the next day travel faster than eight times the speed of light and be that much closer—then move slowly, if not stop dead still? It's impossible to explain." Then after a pause, he said quietly, "I'm ready to say that it's actually possible for it to be here right now, parked in front of us! It's not merely traveling at a certain speed in order to arrive. Its location is possible anywhere. It only appears for us to look at. When something can move that fast and stop, anything's possible. There's no other way to understand it."

"So you're saying it's not so much traveling as it is appearing here and there? Or I should say, there and there?"

"Correct," Jim replied. "But there's a purpose in its movements. I believe its appearances are to get our attention. And they certainly have!"

"No use asking how much time we have. We don't know. Just be prepared!"

"Right."

"But how?"

"That is the sixty-four million dollar question."

The media, of course, was full of every kind of speculation about the object. From newspapers and magazine covers to TV, radio, and internet, the headlines were as varied as the stars in the sky.

William Parker, head of National Aeronautics and Space Administration better known as NASA, also sought help. He was inundated with phone calls, telegrams, e-mails, and the media, and he had nothing definite to give them. He sent notices to seven of the largest observatories in the world in an attempt to gain some sort of understanding that he could pass on with a note of exactness. Desperate for information, he pled with them to send visual photographs of the new object.

The next day, as Jim prepared to leave the LT for the day, he poked his head into the open door of Marcus' office. "Let's see if we can get any pictures of the space object tonight now that it's closer. See you later."

"Right," Marcus replied, ready to act in a moment's notice.

Jim instructed his staff to go ahead and make photos of the object as soon as it was dark enough. He and Marcus planned to return shortly to look at them. Later that evening, he examined the results of the photos. They were BLANK! His staff explained that they had tried everything to get a picture. They adjusted the lens numerous times to account for the brightness of the object but to no avail. Jim turned the telescope to another star and photographed it to see if something was wrong with the computer. The photo came out perfect.

Impatiently he asked as he shook the empty paper, "What are we to make of this?"

No one had an answer. Repeated attempts produced the same results. His mind traveled through the index of his former studies, other occasions when he was stumped, and experiences of his teachers when they faced difficulties. Nothing caught his attention. He dismissed Marcus and remained in his office for some time. His perplexity over this object was growing. He knew others would expect him to clear everything up, name it, declare its purpose, and remove it from being a concern. The sudden move so much closer to Earth caused this man of peace to get the jitters, and he didn't like it.

The Lippershey Telescope's plush office suite and conference room was actually connected to the observatory through a short hall, though not in a way to be used by a crowd. A small team worked throughout the night in the observatory. It was quiet in Jim's office where he leaned back in his desk chair and tried to envision the meaning of this object. He breathed a prayer for wisdom. Was this merely something that was going to pass by like an asteroid and go on its way—a close miss? Was it something that would effect the world? And if so, God would have a plan for it. And if that was the case, the key to handling the situation would be somewhere in the Word of God. It would provide the insight needed. It would give the principles to apply. He had formed a habit of turning to the Bible when he was perplexed and always received the wisdom necessary for the occasion. His thoughts took him to the constellations he loved so much and the stories they told through his study of typology in the constellations and Scriptures. After creating the Heavens and the Earth, grass, and trees, God put lights in the firmament for signs and seasons, to divide the day from the night. He made the stars also.[1] He numbered the stars and called them by their names.[2]

Jim began his thoughts with the Little Dipper and his understanding of it. *Symbolically it represents the Church of which I'm a part, and I'm in God's marvelous sheepfold. I'm protected by the near-by constellation Bootes, the Shepherd, who watches over his flock. He keeps me from the constellation Draco the Dragon that slithers along near the two Dippers, or flocks. The North Star in the Little Dipper represents Jesus. This cubed object came from that direction. Does it have a place in this unfolding drama of star messages? Are there any clues among the constellations? Where and how did it fit into God's plan? Whatever God's doing in His Heavens around His Earth involves me. Our loving Lord wouldn't allow anything to happen like this without letting us know about it. And somehow I believe I'll get the answer from His Word, the Bible. It's His "operator's manual" for this life.*

And he would.

∞

---

[1] Genesis 1:14-16
[2] Psalm 147:4

2

HELLO

A large crowd was assembled at Skyview Community Church in Odessa, Texas. It'd been a couple of weeks since the space object had taken its giant light-year step downward toward Earth. They were there to have a Bible study, but hands were raised as the pastor entered and prepared to speak to them. "Pastor Fleming, what about this 'cube' in the sky?" A member asked, determined to get an answer and rising halfway out of his seat, his Bible folded, keeping the place where he'd been reading, "Can you tell us anything about it?"

"They tell us it's bright, and I suppose by that they mean beautiful, yet it's threatening and scaring us to death," said another, with wrinkled brow, shrugged shoulders, and his arms lifted.

Among the other spontaneous rumble across the chapel, an elderly man, known for his humility and spiritual wisdom, raised a hand with one finger pointed upward. His face was bright and his eyebrows raised. He carefully spoke, "If it's in the form of a cube, I wonder if it has any jewels adorning it?"

The pastor paused, thinking of what to say to his nervous congregation—then cocking his head to the side slightly he spoke to the man, saying, "Hey, Brother Shannon, are you thinking what just popped into my mind?"

"I believe so," the elderly gentleman replied, nodding his head.

The stunned pastor softly said to the gentleman, "Oh, no. It couldn't be!" Then he stood strong and erect, and smiled as he turned to the rest of the congregation, "I haven't seen this block, or cube as it's being called, since a telescope is required to actually view it—and I don't have one. Otherwise I understand all we can see is basically a bright and beautiful technicolored star. I haven't seen a photograph of it, if indeed, that's even possible, so I haven't seen it on television. Nor have I made it my purpose to try to explain it since there's so much commotion, chaos, and guessing. I've been determined not to listen to most of the things that are being said, so as not to be confused." Pausing, he continued, "But now that jewels have been mentioned along with the fact that it's in the form of a cube, it just now came to my mind something that I've preached about from the book of Revelation. Brother Shannon raised the question about it. You remember what it is—the New Jerusalem is described like that! I didn't put the two together until now. As a matter of fact, the New Jerusalem is a cube, fifteen hundred miles long, fifteen hundred miles wide, and fifteen hundred miles high. It has twelve foundations made of precious stones, walls of diamonds, and twelve gates of pearl!"

Then he shook his head from side to side saying, "But, of all things, surely it couldn't be that! It's not supposed to come until after the Millennium. But still, the fact that it's a cube and that same size is astounding! There's never been anything in all of space that was shaped like that. And of course, my beloved people, should that be what it is, then we have nothing to fear. It'll not destroy. It'll bless! What we need to do is obtain all the information we can about this object and see how it fits this possibility. If it turns out to be true, then we have a message the whole world needs to hear. *That* 'cube' is the heavenly City of God; it's the future dwelling place of God and his people!"

"Why would it be coming, Pastor? Is there anything in the Bible that foretold it?" a Sunday school teacher asked, his pen and paper in hand, ready for the study. There was a questioning frown on his face, and chatter in the congregation among themselves. The pastor paused again and said, "Well, we don't know if it is the New Jerusalem. But the fact of its shape is shocking. And, nope, I don't understand why it would be coming now. According to my study for many years, it's not supposed to appear until after the world goes through the Great Tribulation . . . and the campaign of Armageddon . . . and after the thousand year reign of Christ on Earth . . . and after the final destruction of all evil."

"Then what do you make of it, Pastor?" asked a distinguished business man, dressed in his fashionable suit, who was a pillar in the church.

After another pause with his forehead wrinkled he replied slowly for clarity, "Well, if those events are truthfully in the right order, then God would be doing something different from what has been revealed in His Word. It would be a separate plan similar to that of the Church which was kept secret until the Day of Pentecost." Then after a pause, "Of course, God is sovereign and can do what He wants. He could carry out a secret that we don't know about . . . He could even visit the Earth in a different way than that which has been prophesied or that'll still be fulfilled in the future. That is, He could bring the New Jerusalem down to Earth for some other purpose than the one that is yet to come!"

"You mean this could be something that's not even in the Bible?" an astonished young man asked. There was more chatter among the congregation.

"Wow," the pastor continued, smiling, "now, folks, I'm just thinking out loud. This brings up all sorts of possibilities. If this is the New Jerusalem, we need to bring it to the attention of the wise, students of

Scripture within the body of Christ to see what the Lord will reveal to his people. It would be good to have a large-scale call for prayer so that the saints of God could hear from our heavenly Father. We'd have to find out why this is happening. Surely the Lord would reveal his purpose to us. Meanwhile, since this is at least a possibility, let's omit our study tonight on the miracles of Jesus and open our Bibles to the book of Revelation. We'll read the last two chapters, discuss them, and meditate upon them."

"We're with you Pastor!" someone called out as they all reached for their Bibles.

"It's just awesome," Pastor Fleming went on, as he opened his Bible, "to think of what might be happening right before our eyes, and we're not aware of it nor ready for it! What a time for soul-searching and contemplation of what we have before us. I'm amazed, actually, to even *consider* this to be the New Jerusalem. But I wonder if anyone else has thought about that possibility. Later tonight, I plan to give these chapters and some other verses a thorough going over prayerfully. I'd like to bounce this off the minds of some of the most respected scholars. It's going to be difficult to approach the idea without scientific input coming from astronomers who're looking at the object. There's a need to find astronomers who are believers and who know the Bible. If this is verified, then I can use my television broadcast to place this matter before the listeners. Well, all this is for another day. As for now, you can help me as we examine what God has revealed to us about the future New Jerusalem!"

Another helpful member, eyes sparkling with enthusiasm, spoke up and said, "If I may, Pastor. Dr. Jim Waltham, at the Lippershey Telescope, is a believer. He's an outstanding scholar and Bible class teacher at his church. If anyone knows about the space object, it would be him, and perhaps the two of you could get together."

"Thank you. Yes, I know of him, but not personally. I'll be sure to contact him," the pastor replied.

Dr. Rex Fleming did call upon several pastors, scholars, and friends. They would activate the prayer warriors in their churches about the Cube, which became a synonym for the heavenly city, New Jerusalem. These individuals, in turn, would contact others who were humble, gifted students of the Word. The group that grew larger every day was eventually, humorously, termed the "Cubicles." Everyone was electrified to think that they might be in a similar situation to Daniel when he realized that the seventy years of captivity was almost up. He knew God would take the Israelites back to Jerusalem, so he began asking God to do it. It appeared that right now they were at the doorstep of an unknown plan of God, and He could just be ready to answer their prayers about its purpose and their part in that plan to glorify God. Dr. Fleming devoted most of the next three days to the Cube, along with other men who sought the Lord and stayed in the Scriptures almost without stopping. There was actually nothing that could be certain without input from godly and gifted astronomers. They all agreed to find out first-hand what Bible-believing astronomers knew and what they thought about it.

Jim was busy at the office of STSA when he received a call from Dr. Rex Fleming. He explained he was the Pastor of Skyview Church in Odessa, Texas, and wanted to make an appointment with Jim at his earliest convenience to discuss the object in space that had the shape of a cube. "I want to know everything you can tell me concerning this cube. I have been wondering if it could possibly be something in the Bible—the fifteen hundred mile cube in the book of Revelation called the New Jerusalem. Now, that may sound far out, but I'm not a quack. This is just an idea. But I can't dismiss that possibility without further input from someone like you. Should it turn out to be true, then I'm still in the dark as to why it would be appearing at this time. So, I need to know what you're seeing, and if it has any jewels, or twelve foundations, or a wall around it—these are the descriptive items in the book of Revelation. Do you see any of these things?"

"Well, sir, I am putting all the time I can into the object. We actually have no explanations for it yet." He paused, and then said, "But I'd be very surprised if it weren't supernatural. And I'd be interested in hearing what you have to say. I do recall that there's something like that in Revelation, but I'll have to read it again and then examine the object with that in mind. The phenomenon is only just now giving us a break by letting up on its brightness so we can see something besides light! I'd be willing to move my schedule around to explore this with you. Maybe we could have lunch tomorrow and get acquainted then, if that's possible. I would like my associate, Dr. Marcus Loshan, to meet with us. He's an invaluable help to my work. Can you make it here by that time?"

"Oh yes," Dr. Fleming said. "One of my church members owns several planes and helicopters, and I'm an avid pilot. I have free access to whatever's available with his encouragement. He likes to see me use them, though I don't abuse the privilege. And as you know, there's a helipad at your location."

Plans were made to meet the next day. Now that he realized the object could be the New Jerusalem, he reached for his Bible and read the last part of Revelation again. He thought that would be the wildest thing he'd ever heard of—for something like that right out of the Bible to be coming down now! Surely that couldn't be it. That evening he and Marcus spent time on the telescope and were shocked at what came into view.

"Look!" said Marcus, giving the lens to Jim. "There are distinguishing lines around the bottom of this object, but they're not in color."

Jim looked through the telescope. "Yes, I see them," said Jim seriously. "I'm going to count them." When he got to twelve the hair on his arms and the back of his neck began to tingle. He looked with his eyes wide open to Marcus, "There are twelve foundations there! The texture of each of them is different. We're seeing more than ever before because the light is shining differently than it has been. It's radiating outward with a softer hue." He gave the lens to Marcus.

Throughout the next several hours, the astronomers were astounded to account for a high wall around the City, as well as three huge gates on each of the two sides that were visible. The differentiating lines and shapes in the foundation layers could definitely be jewels. They could hardly go to sleep after they arrived home. Besides, as Jim went over the most recent details with his wife Laura and son Keith, she was so excited she couldn't stop talking about it. Jim was drawing pictures of the city on scratch paper as he and Laura discussed this astounding matter. Keith finally had to hit the hay, and Jim's eyes were half-closed as Laura kept on questioning.

The next day, Jim directed Judy Carter, a former university student, secretary to all those working at the Orion Observatory Complex, receptionist, the "Miss do-it-all" and "Girl Friday," to bring lunch from a local restaurant to be eaten in the board room for less distraction. An associate met Rex at the helipad and brought him to the Lippershey Telescope observatory. The LT was an excellent place for the meeting.

Waiting on the meeting to begin, Jim reminisced about how he came to the observatory complex. At age twenty-seven, he became a faculty member at Lyle Thompson University in Austin, Texas, as a physicist and astronomy professor, while Laura Drake, his wife, worked for a financial business firm nearby. During his six years of teaching at Lyle, he received a few invitations from other universities to join their faculties. Up until then, he'd turned them all down. But two offers stayed on his mind. The Space Telescope Science Association, STSA, in Fort Davis, Texas, a cooperative project of eighteen universities throughout North America, was looking for a new head of their organization. Jim's academic qualifications and his experience in the field of space fit the description of the leader they needed. Lyle Thompson University had highly recommended him. If selected, he would enjoy the spacious new office facilities at the Orion Observatory Complex where five observatories were located on five mountain peaks. These observatories used various methods of scoping out the sky: gamma ray, infrared, radio, and ordinary telescopes. His office would be located at the LT, Lippershey Observatory site, since it was the newest and the largest in the world. It was named after the Dutch eyeglass maker whom most historians believe was the inventor of the first telescope. It used a new hyper-generation of interferometers, which allowed stars to be viewed in one hundred times finer detail than NASA's Hubble Space Telescope. And there was plenty of room for board meetings and other larger gatherings for special occasions.

Nearby was the Quad State Astronomical University. He'd also been contacted about becoming an astronomy professor at this school that joined hands with four universities in Texas, New Mexico, Arizona, and Oklahoma. He'd shared the opportunities with Laura, but no decision had been made. Upon further consideration, he wondered about the possibility of doing both jobs. One evening, while the family was waiting for Laura to bring the last bowl of food to the table, he brought it up. He spoke while looking down at his half-filled plate.

"I wonder if I could do both of those jobs in tandem. I could take research from the observatories into the classroom and bring students to the observatories to apply their class instruction."

"Ouch!" Laura had cried out with her eyes opened wide hurrying to get to the table. "I almost dropped the beans! I wish you'd wait till I'm seated before you bring up shocking ideas like that. You're not serious, are you?" She looked into Jim's blue eyes searching for a "nah."

"Well . . . sort of. But let's have the blessing for the food first." Laura stood at the table as they prayed, allowing the two boys to begin eating since she still had the tea to bring from the kitchen counter. After the blessing, Jim began eating in a very relaxed way and spoke as if he was already confident about the job proposal. "I could cut back on my classes and specialize in what I offer. And the STSA already involves students from eighteen other schools, so they should be inclined toward a professor heading up the observatory work. I believe I'll go for it. It can't hurt to make an offer now that I have invitations to both." He looked up calling for a positive response, "What could be better than that?"

Jim was intriguing to Laura and she truly loved this man. He was tall, with lots of wavy hair, and a countenance that emitted confidence. She knew he'd get her approval, but she wanted to have some fun with the scenario, so she stopped close to his chair bending over somewhat and said "You could be two people, that's what . . . in fact, let's go for three! One of you could stay home and enjoy family life while you're at it."

"Yeah, Dad," Keith joined in admiringly, "you're so good, we could use a couple more of you!"

Their other son, Scott, was simply all smiles. Jim reached out to his wife and drew her to his side. "Now don't any of you think that I'm going to slight you for a moment! You know how much I love you," he said looking at them all with a sweeping turn of his head.

"I'm not complaining, darling. You're so lovingly considerate of us all." Then with a look of compassion and raised eyebrows, she said, "My eyes only bulge out when you talk of all that work! It's probably going to turn out to be twice the work of two other men . . . so just make sure the pay is twice as much too."

"What? You mean I ought to get paid to do the things I love the most?" Jim chuckled.

Both institutions were supportive of his intentions and agreed to hire him. It was a dream team offer: President of STSA and professor at Quad U.

Since taking his new jobs, eight years had passed.

∞

3

***

HUDDLE

When Rex arrived, Jim could tell that this preacher was about to burst with information and was hoping for some confirmation as to the idea of the New Jerusalem. Jim had read and re-read Revelation's last two chapters and was still astounded by what they'd discovered last night through the Lippershey Telescope. He'd already conceded to Marcus that this whole thing seemed supernatural. It certainly didn't make sense otherwise. However, it was still so wondrous he hesitated to say anything to anyone except Marcus.

It was refreshing to Jim to learn that Rex was an excellent Bible student and believed everything in it. He quoted Scripture with ease and had a good grasp of prophecy. Jim didn't have much patience with ministers who gave "book reviews" or who whipped up emotion with current events that couldn't be proven to fulfill biblical prophecy, yet they implied or asserted that it was so. Jim believed in the coming again of Jesus and that there were no earthly events needing to be completed by mankind before that event happened. When Rex learned that the Lippershey Telescope was the most modern and powerful one in existence and was especially made for seeing details, he was overjoyed. Marcus was also ecstatic about the potential of this meeting.

The three men enjoyed their time in a relaxed atmosphere. They were seated close together at the head of a large conference table as they ate and got acquainted. Marcus commented on Judy's ability to manage the secretarial work of the complex and her excellent choice of the menu—Mexican all the way. Rex passed on the jalapeño peppers though. "My stomach can only take up to medium picante sauce," he said with an exaggerated smile.

"My weakness is chili con queso," Jim admitted.

Marcus noted that Jim always had an unstoppable dip with chips when queso was around!

When they finished the meal, Rex decided a good place to begin might be the explanation of "biblical north" since that was the direction the cubed object came from, and possibly had relevance to its identity.

Shifting around in his chair, moving his empty plate and utensils to the side, and changing the mood of the meeting, Rex said, "Dr. Waltham, I feel that perhaps I should share several Scriptures with you to bring you up to where I am in my thinking. I don't know if you are familiar with certain details in the Word of God about the direction 'north,' but it's especially significant that this object originated to our sight from that direction."

"I'm open to whatever you have to say, Pastor," Jim answered.

"In Scripture, north is the direction or place of the throne of God—it's not just out in space somewhere. Of course, God lives everywhere. He's omnipresent. And yes, David, in Scripture, said that the Lord's throne is in Heaven. Isaiah also tells us Heaven is God's throne, and the Earth is His footstool. Elsewhere, we're told that the Lord has established His throne in Heaven and His kingdom rules over all.[3] And we know that God is Spirit. Now, having covered all that, there are other verses which indicate that He has specially set up a throne that has specific reference[4] to physical things—that is, Earth. That throne is over all his Creation,[5] and clearly addresses matters concerning this planet. It's called a throne of holiness.[6] It's a throne of Judgment.[7] It's a throne like a burning fire.[8] And there's a Man sitting on that throne! Jesus, the Son of Man, claimed to be that Man in Matthew chapter twenty-five.[9] And one other thing before I forget, we may need to explore this later as to the location of the New Jerusalem. When the New Jerusalem descends, as described in Revelation, where will it land, stop, or take its place during eternity? On Earth—in the place of old Jerusalem? Hovering in the air over the city of Jerusalem? We aren't told that detail in Scripture. We do know in the future Jesus will fulfill a prophecy of Jeremiah which says, *At that time Jerusalem will be called, The Throne of the Lord, and all the nations will be gathered to Jerusalem to honor the name of the Lord. And they will not walk any more after the imagination of their evil hearts.*[10] Here the very city of Jerusalem itself is called Jesus' throne. I hesitate to go any farther in this particular matter, except to say that the constellation Corona Borealis, which is the symbol of a crown, passes directly over the earthly city of Jerusalem with every revolution of the Earth. If the Jews and Arabs only knew the Word of God and the revelation of the stars, they could look directly up into the sky every night and know that someday God's

---

[3]   Psalm 103:19

[4]   Psalm 11:4

[5]   Isaiah 66:1

[6]   Psalm 47:8

[7]   Psalm 9:7-9

[8]   Daniel 7:9

[9]   Matthew 25:31

[10] Jeremiah 3:17

Messiah, Jesus Christ, will take His crown and His seat on His throne in Jerusalem.

Jim's and Marcus's mouths were practically wide open by this time as they were mentally digesting all the references to God's throne in Heaven and on Earth, and especially the bearing of the direction north.

"But the point is this," Rex continued, looking directly at the men before him, "in this present age His throne is not in Jerusalem. And His throne is not *everywhere*. It's north! Polaris is currently the 'fixed' star for north, and represents Jesus. The prophet, Asaph, said in one of his songs, that ". . . promotion doesn't come from the east, nor from the west, nor from the south. But God is the Judge. He puts down one and sets up another."[11]

"Why didn't Asaph say that man's promotion doesn't come from the north? Because that's where it *does* come from. From His throne in the north, He determines who's promoted and who's put down. He taught King Nebuchadnezzar that lesson the hard way after sending him into the woods to live like an animal for seven years. God told him through Daniel, "You shall eat grass like oxen, and seven periods of time will pass over you, until you know that the Most High rules in the kingdom of men, and He gives it to anyone He chooses."[12]

"That's exactly right," Jim agreed, shifting in his chair with keen interest. "If this object is the New Jerusalem, could it be that He's going to change the rulers of this world?"

"That could be, but we don't know anything yet," Rex paused. "And let's consider something else. You know, most people who read the Bible become familiar with the fall of Lucifer, the Archangel who became Satan or the devil. Lucifer wanted a promotion. Isaiah tells us, "For you

---

[11]   Psalm 75:6-7
[12]   Daniel 4:32

have said in your heart: I will ascend into Heaven. I will exalt my throne above the stars of God. I will also sit on the mount of the congregation, on *the farthest sides of the north*. I will ascend above the heights of the clouds. I will be like the Most High."[13]

"The congregation of angels and heavenly beings were gathered around the throne of God. Lucifer wanted to promote himself above all the other created beings and put his throne above them. To do this, he would have to move his throne farther north, farther than the throne that is north—the one that is set up with earthly associations. That would be even above the throne that Christ occupies now over his creation. His prideful ambition was his fall."

"Very insightful," noted Jim. "It's a point well taken, that this object is coming from the direction of north or Polaris to confirm that it's descending from His throne, being the place of God's presence as it relates to His created Earth at this present time."

"Those are my thoughts," Rex said.

Marcus chimed in: "Well, If we could just figure out the purpose of its coming," as he removed his glasses and scratched his head.

"Yes, Marcus, but let me continue with this matter of north," Rex said. "When God ordained sacrifices to be brought to the Tabernacle in the wilderness and at the Temple of Solomon, He instructed that they always be killed on the north side of the altar. 'And he shall kill it on the side of the altar northward before the Lord: and the priests, Aaron's sons, shall sprinkle his blood round about upon the altar.'[14]

"The animal sacrifices were to be put to death in the direction of God's dwelling place, and again we see clearly that God's throne has a reference to Earth. It's northward!"

---

[13]   Isaiah 14:13-14 (NKJV)

[14]   Leviticus 1:11

Jim was pleased with the Bible study they were receiving. "I can see from these Scriptural references that God's throne is surely northward. From all my ability to determine, the New Jerusalem came straight from Polaris, the North Star, and I know that Polaris is the present 'unmovable' star that symbolically represents Jesus."

"That's correct," Rex continued. "The description in Revelation of the New Jerusalem is very specific. It's a cube fifteen hundred miles long, wide and high. To say its construction is spectacular would be a gross understatement. It's a prepared place created by God. It's said to be his personal dwelling place among his people after the Millennium or thousand-year reign of Christ over the Earth. It's the city of God. Its twelve foundations made of all kinds of precious stones, walls of diamonds, and twelve gates of pearl ought to be seeable through your telescopes."

Jim stated, "I'm familiar with the description in Revelation." Jim glanced at Marcus as he was speaking. "Marcus and I looked at and discussed this cube for several hours last night. I can certainly agree with you that it could definitely be the New Jerusalem. I'm so astounded that I hardly know what to do. I just feel like this can't be happening. It's like suddenly I'm in another world with this supernatural possibility. We've looked at the details of the structure, and they do fit the description in the Bible. I can see foundations, the wall, and gates. However, these details are not as clear or dazzling as Revelation describes them, even with our powerful telescope—which doesn't make sense," Jim shrugged his shoulders, "from the physical point of view because the Lippershey Telescope is extremely capable. However, I can *see the jewels* and even some writing appears to be there in some sort of shape or form, like it's waiting to be uncovered. These details have only become visible in the past few days, but we've been unable to put them all together until last night. I've hardly been able to sleep throughout the night thinking about it! There've been some mysterious things about this cube that have stumped all astronomers from its first sighting—shining so bright from such a distance yet without revealing any details. Its identity is still unknown. Even now, assuming that it's the New Jerusalem, it seems too good to be true, and it's not up to all the glorious description written in Revelation.

"Then, of course, it miraculously moved a hundred light years all at once. I wonder if God's holding its glory back at this time, planning to reveal more all at once in due time—or even little by little for some reason."

Marcus added his insight: "It's amazing that the details in the Word of God can be seen in the telescope, though it can't be photographed yet. Jim and I have reached the conclusion that God may be waiting to show more of the City's glory later—that it's being delayed for some reason. The shadowed outline of the jewels, the gates of pearl, and the foundations are definitely visible, but not the beauty, the shining, the dazzling, that we would expect."

"There's no question about it being supernatural," Jim said. "God has to be up to something. He's a revealing God. There's got to be a purpose involved in how He's going about this matter. Surely He'll reveal His plan to His servants—those who faithfully proclaim His Word to the people. Just as man can't know the time of His return to Earth, I expect that as that time approaches, God will have His men proclaiming the certainty of that event during that season. By this, the Bride of Christ will be ready while still not knowing the exact day or hour. One thing for sure, we're going to have to pray and wait to see what He makes known. He'll have to show us what we're to do . . . . Wait a minute! Perhaps because this is not the fulfillment of when Revelation says it's to come, God's sending it in a different fashion at *this* time. He doesn't have to give it all the glory that it'll have in the future. At any rate, I'm convinced that this is the New Jerusalem—strange and bizarre as it may be, it's the best explanation I can think of that fits all the things taking place. And if we declared this to the general public it would probably create enough interest, commotion, controversy, faith, and mockery that the stage will be set for God to give us more revelation. Praise God!"

"I can't believe you've said all that," Rex agreed, smiling and leaning forward across the table shaking his head back and forth. "Those are my feelings and beliefs exactly! My main objective is to get from you, as scientists, what you are seeing, and whether it matches the Bible. Of course, we know that the primary, grand plan of God is redemption through Christ. The New Jerusalem is the future home of the saved. So whatever this is all about, evangelism still is the heart-beat of the Father."

Jim said, "Yes, and since last night, when I knew what to look for, I definitely saw the features of the New Jerusalem in that cube."

"Thank you, Jim. I want you to know I'm just as jarred about this situation as you are. This is phenomenal, off the charts, and here we are taking it at face value and doing something about it. It's so astounding that I could understand why people would be reluctant to believe us. It's bound to sound silly or preposterous to many. I can't wait to see it!"

"You shall tonight!" Jim and Marcus said at the same time.

The three men spent the rest of the day getting better acquainted and discussing everything they could think of concerning the Cube. If it was the New Jerusalem, what should be their response? Have other observatories discovered the same things Jim and Marcus had seen? Should they be responsible to tell the world about it? Is that their business? When should they do so? What would be the expected repercussions of the public as well as the people of God? Why did the Lord reveal this to them?

Jim spoke up and said, "I feel like we're sitting on a bombshell and don't know whether or not to light the fuse . . . and run!"

"Once it's lighted, there's probably no getting away from the aftermath," Rex stated. "We'll be marked men."

"It's something we're going to have to pray about and get the mind of Christ. Servants shouldn't have to make decisions; they only follow orders from the Master," Marcus said.

As evening came along, Jim invited Rex to stay the night at the Lippershey Observatory. "You don't need to return home tonight" he said. It may be late before we finish studying the Cube, and we have a place for you here. One of our trustees provided a gift for a building with several guest rooms. He wanted better accommodations for meetings and local facilities were not up to par. These guest quarters are quite nice, and breakfast will be served."

"That's mighty nice, Jim. I believe I'll take you up on it. That way we won't be rushed when we're looking at what the world will soon be amazed about."

Soon the three men were focusing on the glorious New Jerusalem. Its luster was better than any previous night. If there was any doubt left in any of them, it was removed before they reluctantly gave up the lens and found rest for their bodies.

The next morning the men enjoyed breakfast together and talked about what they should do next. They felt that if God had intentionally included them in this revelation, then He would want them to let His Church know, as well as the general public. It had become their divine mandate. If they didn't do it, God would find someone else who would. They sat around the conference room table in the LT observatory.

"I've been thinking," said Rex, "about what may take place in the next few weeks and months. Perhaps I should warn you—in case you don't already know, that there are many differing beliefs out there among theologians, pastors, educators, and institutions . . ."

"How well I know!" said Jim, bowing and shaking his head.

"Regardless of how we approach this matter, and regardless of what we say, we can expect it to be opposed by others," Rex continued. "There'll be voices raised, academic protests, men strutting around like roosters behind their nests, in this case, desks, who'll deny what we say. There may even be persecution. There are people who will hate everything we do."

"I see you have spiritual wisdom as well as commitment to your calling," Jim replied.

"Just think how many theories and views there are on the Rapture alone. In fact, the New Jerusalem coming at this time like this doesn't even fit my own eschatology!"

"Mine either, though my meager study has only begun compared to yours," Jim agreed.

"I fully expected the Rapture to be the next event on God's calendar, and the New Jerusalem coming down after the Millennium to begin the eternal Kingdom. On the other hand, I'm not going to be a critic of God's miracles right in my face as the Pharisees were in the presence of the Lord." Then Rex jokingly remarked. "He doesn't have to get my theological approval to do anything."

Jim nodded, chuckling in agreement. "I'll say 'amen' to that. The only thing we can do is be submissive to him. Let Him be Lord in our lives and thoughts. Do you have a plan or an approach as to our actions from here?"

"You bet," Rex replied. "I've been musing about it since early this morning. He took pen and paper and numbered his outline to show them. "It involves at least two weeks from this coming Sunday."

Before that time, he would contact a list of scholars, prayer warriors, and close friends, and invite their participation in the plan. Jim and Marcus would compile their findings through the telescope and make them available to him and this group. The first announcement Sunday he would speak to his church and the regular television listening audience of his personal belief that the object in the shape of a cube is the New Jerusalem and encourage them be sure to listen to this astounding announcement the following Sunday when he would speak on that subject. The second Sunday, after addressing the subject to his church and listening audience, he would invite them to hear a full account of his experience with the revelation of the Cube on the next day, Monday, to the general public, by means XPJS TV. Of course, he would contact the station manager in Odessa in advance and let him know that he'd have an announcement to make on the second Monday during the five o'clock news. That would give the three of them time to communicate with the other pastors and leaders who were a part of their investigation, and have God's prayer warriors sending up their petitions and bathing all that they did in prayer.

"I don't want to do something this dramatic on my own as if I were the lone mouthpiece of God. I want as many others to know what we have concluded and why, then let them participate in the event together. After all, we're all the family of God," Rex stated.

"Praise God for your disposition," Jim said.

Now that Rex had met with Jim and Marcus, he wanted to make statements on the news broadcast on Monday *and Tuesday*. Monday would be his personal opinion concerning the matters of the New Jerusalem in which they were in agreement. On that day, he'd do a Bible study by letting the prophets speak from God's Word as it had to do with God's will for mankind and the governments of the world, creating the interest of a greater audience the next day.

Then on Tuesday, he'd make known the common belief that the three of them had concerning the Cube, a synonym for the New Jerusalem. God was visiting them again in a new way, and that there was a spiritual reason for it that would doubtless have many physical and moral ramifications. God wouldn't be dazzling them with this mighty manifestation for nothing. But his lone voice may not make much of an impact. By the mouth of two or three witnesses, a better impression would be established. He'd like Jim and Marcus to be there.

"How would you and Marcus like to be with me and give the listeners your input from the standpoint of scientists on Tuesday?"

Jim's eyes lit up, but his heart sank as he thought about the muzzle Quad U was trying to put on him about the Bible in the classroom.

Marcus declared, "I'd be delighted and honored to be there with my full support."

Jim said, "Well, that will give us a few more days to examine the Cube and further confirm our findings. We should have a better grasp of what to say. I actually don't know of anything I'd rather do."

"Wonderful," said Rex. "We have targeted the date and we'll have time to prepare. I want the station to make this announcement available to all the major news media in America. It should be a huge event. Then it'll behoove us that we stay in touch almost daily to clarify any other thing that we can share with the people. I'll also call for prayer from all the saints of God that we should expect great things to happen from the God of all flesh! The prayer and Bible searching group will be growing daily and should reach throughout most of the States. New developments or revelations that you find should be given to as many people as possible so we can humble ourselves, pray and get ready for what He wants all of us to do."

"I'm touched at your organization, Rex," said Jim. "Obviously you've given this some quality thinking and planning. I don't have anything else to add to your overall plan at this time. I think that's about as much as we're capable of undertaking right now, don't you?"

"Yes," Rex replied.

"It's been a joy unspeakable to meet with you today, Rex," Jim said.

"And what a pleasure to me, Jim and Marcus. What brothers in the Lord you two men are!"

The three men prayed for this plan to be successful in reaching those who needed to respond to accomplish the Lord's will. They thanked God for the privilege of entering into this outstanding work and asked that they'd be found worthy to serve him through every means possible.

It's a good thing they prayed for protection from the Evil One.

∞

4

EARLY CHOICES

"**W**hat a change has been made in my life!" Jim exclaimed to his wife, as he came through the door at home. Reaching out, he gave her a kiss and hug. "Compared to what I used to believe when I was younger, it's like I've come out of a cave into the light. I can't get over how beautifully everything fits together in nature and science. The books I've been studying on the Bible are super! I've even been blessed to see God's handiwork in the Heavens that I love to study. And now we are privileged to see how this astounding Cube is going to mesh perfectly with everything else. My darling, we are on the brink of God's spectacular plans."

Laura affirmed his spiritual growth over the years with a big smile of admiration and grabbed him with another loving hug and in a flash she recalled their earlier life. The couple had married shortly after their graduation from college. She became his lovely, green-eyed, brunette delight. Jim saw her as cordial, with a beautiful smile, with softness in her countenance, a shapely form, and a personality that captivated his attention. There was such a strong sense of mutual attraction that all else seemed to simply mesh together in oneness. Their relationship became even stronger when they both became Christians a couple of years after their marriage. Before that, Jim was an atheist, humanist, and evolutionist, with no need for God. While Laura definitely believed in Him, she didn't try to conform her life to his will. They'd previously had their battles over the matter of religion and finally agreed to respect each other's beliefs and allow their love to take precedence over their differences.

Two years after the birth of their first child, Keith, the Walthams experienced a trial that would both challenge their faith as well as better equip them for handling troubling relationships they would face in the future. They were humbled and their dependence upon God was deepened when Laura's second child was revealed, in utero, to have Down's syndrome. It was a serious blow to them both. They needed God's guidance in this heavy matter. The first counsel they received from their new pediatrician, Dr. Davenport, was to get an abortion. Laura was shocked at the advice. Though she'd only been a believer in Christ for less than two years, she told him it was not an option. Jim noticed her reaction, straightened his shoulders, and joined her in agreement. As they walked down the hall of the doctor's office, Laura saw a place of privacy, pulled Jim into that area and said, "Jim, your support today means more than I can say. I always knew I could count on you, but the reality of it in this situation has filled my soul." She looked him in the eyes and said, "I love you."

"And I love you too, darling. I'm so glad we've always been able to discuss and air our feelings together, and with God's help, we'll learn through this too."

She grabbed him, pulled him to her, and sobbed for a while. "That's what I love about you. That's why God gave me you!"

Together they researched the Bible and shared insights while sitting around the dining table with their Bibles, periodicals, articles, and brochures from various sources. Psalm 139 opened their understanding as they read that God created a child's inward parts in its mother's womb. The Lord's eyes saw its unshaped substance, and all their days were planned and written in His book before a single one of them began. They talked about the call of Moses at the burning bush where God sent a man who had trouble talking to speak His message to the king of Egypt. And the Lord said to him, "Who made the human mouth? Who makes a person mute or deaf, seeing or blind? Is it not I, who am God?"[15]

They realized that God often chose those who were weak, afraid, unworthy, sinful, despised, and unlovely to do His work, so He would be glorified for accomplishing things that otherwise couldn't be done. They discussed the curse God placed upon the Earth after Adam's sin which invaded every aspect of life including the genes of the entire human race. They found in Leviticus 21 where Aaron, the brother of Moses, became the High Priest whose duty it was to bring offerings into the Holy Place of the Tabernacle, as well as other duties there. These responsibilities were to be passed on to his descendants. But the Lord made an exception to anyone in his lineage that had a physical defect. These were disqualified to perform the work! Excluded was anyone who was blind, lame, disfigured, deformed, crippled with foot or hand, hunchbacked, dwarfed, with any eye defect, running sores or damaged testicles. These men were born into the tribe and family whose specially chosen job was to minister in the dwelling place of God. They could still eat the food provided for the priestly family just as all the others. It was only the job assignment that was restricted from them.

Laura got up and brought more coffee to refresh their cups and said, "I can understand that, but the thing that's notable is that the Lord

---

[15] Exodus 4:11

expected such children to be born even into the priestly line! The Lord knew the curse would affect *all* peoples. So he specifically made provision for these situations. He didn't indicate those with defects should be killed or prevented from enjoying their lives. He intended for them to be accepted as they were and respected as equals in all other ways."

"That's quite a revelation, isn't it?" Jim nodded in agreement.

They read widely, researched the internet, attended meetings with those who were experts on the defect, and received advice from numerous sources. They were surprised to know that so many others had faced this same experience and embraced it gladly. Gradually, they came to a strong agreement and commitment that the Lord knew this child would come to them. They would brace themselves for the worst and prepare to give their best. By the time Scott was born, they were ready to meet his every need and give him all the love they had.

Later, when their little bundle of joy was sitting and playing on the floor with all sorts of toys, Jim said jokingly, "I wonder what he's going to think when I take him fishing?"

Laura looked back as she was walking away, "He may not understand how to bait a hook or where fish come from, but as long as he is with you, I bet he'll like it!" Their two boys grew together and learned to get along, and Keith became an important helper to his little brother.

Jim recalled that he used to think he could be a good man as an atheist, just as a Christian could be good believing in God. But his exposure to the large population with Down's syndrome children helped add a fuller dimension to his Christian worldview. And Jim added more girth to his belief. He began studying the origin of the world along with creation scientists. By the time the object in space came along, he was well grounded in the Word of God and had been teaching the Bible in church for over twelve years. Occasionally, he brought Scriptural insights into his university classes when it applied to subjects there.

Jim and Laura learned from this experience to turn to the Word of God again and again to gain direction when a crisis or difficult matter needed solving—a practice they would utilize throughout their lifetimes. It was a good thing; they were going to need it. Yes, his perception had shifted enormously. His delight in the Word of God was appreciated and admired by church members, friends, neighbors, and co-workers—everywhere except in one place where it was despised and resisted.

And the faculty and administration at Quad University were determined to do something about it.

∞

5

ACADEMICS

I n the university classroom, Jim was nearing the end of his lecture. "We've gained this ability to search the Heavens as a result of a Dutch eyeglass maker in 1609, whose children used them to look up at night to the stars. Thus the Optic Tube, that profound, 'miraculous' device which we take for granted today, was developed into what has become our telescope. On your written assignment there are galaxies in and around the Big Dipper's bowl for you to examine. M-81 and M-82 are within one-half degree of each other in the northwest corner. Other interesting sites include Galaxy M-108, the 'Owl' planetary nebula M-97, the barred spiral galaxy M-109, and the double star 'Winnecke 4, also called M-40. Up to now, we're aware of about fifty galaxies, just within the four corners or bowl of the Big Dipper! The total of all the stars in that square is a raw estimate of more than five thousand billion stars. Quite a shock to the average guy walking across the pasture over in Pecos County.

"However, fifteen years ago the Hubble telescope was pointed in a basically empty area near the Big Dipper to a spot about the size of a grain of sand in space. They left the lens open for ten days. When they looked at what it collected, they found that near 'empty' place contained three thousand galaxies. Today it's estimated that there are one hundred billion galaxies in the universe—and counting. No wonder the old time astronomers put on their dress suits when they studied the Heavens. They felt they were in the presence of God and worshipped Him while they worked.

"As a side issue, I've given you the ancient names of the seven stars in the Big Dipper, and we've seen how each name interestingly has something to do with sheep or a sheepfold. The point I want to leave you with is, why is a 'sheepfold' up there in space? Because as I've mentioned to you, all the old constellations that can be seen without a telescope tell the story of the history and future

> *He made all the stars—the Bear, Orion, the Pleiades and the constellations of the southern sky.*
>
> *(Job 9:9 NLT)*

of the human race. Please take note that according to Genesis chapter one, all the stars were created and named before He made man. Who but God could have stamped the information into the constellations by their names, which tell the story He wanted us to know even before man was created? He knows all things in advance, past, present, and future. The stars of the constellations give the same account we have in God's Word, the Holy Bible. Nature and nature's Creator always tell the same story of the Father and His only Son, Jesus Christ, who was sent to be our Redeemer."

"What about the Little Dipper?" a student inquired. "Do the stars in it tell us something like this?"

"Yes, all seven stars in the Little Dipper describe another sheepfold—the Church. We have all the names of the seven stars, but don't know which name goes with each particular star. The Big Dipper represents the saints of the Old Testament, and the Little Dipper, the believers in Christ of this present age in which we live.

"There is so much more to learn about the constellations. But I want you to know that just because we are learning about the billions of stars located in and around the bowl of the Big Dipper, we mustn't miss the simple and profound message that the constellation was put up there for in the first place. There are two folds. The constellation Bootes represents the Shepherd who protects them and whom they are all to follow to green pastures. He also keeps them from Draco the Dragon, the constellation that crawls right between the two sheepfolds, a symbol of the devil, who attempts to lead them in the opposite direction from Polaris, the North Star, which represents Jesus. More on this later. Have a great week-end."

As Jim entered the Lippershey Telescope, LT, and walked passed Marcus' office door, Marcus looked up and motioned for him to enter. Jim came in and sat on a chair near Marcus' desk, leaning forward. Marcus wrinkled his brow as he spoke, "Sir, I know you're already aware of the stir among the faculty at Quad State concerning your religious views. There appears to be a nest of vipers there that are never going to rest until they inflict a poisonous wound to you and your position and move you out. We've been hearing about their jealousy, envy, and hostility for quite a while now. It's amazing that they're so hateful to someone so full of the fruit of the Spirit."[16] Then, smiling, he said, "I thought there wasn't any law against love, joy, peace, patience, gentleness, goodness, faithfulness, meekness, and self-control!"

Jim sat back in the chair shaking his head slightly and seriously said, "It's amazing, Marcus. I hardly say much about the Bible in class. When I do, it fits into the lesson anyway. But we know what it's all about. God hasn't been welcomed in public classrooms now for many years. Today's

---

[16]   Galatians 5:22-23

overly mis-educated elite are smarter in the things of the world than the children of light.[17] So we must be wise in what we do while being harmless in our attitudes.

"It's inevitable that questions should come up about Christianity and the Bible in any class that deals with nature—especially here in the university founded by William Ashbrook, who was not only a noted astronomer but also an outstanding Christian leader. Just look how far an institution can move away from its original rules of operation. Ashbrook required each professor to take an oath declaring his belief in the Scriptures of the Old and New Testaments and promise to explain them with integrity and faithfulness according to the best light God would give him. It was also obligatory that special care be taken as to the moral behavior of the students conducive to the principles of the Christian protestant religion. That historic beginning and tradition has been lost by modern leaders who have outgrown God and substituted transitory science without a foundation for Him."

"You're exactly right, sir. Those high standards were hacked away by the enemy of truth, the great liar in whom there is no truth, so that today that which was cherished is now despised," Marcus replied.

Jim continued, "The old fallen flesh nature has to be intolerant of everything spiritual. Most of the faculty which are dyed-in-the-wool atheists have sensitive antennas and pick up on anything that threatens their insecure stance. I'm sure students bring biblical issues up in their classes, and the professors don't have the background to discuss them except with their usual bland statements. They're hostile against anything that has to do with God. And we should expect such treatment from those who don't know the Lord. But it mustn't catch us off guard. We have the Scriptures that tell us of the devices of the devil. We have

---

[17]   Luke 16:8

to be sweet and submitted to the Lord as He handles the situation. The enemies of Jesus thought they could get rid of Him by crucifying Him. But God used their wrath to bring praise to Him in the end. I'm not going to give up my freedom to live a Christian life in the environment of persecution. If early Christians had done that, we would have never heard the truth. How the rules changed from the foundation of the university is a puzzle. Likely, the trustees slowly moved the Bible out with their new-fangled discoveries that were deemed beyond the Bible, so 'we don't need it anymore.'"

"Why do they have to be so antagonistic over even small things?" Marcus asked.

"Marcus, ignorance is just like darkness in Scripture. It's even punishment to the devil and his followers. God speaks of people being in darkness and having their minds blinded. What are they without? God who is *love* and *light*. Unbelievers oppose Him and thus hate what God is—light. Jesus said they love darkness because their deeds are evil. Christians are the light of the world. If we don't let our light shine, it doesn't bother the darkness. But when we let it shine, it's literally torment to those who would rather be in the dark. They are in love with their own misery. False prophets prophesy lies, and the people love to have it so.[18] Take the devil, for example. He knows God but can't enjoy Him, and that's punishment in itself, for he can't think of God without torment. So it is with Satan's followers who are ignorantly in the dark."

"That's pretty plain isn't it? Well, they want to bring 'charges' against you for living like Jesus! Anyway, friends keep passing on to me the rumble that's in the background."

"Yes, Marcus, I know. Thanks for keeping me informed. I keep praying that God will get me ready for the confrontation or whatever

---

[18] Jeremiah 5:31

they come up with. I believe God's in control of all things. And whatever they do, He's able to overrule it or still use it for my good and His glory. But I don't look forward to it. Conflict is always tough. There's no telling what they'll be up to next."

∞

6

RE-LEARNING

Opportunities at Quad U and STSA were overwhelming. Jim's creative mind wouldn't stand still. Astronomy required so much thought and meditation. Many of the ideas about space were merely theories and guesses, and it took untold hours to confirm the few "facts" that had emerged. He worked hard at his studies and teaching and became an excellent administrator at STSA. His relationship with the students, as well as his scholastic achievements had been outstanding.

But, because of the animosity he received from the faculty and trustees, he perceived it must have come from the hostility they already had toward God and the Bible, and not primarily toward him. History had demonstrated it was always standard procedure for humanity to oppose and disobey God and His Word. The world was still hostile against Him. Jim was merely living in the world that had gone astray from its Maker. After all, if there were a God, they'd be accountable to Him for their behavior. Jim recalled in his mind the days when he delved more deeply into philosophy and humanism and made a mental note of their final conclusions and worldview that left mankind with nothing but smiling into the dark. There was no absolute standard of morality, kindness, wrong, or consequences for any behavior. Relevancy reigned. He concluded at that time the world was actually a bad place for him—worse for most others. Therefore, all he could think of to do was make the best of it, be safe, be cautious, stay healthy, and get whatever he could out of it.

He'd sorted out the hundreds of millions of years it took to form the geological column. He'd studied the fossil record of marine invertebrates and even noted that ninety-five percent of them were mere shellfish. But who was he to dispute the overwhelming claims of reputed scientists and leading educators of the world? Jim could only conclude evolution to be superior to all other explanations of where people came from and where they were going and believed it would be able to discredit all other theories.

But in spite of all the information he'd digested, it didn't mean that he never gave a thought to the limits that evolution and humanism left him with. It meant that he came from nothing and would leave blank. He did consider it strange that the human mind, produced by evolution, should be able to even *think* of these things which were doubtless impossible to experience. How could evolution produce a mind capable of thinking beyond what's possible? Why would people have the ability to reason that which is unreasonable? The desire for "utopia" here or later seemed to be mockery from an evolutionary viewpoint. Or could it be that if there actually was a God, this was His way of telling us there really are two destinies: one promising full realization of every human desire and the other total denial of those desires.

That was then. Today Jim was a spiritual man, focused upon God and His will for his life, blessed and satisfied, content, and involved in the work of his eternal Savior. He was working in an institution composed of fallen men who would inevitably work downward from spiritual truth and persecute those who served the Lord. It was a world-wide dilemma of entropy—the tendency for all things to deteriorate. Quad U had been constituted as a strong Christian school and had now come to disdain Christianity. Conflict was inevitable, but he was not willing to simply walk away and allow students to be overcome by darkness.

Jim and Laura had purchased a new place to live out in the country not far from the Lippershey Telescope, although a little farther to Quad University. It was a haven for the four of them with open acreage all around, plenty of running room for the kids, and a pleasant diversion from the daily routine of work. Jim complimented Laura constantly for the outstanding way she had given herself to raising Scott. Together they had surrounded him with love, and he responded with improvements. His obedience was excellent, his sharing with Keith commendable, and his willingness to learn noticeable. But it hadn't been easy.

Laura's mom, Martha, had come to visit them and stayed a couple of weeks to help out with the move and assist them in adjusting to the new place. She added another dimension to the family. She was an old-time, grandmotherly type that everyone loved to be around; serious, yet lighthearted and kind—the type that, though old, always stayed young. She was a little on the heavy side and the added weight seemed to be full of happiness. She had genuine compassion for everyone and a yearning for them to enjoy the best life possible. Jim loved how she teased him about the Lord in a good way. When Jim entered the kitchen one morning, Martha noticed the weariness in his face.

"You poor dear! You look like you need rest."

"I could use a lot of it, all right. I have a thrilling event to be happy about and at the same time a concern about the university that kept me up most of the night. The faculty can't stand for me to teach that God is real and that He literally created the world."

"Well, the Lord likely has something good in store for you as you worship him. That's when the best insights come to our minds and hearts."

"You're so right, Mom. I'm glad Sunday's coming up," he said.

"Jim, I believe the Lord's up to something good in your life."

"What makes you so sure?"

"I know Him and what He has in mind."

"But that's taking me farther than I can understand right now."

"I know. But He'll get you there soon enough," Martha confidently asserted.

"You always bring Jesus into everything, don't you?" Jim chuckled.

"Absolutely not! I never bring Him into anything. He's *already* into everything. I simply acknowledge He's here and then see what He wants me to do. It's unbelief that keeps Him away from everything He wants to be in for us. God's a gentleman and never imposes Himself upon us. If we don't want His help, don't want Him around, or don't need Him, He'll let us go on our troubled way. Even Christians do that without realizing it."

"Martha, you're something! Where do you get that kind of thinking?"

"From His wonderful Word, the Bible," she giggled. "He explains who He is and what He's like so we can get to know Him. But people only know as much as they choose to know. Isn't it strange that even Christians don't know Him very well? Open your eyes, Jim. This little rumble from the university is just part of the scheme He's got planned for your good future. Even if you didn't mention Creation as the origin of the universe, they'd probably still give you a hard time just for being a Christian."

∞

7

Perplexed

Observatory efforts across the country were still unable to photograph the curious object. Astronomers were puzzled that the only way they could inform people about the mysterious object was by word of mouth, and the only way they could see it was through telescopes or binoculars. Strange!

Opinions continued to flare across the spectrum of "authorities" about the strangely—lighted space object. Dr. Joseph Markel, of the American Atheistic Society declared it to be an Illusion. The outspoken philosopher referred to illusionists who can make buildings appear and disappear. "They dupe the public every day by their trickery. They're very entertaining," he stated, "but something larger than usual is inflicting this illusion upon the whole world. It's probably being done from a satellite." He referred to astronomers who'd reported the object in one place today, and tomorrow farther south in space. "They can't even photograph it. This exposes the truth that it can't be real. It's merely projected into different spots here and there to create commotion and fear. Doubtless the intention is to focus on some religious plan to further capture the futile idea that there is a god."

The International Aeronautics Team took an investigative approach. They were using an astronomy spacecraft with X-ray capabilities to survey the cosmic microwave background radiation from both the ground and from space with the Microwave Anisotrophy Probe, MAP. This was being done in conjunction with the Xron satellite.

Another point of view came from, Emma Van Dosler, head of Psychology department at Berkley University, who said, "We can know that the astronomic movements by this 'object,' 'comet,' or 'space capsule' are a sign of the progress of our humanity. After so many billions of years of evolution, anything's possible. When this phenomenon is over, we'll discover that it's enhanced our growth, understanding, and ability to cope with the future."

Pope Johan Martin, along with William Grahamson, called for world-wide repentance and prayer. Special prayer meetings were being held in thousands of Christian churches throughout the world. Many religious people who were accustomed to using vain repetitions were abandoning them in an attempt to approach God in person. Others who commonly used prayer wheels were learning more about prayer and the Person to whom they were praying. Meanwhile the number of suicides had drastically increased since this "block" in space had been reported.

Television Station XLAD, in Detroit, reported a near riot had been quelled there where the "Justice For Us" group attacked local merchants with a frantic, panic grab of everything in sight. They were taking advantage of the uncertain future to justify their greed. Their sheer numbers overwhelmed employees who had to turn away and hide. Police had arrested about forty-five persons at this point. The leader of the group hadn't yet been found. Consumer Watch revealed that everything in existence that even came close to being a telescope or binoculars had already been bought and was in use. Since the Cube couldn't be photographed, everyone wanted to see it for themselves. Factories were back ordered for two years.

Curiosity had all but "killed the cat" as the unknown continued to be all that people talked about and discussed. Panic and fear ran rampant. The Hubble Telescope was unable to capture a picture of this object. It was invisible to a camera, but only visible to viewers through their magnifying instruments.

The world waited.

∞

8

GROWING

L ife was anything but usual, but it did go on. It was turning out to be a remarkable week for Jim and Laura. She called out to Jim as he was leaving the door for work one morning, "Don't forget Keith's baseball game tonight."

Jim was relieved and encouraged that details of the Cube were becoming clearer. He was able to communicate to Rex, and then on to the Cubicles that the improved view of the New Jerusalem was more defined, indisputable, and even taking on glorious colors! Quad U was maneuvering their strategy to oppose Jim's religious beliefs, as well as his teaching position. Jim and Laura had trusted the Lord through the past fifteen years to raise their Down syndrome child, Scott, as best they could. He showed improvement by putting more words into sentences now, and his understanding had expanded through special schooling. He was somewhat more advanced than anyone had expected. The family was involved in their local church, which had a special needs ministry; their oldest child Keith was outstanding in school and sports; they were reading the Bible and growing in their relationship with Jesus; they were putting what they knew about their vocation and hobbies into practical use by helping others by serving through the church food pantry; and they were experiencing just enough tension to guarantee spiritual growth.

That evening, Jim and Laura were in the car taking seventeen year old Keith to his baseball game. The sky was clear and temperature just right for a great game. Fifteen year old Scott, who was always the friendliest boy in the park, was with them.

Keith leaned forward from the back seat and asked, "Dad, why does there have to be an on-going controversy about God, the Cube, and whether or not to use the Bible at Quad U?"

"Good question, Keith. You see, many members of the faculty claim that there is no God. So when they hear that the Cube came from God, they can't see anything good in it. And they don't believe in God because they don't want Him to be able to tell them how to live. If they deny His existence, they think they can get away with living their own way without any accountability to Him. It's just about that simple."

"How can they come to that conclusion, Dad, with all of creation telling them different?"

"They make it up, Son. The process is called idolatry. Obviously nothing could come into existence by itself. Life in any form is a mind-boggling complexity—far beyond anyone's ability to fathom. By faith, we know it took Almighty God to create the world and everything in it. And He put in on record that He created every physical thing out of nothing![19] Unbelievers attribute God's almighty power to nature, and say 'mother nature' did it—all by herself. Of course, then they have to analyze nature in every way they can, expecting it to prove their case. Since they attribute power to it, they look to it to respond with facts.

---

[19]   Hebrews 11:3

And when she doesn't work, and refuses to cooperate, they make up 'facts' and prefer denial to the truth."

"But, Keith," Laura interjected, "just think of the Cube right overhead; it's a miracle of God, too. And it's there to test and prove the faith of those who love Him."

"Yeah, I know that. But there are some kids in school who don't go along with it. Tommy's one of them and always argues about anything that has to do with God. He parents are unbelievers and I guess he feels he has to think and talk like them.

Jim's fervent study opened his eyes to the fact that the entire universe had God's "fingerprints" all over it. Not only did animals, trees, birds and fish speak of His creation wonders, but the Heavens literally declared the glory of God and proclaimed the work of His hands. There were times when students raised questions about creation, as it had to do with astronomy and the universe. Jim gave them the theories that were on the latest griddle and also contrasted them with the revelation of what the Bible taught. Because of his strong influence on campus, other faculty members were furious that he would even mention God or the Bible, since most professors were secular humanists, atheists, agnostics, skeptics and other freethinkers. There couldn't help but be questions, disagreements, and dialogue in the classrooms. Jim handled their doubts wisely since he had formerly been an atheist, and knew the struggle they had. But, of course, there were a few who complained to their other professors, who in turn took advantage of accusing Jim to the dean of teaching a Bible class!

And the establishment didn't like it.

∞

9

CONFRONTATION

Dr. David Harris, head of the Department of Astronomy, and Dean of faculty at Quad State Astronomical University, approached Jim in the hall and wanted to meet with him to inquire about his teaching and his beliefs. They got together later that day in Harris' office, which was filled with plaques, awards, and various reminders of his outstanding work for the university. Harris appeared to be a "yes man," which means he was in a position he wanted to keep at any cost. It was easy to couch down into what others wanted and expected of him and oppose anything that the majority didn't approve of. He was a middle aged portly man with white hair. He carried an academic air about him and was very committed to his agenda. Jim entered the office and was politely asked to take a seat. Harris got right to the point.

With an air of unquestioned authority mixed with flattery, he began. "Dr. Waltham, your position here at Quad University has been a great asset. There's no question about it. I've always been pleased with the quality of your scholarship as well as the effectiveness of your leadership at the Space Telescope Science Association. However, I keep hearing rumors and accusations that you are using the Bible in your classroom and teaching it as part of the curriculum. Tell me what is going on."

Jim was happy that he would have the opportunity to speak to Harris in person. He thought it would be to his advantage to tell him as much as possible so he would understand his position and motivation.

"Dr. Harris, I'm glad you asked. I appreciate your coming to me and allowing me to share with you personally. Sir, my scientific views have come to encompass more than what merely meets the academic eye. It reaches into the very heart of man. To have studied space as intensely as I have has been an astounding experience. Of course I'm overwhelmed and awed at its vastness, beauty, and cosmic variations. It's wonderful and I love it. But what's the purpose of all of creation, except to understand that it reveals the glory, sovereignty, love, and power of God? Of course, I'm not having a Bible lesson in my classrooms. There are students who have serious questions about evolution, humanism, and atheism. I lay out the tenants of these theories, as they relate to our studies, as well as what the Word of God says. I personally believe the Bible to be superior in authority and find that it's also scientifically sound. These times present a practical application to science that meets the inner need of the students. I treat such questions just as I assume other faculty members would treat them and give them their personal opinions as well."

"Are you telling me that you believe the Bible's simple account of creation?" Harris asked.

"Yes, I find it absolutely delightful—and true to science as well. My knowledge that God is the Creator of all things is exactly what most of the world's most famous scientists have always believed. And there are thousands who still do. It's a logical and beneficial approach to astronomy."

Jim could see that his prolonged and excited explanation was going nowhere with Harris. His heart became saddened to perceive that all Harris wanted Jim to do was to apply mathematical equations to space, toot whatever amazements he could come up with for the rest of his life, and give the glory to Quad U. Harris was lost at sea in his own world of astronomical distractions.

Jim tried to go on . . .

"It's hard for me to understand why you feel the Bible is superior to modern science," said Harris. "The creation taking place in a mere seven days doesn't fit the facts of today's research."

"I'm sorry to disagree, sir. Too many of today's scientists are overlooking excellent scholarly and scientific research by numerous organizations who have abandoned the theory of evolution and Big Bang and present God's account as perfectly accurate. Doesn't every other explanation complicate its own hypotheses, and the more scientists that accept those ideas, the more they disagree with each other continually? What theory can be presented without a large bag of contradictions and unknowns?"

> *Yes, I have more insight than my teachers, for I am always thinking of your decrees.*
>
> *(Psalm 119:99 NLT)*

"That's what further research is about, Dr. Waltham," Harris concluded.

"After a hundred and fifty years since Darwin, aren't there more questions than ever—and fewer 'facts?'" Jim asked. "And has anyone proven the biblical account to be false?"

"It's too childish, amateurish. Too skimpy to be scientific," Harris droned.

"Have you considered that perhaps it wasn't intended to be anything more, sir? It's written so that the common man can accept God's miraculous work by faith. And isn't that what the evolutionist, and Big

Bang proponents require? Aren't other theories even less believable, more complicated, and humanly fabricated? What sort of education would a person have to attain to even plow through all the technical terminology and speculation?" Jim asked. "And I appreciate your time, Dr. Harris," Jim continued, raising his hand as a gesture of sincerity, "but don't you agree we simply have two different authorities? You prefer man's educated approach, beginning with what he can look at, while God begins with nothing and speaks it all into existence. Both demand faith and exclude the other.".

"Exactly!" said Harris. "I'm amazed. I never thought I'd hear such words from you. I felt the criticisms coming from others had to be false and exaggerated. I don't know what to think. This is so far from scholarship, scientific research, and facts that it's hard to believe."

"Dr. Harris, I hope you won't be offended," Jim continued, "but education is primarily about truth. It does little good to present several ways to solve a problem if only one of them works. And it's counterproductive to eliminate one or more solutions without first proving them false.

"If I may illustrate the case, creation and evolution are like two teams on a football field. An evolutionist is given the ball, and he runs out of the stadium for several miles. He thinks he is still in the game because he has the ball. The game is officially sixty minutes, but he calls in and says he needs thousands of years to complete his study of the rules of the game. Then he needs millions of years, then a billion years, then fifteen billion years. He'll never have enough time to finish the game because he changes the rules along with every idea. The original playing field is Genesis chapter 1 and 2, and it's affirmed throughout the rest of authoritative Scripture. If other 'evidence' contradicts this, it's out of bounds, and if someone leaves the field, he forfeits the game to those who adhere to the rules of the originator of the game. I'd like for you to consider the question, is there any danger in telling Almighty God how He should've explained His creation? Haven't men compiled many thousands of pages trying to do so and the volume keeps growing without any possible end in sight? Those who vote on an alternative view get to read up on it as it becomes more contradictory and illogical, and they'll die before science concludes its recommendation."

"The evidence points to another explanation—I choose the Big Bang."

"And there we have it," replied Jim. "One person chooses to let 'evidence' point away from God, when He says Creation points to Him."

"Dr. Waltham, the views you're giving me are unsettling and unacceptable in this University. These statements are contrary to those held by this institution. They'll not hold up under the scrutiny of your peers. As for 'truth,' your use of it smacks of authoritative, fundamental absolutism. We in this generation do not have anything that is unchanging and always true."

After a small hesitation, Jim leaned forward a little, tilted his head, and offered, "Dr. Harris, I've been wondering about something. Doesn't the University itself claim its commitment to truth by its very nomenclature? Its motto is still 'Veritas' or 'truth.' Since 'uni' means 'one,' and 'versity' means 'truth,' what *one truth* was this Uni-versity founded upon? What has it changed to? How did it slip from the seeking of all truth wherever it's found, to disbelieving in anything that even appears to be enduring? What does it now postulate? It used to require chapel attendance. Its mission statement says in part, 'To foster the knowledge of and love of God . . . 'I wonder how other viewpoints manage to discount the creator's own testimony. How is it that mentioning God or creation is now wrong when it used to be expected by all professors?"

"That was before we gained a better knowledge through scientific research," Harris said.

"Yes and such research still goes on . . . and on . . . without conclusive proof, Sir. I wonder did strangers take over the school and remove its original intent? Did this radical change take place by legal procedures, and wide-spread publication? Or is it merely presumed to be 'official' by common consent of those on the board and faculty? I'm only asking for information and facts. I don't understand how the Bible and God were swept out the door and replaced with ever-changing scientific theories. Could it be that Quad wants its professors to be robots for the latest conjectures rather than thoughtful men committed to honesty and certainty?"

Sidestepping the issue, Harris said, "I don't know what to make of your thinking now, Dr. Waltham. I am not one to pounce upon your theology, for I hope you can change back to your former beliefs. But otherwise, there'll come a time when the fire you have started will burn you out of this academic setting."

"Sir, that's not my desire. And as you know, I've read and deeply studied the theories of origins, and they all require an astounding leap of faith to accept. But I've never seen anyone prove that God doesn't exist. Neither have I ever seen anything existing that didn't have a parent. Is it unreasonable to believe God, since our institution claimed to believe in Him when it opened its doors? And as far as origins, sir, how could our origin have taken place out in space for us to discover thousands of years later? According to God, the Heavens and the Earth were created together and were there to be believed from day one. A phenomenal waste of time, energy and money has been lost with that worthless endeavor. I'd appreciate being able to dialogue about my beliefs, and the personal relationship I have with God. They're the same that others have embraced since the beginning of time."

"I think we're through with this conversation, Dr. Waltham," Harris said.

"And I will always wish the best for you, sir."

They parted company—in more than one way.

A few members of the Quad trustees held an informal meeting at the home of chairman, Thomas Fain. After snacks and a few drinks, he asked everyone to be seated and brought up the subject on his mind. "Gentlemen, Dr. Waltham has suffered a psychological set-back, a mental debility, evidently from his conversion to Christianity somewhere in the past. It's usually predicated by a reach for some form of security, and we know religion is the common crutch that fits into the lives of many. Unfortunately, he's bypassed the better resources of science and modern research. His fall all the way down to fundamentalism has now caused him to reach out to students in the attempt to get them into the same boat."

Carl Eckert, joined in. "This literal interpretation of Scripture is what ruins his philosophy. It's easy to see through. Why would anyone keep on denying the fact that Genesis is a myth and fits in with all the other myths of creation? The literal approach to the Bible cordons off the universe into a small cardboard box! That system is so childish and remote that it is an embarrassment to the entire university."

"My sentiments, exactly," chimed in Oscar Huckelby "Why did this have to happen to a man of such influence? I've always respected him as a scientist, but he's going too far with his religion. We have to consider the beliefs of the other students. I'd really hate to see Jim leave the university, but what choice do we have? His position and reputation taint the rest of us. I don't want anyone to think I'm like him."

"Not only that," said Yeats Roberts, "Consider the global impact of exploration and education that involves the whole world and identifies us with his particular brand of morality. I can't stand a man who thinks he is better than we are. I don't know what he's still doing here. I'll miss his congeniality, and yes, he can teach astronomy and make it very appealing to the students. But he has to go."

"I knew you would feel this way," said Fain, "That's why we need to take steps to rid ourselves of his place on the faculty. But we have to be careful and wise about how we do it. He's such a fanatic that he has attracted scores of students to himself."

"Let's cut to the point," said Oscar, "I for one, could care less about the repercussions. We need to eliminate him now. Every day it's more disgusting to have to see his smiling face and know that he thinks his religion makes him equal to or better than us. The next thing you know, he'll believe the Genesis creation account."

After a few chuckles, Dr. Harris injected, "He already does!" This was followed by more surprise and a wave of laughter.

"What a shame and a waste of intelligence," stated Eckert.

"Then we agree that we must intervene and face him, take the first steps of reprimand, and then fire him in the near future," Fain summarized.

They all enthusiastically concurred.

∞

10

Pressured

A few days later, grilled hamburgers were enjoyed at the Waltham home for fellowship and discussion about the Cube and additional subjects on their minds. Attending were Marcus and his wife, Cindy. Other friends included a couple of trustees and three faculty members of Quad U. Jim wanted them to know about the up-coming announcement by Rex and their conclusion about the Cube being the New Jerusalem. They were amazed as well as relieved over the revelation. Jim described what he was viewing through the telescope, and the details that were discernible. As they all neared the completion of the meal, he let them know how pleased he was to get to take part in the television announcement, but didn't know how that would affect the trustees and faculty at Quad.

Doug Ingram, a Quad trustee, turned toward Jim and voiced his concern. "They should all be proud that a member of the faculty is on top of this matter. But I hope they don't fire you, Jim. It's already a tragedy that our university has drifted so far from its initial goals. My father was one of the original founders of the school, and for many years he made sure that all faculty members were sound in doctrine—Bible doctrine, that is, before being hired. The school stood for more than academics and produced godly men and women who made a difference in society. Now, modern fads and fakes take precedence over godliness—and even truth."

"I know what you mean Doug. Unfortunately, as you know, everything tends toward entropy," Jim answered.

"Our school's never had a greater leader than Dr. Waltham," Marcus said. "But I'm afraid the other trustees only want conformity. And Jim is anything but that."

"Hey, now, I didn't call you friends over here for an admiration party," Jim said. "I think it's great to get together with those we love and celebrate along the way. Laura gives me all the support I'll ever need. Keith and Scottie give me understanding and keep me humble! But I never doubt your loyalty, either. That's what real friends are for. I want to keep up with the difficulties each of you face. We're all in the world that's in trouble and need each other's encouragement as we journey along the path the Lord has placed before us."

"The issue of origin and creation has troubled every school and home for the past hundred and fifty years," said a faculty member, as he walked up closer to the group with a small frown on his concerned face. "But I've never found any reason to question the Genesis account. Those who do so are likely hoping for an escape from God's judgment. Even some believers 'accommodate' the assumption of evolution because they've accepted the theories of the pseudo-scientists who follow Satan's ways, claim authority, and promote lies. The same goes for those who reject the virgin birth of Christ or the miracles he worked or the resurrection and his promise to return. Whatever God says, the devil brings doubt and disobedience just as he did to Eve in the garden. He literally called God a liar and is still doing it. But the creation story will survive them all. It's established in Heaven and can't fail."

"There'll probably be plenty of people who won't like the Cube's coming either," said another faculty member with a shrug of his shoulders. "Anything God does is opposed by someone who wants to put Him in His 'place.' But I can't wait for it to get here and find out what He's going to do!"

Then Jim shared with them the Cubicles desire to find out the purpose of the Cube's coming and their possible involvement in that purpose. "We've begun a list of possibilities all based on the Bible. Of course, the Lord could let us know and save a lot of research and brain strain," he said with humor, "but His ways are not our ways and He's good at giving us a challenge as we seek the Holy Spirit's help." He urged each person there to join the investigation and email their input.

The next week, Dr. Harris wanted to keep stoking the fire between Jim and Quad in anticipation of the upcoming disciplinary action or whatever the trustees came up with. He approached Jim again in the hall, which was deserted, so they had time for a private conversation.

"Dr. Waltham, I hope you're not still stirring up the students, getting them all excited about the stars instead of teaching them astronomy."

"I beg your pardon, sir. But aren't stars a part of my curriculum? I don't recall even mentioning the Bible since we spoke. And I wonder what I'm teaching about stars, astronomy, or the universe that's not true?"

"You know what I mean, teaching the Bible. You're bringing the Bible into the stars!" Harris was standing with his legs apart, his hands waving and head shaking. "You're getting away from the teaching of science. Religion and science don't mix. Our university is known for its commitment to the highest standard of scientific research. We're a springboard into the great unknown where students are equipped with the best of knowledge and preparation. To reach back into the past and expect 'flat world' theology to mix with modern technology is absurd."

Jim's heart was heavy, his face sad with concern for the dean. *How could he be so blind and unreasonable*, he thought. He managed to say, "Dr. Harris, without being critical or demeaning, could I ask you if you have personally ever read the Bible through?"

"I grew up in church where the Bible was taught every week," he replied.

"You don't want to answer the question, I guess," Jim lowered his head, giving him a chance to get out of it.

"That's none of your business. I've read it enough. It had a place in the past. Not today," Harris stated.

Jim softly spoke as he looked into Harris' eyes, "You know, I've been reading it through every year for the past ten years, and I can tell that biblical truth mixes perfectly with every other truth in the universe. The Creator is not unscientific at all. 'Flat world' thinking isn't even in the Bible. I'm sorry, Dr. Harris. You're missing the best knowledge in the world. I know how you feel. We scientists are accustomed to accepting concepts of 'science' when they're advanced without proof. An authoritative voice is validity enough. But there's another Authority that is far beyond our intellectual abilities."

Then, Jim smiled and said, "It's thrilling to study the stars, galaxies, and handiwork of His making. That makes it more personal, not mere abstract information stored as usable gigabytes in our brain—with no relationship to the One who created it all and who loves us and wants us to live with Him forever."

"Dr. Waltham, you know I don't want to cause you any trouble, but there's a growing rumbling among faculty members about your beliefs. It's been there a long time now and getting to be a major issue. It's come up several times in trustee meetings. If things don't change, I'm afraid we'll have to let you go."

Jim, with deliberate and quiet resolve, said, "Well, sir, the Bible is not a subject in my classes. It's astounding that if it's ever mentioned somehow it becomes major in the minds of other faculty members. It is counted as anathema. It seems to threaten them. It's intolerable. I guess it all comes down to 'true or false.' They must consider it all false and without any sign of truth, or they wouldn't forbid it. After all, each and every theory postulated on the part of science usually has plenty of questionable—still-to-be-perfected areas, yet it's just fine to protect *them*. Why is that? Why is the Word of God unworthy of its place in the scientific world? Before something is forbidden in the classroom, shouldn't it be first proven false? I wonder if science has ever proven anything in the Bible to be wrong.

"Take me for instance, Dr. Harris. I was as much an atheist as anyone in the world. I never had given God as much as the time of the day in my life. I was resisting Him without knowing it. I was proud of my scholastic achievements and literally felt my knowledge was so superior that I didn't need a god. But I learned that I was very wrong. And I'm so glad I did. My conversion to Christ hasn't made me a numbskull. It's enlightened my entire educational experience. I know how to place the discoveries in a practical and meaningful way into my daily life. I've even found that the Bible has something to say about astronomy. Would it be wrong to mention and discuss that in an astronomy class like it used to be? Where is the mandate to remove all things spiritual?

"And as for toleration, shouldn't all fields of study be open to academic freedom? I think again of our university's original mission statement that says, 'to respect ideas and free expressions of the same in the spirit of cooperation.' It seems that limitations are only placed upon those who disagree with the status quo or the 'politically correct.' You know there are plenty of examples of 'science' being wrong when it went against the Bible."

"I know. I know. But I'm being caught in the middle of a controversy, and I don't like it."

"I understand. And I'm sorry about that. I certainly don't want to make your job any harder. On the other hand, I believe this university will be better off if academic freedom reigns in this department as it used to in the past. Why should it be prohibited without merit? The truth can stand upon its own two feet. Sir, there are plenty of people who are miserable and unhappy because of their prejudices who would love to have us be miserable with them. But they don't deserve that much attention."

"I don't know. I feel there is going to be a showdown of some sort. And I don't like what I see on the horizon."

"Have a good week-end, sir."

"You, too."

Jim could feel the pressure building. He'd been ignoring the growing realization that other faculty members were keeping their distance and short-changing him on friendship. He'd refused to think of what would happen if he were fired from the university. The joy of the Lord dominated his life and he was neglecting other matters that were not pleasant or productive—even if they included his position. He didn't even want to talk to Laura about it, but he couldn't wait to get home into her arms and her comforting disposition. That evening, shortly after supper, when they went out on the patio, he casually mentioned to Laura the conversation in the hall with Dr. Harris.

Jim turned to Laura and said, "Honey, Dr. Harris is doing his best to prevent my ever bringing the Lord into an astronomy class, and the usual faculty members are pushing his buttons to get rid of me. We had a little talk in the hall today. He's such an insecure figurehead that he has to act as the wind blows. Why is it that guys of his type always seem to get into the offices of authority, and then they don't have the leadership to be the man for the job? It's easy to tell what he believes, but he doesn't know what to do with it. He doesn't like to take a stand unless the majority, or the money, or the position requires it. One of these days it's going to blow up in my face. It's not surprising that there's an unwritten law that permeates practically all public schools, and especially universities, that talking about Jesus is off-limits. When atheism and evolution comes up in class, I present the theories and facts and what I believe about them. It's not unscholarly to discuss any view, to share what you know, and either refute it with facts or truth, or leave it to the students to solve it themselves. In all my reading, studying, research, and subjects, no one has ever taken serious issue with Christianity enough to take it doctrine by doctrine and disprove anything. Now the un-refuted teaching I am giving away free is being undermined without basis. It reminds me of something our pastor, Dr. Stone, said, 'Some people might short change you for your work, but they'll hate you for nothing. They despise God without even knowing Him, and they're committed not to read the Bible, His love book, and will go to any length to prevent others from reading it either.'"

From her chair next to his, Laura reached out to him, "I know sweetheart. I don't know how you take the pressure. I wish you could teach in a place where there was real academic freedom, and have everyone falling in love with Jesus like He wants."

"Yeah, well, that will never happen. Besides, there wouldn't be the opportunity to reach those who are in the dark and want out or to defeat the devil on his own territory. And Laura, I'm so glad to have you stand with me when others reject me. I sure do need your love."

"You are such a delight. I love you."

"Not as much as I love you."
"More."
"Never."
"Uh huh," as she kissed him.
"Mmmmm!"

∞

11

ANNOUNCEMENT, CONFLICT & EXCITEMENT

Sixty-one days after the Cube was sighted and reported, another sudden big movement took place. Again it was a one-third integral. The Cube was now two-thirds closer to Earth than it was when it first appeared in the vicinity of the Little Dipper. It had simply showed up there without any explanation as to how that could possibly have happened.

ABC Anchor man, Brian Sanders, began his nightly broadcast saying, "There's a lot of controversy over where this cubed object may hit, if it indeed does hit Earth, and the damage it would do. It's so huge that it would likely mean total disaster. With a fifteen hundred mile impact, it could move the Earth out of its orbit. It could cause earthquakes. It could move the tectonic plates of the continents. It could be literally 'the end of the world.'"

> *Arise, God, defend Your cause! Remember the insults that fools bring against You all day long.*
>
> *(Psalm 74:22 HCSB)*

Turning to his right side, he continued, "We have in our studio today two distinguished gentlemen who may be able to help us get a handle on this phenomenon. Dr. Richard Millikan, physicist and scientist at the University of Texas." Then turning to his left he continued, "And author and psychologist, at the University of Richmond, Virginia, Dr. Wesley Lansbury. Dr. Lansbury has written extensively about space invasions, abductions, flying saucers, and such. He's also been at the forefront with films and documentation of all that can be said about the U.S. Government and its secrecy surrounding the nuclear experimental site in New Mexico where so many mysterious things have reportedly taken place. Dr. Lansbury, we're glad to have you here today. What's your take on this situation concerning the 'block,' or 'Cube' as it's now being called?"

"Thank you, Mr. Sanders. I've been waiting and expecting something like this to happen for over forty years. This is the greatest proof of what I've been saying all along, that there are other beings out there in space. They're watching us, tracking us, making plans concerning humanity. Now it appears that they're making their greatest move. Space crafts in recent history have played an important part in our society. It's a shame that this fact has been swept under the table by so many organizations. Aliens have already abducted thousands of people. They've left undeniable tracks on the ground. They've been seen and reported by reputable persons who've told their incredible stories. But only now will they be vindicated. These aliens are extremely intelligent—far beyond humans. They obviously don't want to communicate with us. They don't need our elementary knowledge. And what they're up to now cannot be viewed as a positive thing by us. We're at their mercy. Whether they're hostile or benevolent we'll have to wait to see, but we're under their power."

"Thank you, Dr. Lansbury," Sanders replied. Then turning to his right side, he continued, "Dr. Millikan, What do you have to say about this situation?

"Well, there are several matters to consider," Millikan replied. "If it's a weapon traveling to Earth with destruction in mind, it'll no doubt accomplish that mission unless mankind can come up with a way to stop it or to communicate with it and reach an agreement.

"Secondly, it's been asked, 'Will it reduce in size as it enters Earth's atmosphere?' The answer to that question is probably, 'No.' It's demonstrated its ability to change speed and direction. Therefore, we believe that it's guided by intelligence. So it could slow down as it approaches Earth, and possibly even go into orbit. That's just an idea to consider, which consequently brings up a spaghetti bowl of other questions.

"Thirdly, its erratic behavior—rate of speed and direction—is totally unusual, even supernatural. It seems certain that Earth is its target or mission. Yet there's no way to calculate when this Cube will arrive at our planet. It appears to have a mind of its own. It's not under the control of nature as we know it, nor of any other atmospheric law or known influence. It appeared out of nowhere. After the amateur astronomer, Jay Smith, spotted it, the object has varied its speed and location intentionally to prevent an accurate time of arrival. But wherever it appears, it's obviously still 'aimed' at us."

"What can we do to prepare?" asked Sanders. "I've heard that people are talking about packing up and moving to Australia, Europe, or even the North Pole."

"That's too difficult to answer at this time. With the little we know about it, the only thing anyone could do—and I'm not one to sound too religious—is, 'Prepare to meet thy God,'[20] as the Bible prophet said. However, this is certainly a time for every living being on Earth to seriously consider the foundations of his or her being. It if were to hit America, for example, what would it matter how we prepared materially? In the worst-case scenario, if it were a solid material block and hit the Earth at a great speed, there'd be no place to hide. And regardless of where it would hit, the rest of the world would possibly have only a matter of minutes or hours before the Earth would become like the Twin Towers of the World Trade Center in New York, on 9/11/2001. It could completely crumble and disintegrate.

"But lest I leave you with only anxiety and panic, just remember this isn't the first time individuals or even mankind, have asked the questions: 'Why, God?' 'Why is this so big?' 'Why us?' 'What now?' 'What am I expected to do?' Such questions have been asked and eventually answered throughout the history of the world. It's a test of our very being, and we must face it as positively as possible. Being a pessimist won't help. Moaning and groaning doesn't produce the 'steel' within a man to meet the forces that try to command us. We must believe in other possibilities."

The following day, written notice was received by Jim Waltham from the Board of Trustees of Quad State University. They issued a reprimand to him concerning his religious views and his use of the university's classroom to expound them. It was noted that, "Sixty-six of the eighty-four faculty have signed a petition agreeing to this action. You are given an opportunity to respond at the next meeting in three days."

---

[20]   Amos 4:12

Suddenly, Jim felt totally weak. He'd hoped to avoid a confrontation, even though it appeared inevitable. He saw the chips stacking up against him, and now his opponents were ready to cash them in. Somehow he didn't feel spiritual at all! He hated such confrontations, but felt the conflict was worth it for the value of having the right to let God speak about His own creation. It wasn't in his nature to simply go along with keeping truth from students. Quad had been taken over by new religions that accepted no competition. The third day would be on Monday, the same day Rex Fleming was to make his announcement about the New Jerusalem! That put greater pressure upon him, but, on the other hand, it would only necessitate that he take the stand in the university that he had already taken in his heart.

He felt competent to intellectually dialogue and debate the issue, but it would take moral and spiritual power to say what he wanted to say. He didn't want to merely win a personal battle. He wanted to re-establish the teaching of truth in Quad U and, if possible, throughout the educational world. All godly scholarship had suffered under the backlash of pseudo-science against God's Word. If he lost this confrontation, it would at most damage his image, position and salary. Though there was a nervousness in his chest, he knew he had to continue in his pursuit of pleasing the Lord and the enjoyment of sharing his knowledge. He prayed, then looked over the charges for which he had to prepare: Teaching unproven religions theories as science; usurping class time to teach religion; ignoring cautions to cease such propaganda; and using the Bible as a textbook.

Jim sighed as he thought, *Of all the times to have to deal with this matter! I'll soon join Dr. Fleming on television to make public our views about the Cube. It looks like when the devil attacks, he always picks an opportune time to further his own causes!* Jim planned to spend every day in preparation for the meeting, but he knew in his soul he needed to break away from all the pressure. He was thankful that he had the confidence to present his stance, as well as to turn the tables on those who oppose biblical truth. He was up for the conflict, but his major concern was that he would control his emotions and allow the facts and the Spirit of God to do the work.

Rex managed to arrange the time slot for two days over XPJS TV in Odessa. He contacted the TV station and presented his plans in person to the station manager. The manager was reluctant to engage all the other news outlets, but felt he had nothing to lose. Air time was scheduled for the evening segment of the five o'clock news on the next Monday and Tuesday.

Jim knew he wasn't the only one having to handle trouble. His family had been under such pressure that they all needed some diversion and fun for relief. Over the week-end they got their four-wheelers out. Scott always rode with his dad. The four of them rolled out to the back of the acreage behind the house where an eight-foot deep, dry drainage ditch awaited their thrills. Keith took off as the others followed the leader. They traversed the ditch up and down both sides, between trees, and through the rough, rained out gullies. Going up steep banks required letting off the throttle occasionally so as not to flip over backwards.

After a tiring satisfaction on the "course," they pulled over to rest. They all had a refreshing drink of water and Keith spoke up about something that had been on his mind. "Dad, what if something goes wrong, and what if the Cube does hit the Earth and destroys the whole world?"

"Oh, Keith, I'm so glad you asked that question. It's bound to be on the mind of lots of people. I don't know why I haven't already done so, but, Son, I want you and your mother to go to the observatory tomorrow. We're going to look at the New Jerusalem together. I should've already done that with you both. You'll see that God's in sovereign control of His Earth. And I want you to realize that He's already told us what will happen to the world in the future, and that's not how it ends. There's always someone fearful that the world will be hit by an asteroid and destroyed or that a nuclear war or some other man-caused calamity will end it. But the Lord has relieved our minds about the future, allowing us assurance that it'll come to a close just as he planned before He created it. There are some things already predicted that will last beyond our lifetimes. Someday this Earth will truly be burned up, purged by fire, and made completely new.[21] Everything here is temporal. It's serving a purpose for the time being, but it's not producing the joy God plans for us later. So there's nothing that can happen differently from what He's already revealed. Isn't it great that we can read the Bible and not fear the future because we already see what's going to happen?"

"Yeah, Dad, I'm glad you know!"

"Tonight we'll read that in detail in Second Peter and Revelation so that you'll know from the Word of God and tomorrow it'll be confirmed by seeing the wonderful City of God. Any other questions?"

"No. That'll be cool! It's just been on my mind because kids at school are saying a lot of things."

"Great. All right honey, it's your time to take the lead," Jim said to Laura as he cranked up his four wheeler. "Let's see how much fun's left in us!"

"Darling, do you feel up to facing the lions on Monday?" asked Laura as they were preparing for bed.

"Aw, my precious, yes. I feel as ready as I'll ever be," he said, walking up to her, taking her hands and looking into her eyes. "I'd rather not do

---

[21]   2 Peter 3:10-12; Revelation 21:1

it. I don't look forward to it, but it must be the will of the Lord, and I know he'll be with me."

"What if they fire you? How will you handle that, and what'll you do next?" she asked.

"If they fire me, I can take it. We still have income from STSA, and then I'll start looking for teaching opportunities with other institutions. But don't you worry about it, okay? It's just not in me to allow error to go unchallenged in an educational institution. So they, my opponents, will probably fire me to get me out of their way. However, I believe I'm fully educated and spiritually equipped for 'come what may,'" he replied.

"I know you are. And we both know that there's nothing admirable about being a professional fool who says there's no God, regardless of how they otherwise may inflate themselves to be.[22] I'm happy to have a man who has convictions worth standing up for. I just want to get in on how you feel. I want to be right with you through this storm, and give myself to you in every way possible where I'm needed."

"You're such a treasure, honey. I cherish every moment of every day with you," Jim said.

It had been a grueling week for Jim, Rex, and Marcus. They worked hard on preparation and contacted many pastors and godly students of the Bible. A large number of believers were seeking God's will in prayer concerning the events that were to transpire on Monday. Rex was ready for the spiritual assignment he faced, with Jim and Marcus right behind him.

∞

---

[22]   Psalm 14:1; 53:1

12

Built For Trouble

Monday morning Jim met with the board of trustees to give his answer to the charges made against him. That evening, Rex would broadcast his views on the Cube being the New Jerusalem.

Jim entered the room at Quad University, where the trustees were set for his "execution." Jim could tell the atmosphere was hostile. It was difficult to relate to them. The mental resistance was more than Jim expected. He could see where it was headed, and it was all bad for him. The only thing he could think of to do was to dismiss entirely from his mind the mood in the room of the trustees and take a giant step of faith in the Savior. The preliminaries of the meeting were all slanted against him. During that time he kept his head bowed prayerfully and blotted from his mind the mischief being launched upon him. When it came time for him to speak, through faith he was able to walk to the podium as if he had just walked into the room with a smile on his face.

"I want to thank the president, faculty, and board of trustees for their support of my professorship during my eight years here at Quad State Astronomical University. While differences of opinions are common in all forms of education, my relationship with this institution has been one of learning for me. I believe I grow each time my mind is faced with a different idea, hypothesis, theory, or proposition. I test them with the foundation blocks that I believe are solid. I accept the unknown as an opportunity to expand my base. I want you to know that whatever is said here has nothing to do with any one of you personally. Regardless of the outcome, I'll treat you as my friends and desire your friendship in return.

"I wish to respond to the charges made against me by inviting you to examine the views that the majority of the faculty members of Quad University hold and test them with the same standards by which my beliefs are being tested. I've been charged with teaching unproven religious theories as science."

Jim humbly but firmly showed the trustees that the university was teaching evolution, a philosophy that required faith to accept its unproven theories. It also approved and taught Secular Humanism which defined itself as a religion and even had a religious tax exemption. The university merely approved certain religions that opposed the belief in God and rejected those that did believe in God. His occasional use of the Bible was a history-tested standard for all schools in the past, and he wondered why there was so little knowledge and appreciation of it in the university, especially since it was specifically encouraged in the founding of the school. He stated that he had been cautioned by Dr. Harris about using the Bible in class, even though it was used infrequently, but he believed such censure to be harsh in an institution where freedom of research and truth was essential. It was the textbook of all of the early American schools. It was the textbook of every early American university. While it wasn't a textbook in the

> *Your commands make me wiser than my enemies, for your commands are my constant guide.*
>
> *(Psalm 119:98 NLT)*

classroom of astronomy, it rightly deserved a place of reference in any classroom, since its teachings had proven to develop better character in all students and teachers. How then, could such a serious book be considered as unworthy of being even an option in the area of origins, since it emphatically described the beginning of all things?

The faculty at Quad were not all atheists. Jim had fellowship with others who were active Christians. But he was aware that the majority of the faculty disagreed with him. He chose to be agreeable while disagreeing with them. He had learned from that time-honored book that the greatest power in the world was love. He told them that from his heart he did love those who disagreed with him and opposed him. He even loved those who may even count themselves as his enemies. Jim said he trusted the trustees to be truly objective about what the meeting was about. If it were merely a concern for the school's academic reputation, perhaps they should set a different example for other educational institutions rather than merely copycat popular policies that promote a false sense of superiority. He would leave that decision to them. It was easy for one to go along with the majority, or the popular. An honorable educational institution would be open-minded to opposing views. A university on the cutting edge of education must seriously face its short comings. Most all run-of-the-mill universities appeared to be coasting on the shoestrings of evolution and humanism which had worn thin for lack of real evidence. Biblical testimony and demonstrable verifications of its accuracy in every field to which it spoke somehow wasn't worthy of consideration. He submitted that Quad was the loser for not opening the door to its message and power.

He concluded by saying, "These are my replies to your charges. I leave the results with you and the prayer that you will seek the best, not for me only, but the best for this institution. That's actually what is at stake isn't it? God bless you."

Marcus was dying to know how the meeting went, and when Jim returned to the LC he jumped on the matter instantly, following Jim to his office walking sideways and asking questions all the way. While Jim brought Marcus up to date, secretary Judy Carter, also came to Jim's office to learn the outcome. They shared their confidence in him and hoped for the best. They were

> *Every word of God is flawless; he is a shield to those who take refuge in him. Do not add to his words, or he will rebuke you and prove you a liar.*
>
> *(Proverbs. 30:5-6 HCSB)*

especially glad for the benefits Jim brought to the Orion complex of observatories.

"Well, there's little doubt that the majority will reject your opinions as well as your convictions in favor of their own," Marcus declared, "but they won't be able to do it from a scientific standpoint."

"My thoughts exactly," agreed Judy.

Meanwhile, in a class at Quad University, philosophy professor Victor Malory was trying to keep the class on the subject while students were more interested in the Cube in space, and wondering if prophecy had anything to say about it—especially the book of Revelation. Malory explained that "the book of Revelation in the Bible falls into the class of apocryphal writings and can't be understood. Allegories, myths, and such have no place in our practical world. They're things hidden and concealed."

"My pastor has preached from Revelation quite a bit, and it seems to be understandable to him," a student replied. "He said there was nothing in Revelation that wasn't mentioned either in symbol, or figure of speech in the Old Testament to give us light."

"My dear Mister Blankenship, such teaching is from the old literal, fundamental school of theology. It has been proven wrong by higher criticism decades ago," the professor enjoined. "There were several apocryphal books written during the so called 'silent years' between the Old and the New Testament. They offer the key to understanding later such writings with hidden meanings."

Blankenship asked, "You mean we're to go to the uninspired writings that have been rejected as being Scripture, to gain understanding of how to interpret the books that are inspired?"

"That is correct," replied Malory. "All books of that sort have much in common, and we can profit from putting them all together and seeing what's similar. Now as for inspiration, that's another subject altogether, and we certainly can't cover it in here."

"Well, I'm not a scholar, of course, but I've been told that 'Revelation' doesn't mean 'concealed,' but *unveiled.* So Revelation shouldn't be classified as apocryphal or hidden," Blankenship said.

"Who is your pastor?" Malory asked.

"Dr. Rex Fleming, pastor of Skyview Church in Odessa," the student answered.

"Oh, then that explains it! I understand he's the one that is joining our Dr. Waltham in trying to bring the Bible into astronomy. Both of these men are a nuisance and blights to modern scholarship. They have the audacity of speaking for science when they don't even know the meaning of the word! These men need to be put into their place and censored for giving out misleading information both in the classroom and to the general public! They're simply scaring the people and trying to get them to turn to religion for their weekly 'opium.' No one should believe their foolish theology. People in official positions in the country should always consult leading scholars on these subjects. Let's not waste our time with their trivialities."

"Sir, would it be all right if I asked you a question?" the student continued. "Have you ever read the entire book of Revelation for yourself?"

"I'm sure I've read most of if not all of it in the scholarly publications that I've studied in detail," was his honest reply.

"Excuse me sir, I don't want to be disrespectful to you, but if you only read God's Word from the viewpoint of others, scholars or not, then don't you think you would be prone to be prejudiced by their writings? Shouldn't the Bible stand alone on its reputation to be read objectively?" the student asked.

The discussion went from bad to worse from that point, and the professor was ready for the bell long before it rang.

Laura welcomed Jim home with a loving smile, hugs and kisses—and his favorite meal of homemade enchiladas. The boys looked forward to the family meal, too. Jim shared the happenings of the morning with them while assuring them that regardless of the outcome, they were blessed beyond measure and the future would be bright.

The television broadcast from Rex began just before they finished the early supper, and they listened to it together.

Rex had armed himself with Scripture. He faced the opportunity with Bible in hand and appealed to the listening audience to give ear to the possibility of the Cube being the New Jerusalem spoken of in the book of Revelation, the last book in the Bible. He discussed the Cube's size and beauty and acknowledged that while he didn't know the specific purpose of the Cube, it would definitely have something to do with the world's ethical—or *un*ethical behavior. He did his best to prepare the people for an unusual event that would doubtless change the whole world. He referred to the Old Testament prophets who repeatedly emphasized the moral requirements of God, the dangers of idolatry, and the justice systems of the nations, including Israel, as tests of loyalty to the sovereign God. Then he impressed upon them to be sure to listen to the broadcast the following evening when scientists and astronomers would confirm his statements.

His talk stirred up an enormous interest that went back and forth across the country over many sources of the media. Most of them didn't take him seriously, but it made a good news story so the content of his announcement found its target.

Meanwhile, the Cube continued to intrude into every conversation. Without an explanation for it, general pandemonium reigned among the world's authorities. The only voice that called for calmness came from Christians who told the public to have faith and rest in God's peace. Although people were crowding into churches in unprecedented numbers, the unknown was still too much for the information to be effectively assimilated.

Speculation had been made that since the Cube had taken two giant steps in two months, it would take the third one this month and it would be upon the Earth itself! But observatories reportedly agreed that the Cube hadn't stopped and continued moving at a rapid rate of speed unheard of before, in the direction of Earth. The speed was calculated to bring it into the vicinity of Earth's atmosphere in less than thirty days!"

Congress was being besieged by emails and phone calls demanding something to be done to protect the nation. Senator Helen Goodrich, (D. NY), along with a number of others, was racing to fund the presently shelved Asteroid Deflection Program, ADP. There was discussion that NASA could launch a nuclear warhead device into extremely high orbit if the president authorized it. Caution was urged, but other military action was being considered on a daily basis. The Pentagon took the precautionary measure of putting nuclear war heads in place, just in case. These could attempt to destroy and scatter the "block" if it were determined to pose a danger to the Earth. So far, no communication from it had been received. On the international scene, all nuclear nations were scrambling to combat any aggression from the "other world." It was difficult to hide the inner emotion of panic that was spreading world-wide. The world stood on its tiptoes, waiting.

The Bible-believing crowd heard Rex's message with an open mind and searched the Scriptures for verification of what was said. Others scoffed, criticizing it as another speculation by a religious zealot, and the scientific community ignored it completely.

But things were about to change.

∞

13

AGONY

J im walked out of the classroom on Tuesday, the day after meeting with the trustees, and into his office. He found an envelope in his box as he entered the door. It was from the board of trustees.

To: Dr. Jim Waltham

This memo is to inform you of the results of your meeting with the board of trustees yesterday with thirty-three of the thirty-eight trustees present. A motion was made that you be placed on probation for a period of six months. After a second to the motion, discussion was opened both pro and con. The vote was twenty-five, "Yes" and eight, "No." This is a two-thirds vote which means it is not subject to appeal. The trustees recognized your academic qualifications, teaching ability in the field of astronomy, and your rapport with the students. They charge you with using your abilities in an unacceptable fashion. You are hereby prohibited from using the classroom to teach the Bible. Of course, it may be referred to in general as good literature, and you may recommend that students read it or certain portions of it on their own outside of the classroom. Failure to comply with the stipulations of this probation may result in the termination of your contract as a faculty member at Quad State Astronomical University.

It was signed, Dr. David Harris, Head of the Department of Astronomy, and faculty Dean, Quad State Astronomical University.

Jim couldn't help but be devastated even though he was certain of the outcome. He felt weak in the pit of his stomach. Sadness enshrouded his spirit as he felt the devil had won the war. He wondered if anyone was watching him right now through the windows. He knew they'd be able to see his anguish. He wanted to sit down and run at the same time. His mind was racing for what to do—especially what to do first. He was embarrassed to leave his office at the moment, but couldn't wait to get out of there. He didn't want to face anyone in the halls. *What time is it? Who's here right now? Maybe if I sit down awhile and wait 'til everyone leaves . . . No, I can't stand to be here that long. And if I leave now I'll be running down the hall.*

After moving around a few seconds in the office, which seemed to be infinitely small at the time, with his head bowed, he took a big breath and sat in his chair. *Oh, I wish I could talk to Laura right now. But I don't want to call her from the office. And I don't want to upset the kids. I can be strong in front of them. They must not feel insecure. I guess I failed in my efforts. But given what I believe, it's hard to think it would've made any difference. There're too many faculty members holding to the false view of humanism. What should I have done, Lord? What do You want me to do if they fire me? I knew this was going to come to a head someday. I must not have been as prepared as I thought I was . . . oh, yes, that feels good—to talk to You Lord. You are right here in my situation. After all, You already knew this was coming today. You always prepare me for whatever comes up, but like so many others, I'm not letting my heart absorb that preparation. Jesus! You are Master of this crisis. I give it to You. Don't let me lose my peace. Thank you Lord.*

Able to be more objective, Jim took another big sigh. He began to trace in his mind the last few years and the opposition he had received from several faculty members. Actually, he had thought he might lose his position a long time ago. *I could actually teach more of the Bible in class if that were my goal. I bring it into the history of astronomy, like I do any other book. It just carries more weight because it's inspired by the Holy Spirit. The faculty and trustees simply disagree with the Word of God, and their consciences condemn them when they hear the truth and realize the students are hearing and accepting it. And some of these students are questioning the lies they're being taught in other classes. That's what's happening. And of course, this is their way of muzzling me now, intending to have me fired later.*

Now, I knew all that. Wow. It sure is good to have the Lord reminding me of these things. I'm already about eighty-percent calmer. Jim felt he could leave now, and if he met anyone, he could treat them as usual. If they knew anything about the memo and asked any questions, he could simply tell them what it's about matter-of-factly and go on his way. *I need to get leadership from the Lord as to how I'll act from now on. I'm sure I'm not going to stop telling the students about God and His blessed Word. It's inevitable that I'll be fired. So I must trust God to lead me to where he wants me to go. I still have my position at the STSA. It has a different composition of trustees, and they have never given me a hint of displeasure—at least not yet. Freedom of belief is obviously dealt with on a different scale. So, Lord, whatever you want is all right with me. Please get me ready for it and grace me with your strength. You said, "when I am weak, then You are stronger in me."[23]*

Laura had planned an early snack for the afternoon because of Jim's participation in the television announcement that evening. Jim's trip home seemed to take too long and to be too short. He wanted to be

---

[23] 2 Corinthians 12:10

there, but wasn't looking forward to sharing the news with Laura. As he walked into the kitchen, Laura glanced his way, then, looked again.

"Jim, what's wrong?"

Jim, shaking his head said, "You mean it's that obvious?"

"Oh, Sweetheart, something's happened. You look . . . different."

"Well, it finally happened. Dr. Harris sent me a memo from the trustees. They want me muzzled. They found it in their hearts to commend me for my academic scholarship, my ability to teach and motivate the students, but I'm using my talents in the wrong way! I'm teaching myths and fables instead of science. And then they were nice enough to allow me to mention Almighty God and His infallible, Holy Word as 'good literature.' That means 'good' like William Shakespeare, Henry Wadsworth Longfellow, Geoffrey Chaucer. I could probably teach everything they said about astronomy, and it would be perfectly alright, because they are famous and harmless authors of the past eight hundred years. But God's Holy Scripture that has shaped the nations of the world for thousands of years and continues to produce freedom wherever it's believed can only be treated like human poetry. Oh, and I can tell the students that they can go home and read their Bibles."

"Jim," Laura asked seriously, "What do they really want you to do, and what if you don't?"

"Actually it's very simple. They don't want God in His own world. They won't admit we're created in his image. They expect people in this country to believe that when we die we merely cease to exist. There's no accountability for our lives. They don't want anything to do with God or his Word and they are determined to keep the students from hearing about him either. He's off limits in any educational classroom. They are carrying out the devil's agenda pretending religious neutrality while stuffing their own religion down the throats of others."

"But what they don't know is that God still rules in his world. He'll call every soul into judgment. They can't win and we don't have to worry!" Laura replied.

"Thanks for beating me to the punch, honey. You're so right. So why don't I react with that assurance all the time? It seems to always take me too long. Oh, well, I guess I'll need to go over my announcement and speech for TV with Rex . . ."

Keith, who had overheard their conversation from the living room, came into the kitchen. "Is supper ready yet? What are y'all talking about, I mean, besides the TV program this evening?"

"Keith, the Lord has handed your father another test. You know, he's always giving them to his students? Well, now and then he has to take one himself. And we're just rehearsing some of the answers."

"Gosh, you mean you get to go over the answers ahead of time?"

"Sure. Don't we go over them with you when you get ready for your tests?" she replied.

Keith smiled, "Yeah. I hope you do good on it, Dad." He looked up to his father with a knowing look on his face. "It must be an important test, and it has to do with the university, doesn't it?"

"That's right," Jim answered. "The faculty doesn't want me teaching anything about God's creation in class. He deserves no voice about the Heavens. If I want my job, I have to be careful that what I say doesn't contradict or compete with the errors which I think they believe. Evidently, their god can't take it. But on the other hand, I could go on through life being a good teacher of astronomy, but, now and then, I like to put more light and fire with my teaching and give more glory to the Lord who created the Heavens."

"Only now and then?" Keith queried.

"Well, I'm only broadening their understanding."

"And they think they are broadening understanding by their vain philosophy," Laura chimed in.

"They don't even understand themselves," Jim said. "But, Keith, don't you worry about a thing. I might not be able to keep quiet enough to suit 'em. And if I don't, just think, I get to find another place to teach. That may not be all bad. Let's finish setting the table for your mother, okay?"

Jim had seriously considered his role in the announcement that evening. It would likely set off a whirlwind of hostility from Quad U. But the outstanding beauty and glory of the Cube couldn't be denied. He was more certain than he ever thought he'd be. The fact that it had moved another one hundred light years distance in one day confirmed Jim's conclusions about it being supernatural. And what else could it be but the New Jerusalem? The possibility of the "any moment arrival" heightened everyone's emotions. A nerve had been triggered in Jim to find out why it was coming and quickly! Its purpose was now an astounding urgency.

He and Laura discussed the repercussions of the announcement and included Keith, so he would understand the likely results. After seeing the Cube for themselves through the telescope, Laura and Keith were emphatically jubilant about the future. They were also saddened about what the TV announcement would likely bring about, but felt the Lord had greater things in store for them. Scott was all smiles from all the love and affirmation he was receiving.

Jim was only home for a short time. He grabbed a bite but would eat later when he returned from the TV program that began at five o'clock.

∞

14

TURMOIL AND CHOICES

J im didn't tell Rex of the meeting with the trustees when they met. He didn't want to crowd his thinking or cause him to have the slightest hesitation to speak his convictions. The two, along with Marcus, met at the radio station in a spare room to go over the main points they wanted to present and the time they had to abide by.

"I don't guess you've received any message from the Cube since yesterday, did you?" Jim asked Rex.

Jokingly Rex replied, "Not a word. I turned on the radio while I shaved to see if anyone else had and kept the TV on while I dressed. Then I checked the newspaper obituary and I wasn't listed anywhere. So I guess we're still on our own."

"That's what I was afraid of," Jim smiled. "This is a gigantic step to declare to the world, and there's no telling what the repercussions will be. But we are simply followers of the risen Christ setting forth our honest findings so the Lord can prepare the people for his stupendous revelation!"

"What a privilege," Marcus added with his eyes sparkling with joy.

When the five o'clock news time arrived, Rex's announcement reiterated much of the things he had already said to the local community. But this time Dr. Jim Waltham's agreement electrified the country. Jim and Marcus spoke from the experience of men who had been viewing the Cube throughout the past two months via the world's best telescope. That gave them a big jump ahead of anyone else in the world! Jim shared with the listening audience how perplexed he was at first. He told them about his journey through research and prayer to the point where he was now. "The more knowledge I gained, the more astounding it all became. We're on the brink of a revelation like no other. I have no doubt whatsoever that this Cube is the New Jerusalem!" Marcus followed Jim with confirmation from his experience of studying the Cube for untold hours and confirming his conclusions with additional astronomers at the Orion Observatory Complex as well as others around the country.

As Rex neared the conclusion of his part of the broadcast, he assured the listeners that they had nothing to fear from the Cube. He urged them to give reverence to the Creator and seek His will for their lives. The Cube was a powerful revelation. "We don't know exactly to what extent it will affect the Earth yet, but there are bound to be many good and great things that will happen. And it could even bring about change in the governments of the world. By the way, remember when God acts, there are always those who oppose Him. Look how Pharaoh stood against Him. And the last time he visited us He was not welcomed by most. He was despised, rejected, and even crucified! Even the coming of the Holy Spirit is still doubted by some. So it's likely that some will respond negatively this time. Please don't be a part of that crowd.

"The time has come for us to stand in faith, not fear. Confirmations of the Cube's identity have come from a number of scientists and astronomers, as well as biblical scholars, who are part of an ever-widening research team with whom I stay in contact."

Jim shared his awareness of the confusion and misinformation that people were hearing from various sources. He hoped to nullify as much of that as possible. "We're being very cautious, desiring to make double sure that nothing be overlooked, and later prove to be un-factual or unscientific. We're confident that the information we're giving you is correct, and that it matches the Scripture in the last book of the Bible. This is not a political show, local magic trick, or prideful show of human achievement. This is Almighty God, who's intervened in the history of man numerous times in big ways in the past. God bless you."

The three men's description of what they viewed through the telescope was extremely convincing. There couldn't help but be a big splash throughout the entire country and beyond. The various news media were especially excited about the story because it combined religion with science. They were ready to ride out that combination as long as possible.

All the major news media pounced upon the announcement and aired it throughout America and abroad. It was constantly being rerun in parts daily. Politicos picked up on it and made it their latest banner, while others their newest sarcasm. Religion, especially the Christian religion, was both praised and criticized. Christians gladly touted the Cube as "theirs" while other religions didn't understand why the Christian God was getting so much attention rather than their own gods. Jealousy and hostility were growing among the masses. Rather than realizing that there was only one true God, those who served other gods found that their traditions and beliefs were being tested.

In spite of being distracted from their daily living, people throughout the world gradually absorbed information about the Cube. They countered with the usual gripes, and self-pity, but the Cube kept interfering with life as usual.

Crazy opinions and ideas surfaced such as underground bunkers and personal anti-alien guns for the home and pocket. Church definitely interested people more than usual. Pastors were pressed to preach on topics that addressed the anxiety of the people. The theological world was in a state of turmoil as various blocks of thought with diverse doctrines tried to hold to their beliefs while defending themselves. They were aggravated at having to keep re-examining why they believed as they did. The media was calling for interviews from anyone who had a place in religion, astronomy or astrophysics. Powerful and influential vocal organizations such as Secular Humanism Inc., American Atheists, American Civil Liberties Union, American Psychological Association, along with others, repeated their steadfast resolve to remain true to their positions.

Dr. Philip Emmett of St. Stevens Theological Seminary in Louisville, Kentucky, declared his opposition to the eschatology being aired by Rev. Fleming and others. The president made the statement that "such tomfoolery was destined to bring sad disappointment to many innocent people. I would urge that every possible action be taken by the United States Government to protect its heavenly borders." He further stated that "the symbolical language of the Bible should not be brought into serious current events such as an asteroid in space. To do so is absolutely reckless!"

Several noted religious leaders and political analyzers spoke out on the topic of the Cube. Unfortunately, the media, as usual, turned to liberal universities and received the bland, blah, isogesis—read-into—explanations of Scripture. Only when the bare, unmistakable facts became evident would they humbly allow Bible-believing teachers and leaders to shed light on the subject. Dr. Bridget McMillan, noted journalist, announced over the Public Broadcasting Association that "religious infiltration in the matters of Government was intrusive, meddling, and needed to be stopped."

Dr. Marcus Loshan responded, "It's alright for anyone to speak their opinions about any given subject, but Dr. McMillan emanates about as much sense as God gave a cocklebur when it comes to the historical events of this Christian nation.

"Those who were there and participated in the founding of this country acknowledged that the great masses of citizens knew the undeniable Providence of Almighty God in establishing our independence and the grounding of America in the fundamental truths of His Word. They embellished buildings and monuments with reminders of God's participation in this government. As a result 'God' is on our money, in our pledges, oaths, and in every historical record. John Quincy Adams, son of John and Abigail Adams, and sixth President of the United States, said, 'The Declaration of Independence . . . laid the cornerstone of human government upon the first precepts of Christianity.' He believed the Revolution that led to our independence '. . . connected in one indissoluble bond, the principles of civil government with the principles of Christianity.' The modern, general public has not only missed the truth when it's needed most, but they're led astray by those whose concept of divine inspiration of Scripture is limited to what they can 'prove' by digging into archeological garbage dumps!"

*   *   *

The next day Jim spoke over the phone and Laura asked, "Who was that, honey?"

"Aunt Clara," Jim replied. "You remember now that we live nearer to her farm, she likes to remind me that she's still alive and wants to keep up with us."

"Oh yes, she is a case! We need to keep up with her too."

"I'm gonna have to take cousin Zeke to the doctor Friday. He can't drive you know—except for the tractor. After a long time of practice, and a lot of patience on the part of Uncle Tue, he finally got it right. He does pretty well at it now. But for a twenty-eight year old, he can't handle much more. It's a shame his intelligence is so limited. But he's a fun guy to be around—at least for a while!"

"Oh my! I forgot about Uncle Two. Why'd they call him that?"

"It's T-u-e honey. He was born on Tuesday, and the name got shortened."

"Oh, yeah. What's wrong with Zeke this time?"

"I'm sure he needs a general check-up, but he's been feeling stomach pain for about a month, and Aunt Clara's worried about it. I told her I'd get him to a doctor."

"It is a wonder they survive out there in the sticks where they live. That family's done wonders to live without the modern conveniences the rest of us take for granted," Laura recalled.

"I know. One third of it is stubbornness. One third of it is refusal to change. And the rest of it is stubbornness, refusal, and choice, if you know what I mean."

"I think I get the picture."

Zeke had never been to a big city in his life. His family had elected to stay at home and let the city bring whatever it had to offer to them, and the city hadn't attempted much. Jim had a wonderful time entertaining Zeke with elevators and escalators. He had an inquisitive mind though, which made it easier for Jim to introduce a few more modern inventions to him. No one knew why his mind was so limited. His parents took him to a doctor when he was young, but didn't get any meaningful information from it.

After receiving medication for an infection, they got on the road home, and Zeke asked Jim about his work at the observatory. Of course, the distances involved in discussing the universe are so staggering that Jim had to modify the conversation to Zeke's capacity.

"You know, Zeke, we look at the stars and planets which are a long way off. Everything in the sky and space was made by God for us to learn something about Him. The Moon is the closest heavenly body to the Earth. It's only two hundred-forty thousand miles away. So if you were driving a space ship to the Moon going a hundred miles an hour, it would take you one hundred days to arrive."

"Leapin' grasshoppers! I didn't know it was that far! That's just hard to believe. It dudn't look like it's that far away."

"That's because God made it so big. The Sun is our nearest star. It's a hundred times larger than the Earth, and four hundred times larger than the Moon, but the Moon is four hundred times closer to the Earth, so you can't tell the difference so easily. The Sun is about ninety-three million miles away. So, if you got on a souped-up space ship going one hundred thousand miles an hour today, you wouldn't get there for over a month."

"Aw, man! How would you eat?"

"You'd have to take enough lunches with you to last that long and it would take up a lot of room on the space ship, wouldn't it?"

Stunned, Zeke reluctantly and quietly asked, "They don't have out houses on it, do they?"

"Yep, right in the back room."

Zeke shook his head back and forth, "Naw. Not me!"

"Well, I don't think anyone would want to go to the Sun anyway, but there are planets beyond the Moon that people are talking about taking a trip to."

"How do they know how big and far away they are? Did somebody go up there and measure 'um?"

"No, Zeke. That is what science does. It figures those things out a little at a time mathematically. It has been going on for thousands of years. God made man with the ability to learn things like that."

"How'd they eat while they are taking so much time to learn it?"

"Sometimes they were paid by others while they studied to find out."

"It seems like a waste of a lot of time. Why do we need to know anyhow?"

"It's fun to learn more about the world that the Lord has given us to explore. That's how we get to know him better. He's able to show us new things—like the Cube, the New Jerusalem, that's coming down to Earth right now. We can see it and tell others about it."

"Oh."

*   *   *

Repercussions of the announcement of the New Jerusalem began to hit home. Keith confided to his parents that some kids in his high school ridiculed Jim for believing something so foreign from common sense that he must be a "nut," along with a few other choice words. Keith didn't allow it to overly bother him, but he felt awkward being around them and wondering what they were saying behind his back.

Two persons had been friends of Laura and Jim for a long time, but Laura heard through another friend that they were bad mouthing Jim for the outlandish announcement. The Walthams were shocked to learn about it, but had to realize the volatile atmosphere around them.

In their Sunday School class, a member asked Jim for information about the Cube, and a couple of members blurted out "this isn't the place for speculation." Such a response chilled the entire class.

Anthony Cagney, a staff member at Lippershey observatory, doubted the reality of the Cube. He couldn't see anything through the telescope, but a bland, asteroid-type block. He heard other staff members talking excitedly about what they were seeing and felt they were only going along with Jim while not seeing anything Jim claimed was there either. Cagney reported his own "findings" to someone in the media, as well as to friends at other observatories. Then he anonymously accused Jim of making false claims about the Cube to the trustees of the Space Science Telescope Association!

Finally, the Waltham family had to get together and have a talk about the facts of the Cube and the various reactions being voiced from those who gave no credence to Jim and what he had actually seen. They entered the den, each selected a comfortable chair or the couch, and they discussed the issue.

"It appears inevitable," Jim explained to Laura and Keith, "that there are people who delight in bringing others down, accusing, slandering, and lying against them. Why they do so is hard to understand. Perhaps they feel they are right, but their jealous attitudes leave no tolerance for others who are willing to dialogue with scientific facts. They seek to elevate themselves into the limelight by criticizing others who get a lot of attention. That's what they did to Job, the best man on Earth, when he wouldn't admit any wrong. They simply invented crimes which they claimed he did anyway!"[24]

Laura said, "It's even sad to see what it's doing to those who criticize us, because it makes them odious in the minds of their own friends who know us better."

"Yeah, I can tell my other friends don't appreciate it when they talk about you that way, Dad," agreed Keith.

---

[24] Job 22:5-17

These experiences drew the family closer together. "We're not going to allow such negative opinions of us to affect our happiness," said Jim. "We're in good company. We know Jesus suffered much more of the same."[25] Scott, or course, was part of the discussion, but all he understood was that they loved him.

Rejection was growing wider among the faculty and trustees at Quad, as well as with astronomers at other observatories. Jim and Rex soon realized they must get together with the Cubicles to discuss whether or not to even take interviews; and under what circumstances to take them.

"We must give careful consideration as to what limits to place upon our speeches," said Rex, "and prevent entering into religious debates, and differing opinions that don't serve the purpose of God. The first order of business must be to learn the purpose of the Cube's coming. Perhaps God will speak to us somehow. But what if he doesn't? Will we be able to discern it from the Word of God?"

They called such a meeting and made it open to anyone who wanted to attend, but they gave invitations to those whom they believed were like-minded. They were blessed with a wide variety of Christian denominations who agreed that this was a supernatural event that merited their serious and humble best. Most of them had been viewing the Cube through telescopes. Those who attended were not there to set forth their particular theories. The group was like a family meeting. There were no rules given, or assumptions made. They simply all volunteered to cooperate to serve the greater public as best they could. Marcus Loshan moderated the gathering, not permitting the group to stray from the purpose they were there for. Much dialogue was enjoyed by everyone,

---

[25]   Matthew 5:10-12

and there was consensus about staying with the facts they had and other truth as it became known. They agreed there should be unity about the information being distributed, otherwise chaos, mistrust, and division would result. There was a sign up booth for sharing by all means of communication and everyone was free to send and receive news as it became a priority.

Jim reminded them, "I believe it's clear that we've been selected by the Lord for this sacred mission. We already know there are confusing reports circulating with the attempt to discredit our findings. We can't allow ourselves to assume that we know the future. We can't afford to run astray from the truth we know and speculate about what might happen based upon our preconceptions. This is God's show, not ours. Let's allow Him to use us as He pleases. While all of this is new, the way we're to deal with it isn't new. And we're already built for trouble! So let's take it as believers."

Rex gave all of them the assignment to dig into the Word for the cause of the Cube's coming at this time. What was His purpose? What was to be accomplished? How long could we expect it to stay? It'll basically come down to 'what's the overall plan of God for His creation and purpose for man? What's He pleased with and what does He want to change?' He urged that there should be a prayer base as large as possible within the entire Christian community, the actual Church of Jesus Christ. We're living in the best of times. It's up to us to make the most of every day. And only through prayer and yieldedness to the Lord can we be participants in his surprising and wise plan."

Immediate suggestions as to the purpose of the Cube were passed around to the group. First, it was God's plan to show His love for the world just as He had done throughout history. How the Cube would achieve this was yet unknown. Next, it would be to bring about a salvation response from people by sharing the Gospel. Thirdly, the Cube would correct the unjust treatment of human beings and give relief to the unfortunate. Since these truths were consistently taught in the Bible, they had to be part of God's purpose now. Other ideas were given but would have to wait for confirmation. Jim roused the attendees by saying they were participants in the Cube's purpose, whatever it was.

"It's up to us to be available as instruments in God's hand to aid in His will being accomplished." he said. "It's obvious since He's beckoned our curiosity, encouraged our investigation, convinced us by his gradual revelation, and motivated us to make the announcement as to its identity. We're a part of His plan!"

But Quad U had other plans . . .

∞

15

STOKING

More serious fallout from the announcement came from Quad. Dr. Harris was outraged when he heard the broadcast. He called for the university trustees to meet and most of them were bristling. Faculty members were fuming. They felt they were being mocked by this man who had just received a reprimand and was now becoming famous the world over for taking his views so public.

> *Do not be far from me, for trouble is near and there is no one to help.*
>
> *(Psalm 22:11 NIV)*

Trustee Carl Eckert, rising from his chair and turning about as he spoke, said, "This is worse than a slap in the face. It's arrogant rebellion. Such delusional thinking makes a laughing stock of this notable institution! I make a motion that he be dismissed immediately! He has no intention of submitting to our authority. He's an embarrassment to all of us. He's not worthy of another chance to 'preach' to us about his wild interpretations! I for one won't stand for it."

Others chimed in echoing similar remarks. Thomas Fain, Chairman of the Trustees, raised his hand and interrupted them by saying, "Ladies and gentlemen, Dr. Waltham isn't using our university or his classroom to broadcast his views. This is taking place from another setting. He's not violated our mandate. We clearly said that he could not use the classroom to teach the Bible. That's all."

Dr. Harris reluctantly agreed, "That's true. Yet on the other hand, he's bringing widespread scrutiny to Quad State that may threaten our accreditation. We certainly don't want to fall from our current position in the eyes of the other great schools who desire our students to pursue other degree programs. They'd look askance at our graduates! Surely there's something we can do before this tarnish gets any worse."

"We'll have to bring him in and tell him he has done irreparable damage to the university's reputation and demand his resignation," said a frowning trustee.

"But that means we'll have to buy out his contract since he's reached tenure!" another said, with dollar marks for eyeballs.

"Whatever we have to do, let's do it. This has gone too far," still another agreed.

Thomas Fain broke into the discussion: "Ladies and gentlemen, let me offer this advice. Why don't we carefully consider our options, go home and cool down, put our sincere determinations and recommendations on paper, and make a decision at another meeting. We're dealing with an issue that has been smoldering for a long time, so we shouldn't allow emotion to dictate how it ends. Haste may cause us to overlook something we could later regret. Let's do a thorough job and establish firm policies. I believe we all want the same thing, but let's do it correctly and not miss anything."

The meeting abruptly came to an end for the time being.

Students crowded into Jim's classroom lining up all around the walls. They were full of questions about his position. Jim had already heard about the trustee meeting, but he preferred not to answer their questions about it since he had no concrete information about the trustee's plans.

"What about the particular object that came from Polaris, called the Cube—what can you tell us about it?" another student inquired.

That presented another awkward situation to Jim, since, if he said too much about the Cube he could count on the trustees to accuse him of teaching something in the Bible.

"Ralph, I'm glad you asked that question. It's a matter that we can't ignore, and of course, this is a good place to give you information about it. I can only say at this time that we're keeping our telescopes upon the object which we call the Cube. All five observatories have been given certain assignments on which to report. As you know by now, it moved twice, gigantic distances and now is continuing at such rapid descent that it's expected to reach Earth from one hundred light years away in less than four weeks. These unprecedented moves alone gave me the suspicion that it was supernatural and that God was behind it. Another amazing thing is that it's a cube in shape and corresponds in total likeness to the New Jerusalem of Revelation in the Bible. But I must postpone that discussion for a later time."

Jim thought the only thing to do would be to meet in another location where he could freely speak of the Cube and answer any questions they might want to ask. He made a quick call on his cell phone to his pastor, Dr. Samuel Stone. Then he informed the students that they could meet that evening at the church where he was a member, Faith Church on the Rock, midway between Quad U and the Orion Observatory Complex. Dr. Stone had been a member of the Cubicles from the start.

After class, Jim called Laura and they made plans to invite Marcus and his wife, Cindy, over to eat some "vittles" while they discussed the meeting that was to take place that evening. Keith could take care of all the children if the ladies wanted to come. By the time the meeting began at seven, word had spread, and the local media had shown up, too. Dr. Samuel Stone, welcomed the people and affirmed his confidence in Dr. Waltham, then passed the podium to Jim.

Facts and scientific experiments made at the observatories were shared with the guests. Jim repeated his strong view that had already been given over television, that the Cube definitely was congruous with the Bible's description of the New Jerusalem. Size, shape and details could not be denied. Therefore, his motive in this entire matter had to do with his belief that God is visiting the Earth in this unique fashion with a purpose. His desire was to inform and urge the people of God to openly participate in that plan when it was revealed. He also wanted to comfort the troubled world by telling them this is a good event, not one that threatened the end of the world or any such thing. Questions began to be asked from the audience.

"Dr. Waltham, it has been rumored that the Quad University trustees have met and are trying to fire you. Is that true?" a concerned student asked.

Jim shifted his position and answered, "I wouldn't doubt that they have that in mind, but so far I've only been warned not to teach anything from the Bible in class. I have no other information about that."

"Can you tell us why the university would have such intentions?" another asked.

Jim honestly stated, "I can only say that there are a number of persons within the university who don't appreciate the biblical views I hold and resent them being 'mixed' as they say, with science. Therefore, I've been forbidden to use the Bible in the classroom."

This information quickened the interest in the media. They played upon it to the limit.

"Just what views do they object to, sir?" a newsman wondered with a hand raised.

Jim could feel the meeting's purpose being led into a different direction. He tried to be careful not to allow the assembly to be branded as a planned means of striking back at the university. That would present a false picture and would override the sincere questions the students had about the Cube. It would further heat up the hostility of the university, as if they needed any more fuel.

"Let me make it clear to the media who are here. You're welcome, although I didn't know you were coming, and I don't want anyone to misunderstand why we have gathered. I didn't call this meeting to criticize Quad University. Those questions about my faculty position at Quad U have nothing to do with the exciting and more important matter of the Cube, the New Jerusalem. I'd like to add that the only teaching from the Bible that I do in class has to do with the origin of the universe, the Creator of the universe, astronomy in the Bible, and God's purpose for it. I feel that nothing I have taught conflicts with true science. I believe that all truth comes from God—even the physical laws that scientists have to use every day. He gave them to us. He's also a moral being. Therefore, He'll hold every living person accountable for their thoughts, words and actions. There's a judgment day coming. Well, enough on that. We're in another atmosphere tonight where freedom of discussion can be freely given about things that bother us most."

"What's the most important thing we need to know and what should we do?" a student asked. They'd come with pen and paper in hand to take notes.

Jim let the students know that salvation through faith in Christ alone was always the priority for anyone. Then, following the will of God and seeking to please him was next. He pointed out the chaos in the world. "Look at the news, see the world leaders, observe the hostility between rulers and religions. This world we live in is in trouble. It could be that the Cube's coming will have something to do with world leaders and how private citizens are being treated. That's a major issue with the prophets in the Old Testament. I believe God intended for all of us to live happily, free to please him, and full of meaning. But until our lives are right with God, it doesn't matter about the Cube. We're losers regardless of what it is or its purpose."

"What would the New Jerusalem be coming to Earth for?" another student inquired.

Jim explained there were no communications from the Cube, so until that happened, and *if* that happened, they should read and reread what God had already said in his Word, the Bible. He began sharing with them the *possibilities* that could come to pass when the Cube arrived. The Cubicles were already discussing this. He wanted them to be excited about getting in on the Lord's plans. Then he described what he had been seeing through the telescope and the breath-taking beauty of the City. He noted that he had seen the design, the shapes and arrangements of the details of the New Jerusalem, and that it was difficult to stop looking at it even though he knew he needed sleep.

"And I don't believe it'll come and settle on the ground, since that would defeat the beauty of those foundations, and other features. I expect it'll stop in the air and be clearly seen by every living person as the world makes its revolutions near to the Cube. Remember, the Earth travels at over one-thousand miles an hour, counterclockwise, as it turns on its axis. It's also moving at about sixty-seven thousand miles per hour in another direction in its journey around the Sun. And the Sun is traveling about two hundred miles per second as it runs its race around the Galaxy. Well . . . , I could go on, but you get the picture. We're talking about an incredible miracle knocking right at our door. If you are not excited about it, you need to see a psychiatrist first thing in the morning!"

After the laughter settled down, he requested that they pray for him and the situation with the university. "I'm facing some difficult matters, but I want to remind you that when you get saved you enter the family of God, and you're built for trouble! Goodnight everyone." Jim lingered with several students and fellowshipped with them; and they let him know their appreciation for the education they were receiving, as well as the fun they were having in his classes.

They didn't know what the morning would bring.

∞

16

EXPECTATION

The next morning began with phones ringing everywhere. Morning newspapers in several cities gave front page headlines as follows: "Firing of Dr. Jim Waltham Imminent;" "Angry Trustees and Faculty at Quad University;" "Science Clashes with Religion;" "Students Meet With Professor."

Dr. Waltham received numerous calls at home and finally told Laura, "Don't answer the phone anymore. I don't know how I'm expected to get dressed with all these intrusions!" Laura was in tears. It seemed impossible that after such a good meeting last night, they could wake up to such confusion. At the office the same thing happened. Jim felt he couldn't receive any more calls. The crashing news hit him before he could imagine the details that must have been given underneath the headlines. He didn't have time to attempt explaining all the news, the students, the Cube, or anything else! He wondered how he was going to get through the day. He felt like a celebrity surrounded by the paparazzi with nowhere to escape. Jim was glad he had Marcus to take the essential calls. He knew Jim's heart and he could explain exactly what had taken place.

Dr. Harris and Thomas Fain were inundated with protests, demands for details, as well as support. They were left in a muddle of matters they couldn't untangle. The scientific community had been stunned with the announcement made by Dr. Fleming and Dr. Waltham, and now wondered if they had been discovered to be wrong. Yet there were no other explanations for the Cube. It seemed that yesterday's activities had launched the devil's usual opportunity to confuse.

Anthony Cagney, a Lippershey Telescope staff member, publically stated his opposition to Jim and the others at the Orion Observatory Complex for their "deliberately concocted" reports to the media. "I haven't seen any such thing, and I've been looking through the Lippershey Telescope for two months, he said in a TV interview. "It's time to stop the confusion and nice sounding promises about this dangerous object." Cagney expected Jim to be fired over the situation, and he didn't want to lose his job too.

Jim was so angry at the accusation he all but broke the computer desk with his fist pounding upon it. He knew he was too upset to speak to Cagney right away, so he waited a couple of days so he could deal with him calmly, as a Christian—if that were at all possible. Meanwhile Cagney was dragged over the coals by all the other workers. When Jim finally called Anthony in, they had a serious talk about his disloyalty and why Cagney hadn't voiced his opinions to Jim. Cagney was sent packing his bags.

Pandemonium reigned among the world's authorities. Pastors were extremely interested in listening to what astronomers had to say about the Cube. They wanted to believe that this truly was "an appearance of God" in some way, but their congregations were growing more and more tense and unsettled, wanting to know what the Bible said about it.

Speculation that the Cube would take its third giant step this month and arrive upon the Earth was laid to rest by the reminder from the Space Telescope Science Association which reaffirmed that the Cube had not stopped this time. It was moving at such a rapid speed toward us that it would be at the Earth's atmosphere inside of thirty days anyhow.

The International Scientific Astronomical Society met each week, and stood by its unanimous conclusions that the cubed object was a creation of "intelligent beings," and that it could reach the Earth in a few weeks and even go into orbit around the Earth.

News about the Cube gained momentum as more and more conservative, Bible-believing pastors, and leaders made their influence known. Many of them had observed the Cube through telescopes and verified what they had seen. While a large number of pastors and leaders "rode the fence," a growing expectation of the coming of the New Jerusalem was electrifying the community of believers locally and worldwide. Prayer concerning the Cube made its way into practically every meeting of Christians. Most were anticipating that God was preparing his people for a meeting with destiny. Others were begging God to protect them from the incoming space object.

Meanwhile other noted religious leaders mocked and ridiculed the idea of a New Jerusalem coming down. They defied the information given out by the Space Telescope Science Association as being totally impossible, unscientific, and condemned it as a ploy for fame and increased church attendance. "Dr. Waltham doesn't even claim to be a theologian and he's postulating all sorts of religious and futuristic jargon," one religious leader stated. "His astronomy has gotten 'out of round,'" another said. They couldn't explain the Cube themselves, but they knew it wasn't the New Jerusalem! Naturally, the secular world was in dismay and unrest. They had no notion of what to make of anything. People turned to the usual "solutions" for help: the U.S. Government, elected officials, psychologists, self-proclaimed gurus, meditation, and spiritualism. There was an increase in those contacting mediums with

"familiar spirits," astrologers, fortune tellers, and other venues of the
Occult.

The body of elders at Skyview Church even set up a meeting with
Rex to inquire what his relationship with Jim was all about. "Dr. Fleming,
we're committed to your outstanding leadership here at Skyview.
However, for your sake we want the assurance that you're not leaning
out too far or being influenced beyond your field by the astronomer,
Dr. Waltham. We wouldn't like to see the two of you go down like the
Titanic over this Cube," one stated.

"I stand as one with Dr. Waltham, and I'm certain of what we have
both seen through the Lippershey Telescope. I can't imagine any other
explanation," Rex assured the elders.

On the political table was a flurry of ideas. "I can assure you that armed
nuclear missiles are at ready for safety precautions," stated Lawrence
Taylor, Secretary of Defense. World leaders offered cooperation and
finances for whatever the "invasion" called for, and stayed in contact with
Alvin Lawndale, Chairman of Joint Chiefs of Staff at the Pentagon. The
entire Armed Forces of the United States were prepared for whatever
might happen that would require their action. Congresswoman, Jeanine
Huntington said, "We can't operate the Government or the Armed
Forces upon religious beliefs!"

When Marcus Loshan heard this, he made a public statement over
the airwaves to Congress. "Tell that to Andrew Jackson;[26] tell that to
John Adams; tell that to George Washington. These men of God who
founded our Republic couldn't disagree more. They feared the day when
the government wasn't operated by Christian religious beliefs! When

---

[26]   The Bible is "the rock upon which our Republic rests."—Andrew Jackson;
       "Our constitution was made only for a moral and religious people. It is wholly
       inadequate to the government of any other."—John Adams;

these men of wisdom and faith declared independence from Britain they made a clear-cut declaration of dependence upon Almighty God! America is truly One Nation Under God. If you took out the direct teachings, laws, and influences of Christianity, and the Holy Bible from our government there wouldn't be anything left.

"What Congress needs is a true American history lesson. It could begin with a daily reading of the Declaration of Independence, The Constitution of the United States, and the Bill of Rights. Then they should look around at the intentional reminders on buildings, monuments, and landmarks. It wouldn't hurt to stop trusting in money and start looking at the 'nudge' printed upon it, 'In God We Trust.' Our government was created with the understanding and acknowledgment that its laws were God's laws. He is supreme. No one questioned that this God is the Father, Son, and Holy Spirit of Christianity. They also believed that those who didn't revere and honor Him would be punished by Him for their rebellion, regardless of how confident they were of their supposed superiority. Perhaps that's why the Cube is coming, to get attention off ourselves and place the focus back upon Him who deserves it all."

The Department of Military Readiness was busy, but what could they do in defense of the unknown? The entire civilized world felt helpless. This object was slowly gripping the hearts of men with fear. Every day the president, his cabinet, the Secretary of Defense, and all of Congress felt like they were walking on egg shells. Obviously God planned on getting the attention of the entire civilized world, and He had them right where He wanted them!

*   *   *

Occasionally Laura would see her neighbor, Phyllis Coe, as they were grocery shopping. Laura had invited her to come over for a visit sometime. Phyllis was always cordial, but Laura could tell she preferred to remain somewhat aloof. Finally, they got together at Laura's house when Phyllis called and asked if she could come over right away. Laura reached out to give her a hug and said, "Come on in. It's so good to see you. It's about time we got to know each other better."

Phyllis was an attractive, middle-aged woman who lived with her husband about a mile from the Waltham's. She was dressed casually in jeans and a top and tennis shoes. Her blond hair was a little blown in the wind and her blue eyes and her face emitted a sense of depression. She was fearful about the Cube. She'd picked up more than an ear full from various sources and couldn't get out of her mind that it was dangerous and might destroy the world. "I know you and Jim are Christians, and that Jim probably knows all about the Cube. But I'm not a Christian, and I'm terrified about the future. Can you help me?"

"Oh, Phyllis, I'm so glad you came. Certainly, I can help you. Can I serve you some tea as we talk?"

"Yes, that would be nice."

"Let's sit down here at the dining table and relax."

Laura served the tea and put some cookies on the table. "Let me peek in the bedroom and check on Scott. I think he's taking a nap."

Quickly, Laura returned and asked, "Do you have any idea about how to become a Christian, Phyllis?"

"Well, I know Jesus died on the Cross for our sins. But that's about it."

"Wonderful. Now let's think about a few things together. Are you the best person in the world?" Laura asked with a smile.

"No."

"Fallen a little short somewhere along the way, huh?"

"Oh yes!" Phyllis replied rolling her eyes with sadness.

"Haven't we all, Phyllis. But would God let sinful people into Heaven?"

"I guess not, but I sure do hope He would."

"Can God completely forgive and change people, Phyllis?"

"Well, I've heard that He can."

"Can He change you?"

"Yes, I believe so."

"Phyllis, your answers show that you do know quite a bit about how to be saved. You have faith that Jesus can forgive you of all your sins because you know He died on the Cross for that purpose. He's already accomplished that for us. What we're supposed to do is pray and ask Him to do it for us personally and trust Him to do it. Are you ready to do that?"

"I don't know how to pray."

"Yes, you do. You're talking to me, and prayer is simply talking to God. Just tell Him you want to be forgiven, and receive Him right into your life to take over. He'll do it."

Phyllis bowed her head, took a deep breath, "Jesus, I'm a sinner." Then relaxing, as if giving up, she continued, ". . . In fact, I'm a *bad* sinner, Lord. I've done so many wrong things that I cringe to think of them. Please forgive me. I need you. I want you to take over my life and change me. I don't even like the way I'm living. I want to be different. I want what you want."

Phyllis broke down with tears and sobbed for a few minutes as Laura put her arms around her and offered her comfort, saying softly,

"Thank you Jesus, for saving Phyllis, thank you Jesus for your forgiveness, praise your name Lord for being so good."

At last, Phyllis looked up and a smile came over her face.

"What about it? Did Christ save you?" Laura asked.

"Oh, yes!" she said exuberantly.

"How do you know?" Laura asked smiling.

"I felt like something heavy lifted off my shoulders."

"I'm sure those were your sins, Phyllis. They've all been removed forever. It was your faith in Jesus and what He did for you that saved you. Not everyone has that much feeling when they trust Him, but it is an extra blessing. You're not perfect yet and won't be in this life, but you now have the perfect Savior living inside your soul! You're ready for Heaven anytime from now on. I want you to delete all those fears about the Cube because it's coming to do good for you and for the whole world. We don't know the specifics yet, but it's a beautiful City, the dwelling place of God, and you are now his daughter! You're ready for the Cube, the New Jerusalem, and for whatever plan God has for you."

Phyllis had a completely different countenance, and the reality of belonging to Christ kept sinking in. The obvious "prison" she'd been living in was gone.

"I want to pray again," Phyllis said.

Surprised, Laura said, "Go right ahead."

Phyllis got down on her knees with Laura beside her and prayed.

"God, I'm so at peace. I feel like a tired person who has been placed in a soft bed. I wish the whole world could be this way. How will the people out there ever know? I wish you'd do something so that everyone could get to know how good you are. Amen."

Laura thought, Wow! *How beautiful! For someone who doesn't know how to pray, she has expressed the very heart of God!*

∞

17

TERMS OF IMPROVEMENT

Jim received a phone call from the office of the President of the United States. The staffer on the line explained that the president and other high level persons requested that he come to Washington for the purpose of sharing with them the basis of his announcements. They were being pulled in many directions; pressure was building; and they didn't want to miss any scientific input about this scary situation. Jim's claim that the Cube is the New Jerusalem was hard for the White House administration to believe, but it was the only identification anyone had offered so far. Jim's public statements were the most exact and confident. His position at the Orion Observatory Complex involving five observatories and home of the Lippershey Telescope, the world's largest, and the fact that the world of astronomy turned to his expertise in matters of space made Jim the most likely candidate for personal input at the White House. Jim made it clear that he'd be honored for the opportunity.

"If there's anyone in America who needs to know this information, it's the President and the decision makers of this country," Jim replied.

It was an urgent matter so he made immediate plans to be there at their invitation the next evening. When he arrived at the White House, he was greeted by the secretary, Mrs. Trudy Walker, who kept President Kenneth Snow on time for his busy appointments and trips.

"Dr. Waltham," she said, "You've already been checked and cleared for this meeting. They've done a thorough examination of your entire life and probably know more about you than you can remember!"

Jim smiled. Flashes of the past shot through his mind about the juvenile shenanigans he had pulled, the times his parents were about to explode over his behavior, and the college days before he became a Christian. He guessed these were probably not known or important. He was glad he hadn't done worse! He praised God for His protection and guidance in his life. He was sure he noticed the secret service personnel everywhere along the way. He felt really special, to be able to walk past them and know that he was accepted, even invited, to give the president and others information that would help them. He realized that there must be numerous "counselors" to the president. He wondered who they were, that is . . . beyond the paid professionals that surround him. Where did the others come from and how much weight did the president think they carried? How much weight would *he* carry? He would be straight forward, truthful, and to the point. It was up to the Holy Spirit to impress upon these leaders what he wanted them to do. The president himself was supposed to be strong enough to stand upon the truth against the loud darts of the devil that he must be sending through the mouths of some of the confused and blinded leaders of note.

The time arrived for him to enter the Oval Office where he met the President. It was even more impressive than the depictions he had seen in the movies—very plush, dignified, business-like, and made Jim feel important. Being there in person made all the difference. The President, who was strikingly handsome and comfortable in demeanor, welcomed

Jim. He rose from the chair behind his desk and walked quickly with his hand extended to Jim. The usual small talk everyone is prone to do eventually found its way into the conversation.

"How's Laura and your two children, Keith and Scott?" President Snow asked.

Jim was impressed, and then tried to recall how many children the President had. *I believe there are three. I should've looked that up somewhere,* he thought! He'd been too focused upon the Heavens and what he was planning to say. He barely remembered the President's wife's name, and after a panicked search through his mind, he said, "And how is your wife, Jennifer?"

They moved into a large conference room, and Jim was introduced to the leading people present. It was truly beautiful and lavishly arrayed with plush chairs and fresh flowers. The president's cabinet, and anyone that had anything to do with defense or closely related matters were there. They were very congenial and encouraging. They seemed hopeful they were about to receive some helpful insights. He was glad they were a ready audience. Jim was guided to a chair next to the President.

President Snow was seriously under pressure with the Cube nearing Earth in a matter of days. Jim could feel his need as he moved from personal formalities to the matter pressing on his heart. "Dr. Waltham, we've heard your statements over the air. We understand about the precise similarities between this object and the New Jerusalem of Revelation. Your statements sound very strong and appear to come from a heart of convictions."

"Thank you, sir," Jim said.

"As you would expect, it's hard for us to understand that this object could be a city sent from Heaven. But as a believer in the Lord Jesus and the Bible, I do know it's mentioned there so we can't rule it out. We have discussed this possibility and read Revelation where it's mentioned.

We must take all precautions and overlook nothing. We accept you as a serious scientist with the most up-to-date knowledge on this subject. First, let's hear from you whether there are any dangerous things that we should be aware of. We've tried to prepare the United States in the best way possible militarily. We continue the attempt to communicate with this object. We want to be certain that there's nothing left unattended that we ought to do for the people of America."

"I appreciate this opportunity, Mr. President. I understand your predicament. Rest assured it's hard for me to grasp that the New Jerusalem is coming too. Your first thought is your responsibility to protect the nation. You want to hear about the bad news immediately! Sir, I'm certain that according to my thorough investigation to discover any such thing about the Cube, there's nothing to fear. There's nothing to defend against. There's not even one negative thing about this whole matter."

"Can you tell me why you feel that there's no danger," the president asked.

"Mr. President, I'm not a theological scholar, but because of the Cube, I've been in constant touch with probably the most godly, humble, and scholarly men in the country for the past two months. I've not only given scientific scrutiny to the Cube, but, along with biblical scholars, we've explored every aspect of this situation and I believe I can give you substantial reasons."

"Good, let's hear them," the President said.

"We believe this matter to be a spiritual one. Its impossible movements and speed define it as supernatural. We're convinced that the New Jerusalem is being sent to the Earth from God with a benevolent end in mind and that it can't be a danger to anyone because of its very nature. In the book of Revelation, it's the designated physical presence of God among His people. On the other hand, if God were going to destroy a vast army, He'd simply send one angel with a spiritual sword and, with one slash, put two hundred thousand of them to death in an instant, as He did in King Hezekiah's day.[27] If God were going to destroy a few cities, He'd simply send a couple of angels as He did to Sodom, Gomorrah, Admah, and Zeboim, and destroy them completely with fire and brimstone. If He was going to destroy one third of the world He could do it by loosening four powerful angels to take care of it as He describes it in Revelation.[28] But no! The Cube is not a weapon of evil design," Jim explained. "Everything about it is glorious beyond words!"

"So you don't see it as being any sort of judgment, or directive for which I need to prepare?" the President inquired.

"Mr. President, so far no one has received any communication from the Cube. Until we do, and it's not even certain that we will, we have God's Word, the Holy Bible, for understanding His plans. He has given us plenty of insights in it. So to answer your question, I don't see that judgment or discipline is in its purpose—and that's not to say that we don't deserve it! I believe there will be plenty of directives you'll need to implement once it arrives, but I don't know the specifics about them. I'm only assuming that the Lord God may take some governing form over His world, and that'll mean those in charge will either be instructed or replaced with someone who knows what to do. There'll doubtless be many repercussions from people and nations because of the Cube's presence."

"Do you have any idea what God's trying to do with this Cube?" he asked.

---

[27]   2 Kings 19:35
[28]   Revelation 9:14-18

"I believe so, but only in generalities, Sir. God's always out to change lives and make them holy. Now, people and religious organizations all over the world have their places which are called 'holy.' Have you ever thought of what that word means? What makes a place holy or one place more holy than another? These are mere designations made by men. It usually has to do with someone having lived there, or worshiped there, or something unusual happened there."

"That's right," commented Jesse Wheeler, Vice President.

"The Bible is rightly called 'holy,' but that has nothing to do with paper and ink. The power of the inspired words is evidenced by changed lives. But again I ask, what is 'holy?' Compared to God's holiness, we have no idea! In the Old Testament there was the Tabernacle that Moses built and the Temple that Solomon built. In these physical places God manifested His presence by a powerful 'shekinah' glory—a shining, a light, a fire, an expression of his excellence. When some men opened the cover of the Ark of the Covenant, God smote and killed seventy of them for looking inside it. His presence was too holy for them to see and live. Today we know that God doesn't dwell in temples made by men's hands. Today it has pleased the Father to dwell in the very bodies of all believers who make up the temple of the Holy Spirit. That's the only truly holy place on Earth. So how human beings made in the image of God are treated is of utmost importance to the Lord."

"Are you suggesting that there'll be a spiritual link between the Holy City and Christians?" the president asked.

"Actually, sir, there already is. The Holy Spirit of God indwells the body of every Christian. Since God will evidently manifest Himself by the presence of the New Jerusalem, and it's the 'Holy City' promised from Scripture, it's the feeling of the Cubicles, a dedicated group of scholars, pastors, professors, and other godly students of the Bible, that his very presence here and its nearness to the Earth will obviously mandate changes in our behavior."

"Well, that makes sense," said the president. "I wonder what kind of changes He'll require and how He'll go about it?"

"That remains to be seen," said Jim. "I'm prone to feel that there'll be all kinds of immediate changes. We can only speculate at this point—whether God will speak directly to His Church, or send angels to give instructions to governments, or what. So I advise all of you to be very sensitive to the Lord God. Open your hearts to hear and perceive His will for your lives personally, this country, and the rest of the world—His Creation. There's no question He'll bring about change—and we can already imagine what some of them will be by simply knowing the Bible. We'll have to wait to see how it's done. Instructions may come to those who are already His servants, proclaiming the Gospel and teaching the Word of God faithfully. We're searching the Scripture for principles and requirements for personal and governmental action. And there will likely be a subtle, if not open rebellion against the changes that God requires.

"Candidly, that will create a predicament for the major religions of the world who don't worship the true and living God and have governments based upon their religions. God has made the greatest revelation of Himself to the world in the person of the Lord Jesus Christ. Unfortunately, not even all who claim to be Christians actually are. There are many counterfeits, and pretenders. It's difficult to tell some of them apart from true believers. That's clearly explained to us in the parables.[29] You can judge a tree by the fruit it bears.[30] I advise you to seek out those who really have a personal knowledge of God in their daily lives. Godly wisdom will greatly benefit you."

---

[29] Matthew 13
[30] Matthew 7:16-19

"Can you give the Congress and me anything else that we ought to know and what our actions should be right now? I want this government to be attentive to God," the President continued.

"I'm so thankful for your disposition, sir. Ladies and gentlemen, you're facing an absolutely astounding new period of time on the calendar. There's never been one like it. In the next few weeks we could all be living in a different sort of world. There is a diverse study group, which we refer to as the Cubicles, that assumes the changes will have to do with the very person and nature of God. They'll have to do with morality, compassion, security, well-being, and justice. After all, isn't that what government is supposed to be about? God can't help but address the things on Earth that are not godly and righteous. Think of how these issues are blatantly twisted and dodged in the United States, let alone those in other countries. Therefore, we anticipate that God's influence and participation in human activity should of necessity affect these areas. He's said too much about them in His Word not to."

"Can you give us specifics about these areas of concern?" asked the president.

"There are at least two basic things that are always on God's heart. He's interested in saving souls so they can enjoy His Kingdom forever—in other words, getting to know God personally, and then living an honest, righteous life as much like Jesus as possible. Christians have the job of living by faith while not being perfect at it. Applying the second part of this revealed will, it's our thought that governments all over the world will likely have to throw off the things that are evil, corrupt, and unjust. The court systems of this country will somehow have to be re-modeled and returned to biblical principles. Crime, immorality of every form, lying, deception, perjury, cheating, embezzlement, idolatry, demonic activity, drug traffic, pornography and harmful use of anything against God's holiness will be targets for change. The sacredness of life will necessarily have to be accepted, and those who destroy it properly judged. Everything that dishonors God will be subject to scrutiny. I don't know how all this will play out, but there's bound to be tremendous pressure upon you, Mr. President, and the Congress. You're going to need help in rightly relating to God's presence and his plan."

"Wow! That's exactly what I'd want if I were in God's place! What should we do? How can we get ready?" one congressman wondered.

Jim thought for a while; then spoke slowly. "The full story is long, but I believe I can at least suggest a few facts as I understand them. Let's consider the appearance of the Cube. It came from God, which is the same as saying from heavenly north. That's the dwelling place of Almighty God and his Throne as it relates to Earth. It caught the world's attention by letting its light shine." Jim was watching the faces of these men and few women. They were not sure if they were hearing correctly or not. They appeared to be listening to a man tell them a simple Bible story that might be told to children. But they were giving him their full attention anyhow. "It's so like God to do things that way," Jim mused.

"After it got our attention, the Cube moved an impossible distance two times to let us know this event is supernatural. I believe God wants us to acknowledge Him as the source so we can exercise faith in his authority and submit to it. There'll no doubt be many repercussions of the Cube. Some of them will require immediate and precise action on your part, but not in the way you would usually expect."

"So you're saying that America and its government should surrender to it without reservation?" the president asked.

"Absolutely," Jim replied. "But it won't be like surrendering to an enemy that has won a war victory. It's submitting to God by faith that He wants to bring about good in your life and into the lives of the whole world."

"That's quite a challenge. I wonder what the American people would think of that?" the president said.

"The people who know God and those who are reasonable will expect you to," Jim replied. "Think about it. The arrival of the Cube was not accidental. It didn't casually float down as if it had no objective. The way it came is a powerful demonstration that its mission has a definite purpose that absolutely will be accomplished. There's no scientific explanation for that speed. It defies all known natural laws. It's clearly supernatural. God wanted us to witness these things so that we can react in a reasonable fashion."

"I guess it's obvious," the vice president spoke up, "if He can do these things we only have one action to take—submit and trust Him."

"You are correct, Mr. Wheeler," Jim said, "but you do have the choice, and that's always the issue with God. Now, my friends, I should point out that Bible scholars throughout the past two thousand years have known that Jesus would come and take His Throne and reign a thousand years over the world from the physical Jerusalem in the Holy Land. Every indication is that after that reign, this heavenly New Jerusalem would come, and it would be the abiding place, or home base, of all the saints, and the dwelling place of Jesus Christ. That's the setting that we find described in the last two chapters of Revelation. However, what's taking place at this present time is not that timeframe in prophecy! Suddenly we have the New Jerusalem, the Cube, coming now, prior to the coming of Christ to reign. So with that information—and this is what you really want to know—why is the New Jerusalem coming at this time?"

Jim paused and let them lean forward for the answer. "I don't know beyond what I've already said." They leaned back on their chairs. "We're at a loss as to the overall world-wide plan for its coming at this time. That's the unknown piece in the puzzle. But don't miss this. God always reveals His plans to His servants who love and obey Him.[31]

---

[31]   Amos 3:7

"So what you're saying," the president inquired, "is that it's no surprise that the Cube, or New Jerusalem, would come, it's just a puzzle as to its coming at this time in history. Is that correct?"

"Yes. And for whatever plan the Lord has, this heavenly New Jerusalem is knocking at our door. The Cube's coming at this time is not something that is predicted in Scripture, from the best we can determine from eschatology—the study of things to come. Therefore we're obviously limited as to its reason for coming at this time since there's nothing written about this particular event. It's similar to the 'hidden mystery' of the Church, which was not made known to anyone until after the coming of the Holy Spirit on the Day of Pentecost, which followed the Resurrection of Christ."[32]

"Just what is the purpose of the New Jerusalem as it's found in the book of Revelation?" the vice president asked.

"That's easy. In that book the last battle on Earth has been fought. Christ has judged the world and banished all evil from His presence. He's completely renewed the Heavens and the Earth, and they're populated only with godly people and angels who love God with all their hearts. So the City's a physical manifestation of God's presence, the abiding place for all the saints where worship takes place forever, and everyone beholds its unspeakable beauty."

"So then, you think its purpose is different today, is that right?" asked Lawrence Taylor, the Secretary of Defense.

"Yes, it has to be different. The first Heaven and first Earth have not yet passed away.[33] Evil's still present everywhere. The Church is still involved in world evangelism."

---

[32]   Ephesians 3:3-6
[33]   Revelation 21:1

"Can you see what the New Jerusalem looks like through your telescope, Dr. Waltham?" asked Taylor.

"Yes, Mr. Taylor. There's no other known object in all of space with that shape. Now that it's moved another giant step closer, I can see the foundations, the walls, the gates as Revelation describes them. At first, I was so excited that I hardly knew what to do. It was hard to contain! And since God often does things in threes throughout the Bible, corresponding to his essence—Father, Son, and Holy Spirit—we expect its third stop will put it right at the rim of our atmosphere. In fact it continues to move at a rate of speed that will bring it here in approximately three weeks.

"So you can describe it to us?" asked congressman Herman Jennings.

"Yes, but strangely, we weren't able to pick out anything but light for about the first fifty days. Yet the New Jerusalem was so close to us even two months ago, that we should've been able to see all of the beauty and glory of this indescribable City. Our Zoph XT-four extractor should've been able to lift every minute part of it right before our eyes! Amazingly, we could only see a little of it. For His own reasons He has determined to let its glory be observed more and more only as it descends. Now we're viewing the actual description found in the book of Revelation that you have been reading for yourselves. I hope you understand that several of us back in Texas have given much study, prayer and meditation upon this matter. We've come to believe this is His plan—to give us answers as they're needed. In other words, this visitation is to be learned one day at a time, like the Christian walk is and always has been. We know Him as we live with Him on a daily basis."

"And what if there were some hostile moves from the Cube," Secretary Taylor pressed, trying not to leave any negatives uncovered, "what would you suppose would be the nature of them?"

Jim shifted in his chair and relaxed more, then replied, "Well, if it were a space ship or alien object from another universe, it obviously would be far ahead of our scientific world. If it were hostile, it would be capable of getting around our best defense, which to it, would be puny. Of course, in such a case we'd still probably do anything we could to overcome it for safety's sake.

"If it were science-fiction, we could expect there to be war by fighting, killing, abductions, intergalactic intrigue, and so forth. We automatically think that if there are others out there in space, they must be violent, warmongers, and wicked like the human race. But my friends, this is not science-fiction. This isn't a creature orchestrated event. If this is the New Jerusalem, it's our Creator who is paying us a visit. I should remind you that He's paid us many visits in human history. Some were visits involving judgment: Noah's Flood, the Exodus, numerous armies supernaturally destroyed for

> For You, Lord, are
> kind and ready to
> forgive, abundant
> in faithful love to
> all who call on You.
>
> (Psalm 86:5
> HCSB)

or by the Nation of Israel, as well as judgment upon Israel for her failure to obey His commands. However, the New Jerusalem as it's now being seen is a partial revelation of His glory, and I'm personally convinced that it is all good!"

Jim felt he had likely given them more information than they could contain at one sitting. He sat back in his chair and said as much, "I realize I'm probably assuming too much, expecting you to be familiar with the Word of God, and taking you farther in the Bible than you may be acquainted with, especially in the area of prophecy as I understand it. If so, please ask questions, and I'll try to draw you a picture and simplify things as much as possible. I've been brought to the White House, not to speak so much on biblical themes, but to give you scientific information from an astronomer who's been looking at the Cube consistently for the past two months. The more I study the stars, the constellations, the Cube, and the Bible, the more I believe that all these things go together. This is an unexpected appearing unrevealed before."

Then the president turned to those in the room, "From what I've heard, we need a lot more input before we're going to get up to speed for this event! I'm feeling pretty helpless and unnecessary!"

"That makes the rest of us feel better, Sir," said a Congressman. "We all felt we were the helpless ones. Where should we begin?" he asked, turning to Jim.

At this point, two men rose to leave the room, appearing to be somewhat exasperated with the meeting. A few other were looking at each other as if this might be a good time to go too. But the President looked at them with a determined face and said, "Hear him out!" They all returned to their seats.

Jim surveyed his listeners and then stated, "There are people who know God very well. Others hardly know anything except what they've heard from relatives or fairy tales of the past. Even many Christians in America, who've received His salvation and forgiveness, have stagnated in their spiritual growth because of neglect. God never forces Himself upon us. He appeals to us, reaches out to us through circumstances, draws us to Him so we can have the pleasure of knowing Him more and more as we open up to him. Every believer has the potential of gaining exceptional knowledge of Him. But few are willing to give Him the time. You see, we're all just as spiritual as we want to be. If we really wanted to be more spiritual, we would be devoting ourselves to those biblical disciplines that bring about spiritual growth. But most of us are content to be mediocre."

Jim's discussion of these matters literally held most of those in the conference room spellbound. Their concepts of God, government, righteous living, and personal accountability were brought to light. Intercession by the band of prayer warriors back home and those scattered around the country was being answered.

He continued, "I don't know your hearts, whether you're believers in Jesus Christ and what He did for you on the Cross or not. I do know He loves you. He died to pay for your sins. He arose from the dead and is now preparing to bring more of His eternal plan for man to pass. This New Jerusalem is a powerful, and probably, a last call for many to be saved from sin and hell. If you've not been saved yet, today can be the day of your deliverance from sin and your reconciliation with God. Face the fact that you're unable to go up into Heaven by your own efforts. That would be as impossible as it would be for a gnat to fly up and land on the sun! Face the truth that Jesus is the one and only Way for all people to be forgiven and become children of God."

"Isn't that a narrow view?" asked a participant, with a doubtful countenance.

"It's a narrow way, yes, but not a prejudiced way. It's open to every person, every nation, language, and tribe. Jesus Christ is your Way. Call upon Him, give yourself up to Him as your Lord and Master. He'll answer your prayer of trust and change your heart and life right now! Then, you, too, will be able to learn why the New Jerusalem is coming and get in on the full benefit of it. That's where you must begin. Those who 'wait and see' will likely be overwhelmed by the issues that'll have to be faced. You'll be able to discern them better as God's children in His family."

Jim bowed his head and prayed: "Father in Heaven, bless our president and his cabinet, those who minister to him in numerous ways. These people came to learn of your City. They're open for answers. Let them begin by receiving the One who has every answer into their lives. Come be their King and Savior as they pray. Let them know the joy and meaning of being in your family by faith in the living Christ, in Jesus name, let it be so."

Jim had presented what he knew as a scientist and a believer in Christ. It was his belief that God was the Author of all truth, physical, scientific and spiritual and that it all fit together perfectly. True science was merely using God's laws to enjoy His world. He explained that all human beings were still rebellious, stubborn, skeptical, and resistant to Jesus and that the Bible told us that about ourselves. He asked for questions.

The president and others did have questions.

One participant impatiently asked, "Dr. Waltham, your explanations sound good and meaningful, but they are so simple that I wonder if it can possibly be—that God's in control, and all we have to do is sit around waiting for Him to take over the world and all will be fine. Isn't there more to it than that?"

"Yes sir! You can't just sit around. I believe God expects us to be busy seeking to get our lives clean and usable. Turn away from all known sin. Right every wrong you have committed. Treat every person with respect and worthy of highest value. This will take some time. You can't complete it in twenty-four hours! Who have you lied to? Whose heart have you broken? Who have you offended? Who has suffered loss and you need to make repairs? I understand all of you tend to have a nationwide perspective, and that is good. But you can't expect to impact the nation while there are personal offenses, atrocities, unforgiveness, or even 'petty' sins that you overlook and try to sweep under the rug. What I'm saying is, God Almighty wants to begin right here in this room and in your hearts and mine, to get ready for something larger than your imagination. And it'll mean the most to those who are pure and ready to be used in his work."

Another person asked, "Dr. Waltham, suppose you are wrong about this object. What if it's not the New Jerusalem, but a serious, wicked intruder intending to destroy us, manipulate us, take us captive, or something like that? Shouldn't we consider other options?"

"Yes sir! But am I not correct in believing that you've already considered every option that you can think of?" You did that before you called me. Then, smiling: "Who turns to God, or religion, or spiritual help until he exhausts everything else?" That brought a little laughter from the crowd. "Do you think I haven't considered everything else as well? I've racked by brain over and over. I've tried to figure out if this could be a counterfeit from the devil, the master deceiver. But nothing else makes sense to me. The whole thing is too obvious to miss. It's just as I've presented it to you. I only wish I knew more to share with you at this time."

Their conversation lasted a little longer and only ended when the next important meeting had to take over their time. President Snow was obviously moved by Jim's candor and confidence. On the safe side, they would still have to consider all other options. The New Jerusalem was a real shocker to all of them. But at least they now had the story from an expert and didn't have to rely on hearsay. There was an openness in Jim's heart and the president wanted to get to know him better. That opportunity would come in the near future, but for now, he had other pressing issues to deal with.

Jim felt like a father leaving his children when he departed the White House. There was so much more he wanted them to know. His mind kept running along with all the things that he wished he could have shared. He consoled himself with the fact that he did accomplish what he came to do. *At least they know what I know. And they'd better look to God for what else He wants them to know!*

∞

18

WHERE TO FOCUS

Back home, Jim and Marcus discussed their frustration with so many issues to deal with. They explored the Cube as much as they possibly could. They were thankful for the excellent staff that was at the cutting edge of astronomy and who conferred with them daily. The Cubicles constantly studied, sought for what God wanted to accomplish, and examined their hearts. Jim was also engrossed preparing himself for whatever the trustees at Quad U might come up with.

Jim went ahead with his classes as usual. The students were always full of questions, so he had to guard himself as to what to say. But he didn't shy away from revealing at least all scientific findings to them. The New Jerusalem was still rapidly descending at super speed indicating that it would be at the Earth in less than three weeks!

Dr. Fleming stated over the air that every moral precept that's found in the teachings of Jesus, the New Testament, as well as the Old Testament's prophetical books were important for them to know. God's word to Israel was a constant reminder to them of caring for the poor, taking up for the downtrodden, lifting up those who were oppressed, and seeking right judgment for those wronged. There needed to be a biblical approach handled unlike the welfare America was familiar with. He stressed his belief that these precepts were pertinent to the Cube's event. His contact with seminary faculty members enriched his thinking. He and Jim got together at the LT office again to sharpen their thoughts and theology as to what God might have in mind by this visit.

Coffee and cherry cheesecake were on the end of Jim's desk, and both their Bibles were open. They were relaxed and engrossed with their Lord and with each other. Jim admired the knowledge of this man of God and wanted to visualize future events with the Cube's imminent arrival. "I know," Jim said, as they re-examined Scripture, "the New Jerusalem as it appears in Revelation is coming to an Earth that's already been re-created and new, along with a new heaven. So the only persons on earth at that time are the ones who know and love God. Everything is perfect. The redeemed of all the ages will be worshipping and serving Him with all their hearts."

> *As iron sharpens iron, so one man sharpens another.*
>
> *(Proverbs. 27:17 NIV)*

"That's right," Rex agreed, as he leaned back in his chair calling on his vast knowledge of God's Word, "but think of the changes that belong to the new Heaven and Earth. There'd be no more devil, he'd have already been cast into the Lake of Fire. There'd be no more curse on the Earth, so everything in the world would be operating at maximum capacity like it was before Adam and Eve disobeyed."

"Yes" Jim said, "And the changes that are to take place when the Cube arrives here remain to be seen. I keep wondering if He'll speak to the whole Earth with an audible voice. I wonder if He'll send visible angels to communicate with us. I wonder how He's going to get across to us his plan and will."

Rex reflected, "Throughout the Bible God made himself known to His servants, the prophets, and others in various ways: dreams, visions, theophanies, angel messengers, answered prayer, and vocally. We're going to have to wait and see . . . but isn't it hard to wait?"

"Amen," Jim agreed.

*   *   *

Later that evening the backyard of the Waltham home was the gathering place for friends to unwind and overcome some of the present tension. While the kids were playing "hide and seek," four year old Asa, son of Marcus and Cindy, came crying to Jim saying, "Keith scared me!"

"How'd he scare you, Asa?" Jim asked while reaching out to him with a one-armed hug and acting overly surprised.

"He jumped out of the bushes and growled at me," Asa complained, his face twisted up like only children can do—reflecting hurt, fear, anger, pretense, and the need for comfort.

"He did!" Jim said with pretended amazement. "Why that meanie!"

When Keith saw he was being tattled on, he hurried over to his dad laughing and interjected, "I was just playing."

Jim advised little Asa, "Why don't you just scare him back? Growl at him."

Asa, changed his frown to a half-smile, caught the idea and turned to Keith growling and running after him. Keith joined the fun screaming in fear and said, "Oh, no! Don't get me!" They disappeared in the distance as all the adults laughed.

"Daddy, what's the Cube object?" eight-year-old Kristin, daughter of Marcus and Cindy, cautiously asked, her face emitting fright. "The kids at school say it's an invasion from Mars."

Smiling, Marcus put his arms around her and pulled her to him with a hug and replied, "No, Kristin, it's not an invasion from Mars. People are prone to be afraid of just about anything that comes along. They have to cushion themselves with exaggerated possibilities, hoping it surely won't be that bad. But we don't have to be afraid of anything because we know who God is and what He's like. One thing we know is that it's the New Jerusalem, a place where God will show us some of His beauty and glory. And since He's there in a special way and loves us, the Cube has to be for a good reason."

As Kristin happily skipped away, Marcus smiled and commented to Jim, who sat on the bench of the picnic table, "It's hard to wait for more information about the Cube, isn't it, Jim? What a dilemma. Too exciting and too unknown at the same time!"

"Yes, but soon we may have more information than we can handle!" Jim replied. "He's got a reason for not telling us all we want to know before now. People always want all the answers ahead of time. But God's ways are different from ours. Remember how he promised Abraham a son? I'm sure Abraham had difficulty in waiting twenty-five years to get him! Moses wanted to deliver the Israelites from slavery in Egypt and took steps to get it started. The Lord let Moses herd sheep in the desert land of Midian forty years before He appeared to him and gave him that assignment. Sure, I'd like to know all about the Cube today, but I'm thankful for what He's already shown me. I already know more than I knew two months ago. I'm not going to presume about what I don't know."

"Yeah, me too. It's enough that we know it's actually the New Jerusalem! That information is far ahead of what the rest of the world knows." Marcus replied.

"Yes, and He's allowed us to learn much about His universe. But what have we done with our knowledge? People are so typically impatient they want to know everything by five o'clock today. When God doesn't give them what they want, some people make up their own answers and claim them to be 'spiritual' or 'scientific.'

"Meanwhile our true knowledge is largely wasted on things like evolutionary musings. The bulk of education is off on a rabbit chase that doesn't even have a rabbit! What does God want us to know about his universe? Perhaps he would appreciate it if we took the information we already have on hand and laid it out in sensible outline. Maybe we could come to some very simple and general conclusions that are really profound and begin putting them into practical use."

"What kind of things do you think we could already know, Jim," Cindy curiously asked.

After a pause to think about it, Jim got up off the picnic bench, chose a more comfortable chair and continued, "Well, for example, first, we know the universe is vast! God's bigger than we thought. That truth alone could fill in a lot of blanks in the average mind since most people are perplexed by the smallness of their God.

"And of course, we know that space objects are all moving—at enormous rates of speed, and God's bigger than space. That tells us that God's an active Person. He's not merely sitting around, scratching His head, wondering what to do. He's involved in His Creation, and will bring it to his desired future. He's closer than we thought.

"And then, the universe is so captivating! No matter what direction you explore there are things that can intrigue you for a lifetime. That concept should put humility into our souls. He deserves to be worshipped. That's what happened to David. He said, 'When I consider Your Heavens, the work of Your fingers, the moon and the stars which You have ordained, What is man that You are mindful of him, And the son of man that You visit him'?[34] He's wiser than we thought.

---

[34] Psalm 8:3-4

"Also, we know that Earth, space and its objects are orderly. God planned every detail of life in advance before He created them. It may not seem that way to the casual observer, but they are to the serious students. All of His doings are meaningful to mankind. Learning His natural laws has helped us to become modernized with inventions and discoveries unthinkable just one hundred years ago. We have the resources to make Earth a paradise. But they're mostly wasted by selfish living, petty thievery, self-righteous and prideful prejudices, covetous dictators, warmongers, and uneducated multitudes who've been robbed of their potential. Therefore, life in general is a maze of confusion, worldwide. We're more sinful than we thought."

"Hey, is any of that written in a book?" asked Cindy, as she leaned forward in her chair as if to get a notebook and start writing.

Laughing, Jim said, "Probably. I'm just running off at the mouth, thinking out loud. I haven't ever written this down myself."

"Hello! Anyone for another barbeque sandwich?" Laura called, with a threatening smile.

There's still a lot of stuff here that needs to be eaten. And remember, what you don't eat you have to take home with you!"

The Cube was close enough now and allowing more of its beauty and glory to be seen, so small amateur telescopes were delighted with its detailed features. There was widespread excitement as well as fear reaching the media every day. Reports differed, too. It was like the testimony of four persons who witnessed the same car wreck. "How could there be such confusion and difference in what they see?" Jim said with dismay. "Astronomers in other observatories must be desperate and making up lies to come out with such rubbish! But why would they do it? Are letting their emotions clouded their logic?"

The Pentagon reported that every nuclear warhead directed at the Cube had ceased to function! General Lawrence Taylor, Secretary of Defense, announced, "Not a single switch works. Power is still connected, but none of the switches will operate." He also received reports from other countries of similar failures of their defense weapons. The Cube had obviously disconnected all opposition. Defense personnel in charge were panicky. Pressure was at maximum force, and there was no one to turn to for explanations.

Action was taken by at least one cult. Omni-worshippers were calling for all their followers to meet at the Continental Divide between Helena and Butte, Montana, wearing white robes beginning next week. They intended to wait out the coming of the "Flying Skiff" that would be sent from the Cube to pick them up and take them to paradise, separating them from the rest of the world. It was estimated that their number of about five thousand would swell to several times that size during the next two weeks, creating major traffic jams and a run on hotels, camping areas, and food establishments.

> I will destroy the wisdom of the wise, and I will set aside the understanding of the experts.
>
> (1 Corinthians 1:19 HCSB)

The mayors of Helena, Butte, Great Falls, and Anaconda were rushing to try to provide for, as well as contain these areas with necessary personnel. They appealed to the governor for help from the National Guard for major traffic control, security, and aid to the suppliers of necessities to the communities as every store would likely be depleted in a few days. A state of emergency was declared. The National Guard could also help prevent the possibility of mass suicides that resulted from similar events in the past such as those involving Jim Jones, David Koresh, and the Haley Bop comet fiasco.

At the same time everyone who lived there was keeping an eye on their family, so as to stay on top of this event and to care for their own loved ones. Magazines were offering huge amounts of money for the first person who provided them with a photograph of the Cube.

Earl Wilson, Chairman of the Objects In Space Association, announced over the news media that this was the coming of the ultimate spacecraft. There would not be one human being left on Earth after it completed its series of journeys. He declared, "There'll be more of these invasions to every planet in space. There's a world out there that we only have a slight glint of understanding about. It's a world in which inhabitants from every reach of space will be gathered in the Numadome of the Mother Galaxy where they'll participate in inter-exchange of creation and the making of the crowning species."

There was a run on every kind of food at grocery stores. People didn't know what to expect and were operating on adrenalin. There seemed to be no place to hide. The Cube had blanketed all other news reports.

Scientific organizations scoffed at religious leaders. Evidently those who didn't believe in God were just as fanatical as some religious "kooks." They set forth numerous theories of aliens. Atheists were hoping that, whatever the Cube was that it would prove that there was no God. But they couldn't figure how this invader evolved so far ahead of them. Division abounded in every field of study, each wanting to be "right" in their guesses. The pride of man was sticking out everywhere. Some were learning the basic truth about quacks. A hard-working man in jeans and a hard hat with common sense, with a stern face walked by a news microphone and spoke up, "Just because a person has a degree in science doesn't mean that his work is scientific. There are procedures that are necessary before their findings can claim to be scientific. Even so, there're many religious people whose life and teachings don't reveal much about God. After all, not all auto mechanics can fix a car either!"

Every profession seemed to be put to the test as to its authenticity. The origin of the world and the billions of galaxies were constantly a matter of debate.

Dr. Claude Moreau, pastor of Ohio's largest mega church said the reason people are in panic mode is their lack of confidence in the Creator. He spoke to the issue of origins in his televised broadcast the previous Sunday and said, "To try to arrive at 'where we came from' by examining the core of an asteroid is a slap in the face of God. It makes about as much sense as asking a duck to take an oral exam in chemistry. 'Quack, quack, quack,' and a professor says, 'Wow, did you hear that? I believe he passed!' So we have schools passing one bag of ignorance on to another person's ignorance and calling it education. Someone goes to Africa and finds a few bones, part of a skull, and a couple of teeth, and declares that he's found the link from prehistoric man to modern man! Another thinks he can find the origin of the world through his telescope and bases his entire view of the universe on that man-made looking glass. How silly and non-productive. He may as well dip a jar full of ocean water and declare that rubber tires came from that. Where is the science in such foolishness?

"Physical things don't tell us where we came from. They only indicate that we were made! Scientists can study apes, galaxies, mud holes, black holes, and even DNA, but none of these will ever reveal our origin! God told us He made man from the dust of the Earth and placed him in Eden located near the Tigris and Euphrates Rivers. He's the Source. Mankind continues to announce 'new ideas' of our origin, all of which are just another way to rebel against God. It takes a lot of love for God to patiently knock at wicked hearts so He can bring them back to His simple, absolute truth where they can find rest from their weary

efforts. The Holy Bible is the only book in the world that reveals to us
God's Creation, where we came from, our purpose, and destiny. Its basic
story has to do with God, Man, Sin, Satan, and Salvation through Jesus
Christ. All other attempts to explain our origin and purpose are just so
much gobbledygook."

Certain groups of philosophers, scientists, politicians, religious cults,
and financial giants formed "think tanks" to pool their wisdom and to
preserve their status. Theories from these pools were streaming over the
internet as well as headlining magazines, newspapers, and other media.
If there ever was a time when the entire world focused its efforts, and
knowledge ran to and fro throughout the world—it was this time.

Third world countries struggled to gain solid information about
the threatening situation. There were too many authorities. Which
one or ones could they trust? It came down to the opinions of friends
in more developed countries that they relied on most. The majority of
the smaller countries suffered greater terror of the unknown, and their
leaders appeared to be too handcuffed to help. All they could do was
plead with the big nations to please protect the world with their nuclear
arms, defense plans, and technology.

Meanwhile among Christian churches, the atmosphere was changing
to that of positive praise and shouts of joyous anticipation. "Praise the
Lord," "Come Lord Jesus," and "maranatha,—the Lord is coming" were
phrases that were taken up by those who previously were not so vocally
spiritual. Christians around the world celebrated while all others were
afraid of the inexplicable. Informed ministers throughout the world
tried to bring the message of peace to their cities. But there seemed to be
a natural animosity, skepticism, and prejudice against the Word of God.
Large groups of believers gathered to pray for God's will to be done on
Earth as it was being done in Heaven. They were especially anxious to

see if the New Jerusalem would actually go into orbit and how it would affect the world.

Jim received word through the grapevine that the trustees of Quad U were finally going to dump him. Since he had clearly not taught the Bible in class after their reprimand, they evidently wanted to confront him with his general snubbing of the "spirit" of their contention. They wanted control over what he had to say outside the classroom, for he was still a faculty member and in a sense represented the school wherever he went. Jim realized he had his hands full of many responsibilities and couldn't sit down and spell out the answers he'd like to give. Instead, he spent more time in prayer and claimed the statement that often came to his mind that Jesus gave to his disciples, "And when they shall lead you to judgment, do not worry what you are going to say. Don't even premeditate. But whatever is given you in that hour, simply say the words you are given when the time comes, for it will not be you who speak but the Holy Spirit."[35] What a relief! Jim knew he could count on the Lord when he didn't know what to say.

The New Jerusalem was only two weeks away now—assuming it would continue descending at the same rate of speed—from the supposed landing, orbit, or whatever it would do. Jim and Marcus were ecstatic about the details outside the Cube which had become so distinct. The beauty of the jewels was amazingly awesome in the twelve foundations and clearly distinguishable. Powerful telescopes now brought it all right up to their eyes. Jim was committed to let the public know what they saw all along—after first giving their findings to the group of like-minded believers, the Cubicles, who stayed in communication with him from the beginning. That way, the others were free to disseminate the information locally at the same time. This deeper, on-going revelation caused great

---

[35]   Mark 13:11

joy and assurance to those who trusted the Lord and confirmed that they need not be anxious.

Against these findings were the usual astounding contradictions from many opposing fronts claiming that what was reported by Jim Waltham and his staff was merely religious lies. There were plenty of negative voices that didn't hesitate to criticize him personally. The influence of Anthony Cagney, the recently-fired former staff member at the Lippershey observatory, was evidently still being felt among astronomers at other observatories. Jim and Marcus didn't know what to make of these complaints. All observatories were looking at the same thing. "We'll just have to write it off as disgruntled, jealous misfits who can't stand for God to be at the top of the news," Marcus stated.

And another enemy was arriving on the scene.

∞

19

LOOMING DANGER

One of those voices of opposition was none other than Margaret Thames, a college girl who had her mind on Jim, but failed to get his attention while they were in school together. He was happy he didn't respond to her innuendoes, but occasionally during the semesters she would catch his eye as he walked across the campus. Margaret was a red-haired, persuasive, pushy, sultry egotist who was interested in Jim. She let him know in some way every time she saw him. Often it was that "come on" look she gave him as she walked near or that long stare when their eyes met or that big smile that said, "I understand. I'm what you want. I can make your dreams come true and you know it. And it is all going to be my way soon."

"Hiiii, Jim," she would say, with a wide smile when they passed each other.

"Hello. How are you?" Jim would reply, nodding without stopping to find out.

Jim was drawn to her in a sensual way, but he could tell being together with her would be a temporary destiny. It might be exciting, but not worth it in the long run. The more she made overtures toward him, the more he grew repulsed by her personality. He wanted "soon" to be as far in the future as he could make it. Sometimes they spoke with each other when circumstances brought them near. He didn't ever do or say anything to turn her away, not wanting to hurt her feelings—which might happen regardless of how he reacted. So, he smiled and treated her nicely, as he would anyone else. He could tell, though, that she didn't appreciate not being more appreciated!

Margaret had a charming, outgoing personality. She had lofty goals for herself and an eye for anyone who could help her get there. She also wanted others to play with while on the way. She majored in communications and knew how to use her talent. Desiring to make her mark through the media, she'd already worked at a local television station as a back-up to one of their reporters. *Yes,* Jim thought, *there's no telling where I'd be if I had been involved with her—especially if I had married her.*

By now she'd pushed and shoved her way to the news anchor position in the mega city of Atlanta, Georgia. When she picked up on Jim's name in the news, she determined to vent some of her red-haired vengeance upon him just for good measure. It would serve him right for ignoring her alluring and persuasive personality. She'd learned the ropes perfectly and knew just how to manipulate stories to appear whichever way she wanted.

Margaret immediately began gathering stories and speculations, airing them to suit her subtle purpose. Her research revealed the details of Jim's long-time involvement in religious affairs. She was able to fabricate and publish the suspicion that Jim was using religion to advance his career in the field of science, pretending he was a spiritual leader. And now there was a questionable, religious element being brought into the science of astronomy concerning the object called the Cube. When the story came out in the local newspaper in Ft. Davis, eyebrows were raised by many who didn't know Jim, and the "mafia" at Quad U was spurred on with their intention to fire him for his rebellious ideas against their philosophy.

Margaret received permission to go to Quad University on assignment to gather more information on Jim Waltham, the Cube, and whatever else was there to make a smashing news story. Jim was unaware of Margaret's recent news item. When he entered the door of his home that evening, Laura took him by the hand, sat down with him and shared the story about what she had heard and quietly asked, "Honey, what's the meaning of this insinuation?"

It was so preposterous that his face turned white, then red with anger. He was unable to contain all the profanity that boomed in his mind, but he did control most of it as he got up from his chair and walked back and forth in the den, waving his hands up and down. Then he hung his head in grief that someone would purposely ambush him with something that twisted. "I'm utterly amazed that anyone could be that blatant—especially someone who obviously has no first-hand knowledge me. She had to go way out to come up with a story like that. Apparently some people will do anything to bring another person down or into suspicion. Being in the public eye has more hazards than we can imagine!" he said. "Forgive me, Laura, I had no right to vent my anger in front of you . . . and for no good reason."

"I understand perfectly, honey," Laura responded. "We're victims of a vicious attack from spiritual wickedness in high places."[36]

Quad trustees met and discussed the problem of Jim's involvement with the media. He was reporting to the stations regularly his findings

---

[36] Ephesians 6:12

concerning the Cube. Some of the trustees agreed that the Cube did indeed have the characteristics of the New Jerusalem as described in the book of Revelation. But others loudly retorted: "Are you guys from Orion too?" referring to the world's greatest telescope a few miles away. "Anyone knows that there can't be any such thing as a City coming down from the sky!" they shouted. Heated debate followed so they couldn't continue their meeting. They would reschedule in a few days.

Jim was relieved! The whole world seemed to be heating up over the Cube. He was certain that there ought to be plenty of heat over this event. But too much of the heat was coming from the wrong furnace! He countered in his mind that God's heat ought to out-burn the devil's!

∞

20

***

PAINFUL WAITING

As the last few days approached and the Cube drew closer to Earth's atmosphere, more and more contradictory information hit the news. It was as if confusion was king! Jim and his staff were scratching their heads about the puzzling reports coming from otherwise stable and reliable sources—observatories, scientists, and qualified personnel. It didn't make sense. It was all Jim could do to hold down his anger at what was said about his reports as well as himself. The Lippershey Telescope staff kept re-studying every statement they made for accuracy. They went out of their way to make sure they didn't exaggerate or read into the facts their own beliefs or ideals. Everyone on staff had seen the Cube personally. They worked hard to be totally objective. Yet they read the news and even received reports from observatories that clashed with their own. The contradictions were so blatant they had to be intentional.

On one hand, Jim Waltham and his staff reported on the wonderful City of God, that it was beautiful to behold. Its details were spectacular. It was peaceful in its approach. There should be no damage expected, nothing to fear, the Creator Himself was in charge. On the other hand, other observatories reported, "This Cube has brightness alright, but it's a bland form with no beauty that would make it appealing at all. It appears to be more man-made than supernatural, and it could truly be an alien invasion!"

This was such a flat contradiction that it was shocking. "The governments and media are receiving the same information from both of us," Marcus said, "so there can only be confusion in the news! What should we do about it?" What could Jim and the Cubicles do about it was that they could pray!

A bright student in Jim's class asked, "Sir, what makes you and others at the Lipppershey Observatory say that more beauty is observable from the Cube as it gets closer to Earth?" Others in the class perked up at the question too.

"Well, I'll have to start at the beginning," Jim answered. "That's why we are so careful about what we say. But the Light within the Cube is . . . , and this is hard to explain . . . it's as if the Light within . . . is alive. Yes, that's it. Like it's moving, pulsating, or appearing to be ready for action, and powerful enough to explode with purpose—sort of like a volcano preparing to erupt. No, that's not it—that would make it sound dangerous. You know, after having looked at it for so long, I keep trying to put into words what I see, and it's different every time. It gives us the feeling that it's alive and can't wait to do something—and what could that be, but shine brighter or clearer, or perhaps I should say, even more dimly—so we can see the jewels in better detail. You see, at first, it was extremely bright. Now it has a softer glow, enabling us to see more of the intricacies of the New Jerusalem—they're more recognizable. There's an absolute spiritual aura about it. I never want to stop looking at it! You see, I'm having trouble describing it very clearly right now! That's why we've cautioned our staff to report only the facts. We don't want to overstate the accuracy or declare our feelings. But the basic truths and details that match Revelation are undeniable. And we're seeing more today than we did last week. Does that help?"

"Yes sir. I think I see the situation you're in, and I appreciate your truthfulness and commitment to the absolute facts!" the student replied.

The Christian community was growing, bulging with seekers and inquirers. Faith was being shared with multitudes. This was the one facet in the world that largely was in one accord.

Observatories commonly invited guests to tour their facilities and learn more about the work going on in them. But because of the Cube, every observatory was being overrun with visitors wanting to view the Cube. It was such a problem that they all had to make policies limiting visitor inquires in order to conduct their daily business. Also, crowds wanted to talk with the astronomers themselves and hear their latest findings; they had many questions and searched for answers. Jim had to deny personal interviews, in order to manage his busy schedule. He made it known that he'd give regular reports at certain hours of the day and update each report as necessary. Visitors were directed to these scheduled announcements. Every report became a strain—because of the opposing reports. Jim wanted to shout the glory and details of the City, but others were contradicting everything he said. *What a strange situation*, Jim thought. He didn't want to come right out and make his comments critical, call them liars and deceivers, but that's what they were.

As if there wasn't enough trouble to handle, Quad U called for another meeting with Jim Waltham. This time they were determined to remove him somehow from their faculty. They had various ways to approach it. They began with another reprimand for dragging the University into the foray of controversy with the Cube, even though indirectly. They charged him with doing irreparable damage to the otherwise spotless reputation and image of their institution. They felt his actions were severe enough to ask for his resignation immediately.

Jim met with them, took his time to reply, taking deep breaths, and trusting the Lord to give his answer to these blind leaders of the blind. But he wanted to do it with a gentle spirit.

Jim stood before the group and began his remarks speaking softly and thoughtfully, as if they were going to have to listen closely to hear it. "The root issue we face today is whether there is a Creator who created the world and everything that we know about as described in the book of Genesis. If he did, then everyone ought to pull together in one accord to publish that truth to the entire world's population. Since we weren't there at Creation, however it was accomplished, we can only look at our resources for the foundation of our beliefs. Some choose to turn away from Genesis, as God gave it to Moses to write down for our education. They'd rather look to a more distant place for an origin—objects in space—and theorize that somehow life came from non-life. They postulate the notion that everything somehow began small and grew large, was dead but became living, had no intelligence and became smart. Some unknowingly admit they are empty handed by making such statements as, 'Just imagine how stupendous it would feel to find something out there in space,' as they search for 'something' that exists only in their imaginations. Meanwhile, the world goes on to its grave hoping science will hurry up and tell them how it happened so they can act upon it. And Almighty God, who cannot lie, still waits to be believed."

Jim shifted his position and turned to one side of the room as if they were the special ones chosen to hear his next utterance, "What I have to say today will take only a few minutes, but I hope you'll hear me out, for it'll clarify why we're meeting and determine what your actions will be about me."

Jim explored the flaws in the "Big Bang" claim that the world and everything in it came from an explosion billions of years ago. It was without any factual support, and nothing was proven about the development of life. He explained that every scientific graph used to indicate the past brings along with it a margin of error so enormous that no rational person would seriously think of accepting it with certainty. Astronomers continued to be astounded with galaxies so tightly compact that they destroyed all previous notions about the assumed age of the universe. Since the Earth was created by the infinite, eternal God, whose fingerprints were visible only to the eyes of faith, it would always appear to be older than we could imagine. He mentioned the common use of leading cosmological models that recklessly employed dark matter and dark energy to their various conclusions, even though no one had ever directly observed them, and no one actually understood either of them. And he pointed out that every person in the room would die and be long gone before any definitive 'truth' of origin from space was found. Precision in these studies was non-existent. Trying to formulate finality on anything in space would be presumptuous.

Then he asked, "Meanwhile, what should you rely on for what's beyond this life? Is such guess work what we want to tell people to rest their eternal destiny upon? It's like an ant climbing to the top of a bush and declaring to his colony below that the world is bigger than they all thought. He sees hundreds of other bushes and some tall trees far in the distance! As for origins, the bushes and trees wouldn't offer any actual information any more than one more group of galaxies or other objects in space offer the scientist."

Changing his position again, and moving a few steps in the other direction, he continued, "In 1881, advanced science declared Pluto to be a planet. One hundred years later, in 1981, Voyager II did a fly-by pointing out its fifteen moons, its complex of rings, and its various satellites. But today's advanced science declares it to be merely an asteroid. What will future scientific investigation determine all our educated declarations about the origin of the universe to be? They may all be laughable.

"Recently the Phoenix Mars Lander spacecraft obtained a teacup of soil from Mars. Scientific experiments were performed on it. Like the other five landings on Mars, there were no signs of anything from that barren terrain that could be 'the building blocks of life.' Scientists had formerly conceded that radiation there is so intense that even if there were any molecules of life, they would've already been destroyed. But still it was declared to be 'similar to Earth!'" Jim stated these space trips and experiments proved nothing about our origin. They could tell us that our wise Creator used a similar model for some planets as He did for Earth. He used a similar model for humans as He did for animals, but animals had no eternal soul and spirit as man did. A praying mantis had similar characteristics to a buffalo, ground hogs, other animals, and even humans. There were eyes, legs, a heart, and so on—but each creature was different for a specific purpose. They were helpful to gain understanding about God's Creation, and even for learning something about ourselves, but they told us nothing of our *origin*. Neither could we learn anything about the magnificent truth of origin out in the movements of a black hole.

Then Jim turned his head with a bright expression, with one finger raised, as if he were passing on some great importance. He said, "Our New Department of Astrobiology is a commendable and interesting thing. I am not against research in the area of possible life on other planets. It's common for men to conceive of such a thing. Meanwhile, we must admit that astrobiology is a science without any data in support of the science."

He hurriedly lowered his head and kept on talking, "There are those without a clue to the beginning of the world, who feel the Earth was 'seeded' by beings from some other planet. They don't know which planet. They don't know how these beings got here or where they went. They are without one shred of proof. It's just an idea in someone's head. Still others turn their magnifying glass to the slime of a water hole and believe all life came from there.

"Bold assumptions on the part of evolutionists, with scarce scientific input, have led to the fabrication of a lie that has to be propped up with every sort of impractical speculation available. And every support keeps on crumbling out from under it. Those who hold to these hypotheses continue to disagree with each other. DNA will not allow cross breeding with any other 'kind.' The two hundred seventy-five species of sparrows are all still sparrows. A sparrow can't even cross breed with a cardinal to produce another kind. Humans can't breed with monkeys. We didn't come from apes. It's impossible because DNA prevents it. The absence of true scientific input leaves evolution as a pile of deceptions.

"These and numerous other guesses abound and change with the passing of time. None of them can be proven. It's doubtful that anyone even expects them to ever be proven. Just the self-satisfaction of knowing that these theories are viewed as being 'scientific' and that Dr. Doomafloche gets the

> *All day long I have held out my hands to a disobedient and obstinate people.*
>
> *(Romans 10:21 NIV)*

credit is good enough for those who seek an excuse for rejecting God's claim upon all life. Which guess would you want to put your stakes down into and trust it to be 'true' forever? All such musings offer zero help for the world depending on science for its answer."

Jim lifted his head and spoke humbly to the group, "Not even Genesis can be 'proven' scientifically, for we cannot repeat it. We can't duplicate any of it in our laboratories. So regardless of our position on this issue, we have to trust that our facts will stand up to the faith we place upon them. You have the right to believe whatever you choose.

Though I disagree with these other theories, I still respect your freedom of choice and I expect you to respect mine. I simply choose to walk out of the dark and into the light.

"I was an atheist for half of my life. I lived by relativism, humanism, and materialism because I'd refused to objectively look at the Light. I was pursuing happiness with blinders on. We all have the right to seek fulfillment our own way. But we can also simply trust God's way and finally learn that happiness isn't to be 'found,' it's to be received as a gift from God.

"I believe when God said, "Let there be light," the light came on. He didn't have to wait hundreds of light years for the light to reach the Earth. He flipped the switch with His Word, and there was light. Natural laws only began working as He completed each phase of His work. 'And God blessed the seventh day, and sanctified it; because in it He had rested from all His work which God created and made.'[37]

"When He wanted to create man in His own image, He didn't make a baby and wait for him to grow up. He was a walking, talking adult in an instant. Immediately he was able to name all the animals God had created. Now, what's wrong with me believing that? Moses believed that. The prophets of God believed that. Peter believed it. Paul believed it. Jesus believed that. How can I claim wisdom greater than these?

"Ladies and gentlemen, no one has ever proven anything in the Scriptures to be false. So if it's flat wrong to have faith in the Word of God, if you don't want a faculty member to have faith in Jesus and His death on the Cross, if you are absolutely sure of your foundations about our origin, and if you prohibit academic freedom in this area where the Creation itself offers the best scientific laboratory for research, then I think you ought to put it in writing and fire a simpleton like myself. I

---

[37] Genesis 2:3

choose to reject having to believe in something that has more problems than can ever be solved, a foundation that has changed dozens of times over the past hundred and fifty years, and theories that are forced upon my better judgment and my conscience. I leave this matter in your hands. You get to make the choice.

"And as for the image of the university, the reputation of an institution in mere conformity with others who would like to dismiss God from their roll, your legacy won't be written next year. It'll be reflected upon by the wisdom of those who follow the paths of enduring light, by those who've learned what happens when new cloth is sewn into an old garment, and who declare that the old wine is better than the new.[38]

"And by the way, when you cash and spend your checks, please notice the date on each of them. They refer back to a time when all civilized people on the Earth recognized that something supernatural had taken place."

Then, pausing, he noticed that a hush, a holy "surrounding" seemed to have taken over the atmosphere.

"Unless you ladies and gentlemen have any further need of my presence right now, I have some exciting business to attend to. There's a New Jerusalem coming down from God that's about to establish its dominion over this planet in just a few hours! Good day."

It seemed as though every member of the board was petrified by his statements. They didn't begin to loosen up and come back to their senses until he had exited the room.

When Jim felt the fresh air of the outdoors, his heart rejoiced. He hadn't known what he was going to say, but the Lord put the words into his mind. He felt exuberant in heart. He could only imagine how they

---

[38]   Luke 5:39

would react and refused to waste time guessing now. They could fire him. They could postpone their deliberations. They could sit around and argue. He didn't care. He felt free to be in the will of God and would accept their decision like turning a page. It would have no consequence in eternity. Praise God! What a Savior! He was so glad that when he gave his life to Jesus he didn't bring God's worldview into his puny one and force it to fit. Jim took his position, seated in heavenly places in Christ, and assumed the worldview of Christ!

Laura and their oldest child, Keith, along with Marcus and Cindy, had planned to wait at the university during the trustee's meeting as support for Jim, but he persuaded them that it wasn't necessary. He was sure the Lord would provide all that he needed. Now, he wanted to share with them the peace he had. The red light changed to green, Jim looked both ways and began entering the intersection. Out of the corner of his left eye he saw something move. It was a speeding car running the red light. Jim slammed on his brakes and stopped just as the car hit his left front wheel. Jim's car spun around to the right and he was thrown against his left door. The air bag hit him in the face, and that's all he could remember for a few moments as the dust settled. He just sat there awhile evaluating his physical condition and wondering how he was going to get out of the car. Several people approached his vehicle to see if he was all right and to help. Someone had already called the police and ambulance with a cell phone.

"There's no gasoline leak," a man affirmed, speaking through a broken window, "You should remain in the car until paramedics arrive."

Medical personnel tested him by various means before allowing him to move across the seat to exit the right door. His head and left shoulder were bruised from the left door since it didn't have side air bags. After examination, a paramedic said, "Sir, we don't believe you to be seriously injured, but we want to take you to the hospital emergency room for X-Rays and whatever else the doctor in charge would recommend to see if there's anything we can't observe ourselves."

Jim didn't want to do that, but better judgment told him that would be the safest choice. The other driver was also being treated. After giving information to the police officer, Jim rode in the ambulance to the hospital, but not before calling Laura and assuring her that he was alright. He was going as a precaution only.

This was to be the night when the New Jerusalem could reach its lowest altitude over the Earth. Jim had planned to be at the Lippershey Observatory with Marcus and his staff just in case there were changes in the direction, or a stop to the descent. Of course, no one could predict precisely where the Cube would stop because they didn't have any information to indicate any such thing. It was all speculation on that issue. But at least for the next few days, anything could happen. Excitement was running high. The last place Jim wanted to be on this night and the following evening was in a hospital.

∞

21

OPPORTUNITY

Waiting in the room for tests, Jim struck up a conversation with George Riddle. They were in chairs next to each other in the x-ray hall. Comments on the Cube came up, and Jim learned that George had a telescope and loved to watch the stars. When he learned that Jim was head over the Orion Observatory Complex, George was all eyes and ears! He wanted to learn more about Jim's news releases.

George was a man in his sixties, a little overweight, with balding gray hair, and glasses. He appeared to be very energetic. He was aware of the prestigious telescope at LT, as well as the position Jim held. He turned with sincerity and obvious intent saying, "I wonder why the reports from your office are so exaggerated," he began. "I have a twelve and a half inch club-built Cassegrain telescope with a four inch coronal camera. It should show up the same features your giant telescope sees. But the details you give are unbelievably described. It appears that they're greatly embellished in the press."

"Sure, George, you should still be able to see the details, even though not as clear. I don't understand why you can't. We're extremely cautious not to report anything that's not both accurate and exact. My staff knows how tough I am on honesty. We've been astounded at the other reports that contradict ours."

"You mention twelve foundations and twelve gates, and details of these. Also the beauty of the various stones the City is built of. Where do you get these? I don't see any of them. I can only see a large Cube with non-descriptive features of some sort. But nothing that would indicate what they actually represent."

Jim was dumfounded with a frown on his face. "I don't know how you can possibly miss seeing them!"

Both men are silent for a while, in deep thought.

"By the way, George, are you a Christian?" Jim asked.

"Well, I certainly do believe in God. I know it took Almighty God to build the universe and all that we see. But I've never been baptized, if that's what you mean."

"No, you don't have to be baptized to be a Christian. But you do have to be born of the Spirit of God."

"Well, just how does a person become a Christian?" George asked.

'I'm glad you asked, George. Have you ever read John 3 in the Bible?"

"Probably not. I don't remember what's in any chapter of the Bible."

"It tells us of a man named Nicodemus who was a master teacher in the nation of Israel. He acknowledged that he believed Jesus was sent from God because of his mighty miracles. Jesus knew he was a sincere man seeking the truth, and that he wasn't going to find it among the Jewish leaders or schools. Then Jesus told him he must be born again in order to see the kingdom of God.

"Nicodemus didn't understand. Jesus was, of course, speaking of a different kind of birth, a spiritual reality, not physical rebirth. He needed to be spiritually born into God's family by the power of the Holy Spirit.

Then, Jesus used an example of the Israelites in the wilderness who were grumbling against God and murmuring against Moses. The Lord sent poisonous snakes to bite and punish them, and the Israelites were dying of snake poison.[39]

"Then God told Moses to make a snake out of brass, the symbol of judgment, put it upon a pole, and tell the people that whoever looked at that snake would be healed. And it came to pass as the Lord had promised.

"Here in John 3, Jesus said, just as Moses lifted that serpent upon a pole, so must Christ be lifted up on a Cross, and everyone who looks at Him, with faith, would be saved. Nicodemus probably recalled a reference in the Old Testament where God said, *Look to Me and be saved, everyone to the ends of the earth; for I am God and there is no other.*[40] We know Nicodemus, an Old Testament scholar, came to understand and believe that Christ was not only sent from God, but that He was also the one Sacrifice that God demanded for payment for the sin of the world because when Jesus was crucified, Nicodemus helped take Him from the cross and bury him."[41]

When Laura arrived at the hospital and found Jim, she couldn't wait to embrace him, kiss him, and get answers for her questions about his condition. Jim assured her of his wellbeing. He then introduced her to George. She knew they were both awaiting tests and took a seat near Jim.

Jim continued, "George, God calls everyone to look at Jesus, His Heaven-sent Son. Jesus was Almighty God Himself walking around in a human body so that He could become the Sacrifice for the sin of mankind. But forgiveness isn't automatic. You must turn to Christ and receive him personally into your life to be saved. When you do, the

[39] Numbers 21
[40] Isaiah 45:22
[41] John 19:39

Holy Spirit of God comes into your body to live. He's the One who inspired the Scripture to be written. He's the Teacher that gives you understanding. He's the power of God that brings about spiritual new birth. And it takes place instantly when you yield yourself to Jesus. Is that clear, or do you have a question about what I've just said?"

"Man, that's very clear! I never thought of forgiveness as coming to me as I actually invite him into my life. You're telling me that I have to trust in Christ by faith, that's obvious."

Blessed are those who hunger and thirst for righteousness, for they will be filled.

(Mathew. 5:6 NIV)

"George, you're exactly right. You're to trust and pray, asking for forgiveness, and believe that He'll immediately provide it. God will do for you just what He has promised."

"Then I'll do it," George stated, as he turned his face away.

"Let's do it right now," as he looked at George in the eyes for approval.

George gave it, and they bowed their heads.

Jim prayed, thanking the Lord for what he was going to do and George prayed. George asked for God's forgiveness of his sins and for the salvation of his soul. The timing was right, for as soon as they finished praying, an attendant came to take Jim in for his tests, and another came and told George that his tests would be in just a few minutes.

X-Rays and an MRI showed Jim had no permanent or dangerous injuries. The admission, preparation, and tests took several hours and left Jim fatigued. At last they arrived home, and Jim decided the best thing to do was go to sleep—though in his inner soul he desperately wanted to be at the observatory. He was glad that he hadn't received any calls from Marcus or his staff about the Cube, so maybe nothing of significance had happened.

In the morning Jim told Laura, "Now I know the meaning of the saying 'I feel sore all over more than anywhere else.' It was a real chore just to get out of bed." He crept around most of the morning, spending considerable time on the phone to the University and the Phoenix Complex. He explained his accident, tests, and that he thought it best not to try to work that day. Still no pictures were possible of the Cube, but the details of the City whose Builder and Maker is God[42] were clearer than ever through the telescope. The LT staff didn't know how they could become more glorious! No communication from the Holy City had been received as far as anyone knew. Jim decided this day may be one ordered by God to rest, pray, and contemplate what might lie ahead. Perhaps this was best for the event that was about to happen.

∞

---

[42] Hebrews 11:10; 12:22-24

22

To See or Not to See

The next night, observatories received the shock of their lives. After traveling at an enormous rate of speed for the past month, the Cube had stopped its descent and had not begun to orbit on the opposite side of the Moon as speculated, but had taken a sovereignly selected spot in space *beside* the Earth. It was traveling along with the Earth all right, but not circling the Earth in orbit. It was later observed that the earthly city of Jerusalem passed beside it with each revolution. The heavenly Jerusalem was stationed so that with each turn of the Earth most of the entire world would be able to see it.

The brilliance of the New Jerusalem was more magnificent than ever before. It was literally breathtaking! A light of splendor showed through it. Bright colors radiated from the precious jewels in every direction. The City's wall, two hundred feet tall, was sitting upon twelve foundations. These foundations had the readable names of the Twelve Apostles of the Lamb upon them, surprisingly written in English! The two visible sides showed three large inset portals with recessed spheres in each portal. One engineer described them as "resembling gigantic transparent Teflon ball valves." These were half of the twelve gates to the City, and each one had the name of one of the twelve tribes of the children of Israel clearly written upon them, again, in English. At two hundred feet in diameter they were indeed gigantic and resembled huge Pearls. The outer "shell" or "hull" of the City seemed to be as transparent as the finest clear glass.

This report was compiled by the staff at the LT in conjunction with the four other observatories and was sent by various means to the supporting body of Cubicles that was formed earlier in the year to work together informing the Christian body and the general public, then sent to all news media outlets. Jim had the pleasure of getting to the observatory early in the wee hours of the morning and approving the report. He was beside himself with joy, and hardly noticed the pain and soreness that was there with every step and movement! He included the following information for clarification to the public:

> The New Jerusalem is estimated to be 21,500 miles to the side of the Earth, far beyond the last sphere, or exosphere, before entering outer space. To help visualize the New Jerusalem, the Moon and the Earth, consider the following:
> The Moon has a mean, or average, distance of 238,857 miles away from the Earth. The Moon has a diameter of 2,160 miles, and the New Jerusalem, 1,500 miles. The Earth has a diameter of 7,926 miles. If the Moon had moved eight times closer to the Earth, it would be about the same size to the naked eye as the New Jerusalem is today.

Jim went on to say, "The New Jerusalem is astoundingly more dazzling than I could have ever dreamed," He declared, "and just think, according to what I understand of the Word of God, this Golden City is the future destiny, dwelling place, or the many mansions[43] of all the saved

---

[43]   John 14:2

throughout eternity, who trust in Jesus and follow His Word. The whole world is getting an advanced view of what it looks like up close!" Jim also noticed something else—the Cube was turning slowly as it traveled, so that eventually all four sides would be observed by those on Earth.

Notification from other countries reached the Orion Complex with jolting news. Astronomers were claiming that the names of the Apostles and Tribes of Israel were *not* written in English but in German, Chinese, Russian, Japanese, and whatever country was viewing them! Could it be that the names were supernaturally understood by every individual in their own language? Extensive investigation through observatory networking proved that to be the case, with one exception—some people couldn't read any names!

For anything that big in space to drive up and park so close to Earth would jolt the entire world. That's exactly what happened. In spite of informative reports the media had received and given to the public for the past three months, nothing could have prepared them for the panic that resulted. Billions of people trembled and asked, "What now?"

Just like the reports that previously contradicted Jim's, there were other reports that were aired over the news media quite differently from the one sent from Jim's staff. It stated similar estimates as to the distance from the Earth, and the location in space, but its description of the Cube was totally divergent from the one from the Orion Observatory Complex.

One such report stated, in part:

"It's a large fifteen hundred mile cubed object of bland asteroid color. Various unidentifiable markings are on the object in several places that are impossible to decipher. The purpose of the Cube is yet to be determined. We cannot tell if it's friend or foe. We urge all governments to be prepared for anything!"

Jim couldn't believe his eyes and ears. How could they be reporting such lies? Didn't they realize they would be exposed in the future and bring shame and humiliation upon themselves? What were they up to? Is the devil that stupid that he would try to fool the entire world and keep it from eventually finding out the truth? He trusted in God's wisdom to prevail over the enemy.

And it would.

The next day a phone call from California was forwarded to Jim as he came through the door and headed toward his office at LT. It was from Jeremy Green, an amateur astronomer who'd been watching the Cube beside many others all through the night.

"Dr. Waltham, I'm so glad I'm able to reach you. I have something that I think will be of great value to you."

"Glad you called, sir. Go ahead."

"Several of us have been working side by side on several telescopes. Some of these are Christians and some are unbelievers. We were all looking at the same thing. As we described the Cube, I was excited to see its beauty, while the man next to me said, 'You must be crazy. It doesn't look like that at all!' I would look through his telescope and he through mine. I saw the beauty through both and all he could see was drab and unattractive. We both thought we were tricking each other. But then we became extremely serious. He said, 'What do you have that I don't have?' I said, 'I don't know unless it's Jesus. I know he's my Lord and my Savior.' Immediately the man was smitten with conviction and dropped to his knees, crying out to God to forgive him and save him. After a time of gathering his composure, he looked through his telescope again—and guess what? He saw the beauty of the City of God!"

"My God and King!" Jim exclaimed. "That's so wonderful I almost can't believe it! But I can see that it's true. That must be the reason why there are two contradictory reports being given. One from those who truly see God's beauty and the other from those who are spiritually blind! Mr. Green, you've solved a problem that's more important to me than you supposed! Thank you so much!"

"You're welcome sir. God bless and have a good day," said Jeremy.

"I'm already having a good day, but you've made it a great day! God bless you too," Jim said.

As he was hanging up the phone, Judy was forwarding another call, this time from George Riddle, whom he had met in the hospital.

"George. How are you doing? And how'd your tests come out?"

"I'm doing fine, Dr. Waltham. But my tests showed that I've got a couple of dark spots on my lungs. They're pretty sure it is cancer. I've smoked for most of my life, and quit a few years ago, but I guess I didn't quit soon enough. I'll probably have to take radiation or chemotherapy soon."

"I'm so sorry to hear that, George. I'll pray for you that the Lord's best will be done in your life, especially now that you belong to him."

"Thank you sir. What I really called you about is I looked through my telescope last night and I saw the beauty of the City that you described to me. I couldn't believe that it could be so great. I don't know what was wrong before. I had the same adjustments as I always have . . ."

"George! Let me tell you what happened. I just now received a call from a man in another state who said that a friend of his couldn't see any beauty either. But he prayed and received Christ as his Savior, and then looked again through his telescope and he could see all the details that I've been talking about! Isn't that something? The same thing has happened to you!"

"Man, I never thought of that! It is a spiritual thing, isn't it?"

"More spiritual than you and I will ever know, George. I really appreciate you calling and telling me of your experience."

"You're welcome, Dr. Waltham. I don't want to take up more of your busy day. I hope you have a good one."

Jim was so excited he thought he would explode with this new information.

"It was already great, George. Now I'd like to use the old expression, it's supercalifradulistic and expialidochus!"

Jim didn't know who to tell or call first. He began with Marcus and his staff, then, assigned to them the joy of passing the story on to others; all the prayer warriors, Bible scholars, and the Cubicles who had been working together and needed to be informed.

Jim was about to burst from excitement. He wanted to call Dr. Fleming, Laura, the news media and a lot of others all at once to explain about the different reports and why they were contradictory. It was a difficult predicament. His staff was already passing on the message to the believers, but he felt left out of the exciting response. He also knew that he ought to take time to give himself to meditating in the Scripture so he could base his understanding solidly upon it when the media was notified.

But before he could make a call to anyone, Doug Ingram, a supporter and trustee at Quad U was on the line. "Jim, you know I've been pulling for you all along, and count it a joy to be your friend. I wanted to let you know how it went after you left the trustee meeting."

"Yes, Doug. Thank you for calling. I haven't heard anything yet."

"Well, your speech penetrated the trustee body like a powerful javelin. It took a few minutes for the group to come back to their senses. Or I should say to get back out of their senses. After you left, the holy hush left too, and the mumbling turned into burning hatred. It was so inhuman that I thought if I objected to anything it would cause a fist fight within the group. They were literally gnashing their teeth. Of course, there were a few others like myself, you know. Carl Eckert jumped to his feet with a motion that you be fired immediately. It was seconded. Then Thomas Fain, Chairman, had to pound the gavel to regain order. The opposition to you was arrogant and emotional. And you know how it is with a room full of followers who are swayed by whoever shouts the loudest and longest! You were branded as arrogant, having lack of commitment to the University, being in opposition to the scholarly standards of the institution, having an unscientific approach to astronomy, branded as a religious bigot masquerading as an educator, and a liability to the legacy of the finest University in the area of space exploration.' The vote was just like always, with the two-thirds majority ruling the day. The few of us who voted against it were sneered at with their noses in the air.

"Oscar Huckelby gave the usual chloroform statement that 'Evolution is a fact, easily observable and documented beyond any reasonable doubt.' Somehow he left out the truth that every leading evolutionist disagrees on just about every fact, and observation. The trustees at Quad would disqualify God from explaining His own universe! Jim, this is a sad day for everyone. This University has not only lost one of the finest scholars on Earth, but it's cut its nose off to spite its face! I am sorry to be the one to tell you, but I didn't want you waiting in the dark without a word. And Jim, you know I'm here for you and will stand behind whatever you choose to do. I'll give you a strong recommendation. I'm willing and desiring to call other schools in your behalf and to look for a better place for you—if that is what you would like."

"Doug, I really appreciate your help and value your advice. Right now, though, it's probably best that I'm not to be there any longer. I just feel for the students who were learning so well in my classes. I hate to let them down. But, on the other hand, Doug, God is still Governor of the universe . . ."

While Jim was speaking, his inner soul was absorbing a vicious blow, and his mind was speaking what he knew to be the truth, but he felt awkward and shocked because he didn't know what the repercussions would be. People in public positions were often so unpredictable they created constant uncertainty for others; like Harris, dragging his soul down while the Lord was pulling it up, though Jim was fairly certain of Harris' plans! But he continued, "He hasn't lost his place. And I'm at His service. He has a plan. It'll all turn out for the good somewhere down the line. He's given all of us that promise in Romans 8:28, you know."

"Exactly right, Jim. You're a man of faith, and you can't lose. You're like a cat that's dropped up-side down, but always lands on its feet!"

Laughing, Jim replied, "You're so right, by the grace of God! Thanks for calling."

Not long after that, a "Special Delivery" letter arrived at his office. It was from the Trustees of Quad U. It verified all that Doug had said and stipulated the terms of Jim's dismissal. The contract of his tenure would be paid for, but his teaching responsibilities were now over. He had two weeks to clear out his office at Quad. He couldn't help but be alarmed. He had enjoyed his teaching so much and loved the students. He had the practice of keeping his emotions tightly contained, until they were relieved by his yieldedness to the Spirit. He recalled that in his beginning years, his motivation revolved basically around himself, and now it reached out in compassion for others. He consciously acknowledged this change had come from the Holy Spirit, who bore witness that he was a child of God. He thought, *If it weren't for the New Jerusalem occupying my mind, I'd probably be depressed. But the excitement of the current status of the City Foursquare overwhelms all else.* He truly couldn't get upset over it all. He wondered if he would go through a low time in the future. *Oh well, this is not the time to wonder about it anyhow.*

No, he would have something else to intrude on his thoughts.

Margaret Thames had arrived in town on the same day Jim had met with the trustees. The following day the entire university was buzzing over his firing. Everyone on campus wanted to be filled in on the details. Margaret was amazed that she didn't have to ask questions, all she had to do was eavesdrop on conversations! There were those who took sides; others who said it was all up to the trustees to do what they wanted. She was free to pick and choose which parts of the conversations that suited her purpose. She learned quickly which faculty members were against Jim, and interviewed a few of them. She even met with a couple of trustees who were glad to give her an ear full.

Margaret compiled her news story and expeditiously e-mailed it to Atlanta. She gave a savory account of how Jim had been ". . . a cancer to the educational system at Quad, and had finally been excised." "His forbidden religious indoctrination of students had been an issue for years;" and "his 'attitude of superiority' could be tolerated no longer." But she was not satisfied with the information she had heard and thought that a visit to an observatory, where she assumed the same attitude would prevail, might produce more fodder for her donkey appetite.

"May I help you?" Judy asked, as Margaret approached her desk at the LT.

"Yesss," she said as she handed Judy her card, with a pasty smile, and head slightly tilted, "My name is Margaret Thames, reporter from television station XURB in Atlanta, Georgia. I'm on assignment to cover the story of the firing of Dr. Jim Waltham from Quad University. I wanted to talk to a few people about this matter so I could gain a more thorough understanding of what took place and why."

"Well, you came to the right place, Ms. Thames. I hope the media gets the right story. Dr. Waltham is one of the most outstanding scientists and astronomers in the world. His firing was a tragedy and great loss to the students there."

Margaret showed no sign of inner recoil when she heard that statement, but knew this girl was not the one she wanted to speak to!

"Thank youuu," she replied, holding on to that same smile. "Are there any others here that I might speak with who know Dr. Waltham?"

"Well, at this time of the day, we have . . ."

At that moment, Jim had just reached Rex Fleming on his cell phone, as he was walking out of his office in the direction of Judy's desk.

"Here's Dr. Waltham himself, you're lucky to catch him here," Judy said.

Margaret hadn't expected to see Jim there. Out of five observatories, she wondered how she happened to pick this one!

Jim was speaking excitedly as he said, "Rex, you won't believe what I have to say, it is so fine! Lost people cannot see the splendor of the New Jerusalem . . ." Margaret turned toward him and their eyes met as he neared the desk. He was shocked to see this woman he had met in college and who had aired such notorious slander against him. Both were somehow able to maintain their composure. Margaret, out of the strength of years at being cruel, had conditioned herself to such face-offs. Meanness seemed to come easily. Jim on the other hand, learned the hard way to turn crisis situations over to Jesus and was thankful that the habit paid off at this moment. He could feel the conscious necessity of letting the Holy Spirit take charge.

"Rex, I'll call you back later," said Jim, as he closed his cell phone. "Why, Margaret Thames, what a surprise to see you here."

"And what a pleasant surprise to see youuu here, Dr. Waltham! You're just as young and handsome as ever. I guess you still have all the girls running after you."

"Only my wife," he replied. "And what brings you here?"

"Oh, I'm just following the flow of newsworthy events. I'm doing a little investigation concerning all the things that are going on in Fort

Davis, and Quad University, and the object in the sky, and the news that you've been fired from your position at the university. What a shame. I know you must be aawwfully disappointed," she said, sort of frowning, yet hoping she had gotten it right.

"Not as much as you might think," Jim said. "The Lord seems to have a way of putting me right where He wants me, and I always enjoy the surprises He has in mind. I thought you might have come to take a look at the Cube."

"Wellll, . . . I would love to. How long would it take?" she asked, cocking her head, as if a little peak would do.

"It'll take several hours before it's dark enough. Then, you'd have to 'cut in line,' if possible. There are lots of people around here after dark, and they spend the entire night studying it." If you are interested, I might be able to help you out."

"Well, that sounds exciting! What should I expeeect?" she asked.

"I probably ought to prepare you for it in some way. You're welcomed to relax here until then if you desire, or you could come back right at dusk. There are a few things that'll be essential for you to understand to get the most out of it. I guess you could call it a briefing. Then you can see with your own eyes what you're reporting about. I've urgent business to tend to until then."

"I would be delighted!" she faked.

"Judy, would you take Ms. Thames to the lounge and show her where the coffee is," he instructed.

"Yes sir!" Judy replied.

Margaret helped herself to refreshments, then circulated around the observatory hoping to find someone interested in sharing their disgust with Dr. Waltham. She was repeatedly disappointed in them all!

Jim was momentarily oblivious as to where he was going when he walked out of his office a few minutes ago. But he knew he had to make at least two important calls, one to Laura, and the other to Rex!

Back in his office, he dialed his wife. "Laura, guess who's here at LT!" He didn't know if she was able to detect the quiver in his voice.

"Who, honey?"

"Margaret Thames!"

"What on Earth is she doing there?"

"She's on assignment from her TV station to investigate the things taking place here, the Cube, my being fired, and such. She's probably scratching around searching for more gossip, misinformation, and lies to report to her Enquirer type, pulp station."

"Aren't you being a little flattering? It's bound to be worse than that."

"Yes, you're right. Only God knows what she'll find to exaggerate, misinform and destroy before she leaves. I just don't know what to expect. I thought she might've come to get a take on the Cube. But surely she doesn't have any intention of reporting the truth."

"She wouldn't recognize the truth if it ran over her. Be careful what she sees and hears. How long is she going to be around?"

"I have no idea, but I'm going to show her the New Jerusalem tonight right after dark. I've decided that I'm going to be so nice, to the point, and correct in my every statement that she'll have to do back-flips to slander it."

"That won't be too difficult for an expert lying linguistic gymnast. Just watch your step."

"I will. Oh, I almost forgot to tell you the most exciting news I have heard in years! Lost people cannot see the New Jerusalem; only born again believers can actually see its glory, its gems, its gates, and the other details. To others it appears drab and unattractive."

"What? What do you mean?"

"You know. That's why there're different reports being aired by the media—they're receiving information from believers and non-believers. Some observatories see its glory, and others can't. It's causing chaos and accusations. No wonder the devil is said to be the author of confusion. You remember George Riddle, whom we met in the hospital?

"Yes."

"He called to tell me since he became a Christian he can see all the details that were bland and meaningless beforehand! I received another call today from a man named Jeremy Green, an amateur astronomer from California, who told me the same thing. He's a member of a star-gazing group that was looking at the Cube. There were several telescopes next to each other. One man was astounded at the beauty, and the man next to him thought he was teasing. When he realized it was no joke, he became so convicted that he dropped to his knees and got saved. Afterward, he looked through the telescope and witnessed the beauty for himself! Isn't that fantastic?"

"Wow, isn't God wonderful? He's always doing things that are surprising and delightful. That's just like him."

"That's Jesus, all right. Laura, I can't wait to get home to see you. I will be there as soon as I give Margaret Thames her bit of scoop of the truth. There's no telling how she'll report the fact that there are two groups of people on Earth—saved and lost, some can see spiritual things and others can't. She'll reveal which she is when she looks at the beautiful New Jerusalem! It'll be interesting to see how she handles that. I love you."

"I love you, sweetheart. Hurry home."

Jim could hardly catch his breath before he dialed Rex. There was so much to say and so many others he wanted to tell the story to. He was grateful for the cadre of competent staff members who would take care of most of it. Thankfully, Rex was still at church and available. It was one of those desperate moments when Jim felt he just had to have input from this spiritual giant, and he was anxious thinking Rex might not be there.

"Rex, I apologize for needing to hang up a while ago, but I really have some astounding news. Only saved people can see the New Jerusalem! The lost are blinded to its beauty! Isn't that something? This is a spiritual revelation beyond being a physical one. I think we need to get together and discuss this before we attempt to explain it to the media. That's why they're receiving two conflicting reports. I don't think they'll understand even when we try to explain it. What should we do?"

"Well, that is quite an eye opener to learn. And it clears up the confusion doesn't it? Several verses come to my mind right now. We know that the natural man is unable to receive the spiritual things of God because they have to be spiritually discerned.[44] And, of course, Jesus told His disciples that it was given for them to understand the parables and not for the world. I can see that there could be a definite need to think this through in order for us to explain it to the public! And you're right. We need the mind of God in this matter. What we say to the media and how we say it may be tremendously important and may determine the way it's received by those who don't know Christ. If they get the idea that we think we're 'holier than they are,' they might reject the truth because of our perceived lack of humility. And we can't let them think they're looked down upon by us. After all, we're only saved by grace and willingly sharing with them where to find the true Bread of Life."

---

[44]   1 Corinthians 2:14

"Those are my sentiments exactly, how about tonight, Rex? I feel like it's urgent!"

"Well, I'll have to cancel some prior plans, but I believe this has the greater importance. At your office?"

"Yes. Let's get an early start. I'll have snacks and drinks in case anyone doesn't have time to eat. Six-thirty okay? Mobilize the local Cubicles and bring whoever you want."

"See you then," agreed Rex.

The two men hung up; then Jim remembered:

Whoa! I got so caught up about the Cube that I forgot about Margaret! He didn't want to miss this time of study. It was too important and necessary before beginning to explain to the media and the world about the fact that some can see the glory of God and some can't! He either had to call off the time with her, or maybe she'd come to the Scripture study, too. Now that would be a predicament for her! It'd be good for her to meet those who are working with this great revelation from God. That's what he decided to do. On the other hand, he was concerned that she might stir up trouble and get in the way of the study.

Then he prayed, *Lord, I leave it up to you. If you don't want her to come, just let her give an excuse and that will settle it. If you do want her to come, I ask that she be informed from your Word, come under conviction and desire Jesus as her Lord and Savior, and please keep her from disrupting us from reaching the important conclusions we need to reach with the study group. Thank you in advance for answering this prayer, in Jesus' Name.*

Jim buzzed Judy's desk and explained the situation to her and instructed her to pass the conflict of scheduling on to Margaret. Urgent, breaking news had just been received, and a meeting had to be arranged as soon as possible. She would have the opportunity to come and see the "behind the scenes" details of what was going to be given to the media, firsthand. If she couldn't come, then Judy was to offer his apology. After that, she might still be able to look at the Cube the next evening. Now Jim had to call Laura and let her know of the meeting and tell her he would like her to be there if she could shuffle the kids' schedule around.

Judy took care of preparing the room and made a run for the food. The Bible study was composed of Jim's family, Marcus and wife, university students, some faculty friends, a number of Cubicles, Rex, and some others he brought—about twenty-five persons—including Margaret. The dialogue focused, of all things, upon the difference between the natural man and the spiritual man!

When most were finished eating, Marcus, ever the effective master of ceremonies, began the meeting explaining why they were called together.

"The difference between a child of God and a lost soul shouldn't be new to any of us." Marcus began. "We know the natural man is unable to see spiritually. But is there any way the media should be approached to help them understand when they're told that some won't be able to view God's glorious City, the New Jerusalem, because they're not believers in Christ? Obviously, they've had difficulty reporting it already. In a way it's funny that we have to explain what God's doing! But perhaps it's best that we agree not only on what to say, but what not to say to those who are still in darkness, in order to get the most mileage out of the truth, and prevent any offense that may come from an improper explanation. In fact, I'm thinking it best not to tell them anything except what the City really looks like and let their believing friends do the explaining."

Rex began addressing the topic with a smile and his discourse was full of Scriptures. "Ladies and gentlemen, communicating the Gospel is what we all do best. We lay the facts before people, and the Spirit does the work. Whatever we do will seem awkward. We'd like to soften the blow to their ego, by changing God's requirements, but that won't work. It's going to be impossible for the media and the majority of the world to accept what we tell them. However, we didn't create the problem. Our assignment is to be honest and loving in the face of the fact that many of those we speak to are going to be prejudiced against it. However, it's up to them what they do with truth. We can't believe for them. It has pleased Almighty God to require faith in his Word. So, all we can do tonight is come up with some simple verses of Scripture to reinforce our understanding and theirs.

"The issue we face today is simple. God is Spirit.[45] In order to communicate with him we must have a living human spirit. The person without Christ has a living soul with a dead human spirit. When Jesus told Nicodemus that he must be 'born of the Spirit,'[46] He spoke of the Holy Spirit's power to raise the human spirit back to life, thus enabling him to be renewed in the image of God,[47] talk to Him in person, and receive illumination from his Word. Every born again believer has the Holy Spirit dwelling within,[48] and Paul said our bodies are His temple.[49] Unbelievers, on the other hand are limited to the material world. They cannot see, perceive, or discern the things of God. Therefore, they have a predicament on their hands. They must be born again to see spiritual things."

"Isn't that what the Gospel is all about anyway?" a Cubicle with a list of Scriptures written down on her note pad asked. Jesus said, 'Unless a person is born again he cannot see . . .'[50] Jesus told the Jews that he had come so that the blind could see, and that those who thought they could see might be made blind—that is—make it obvious that they were unable to see spiritual truth."[51]

---

[45]   John 4:24
[46]   John 3:5
[47]   Colossians 3:10
[48]   Romans 8:9
[49]   1 Corinthians 6:19
[50]   John 3:3
[51]   John 9:39

"Exactly," Rex replied. As the conversation moved along, Rex asked, "Does everyone see the simple truth that we are discussing?"

"What is this book that you keep quoting?" Margaret asked.

Dumbfounded, Rex said, "Why . . . it is the infallible Word of God, called the Holy Bible."

"You mean you're going that far back into the past and using a book to explain human behavior and objects in space today?" she remarked.

"Absolutely Ms. Thames," Rex said. "There's no other source so authoritative and accurate."

"Well, I've heard about fundamentalism and the far right for years, but I never guessed that it was like this," she interjected. "That must be why so many people are turned off about Christians claiming to have the only truth. It's so old it must be outdated, and unscientific. And you're going to purpose that the news media accept such foolishness and sincerely publish it? It sounds like a fairy tale. Only little children would swallow this teaching."

"Actually, Ms. Thames, the Kingdom of God is full of educated people, even scientists, who have entered the family of God with child-like faith,"[52] Rex stated.

With that, Margaret stood, and, in disgust, excused herself and left the building in a huff. A member of the Cubicles began praying for her soul as others joined in with compassionate concern for this woman.

"Lord," she prayed, "This lady's attitude demonstrates what we as a group are up against with an unbelieving media who've been educated beyond their intelligence. The god of this world, Satan, has blinded the minds of them that believe not.[53] We realize, of course that there are many outstanding and believing persons in the media, but they are

---

[52]   Mark 10:14
[53]   2 Corinthians 4:4

simply swamped by the spiritually dead majority. Oh Lord, please open their hearts and eyes."

After the prayer session Rex and the Cubicles continued expounding on Scripture that was pertinent to their meeting.

"Friends," Rex stated, "we've seen an example of what it costs to live by faith. All of you remember how it was before you were saved. Unbelievers struggle with their old human nature that's dead in sin.[54] In fact, it's usually a surprising disappointment to new Christians to realize that they still sin! Therefore, when we tell the media that those who don't have Christ as their Savior can't see the New Jerusalem for what it is, they still won't believe it."

"That's what I was thinking," Jim agreed. "You know, this is really not any different from the way it was before the New Jerusalem appeared. The blinded world never has seen the value, the beauty, the glory of Christ or his Bride, the Church. They drive by church buildings and think, 'It must be boring in there.' And actually it is . . . to them, since they don't have a spiritual capacity that can appreciate it."

> *Indeed, the Lord God does nothing without revealing His counsel to His servants the prophets.*
>
> *(Amos 3:7 HCSB)*

Rex continued with a knowing smile, "So, what shall we do about the New Jerusalem and our reports?"

"We're so blessed with the promises of God," a Cubicle said as he quoted the Psalm where David said that "The secret counsel of the Lord is for those who fear Him, and He reveals His covenant to them.[55] And Solomon said, the devious are detestable to the Lord, but His intimate

---

[54]   Ephesians 2:1
[55]   Psalm 25:14 (HCSB)

counsel is with the upright.[56] God is faithful to show his servants what his plans are and what he wants them to do with it."

"Well, then, let's just tell them the truth, as is." Jim said. "That's what we've been doing all along. At least we know now why they haven't received it. The Lord will do His work. It's ours to be faithful to His Word. Until He speaks to us otherwise, let's keep on doing what He's already said."

Marcus added, "You know what this reminds me of? I was in Arizona visiting the Meteor Crater, where they had a small building like a museum with a collection of rocks. They were just rocks that were picked up around the area. None of them had any particular shine. They were dull, unattractive, undesirable rocks. I wouldn't have wanted one if they'd offered it to me. But then, the person in charge said, 'Let's see what they look like under a different light.' She then turned out the natural, incandescent lights and turned on a black light. Every one of those rocks lit up like a skyrocket! They were so desirable, so full of all kinds of bright and deep colors, that I could hardly believe it! I would've never thought they could appear that way. So that's the way God is to those who are spiritually blind. They can't see the real thing. They need to view it from a different light. The light of the New Jerusalem is Christ. Only through Him will anyone be able to see His beauty and see spiritual reality."

"Very good, Marcus." Rex said. "Quite a striking illustration. Since most people view Jesus and the Christian life as very dull and undesirable, they'll perceive the New Jerusalem in the same way. They'll claim religious fanaticism to those who see it for what it is, but His glory is hidden from their eyes just as Jesus quoted Isaiah, saying, 'They

---

[56]   Proverbs 3:32

have eyes to see, but won't see. They have ears to hear, but they won't hear.'"[57]

"Then, we're in agreement. We'll keep on reporting the things we see to the saints and to the public. It's up to the Holy Spirit of God to open the eyes of those who want to see," Jim said.

"Yes," Rex agreed. "And we can expect to be persecuted for our faith. The world hated Jesus without a cause, and we're certainly not as great as He. But we'll have lots of fun serving our Lord, along with our broken hearts over their lost souls."

∞

---

[57]   Matthew 13:13-16

23

WORLD-WIDE CHANGES!

Margaret Thames began to present her first hand report from Fort Davis and Odessa, Texas. It couldn't help but upset Jim and his supporters while confusing others who weren't sure what to make of it. She had "seen with her own eyes and heard with her own ears" how Quad University had fired Dr. Waltham for "his simpleton views of astronomy and scientific ballyhoo." She reported how "the study group, composed of Bible scholars, and pastors were passing laughable explanations on to unsuspecting simpletons, expecting the world to give them audience." She further mocked and ridiculed Jim and the Cubicles for their claim that only Christians could see the glory of the Cube, while others couldn't. "Nobody would believe that," she said.

Margaret was not content to air her hostility and criticism of the staff at the STSA, but wrote to the trustees of the organization setting forth her disbelief that they were still giving credence to and paying a salary to Jim. She had urged others to write similar letters and to send e-mails of protest. Jim was being attacked from all sides in one way or another. There was an ongoing opposition to all LT's reports. Jim was slandered as an opportunist hungry for attention and fame.

Jim was easily angered when he learned of these things. "Why are so many Americans gullible concerning the blinded media? Their minds are made up to believe what they hear or read as if it must be so even if their closest friends, relatives, or solid authorities try to convince them otherwise!"

Laura had to remind him of the privilege of suffering for Christ. "It's not something to take lightly," she said. "I believe the ones who truly suffer for righteousness sake are those God has blessed to have the higher stake at unthinkable rewards."

In addition, Your servant is warned by them; there is great reward in keeping them.

(Psalm 19:11 HCSB)

"Laura, you are exactly right. How precious you are to stand beside me with wisdom."

The governing board of Space Telescope Science Association contacted Jim. They wanted to discuss his relationship to Quad University, his firing, and how it affected his position at STSA. "After all," it was recalled, "it was your idea to combine these two institutions together to utilize them both for educational purposes."

Jim was stunned, but agreed to meet with them. The board chairman said he could bring most of the twenty-six members together by Thursday. It was now Monday. They would assemble in the spacious new conference room at the Orion Complex.

It seemed impossible that the Lord would allow him to lose this place of service and influence, especially at this time when the world was in such turmoil and his input was so strategic. Doubtless, the enemy of darkness was on the rampage to put him out of business one way or another. He'd have to pray and seek the mind of God in this matter.

Submission to authority and readiness for action was always the best way, he concluded. He knew God wasn't through with him; it was just a matter of where and how he wanted to use him next. Every day was filled with such excitement and new information he didn't have a spare moment, and he certainly didn't want to lose his position at the LT.

*   *   *

Meanwhile, something miraculous began taking place.

One evening, Laura came to Jim, looking strange. She was wide-eyed, and said, "Jim, Scott's language is suddenly excellent . . ."

Jim looked up puzzled as to what she was talking about. Then it struck him. "You mean . . ."

She nodded.

Jim fell to the floor praying in tears, "Oh Father, Your will be done. You know Lord that we've accepted our son just as he is. We love him. We trusted that he was your gift for us to give unconditional love to all our lives. Lord, what do you want? I thank you and trust you for your best. If you're healing him, then may your blessed will be done! I thank you, I praise you. Jesus, you know we've gone through a lot. Lord, it's almost too good to expect. I just want you to get us ready for such a change. We'll wait upon your love."

Jim could hardly stop praying. He had to get up off the floor and hold Laura. Together, they looked at each other, wondering. They hadn't even thought about the possibility that the improved health and healings being reported by so many would include their son. Scott's Down syndrome had been instantly healed, but since motor skills and language are learned developments he had a bit to go.

Laura's mother, Martha, who lived in Houston, Texas, was on a field trip with a group of senior citizens when their bus stopped at a shopping mall to eat. All around them were people of different ethnic origins speaking in their native languages.

However, Martha understood what they were saying! She turned to a small group of three or four ladies and said, "Did you know I understand what you're saying?" The others looked puzzled, and one said in her native language, "We don't speak English, but I understood what you said to." They all giggled with joy! What a shock. They were speaking a different language, yet everything was clear. It was another miracle that the Cube had brought to pass. Martha called Laura and explained what had taken place. Laura passed the information to Jim, who called Rex.

"Yes," said Rex, "we just learned about it ourselves. We have a Vietnamese congregation that meets in our church facilities, and the pastor said very few speak more than a few words in English. However, last Sunday everyone understood both languages perfectly without having to learn anything! Can you imagine what that will do to our mission efforts? No more language classes, no more frustrating mistakes and hindrances. Praise be to God for His wonderful works! I'm sure travel will increase multiple times this year as visitors more completely enjoy the company of each other all over the world."

> ON *that day I will purify the lips of all people, so that everyone will be able to worship the Lord together.*
>
> *(Zephaniah 3:9 NLT)*

Strange things were also happening. One afternoon after Keith had gotten home from school Laura glanced out a window and saw a vehicle in their driveway. It was five hundred feet from their house to the highway and the car was stopped halfway. Laura called Keith's attention to the car and asked if he knew who it was. "I'll get the binoculars and see if I can tell," he said. Looking through the window he could only see two unidentifiable persons in the auto, so he focused on the license place and wrote down the numbers—XTS 4TJ. Then he left through the back door, without his mother's knowledge, grabbed his .243 Winchester rifle, slung it over his shoulder, and rode out toward the auto on his four-wheeler. When he came into the view of those in the car, it suddenly backed up doing a turnaround, and spun off toward the highway. He thought about shooting out the back tires, but instead looked through the scope, which would have been enough to put the fear of God in their minds!

When Laura saw what had taken place she scolded Keith, "You could've caused them to shoot at you, or you could've possibly shot one of them without even knowing who they were!"

Keith replied, "No, Mom. I only felt that if they were friends, they would've stayed there and talked with me. If they were trying to intimidate us, I would at least scare them off."

"I just don't know what to think of this," Laura said. "Who could want to put anxiety upon us but someone at the university?"

"Could be, Mom. You know how people get desperate when they get trumped by love. They can't stand that Dad's love for God and his students have put their puny little kitty-carts to shame. They're probably so under conviction they don't know what to do. God's dealing with them in a powerful way."

"I believe you're right, Keith. Oh, my! I hope your Dad isn't too hard on you for taking that gun with you."

"But Mom, I take it for rides on my four-wheeler all the time. That's the custom around here. They're the ones not used to it because they didn't have any business here," Keith pleaded.

Later when Jim gave a report of this incident to the police, they traced the license plate to a Quad trustee. By questioning him thoroughly they learned that a faculty member was the other person in the automobile. They had no credible reason for being parked so far down the driveway on private property and were cautioned by the police that they might think twice about doing it again.

One day Keith noticed that their acreage was producing what appeared to be bumper crops coming up everywhere. He asked his dad why the entire yard was full of "bushes."

"There's not even room to drive my new four-wheeler without mowing a trail through it!" he said with frustration.

Jim came out of the house and looked it over and pointed out that there weren't any weeds growing along the fence line either. There were no weeds! Thorns and thistles, ragweed and other undesirable vegetation had died out. "I wonder what else must be taking place in the world?" he asked as he and Keith walked back to the house.

People had to be careful where they parked their cars so as not to run over anything growing that was edible. Seeds recklessly sown in the past were now crops ready to be reaped. Every kind of seed had a fast starting shoot that came up in just a day or two!

Other revelations also came to light. A nine year old neighbor child came running into his house shouting, "Daddy, there's a snake out in the yard. And it has one of our rabbits."

"Wait right here 'till I get my gun," the father said as he retrieved it from the bedroom. "Now come with me and show me where it is."

His mother held the boy's hand as they cautiously went outside. But to their surprise, the snake didn't actually have one of the rabbits they raised in the elevated pens in the back yard; the rattlesnake seemed to be "playing" with it! The baby rabbit had fallen through a crack in the cage door which hadn't been properly latched, and the dangerous viper was rolling it back and forth on its back. The rabbit was walking on the snake and crawling right over its head! Furthermore, Little Bit, their wiener dog, who was usually an excellent snake killer, was right in the middle of the frolicking and licking the snake's head!

"If that don't beat anything I've ever seen," the dad said. "Look at that! There's something wrong with that snake!"

The little boy heard Keith's four-wheeler in the distance, and jumped on his bicycle to get his attention to come see the snake, for they lived on property next to the Waltham's.

The rattler began crawling up the leg of the rabbit pen in which there was a mother and daddy rabbit and three more babies. The man came close to the snake and said, "I'm going to see if it threatens anything in the pen before I shoot it." The whole family, along with Keith, was practically speechless and dumbfounded as they watched breathlessly. The snake crawled about in the pen, and the rabbits were not afraid, but walked right up to it and stepped over it. The snake made no attempt to coil or to strike. It was all the man could do not to shoot as he watched with amazement.

"We've found a pet rattlesnake," he announced. "Honey, go call the TV station and tell them about this. I bet they won't believe it and would like to come see it for themselves. This snake has seven rattles—so it's seven years old!"

There happened to be a television unit in the area covering another event, and within a few minutes, local TV personnel came and watched in disbelief. Before they arrived, the family actually saw the snake eating some of the grass they had put in the pen for the rabbits. Keith had a startling experience to announce to his parents that day. The TV crew shot pictures of the whole show and aired it that night on the news with

Keith enjoying the whole episode. This sparked numerous other calls to the station reporting similar weird situations.

One of the calls had to do with zookeepers who were puzzled as to why they couldn't get their animals to eat their meat, but were devouring grass like it was dessert.

Jim commented to his family, "Isn't this great! Things are happening all around us and we're just beginning to understand the scope of God's plan through the Cube."

Claudia Webster was riding in her Jeep on a search for a morning shot of wild animals hunting their prey. She was a photographer and writer for the National Geographic Society in Tanzania, East Africa. She often rode for half a day before happening upon the ideal predator attacking another animal. She took a second look as her eye caught a female lioness on her back with a gazelle fawn that seemed to be playing with her!

"Look at that!" she said, pointing and rising up somewhat out of her seat. Gene Rollins, her photo assistant, grabbed the camera and had film rolling within seconds. James Davis, the driver, drove slowly upon the two as they all stared in doubt, hardly willing to believe their eyes! Even more shocking was the mother of the fawn who was eating grass nearby, totally without concern. All the animals ignored the vehicle which finally came to a stop within thirty yards of the action, and they filmed what they felt was the shot of a lifetime.

Claudia said, "This is such a rare sight it's going to big splash in the news the world over. Who can explain such a thing?"

Finally they moved on only to come upon a fifteen foot giraffe bending down to lick the face of a male lion! "If there ever was a setup for the perfect kill, this is it," Claudia said. "All the lion has to do is grab the giraffe's neck with his powerful jaws and there would be lunch, dinner and supper for the whole family and then some!"

To their amazement, the animals continued to play together until Claudia grew embarrassed that she was getting the lengthy filming of such an unusual event. She phoned her boss in New York who was so excited he told her to get the film to him immediately. "It'll truly be a sensational story worldwide," he said.

The crew decided to get back to town to get the digital film off as soon as possible. But on the way back, the photographers filmed several similar sights of fierce beasts befriending their prey while other animals enjoyed a frolicking time together! Before these images had even reached New York, Claudia's boss learned he'd already been scooped by local amateurs who had videoed wolves, poisonous snakes, eagles, and other beasts of the wild with helpless rabbits, puppies, and babies of the field, and there was no animosity between any of them. These videos were being shown repeatedly over the television.

Something had happened to nature!

For several weeks, Jim, Rex, and everyone else found out more each day just how the New Jerusalem was affecting the world. It influenced every aspect of life. The entire world was jarred by new discoveries. Some changes were immediate, while others were more gradual. This divine intervention revealed the kind of being God was, and pricked the consciences of all mankind.

Since the Cube had taken its position and begun its journey along with the Earth around the sun, the Cubicles took note of first—hand experiences and news reports of strange things that were coming to light throughout the world. They accumulated the information on a list and shared it with all other Cubicles along with documentation of where and how the information was obtained.

Jim, Laura, Keith, and Scott read and witnessed with amazement miraculous changes which they discussed together. Their own lives were also a testimony of God's blessings with Scott's healing. The purpose of the Cube was unfolding right before their eyes and included them personally. God's plan for humanity and the earthly conditions of the future were being lived out in part every day.

Initially, many things were still taking place on the dark side; the elements that disrupted peace, honesty, love of neighbor, and general godliness hadn't ceased. Abortions, rapes, murders, robberies, adult video stores, drug use, children being molested, kidnapping, crime of all sorts, families broken up, even the lack of Bible reading and prayer in public schools still made the news. It even appeared that some evil behavior was on the rise, hinting that things people usually considered by God to oppose were calling out to them in a stronger way, as if to say, "Get it while it lasts."

America had come a long way from the days when the Bible was in every classroom, and congressmen had prayer meetings and church services together in government buildings and attended revival services together. No generation was ever perfect, but senior citizens wondered how this present generation would ever know the abundance of enjoyment they experienced as children and how good God really was. The majority of the world was basically destitute of so many character traits that were commonly found in the lives of earlier generations of Americans. Few knew the fact that full freedom is enjoyed only in Christ. Some of those changes caught the attention of the Waltham family and they gathered to discuss them with complete interest.

God was doing a variety of things to get the attention of the world. There were selective miracles that made the news because they were so hard to believe.

At a local convenience store in Dallas, Texas, a young man entered with no other customers present. He pulled a mask over his face and pointed a gun at the clerk. "I want your money!" the robber shouted.

The clerk was so surprised and shocked that she froze.

"Get that money out!"

The clerk was hesitant to even move.

"Get out of the way, I'll take it myself!"

As he reached over the counter, the register till opened of its own accord. Both of them were shocked. The thief was delighted and grabbed some money. Suddenly there was a blur of movement behind the register, and the drawer shut quickly on his hand so hard that he couldn't remove it. It hurt so badly he dropped his gun. The clerk realized that she had a chance and kicked it away; then didn't know what to do.

"Ouch! Open this drawer! The thief cried. "Open this drawer. It hurts! Do something right now!"

The clerk reached for the phone, called 911 and reported the crime that was underway. In a few minutes the police arrived. They were amazed to find a thief caught with his hand in the register till! As soon as they took charge, the drawer opened of its own accord. The clerk felt that she had seen a ghost! Her knees were knocking. She couldn't even speak. After the police took the criminal into custody and drove off, the clerk eyed the register curiously for a long time. She kept her distance. Sweat was dripping from her brow. Slowly, she took a few dollars from her pants pocket, reached to open the register, but it opened again by itself!

She cautiously put some bills back into the till that she had been skimming and closed the drawer. Then she backed away slowly, looking at the register with great respect. Suddenly the cash drawer slowly opened again. The clerk jerked her head toward the register and looked with wide eyes as her blood drained to her feet! She reached back into her pocket and drew a few more dollars out, timidly placing them in the till, which then closed. She was limp as a rag and had to sit down. It took several minutes before her mind returned to her duties.

At the police station, the officers told of the strange case of the register that caught the robber. The media took interviews from the officers and the clerk, and the incident shortly made news throughout the country. "Perhaps the cops thought it would make a difference to other would-be robbers," readers said. But most people concluded it was simply exaggerated.

Outside a grocery store in Lafayette, Louisiana, a man approached his car carrying groceries when someone with a gun ran up to him and demanded his money. He dropped the groceries, then reached into his pocket and pulling out his money clip and threw it over the car.

"There it is. You can have it all."

But the robber was irritated and pulled the trigger. The gun wouldn't fire. He tried again and again to shoot the man, who realized he now had an opportunity. He drew his own concealed weapon and fired, wounding the robber. He then kicked the thief's gun that had fallen to the pavement away under a car and called 911 on his cell phone. When the police arrived he explained, "It was the defective gun that allowed me to pull my own and save my life."

Later the gun was tested by a ballistics specialist. Thirty-four shots were fired, and there was nothing wrong with the gun. When this report came out, news personnel again reviewed the story and publicized it. Word got around fast that such things were happening, and those who heard it began wondering if the Cube had anything to do with it.

Rumors began surfacing in Nashville, Tennessee, that some weapons wouldn't fire. A few police officers reported that theirs wouldn't work. But when the weapons were checked out by a gunsmith, the weapons functioned fine. So many stories were being reported that the police departments across the nation were putting together what seemed to be principles that were involved in the various incidents. A certain police officer brought his gun in for repair, claiming that it wouldn't fire. The quartermaster looked him in the eyes and inquired, "What were you trying to do when it wouldn't fire?" When the officer

> *But if you fail to do this, you will be sinning against the Lord; and you may be sure that your sin will find you out.*
>
> *(Numbers 32:23 NIV)*

stammered, trying to come up with an excuse, the supervisor knew he had a bad cop on the force.

Several calls were made to the police in Orlando, Florida, about slim-jims found in the windows of their car doors. Evidently when the car thieves attempted to unlock the cars, they couldn't make the tool work, and couldn't get it out either. Police personnel were amused, imagining how the thieves must have looked around deciding to run while it was taking so long to unlock the door, but were unable to get their slim-jims out! Some crimes were still being carried out as usual, but a noticeable number of them were somehow being prevented. Others were easily solved, and justice served to the offenders. It was obvious that more cases were resulting in convictions and were punished by law.

In New York City, gang members didn't read the newspapers and plotted their usual evils. They made absolute fools of themselves time and time again. A frustrated group of them sat around wondering how they were going to get some money. Half of their members were already in jail. No one could come up with a plan that worked. Later, they were seen standing in the food line at a local mission center.

Jim and the Cubicles learned through the presence of the Cube how God was dealing with His world by these examples. They knew the Lord hadn't come to fully judge all people at this present time. Otherwise people would serve him out of fear. The final judgment day was still in the future. Meanwhile, He wanted an obedient response to the great sacrifice He had made for sinners, and a loving recognition of His world-wide shower of blessings.

The Lord was especially dealing directly with His children. The Holy Spirit in them was bringing conviction to their better knowledge of living right. In Los Angeles, California, word spread about how many live-in couples couldn't seem to get along. Some of them couldn't even stand each other anymore. Actually, Christians were scrutinizing right and wrong from a different and correct perspective. It seemed that someone was actively watching them, and it affected their moral base—which in many instances had a cracked foundation. A woman gave her male friend a "come-on" at her home. But as he moved in her direction, he became awkward with his conscience convicted. He knew in his heart he shouldn't even be there. He gave her a lame excuse and prepared to leave. The woman became angry, blaming him of not caring for her. He surprised himself by saying, "Maybe the Cube has something to do with it." She responded, "You mean we can't even have pleasure anymore?"

In Cleveland, Ohio, a man said to his buddy, 'I'm getting so shocked and surprised at what I'm seeing in the movies that I can't stand it. The vulgarity and language is unnecessary and repulsive. It didn't use to bother me, but for some reason I seem to be more sensitive. Is there any way they could become more evil?"

"I know," Charlie responded. "The moral rottenness and boredom of violent sex scenes have reached their peak, and I, for one, would like to shut 'em down. Bugs Bunny and Yosemite Sam were better than what we're getting!"

In Madison, Wisconsin, a group of computer employees were in the same room when they heard a clicking sound. It began softly, then increased harder and louder like hail on a tin roof. Soon it was unbearable. The owner rose to his feet and shouted, "Everyone take cover!"

They all became fearful, scrambled for security in the halls and under desks and remained there until it grew fainter and finally went away. The next day, Mr. Branson, owner of Maxim Computer Corporation, noticed that a computer program worked. He tried to use it the day before and determined that it obviously had a glitch or a virus. He wondered how it possibly came to be restored. By networking, he learned that all glitches had been removed from every computer! Not only that, but three individuals voiced complaints that someone had erased all their porn sites. Within a few days, the news reported that every porn site in the country had been purged! Protests were lodged openly, but no one could produce the culprit. Multitudes mentioned something about a clicking that became unbearably loud like hail, which evidently passed throughout the entire country—or perhaps the world! Apparently the Cube had corrected all the imperfections and blotted out sin like the sun dries up rain.

In Bowling Green, Kentucky, Mary said to her husband, "Bill, I've hardly heard you use any bad language in three or four days. Are you trying to stop? Is something the matter? Did you make a decision not to cuss anymore?"

"No, actually, I still think the words, but for some reason the last few days I've felt differently. That is . . . I don't know why, but it just doesn't seem as appropriate as it always has."

"What?" Mary exclaimed, "That's a strange thing to say."

"Yeah, it's weird. I have no particular reason except that it just doesn't seem as fitting. It doesn't serve the purpose it always has in the past. It's like I'm an adolescent, you know, when I first began saying words that I heard others say. It didn't seem fitting coming from my mouth then either."

"Well, I think it is a wonderful change. I'm glad. In fact, my language isn't always clean either, as you know, and I've been dodging the slang and cussing that I do, too! I wonder why?"

"You think it has anything to do with the Cube?" he asked.

"I don't know. I wonder if other people are feeling the same way we do."

Bill and Mary didn't know it yet, but the holy presence of God's City was exerting His influence upon all the believers in His family. When someone acted against their conscience a pattern was set up for repetition. The Cube removed that pattern and restored the innate resistance to sin making temptation easier to escape. Non-believers even found it increasingly awkward to act as they were accustomed to doing around Christians. It was as if someone was listening; yes, maybe God was listening!

∞

24

COME AND SEE

After scheduling a meeting with Jim, the governing board of STSA met on Thursday as planned. There were already divided opinions of what to do with Jim. Religion was the issue. Jim gave his testimony of being an atheist and how his life was changed when he came to know the Lord personally. He began to understand how God created the world and all the universe, and how it not only fit into the scientific world, but brought positive acceptance to the students. The more he learned, the more meaningful it was to tell others about the Lord and His Creation. It was surprising how scientific God was.

The Board could see that Jim's position was an all or nothing matter. He wasn't going to be open to compromise between science or religion, because he saw them as compatible.

The shifting of members in their chairs with bored countenances told the tale. As Jim neared the end of his testimony, one man had waited for an opening and leapt to his feet. He was obviously a leader in the group, a middle-aged man with much business experience and little patience for anything not going his way. He said, "We appreciate your explaining to us your religious experience, Dr. Waltham, but it appears clearly that you would probably feel better if you were teaching in a religious institution, rather than here at the astronomical steering wheel of science. I'd like to offer you the opportunity to resign and seek a position that would allow you full freedom to explore religion at your pleasure."

"Oh, let's not be hasty in this matter," said another man with a soft voice and gentlemanly countenance. "Dr. Waltham has distinguished himself in many ways here over the past several years, and I believe he has too much to offer to lose him."

> *I have a better grasp on truth than have the elders, because I have kept Thy precepts.*
>
> *(Psalm 119:100 TBV)*

Many persons were getting heated up in the ensuing debate, and they all wanted to speak at the same time. Jim raised his hands and addressed them.

"Ladies and gentlemen, I'll gladly comply with whatever you officially vote to do. But I have one request to make of each board member—that you first look through the Lippershey Telescope at the Cube. Then you can do what you will."

They looked at each other, thought it was a small thing to ask, then agreed. The group packed into the observatory room that wasn't made for a crowd, but they wanted to get this matter over with as soon as possible. The first member to view it did not take long. "I don't see much," he said, "just an odd looking object in the atmosphere."

The next one was so excited he could hardly catch his breath. "So beautiful! It looks beyond reality! I have never seen such a sight in all my life." And he didn't want to get out of the chair for others to see. This stirred anticipation on the part of the rest who wanted to settle the difference of opinion firmly, one way or another.

The next person also exclaimed its glory. She and her husband were both board members. Her husband was next. He saw nothing outstanding. On and on, each member looked at the Cube with different responses, until all twenty-four attending were through. There was twelve positive, and twelve neutral or negative responses.

"Isn't that interesting," said Jim, when they had returned to the conference room. "The fact is that only true Christians can see the beauty of the Cube, while others see nothing unusual."

They looked at each other.

"Are you serious?" asked a board member.

"Aw, that's preposterous!" exclaimed a board member with irritation in his voice.

Others spoke their responses at the same time: "I never heard such a thing!"

"Are you kidding?"

"What are you talking about?"

"No, it couldn't be."

"I'm a Christian, and I didn't see any outstanding beauty," said another.

Jim explained, "You should know that being a Christian isn't a matter of church membership, merely being baptized, or trying to live a good life. It requires literally giving your life to Christ and allowing Him to be your Lord."

One lady with gray hair and a fashionable dress turned to her husband and said, "See Leonard, you know we discussed your uncertainty about salvation. I saw its beauty, and you couldn't see it."

"Shush, woman!" Mr. Sims responded. Then the embarrassed, angry man arose and quickly walked out the door. They could hear his wheels burning rubber as he left the parking lot.

"That must be the answer then," said an older woman, accepting the situation at face value. "I wondered why so many of us couldn't have the same excitement that the others had."

"Then I want to be saved!" said Bruce Coulter, a young, active, and leading member of the trustees. "I didn't see anything outstanding either."

Jim gave him the opportunity and told him, "Give your life to Christ and call on Him to save you right now."

He bowed his head and prayed aloud for Jesus to save him right on the spot. "Lord, I've been a hypocrite. I knew I was not a true believer. I'm ashamed of not coming to You long before now. I've been a coward. Come into my life and forgive me. I give my life to You now."

Board Chairman, Larry Atwood, a distinguished and respected man, tried to enter the fray, but it was difficult to get their attention. Finally, he said loudly, "Friends, we are here to discuss and determine Dr. Waltham's position at STSA. I realize that there are two opinions . . ."

"Before we do anything," said Bruce, "I want to look through the telescope again, now that I have called upon the Lord to save me."

That idea got the attention of everyone, and they quickly agreed. They all got up and returned to the telescope. When Bruce looked they could tell by his bodily reaction that something had happened. He started shouting, "Thank You, Jesus! Praise Your Name! Oh, it is so glorious!" They had to practically tear him away from the telescope.

The Board's opinion began to solidify in Jim's favor right on the spot; then they made their way back to the conference room.

"I'm sorry to interrupt," said Judy Carter, "but there's an urgent phone call for Mrs. Sims."

Molly Sims had been left behind when her husband sped off earlier. She was expecting to have someone drive her home. Molly answered the phone and heard, "Molly, I'm sorry about the way I acted. I know.

It was my pride. I had a wreck going around a corner and hit a guard rail. I'm not hurt, and the car's being towed to the repair shop. But something else happened. When God finally brought me to a stop, I humbled myself, repented, and asked Him to forgive me and save me. I feel so much better that it's hard to explain."

"Oh honey, that is marvelous! I am so happy."

"Is the meeting still going on?"

"Yes. It's been pretty complicated around here since you left. But it looks like God is getting everyone straightened out."

"Well, if they take a vote, tell them I want Jim Waltham to remain there for as long as he wants. He has my vote."

"Mine too, honey."

"The wrecker driver said he could take me home. Can you get a ride from Bruce?"

"Yes. And guess what? Bruce just got saved, too!"

"You're kidding! Well, if that don't beat all! You'll have to tell me about that."

"I'll see you soon, honey. Bye."

By the time Mr. Atwood reassembled the group, everyone knew it was a "done deal." Jim was in the driver's seat and holding the steering wheel of astronomical science.

*   *   *

One day Scott and Jim were lounging in Scott's room when Scott had a question. Jim was sitting on the bed spinning a football with his hands. Scott was in the chair in front of his computer and turned around as they talked.

"Dad, do you think there're people living in the Cube now?"

"That's a good question, Scott," Jim answered. "Let's think about it a minute. It's made for the habitation of the saved, so there absolutely will be someday. But even if there are saints there now, we couldn't see 'em even through our telescopes. They're souls awaiting the First Resurrection for their new bodies. That'll happen at the Rapture of the Church. I wouldn't be surprised if there are people there now, enjoying the street of gold and the River of Life. On the other hand, I suppose they may not be there yet, but are in Heaven around the Throne of God awaiting the day when He'll bring His final judgment upon the unbelieving world, and then usher in the millennial reign under the same conditions in which we live right now, except Jesus will be ruling from the City of Jerusalem in person."

"Wow. It's just incredible that we are having all these miraculous things happen here now. I can't wait to see Jesus when he's King over the world."

"And there's something else I want to share with you. I think we're sort of getting teased by the New Jerusalem."

"What do you mean?"

"We believe the Lord's having fun with us about what's going on in the City by allowing us to see movement and partial images that evidently are spiritual rather than physical—like the golden street. The street appears to be a moving street that reaches everywhere in the City. It's a real street, but probably what we are seeing is beyond explanation or description. There're images like a river and trees growing on each side of it as Revelation presents them. But the more we try to conceptualize them, the more they move or change. So it's our guess that the Lord is teasing our curiosity. The same is true of the 'mansions.' They are there, but we'll never know the actuality of their appearance until we have our resurrection bodies! Isn't that something?"

"Awesome! I want to go there right now!"

"You know, Scott, there're some things that are impossible for us to know here in these bodies. They're reserved until we get into God's presence. Paul was caught up into the third Heaven and heard things that were unlawful for him to tell about.[58] Think of how difficult that must have been for him—to see and hear things so glorious and yet they had to be kept secret from us, and he couldn't even talk about them! That's what I think we are seeing in the Cube, just a wisp of unspeakable thrilling things that can't be fully disclosed until we are ready for them."

"I'm sure glad He let us see the New Jerusalem. That ought to knock the socks off anyone who has any doubts about what we're going to enjoy."

"And what a solemn thing too, Scott. Remember that only the saved can see that wonderful revelation parked out there in space. Lost people only see bland, undisclosed things. Amazing!"

"I know. It's sad that they're missing out here and there, too. And we get the best of both worlds. I love God for letting me in."

"The Lord's showing the world what His plan for humanity's like so they'll perceive His wisdom and trust Him from their hearts. These days are a preview of the future, aren't they? Those who reject His merciful revelation now only show the power of sin to blind their minds and rational thinking. Yes, the whole world is invited. Not many come to Him, but the followers of Christ will enjoy everything God has ever made!"

Someone else was looking for help, too.

∞

---

[58] 2 Corinthians 12:2-4

25

RESPONSIBLE LEADERSHIP

The President of the United States again called Jim, inquiring how the present government could and should respond to the Cube in ways that would please God. Since he'd received no communication from the Cube, he believed Jim could provide wisdom and insight concerning this matter. It was obvious that the Cube's presence had to be addressed by the entire world, but especially the leaders in the United States. The world was changing, but God's blessings were obvious upon the ones who sought to obey him. Governmental restrictions throughout the world still bound their citizens from the full liberty that America had from its beginning, and it was noticeable more than ever.

It had been several months since the President had implemented the principles learned during the seminars taught by Jim, Rex, and the Cubicles, and the results were dramatically evident. It was an uphill battle, but the Cube's holy presence and divine providence, combined with willing hearts did what only God could do. Government waste had declined; Christian freedom again permeated the land; acknowledgement of God's blessings were made and glory given to

Him. Atheistic, humanistic, evolutionary philosophies were easy to refute and found harmful to mankind. There was joyful creativity in the development of new products and manufacturing where individuals and companies worked without restricting regulations imposed by impersonal governmental hirelings.

President Snow received plenty of criticism from inviting Jim, noting that he had recently been fired from Quad University. The President responded, "I've already heard from numerous other noted individuals who used a lot of high-sounding jargon without any practical meaning. It seems clear that many in the academic world never tire of creating their own vocabulary without substance. Like so many others, they love to receive recognition for their positions, while betraying the very profession they claim to represent." He accepted Jim as a genuine educator who had personal experience of what he was talking about.

While they were on the phone, the President commented to Jim that he knew he had some enemies. Jim replied, "Yes sir, so did Jesus, who also said a few things in that regard. 'Woe to you when all men speak well of you, for their fathers did the same thing to the false prophets,'[59] and in another place: 'If the world hates you, remember that it hated me before it hated you.'[60] And from what I've heard, it sounds like you have one or two also." They both laughed.

After hearing what the President had in mind, Jim said, "President Snow, I'm so glad you called, and especially for the purpose for which you stated—to please God. That should be the goal of every government since they're all the servants of God.[61] As you know, our nation was established by men who were fully committed to pleasing God. There can be no other explanation for her outstanding successes in just about

---

[59]   Luke 6:26 (NKJV)
[60]   John 15;18 (NKJV)
[61]   Romans 13:4

every field of endeavor, along with world-wide influence, than the 'God of Providence,' as they so often referred to him. Therefore I believe it's essential that we become thoroughly acquainted with the principles, errors, and victories of America. God honors those who honor him."

"Well, I'm going to use that religious word, 'Amen,' Dr. Waltham."

"You're not worried about complaints for teaching religion at the White House are you?"

"Jim, I'm very familiar with how this nation was founded and how history acted within its founding documents. The first English Bible printed in America was paid for by Congress for our schools and recommended for all people to read. The Bible was taught for over fifty years in the U.S. Capitol where worship of God took place every Sunday for some two thousand people. Four churches used the Capitol building as their place of worship before moving to their own location. We're way behind in understanding and practicing what godly people did back then before we became ashamed of the God who provided our freedoms. There were always some who were offended at Jesus when He taught, but it didn't bother Him. He just turned them over to the Father and kept on doing what was right."

"You're always accurate, Mr. President. I like that." Jim went on, "Until the Lord chooses to speak to us from the Cube or some other way, I can only believe that He expects us to go by His Word, the Holy Bible, which already expresses His will. Since He has ordained that there be governments, His Word should of necessity be followed and applied through the laws of the land. The Cubicles feel that America could possibly be the 'model' for other governments to follow since our Founding Fathers in 1776 did that very thing. They incorporated the teachings of His Word into every aspect of life, legal practices, the settling of judgments, the court system, the qualities to be sought after in leaders and officials, and the checks and balances of those we select as our servants.[62] They believed the Bible to be essential to all education. Why don't we do what the Founders did? Perhaps a thorough review of what they've already done would serve us well. We know God has blessed their obedience and sacrifices."

"It sounds very appropriate to me, Jim! I'd like to see this nation's government make a giant move back to God," President Snow responded.

"You and me both, sir. We are not in the Millennium yet, but we are experiencing many of the same conditions of those glorious days to come. And while God's beautiful City is right above us our efforts will likely be powerful and effective. I believe He'll affirm America's Independence, the unalienable rights He's given us, the liberty of true worship, along with just and righteous courts based upon His laws. Our administration is already patterned after the will of God. But it's slipped far away during the past seventy years or so."

"I believe that's a fact, Jim. We've got big problems. In my background of law and politics, I've plowed through an unbelievable record of contradictions and foolish judgments on our books. We've accumulated a 'junkyard' of laws, loopholes, and frivolous legal wranglings that needs to be removed! I can just imagine the chaos of other governments in the world whose foundations are so far from God's revealed will. God will indeed need a template for them to follow. Of course, they're gonna have to be motivated and see an example first, and that'll require the intervention of God to bring it about. Otherwise, it's all impossible. The best means I can think of is the example of the life of Jesus. I believe

---

[62]   "Liberty cannot be preserved without a general knowledge among the people, who have a right, from the frame of their nature, to knowledge, as their great Creator, who does nothing in vain, has given them understandings, and a desire to know; but besides this, they have a right, an indisputable, unalienable, indefeasible, divine right to that most dreaded and envied kind of knowledge; I mean, of the characters and conduct of their rulers."—John Adams (Dissertation on Canon and Feudal Law, 1765)

He taught it was the will of God for people to be safe, peaceful, happy, whole, and living a meaningful life."

"You're right on target there Mr. President! What a great assignment for devoted people of God to tackle. Well then, I would suggest, sir, that a few others come with me to Washington D.C. and lay out to your selected members a seminar setting forth from the Bible and the history of the founding of this nation, the things essential to practice in order to best please God. I'm sure we won't be able to do it perfectly, but we can at least make a start with what God's Word clearly says and how the Founding Fathers put it all together. Now that the New Jerusalem is present, it'll obviously keep on exerting the same holy influence upon the world which has already resulted in benefits for all and it's inconceivable that there would be outright rebellion or war. So that'll give you time to adjust your responsibility accordingly. And, admittedly, I haven't thought about it before, but we don't know how long the Cube will be here, but it's certainly not going to stay here forever. So before it leaves, we ought to have the best form of government possible—especially if it stays for a thousand years!"

"I am deeply impressed by your foresight, Doctor! Do you have anything in mind that could put our government more into the will of God? What do we lack? What do we need to get rid of? How can we go about implementing specific things that line up with His good pleasure?"

"Wow, that's a large order, sir. Now, I'm not experienced in a wide range of subjects that might fit into such a curriculum, but there are at least four primary areas of study that come immediately to mind. I have no idea how well they would be received and acted upon in general, but they would cast a lot of truth in the direction of those who are open to God. These suggestions could be changed or adjusted as needed. I know your time is limited, so I'd propose, let's say, a three day conference with five or six hours, more or less, for each subject. Then if the President so desires, a larger group could be taught at another date in greater depth to whomever you'd want to attend. The four areas could be the basics of Christianity, the history of Israel, the place of Christianity in American history, and perhaps eschatology, a study of things to come. The scope of these areas could be expanded to a full college course."

"Everything you say, Jim, sounds delightful to me," said the President. "Why not begin with what you've suggested? Give me a little about these four areas so I can understand how to present them to my advisors."

"I believe what the government lacks is a proper focus upon the things that matter most in its foundation. Our Founders knew who God was and desired His help in crafting the documents that would receive His approval and blessings. They knew He was the Creator, and they trusted Him to create this nation. That's why they were successful. The truth of the Gospel must be understood. No one is forced to commit their life to God because they have a choice, but they ought to at least know how. Those who do will have the Holy Spirit guiding them into the truth necessary to meet today's demands.

"After all, if Jesus is who He claimed to be—God the Son, who came from God the Father—sinless, keeping every law to perfection, teaching a superior way of life above all other religions, who will be the Judge of all individuals and nations, blessing those who follow him, and those who reject him suffer hardships and untold loss—we must align our country to Him again regardless of the cost and opposition it brings. This nation put his Word into its government and has reaped benefits beyond all other nations combined! Since these facts are irrefutable, who cares how the world reacts to renewing our commitment to Him again?"

"You're exactly right, Jim. Political factions, and prejudices won't go away, but they're not going to overrule what God wants. I believe God is the main character in His Word and everybody else is included to show us more about Him."

"That's the truth, sir. Our country needs a lesson on Christianity and how God intervened to bring America into being. Basic instruction with that in mind could include God—Father, Son, and Holy Spirit, Creation, his revelation through Scripture and the life of Christ, the purpose for mankind, the entrance of sin, the deception of Satan, the necessity of reconciliation, the free gift of God's grace through Christ, and the Church. The details of these lessons can be applied as needed to each class."

> *And this is his command: to believe in the name of his Son, Jesus Christ, and to love one another as he commanded us.*
>
> *(1 John 3:23 NIV)*

"Isn't that the overall plan of God, Jim," the President asked, "that all people have the opportunity to enter His family?"

"That's correct, sir. He wants everybody saved and growing in spiritual knowledge. The second area would be the history of Israel. No one can claim to understand how God treats the world today unless he grasps the principles involved in the way God has treated Israel in the past more than three thousand years. They're the key. After all, from Genesis 12 to the end of the Old Testament, the Lord has given a running history of not only His love for Israel, but for the entire world. From Abraham to Isaac and Jacob, to the twelve tribes, there is a wealth of information, revelation, and admonition to all nations. Then the New Testament begins with, Jesus Christ, the son of David, the son of Abraham.[63] The twelve Jewish apostles were responsible for taking the Gospel to the Jews and Gentiles, and the Church, to the ends of the Earth."

---

[63] Matthew 1:1

"Our nation is the result of that message isn't it Jim?" the President asked.

"You're right, sir. God is not through with Israel, either. Their Messiah, who fulfilled the Scriptures of the Suffering Servant in Isaiah 53, will come again, be recognized by those alive at that time, and He'll take up His rule from Jerusalem. He disciplines the heathen and chastises His own.[64] Their success and failures, God's long-suffering love, along with His chastisement for continued disobedience—these offer today's leaders amazing insights of how He deals with all nations, families, and individuals even now."

"I certainly need that history lesson," said the President, "I can hardly wait to soak it up like a sponge!"

"Yes sir. It will serve an ongoing purpose in your worldview for the rest of your life. Another area is the future of the world. The Bible reveals much about what's going to happen. At least, a brief study of unfulfilled prophecy that'll come to pass in the future would be like icing on the cake. It gives the followers of Christ assurance during uncertain days. While this is usually a controversial area of study, it would be worthwhile to explore the basics. The primary issue is the coming judgment. Our Founding Fathers knew that every individual and nation would face God and give an account for their behavior and choices. This truth is largely missing, both in our government and in society today."

"I would certainly like to have a sure grasp on that subject," the President said.

Jim reminded the President that America had been a marvelous example of how God would bless any nation that truly believed and honored Him by their treatment of others. America had consistently come to the help of millions of others without requiring any payback.

---

[64]   Psalm 94:10

The influence of the free Gospel motivated that to come about. However, for years, we'd failed to give God the credit for our humanitarian aid to numerous countries. And besides, it'd grossly been stolen, misused, and consequently unappreciated by the bulk of individuals who received little of it. This area would be the practical application of all of the above.

Jim stated that the Founders were highly educated and spiritual men who'd thoroughly studied what every type of government had to offer and patterned their ideas from the Word of God. Therefore, most of what God desired from a government had already been drawn out for today's government to follow. America had plenty of strong, solid laws, but they'd been largely discounted and even rejected at everyone's loss.

"What about other religions in America?" the President asked. "How do they fit in?"

"Wow, that's a very important matter that the country must come to understand. Our Founders believed foreign religions restricted people from the freedoms America enjoys by not recognizing their unalienable, God-given rights. They hindered and held back personal talent and ability, forcing people to be under the control of other men. Our Constitution, based upon Christianity, liberated its citizens from intrusion, protected individualism, created free enterprise, promoted science and inventions, and motivated citizens to help others, while being blessed in the process.

Blessed is the nation whose God is the Lord . . .

(Psalm 33:12 KJV)

"Of course, America hasn't done well with requiring responsibility along with our liberty, and today people are running wild claiming they are free to act sinfully against the God who gave them liberty. Other religions trample upon the unalienable rights of God, forcing citizens to conform to unrighteous demands. Even in the United States, men have written over thirty-five million laws trying to curb human nature. These laws are so confusing that often judges can't even determine common decency. On the other hand, God defines our total obligation in two verses of Scripture[65] requiring whole-hearted love of God and love of others—the first two greatest commandments. If we practiced these, there would be no need for any other."

"That's just what I thought," the President said. "That's what I've always believed."

"Mr. President, our Constitution was constructed by men who believed Christianity was the greatest religion on Earth, and the only true one. Jesus Christ was the only flawless person to ever live a perfect life from birth to death. Thus, for someone to oppose Him and His teachings exposes their own wicked heart. To prefer any other religion would be to resist the Holy Spirit. To try to implement any government that leaves God out reveals man's unwillingness to try the best and highest way. There's not another perfect person who has ever lived. No Christian is perfect at living by faith, so that should lead us to humility. But there ought to be an obvious difference between us and those who aren't. It's not an easy way because it's the perfect way."

"That must be why many people criticize Christians as well as the Constitution because the teachings and concepts are above them," the President said.

"You're right on, sir. When men fail and compromise their lives, they usually justify themselves by insisting that *their* own way, or opinion is best. Most people resent Christianity because it restricts their fleshy appetites. There're some members of our government who belittle Christian teachings preferring their supposed superior ideals, and their extravagant, corrupt, dishonest lifestyles. They hypocritically treat others as inferior to them simply because they despise God and don't know Him."

---

[65]   Mark 12:30-31

The President understood there could be no successful government without true religion. He believed Christianity was the only atmosphere in which freedom and the 'pursuit of happiness' could be sought and experienced. It was also the only religion that was strong enough to allow people the freedom to practice other religions without imposing or forcing Christianity upon them. He also believed that the farther away from the Constitution the nation drifted, the more it came to be controlled by man-made ideals that led to slavery. He realized today's leaders needed to hammer out from God's Word what's best, as the Founders so admirably did in the beginning.

"Other details are too many to cover by phone," Jim said. "I hope this is enough information to at least give you a sketch. Sir, what would you like to do about this proposition?"

"Dr. Waltham, I'm motivated to see all these things implemented. I'm very aware of the influence of Christianity upon the government of America. It's irrefutable that this nation was built upon God's Word and was intended to be the best for all people. It even left the way open for improvement by amendments which abolished slavery and gave women the right to vote. I'll make plans to do exactly as you have said, Jim. And don't let the media or any other source discourage you from this matter. I want America to be what God wants her to be. And I'll fight to see it come to pass!"

"Praise God for your position and commitment. I'll immediately contact others that I believe will be able to satisfy your request and let you know when we can all come together, as soon as possible."

"You're my kind of man, Dr. Waltham. I'll anxiously await your contact. Goodbye and God bless you."

"And you likewise, sir."

The presidential office later cleared the calendar and put the three day convocation on the first possible date. It was to be well attended

by numerous individuals and departments throughout Washington
D.C. Jim was to be assisted by several Cubicles including Rev. Fleming,
Rev. Stone, Marcus Loshan, Dr. Nathan Amelang, expert on American
history and author of *Christianity and the Civil Institutions of American
Government.* And Dr. Roland Mayfield, noted Bible scholar and author
of *God Is Ready, Israel,* was also committed to come.

Immediate outcries came from those who were offended that the
President of the United States would call for such a meeting, especially
exalting Christianity and placing it over all other religions. They had
plenty of criticism to vent against those who were invited to the White
House to present their "prejudices" and religious "hatred" in a seminar.

But President Snow spoke to the objectors and the whole country
through a national address.

"My dear friends and countrymen, the truth
is that no government is free from religion. God
ordained that every country should be governed
for the good of the general public. Now, it
doesn't have to be a Christian government to
be recognized by God, but I'll tell you one
thing for sure, He'll hold all government leaders
accountable for the way they behave and how they
treat the people. And His Word, the Holy Bible, tells us how He will
judge them—according to their works, influence, and motives. Therefore,
it's wise for us to trace the steps in our great country of America to its
beginning and conform ourselves to what's best for all. Our government,
based upon His principles, righteousness and justice will continue to
outrank every other nation in the world. We're not under the law of
the Old Testament, but it's a treasure house for knowing His will. Our
unalienable rights have produced the greatest freedoms the world has

> *Behold, the
> righteous will
> be repaid on the
> earth, how much
> more the wicked
> and the sinner!*
>
> *(Prov. 11:31
> TBV)*

ever known. The New Testament and the life of Jesus are the greatest revelation of Himself and His will.

"The Founders expected Christianity to be manifested everywhere because the people here knew the truth. They could easily see the weaknesses of other governments because of the infusion of inferior religious teachings they contained, as well as the rejection of the teachings of the Bible. The common practices of our early government clearly expose the false, 'politically correct position' predominately promoted by many leaders in America today, trying to keep Christianity out of government.

"Our Founding Fathers wanted all denominations to be free from the pressure to conform to each other. It literally took creative genius and the leadership of the Holy Spirit to bring this about, and only in the atmosphere of Christianity could that opportunity have been provided. They considered our nation to be 'Christian,' but without a church wielding the power of the government through any particular denomination. They also knew that our newly formed government had its enemies and was vehemently resisted from the very beginning by those who were ignorant of the New Testament and motivated by their pride and prejudice against God's revelation.

"That's why Americans have put so many reminders of God's Word and teachings on buildings, money, monuments, and historical records, hoping that would counteract the resistance that endangered our liberties. They firmly believed that those who rebelled against God would be punished after they died.

"My dear friends, I am committed to dig back into our history—that's so eloquently and exactly preserved in our libraries—of every discussion and detail that brought about our great government of the people, by the people and for the people. God loves all people and wants them ruled by godly principles. He hates evil and will judge those who balk at His will and serve their own selfish ends. He's here above us to make the adjustments that will bring about the greatest good to His world. And I intend to see it through in America. We may not be able to do it perfectly, but by God's help, we're going to give it our best to please Him.

"I won't be surprised if there're those who'll oppose this intention fiercely. But I don't have to fight their obvious resistance. God Himself will take care of that. Let's all join Him in what He wants for a change. We've had too much of this man and that man's ideas, philosophies, opinions, and criticisms. This is the time for God to rule while He is over us in His City, the New Jerusalem."

Numerous organizations made their move to stop the seminar before it got started. They sought court injunctions against the President, Jim, and others he planned to use. They made threats against them and sought to dig out any slanderous information they could about the seminar leaders. The leaders became troubled as to whether court injunctions would be issued, but the Providence of God kept all attacks at bay. The study went on as planned.

One particular issue that had been fully examined and agreed upon by the teaching staff was the effect that America's Republic had upon non-Christian religions. They believed God had provided the best examples of what religion could do for or against people through his Word that covered thousands of years. Even when God provided a theocracy of rule from Heaven for Israel, the people still turned away and managed to lose it. The religious freedom America enjoyed was as close as men could design it using the Word of God. Even God's law allowed pagans to live with Israel. They just couldn't participate in His worship without giving Him their hearts. Likewise, mixing other religious beliefs and forms of government with those of America would eventually destroy the freedom America enjoyed because its Constitution was based upon the Bible. America's freedoms, or unalienable rights, came from God, and the denial of those rights lead to bondage and oppression in the lands where they are forbidden. These freedoms are what attract those of other religions to America.

Christianity, on the other hand, should not be forced upon others. Though at times, it had been used by force in the past, it was only done by those who either didn't understand the Word of God or even know Christ themselves. God was the One who originally gave mankind freedom of choice. He didn't want anyone serving Him out of fear or oppression. He blessed those who served Him with gratitude. Other religions might not agree with these practices and even look upon them as restrictions, but they had to understand how and why the U.S. Constitution came into being and why, of necessity, it had to be enforced. Governments and religions had the potential power to wield unlimited force, inflict harm and commit injustice upon citizens. Therefore, individuals and families needed to be protected and secured under the Law of God against those who could wrongly use their legal authority over their very lives. The concept of protecting individual rights with an equal obligation of all individuals and institutions was unique to Christianity. It came from God. No other religion or philosophy had that concept. Atheism, Marxism, socialism, evolutionism, Islam, Buddhism, Hinduism, natural law, and others were void of such a thing. Therefore since Christianity offered the highest form of freedom possible. America's Republic only limited freedom when it jeopardized the Constitution or the overall freedoms that Christianity insured for all citizens. And there was a way to improve upon the Constitution through amendments by the will of a large majority.

Religious freedom in America didn't mean that any religion could offer human sacrifices! The law against murder would eliminate such practices. Neither could a religious group practice 'prayer only' for healing from serious illness of a child. If a child died for neglect and endangerment from such practices, the parents could be charged with a criminal offense. Neither could any religion oppose the government and promote tyranny or terrorism. That would be treason, betraying the country they owed allegiance to and jeopardizing the basic freedom of all others to life, liberty and the pursuit of happiness, as it was known under this Republic. Islam couldn't practice or enforce sharia law, since it imposed another set of standards for judgment and prevented freedom and equality of all people, male and female, who are made in the image of God. Neither could a religious group practice the teaching that their god would bless those who murder innocent people because they were not members of their religion. Such a thing would bring chaos and confusion to common sense and just law. A person couldn't use their religion to force others to join their religion. That would eliminate the element of choice, a God-given, unalienable right. Americans had enjoyed the greatest liberty and creativity in all history because their laws were based upon God's highest revelation. America's government was never thought to be or proclaimed to be perfect, but it was the aim of the Founding Fathers to get it as close to the Bible as possible. These facts and principles were agreed upon by all conference leaders and it was their objective to make them clear to the participants.

And what lessons they were to learn.

∞

26

REMOVING THE VEIL

As the conference got under way in Washington, there were four groups meeting simultaneously studying the four areas agreed upon and rotating at specified times. All four areas of study drew great interest and discussion, but the influence of Christianity in American Government was an area the attendees felt they were especially lacking. They'd never been able to investigate this matter outside a controversial setting, so the benefit was always less than desirable. In this objective atmosphere they were able to explore all their questions. The truth about how God providentially guided the formation of America was made clear.

There were conflicting views discussed in the conference and the leaders welcomed all questions. Every idea and ideology had a base of origin or authority. The leaders reached into that base to throw light upon the difference between other political and governmental examples and those of America. Their thorough preparation enabled the sessions to move through each and every differing opinion.

The participants learned about the Founding Fathers, who they were and why they were so important. They were introduced to The

Federalist Papers and their significance. They learned the dangers the
Founders warned about if the Supreme Court treated the Constitution
as if it were a living and changing document. They found out that the
wise men who framed our government were not mere copycats with
a university brainwash. They were deep thinkers, well-educated, and
men of faith. Twenty-six of the fifty-six signers of the Declaration
held seminary or Bible school degrees. They heard the truth about Ben
Franklin, whom some today labeled a deist, but who called for prayer
meetings and for the Gospel to be preached and believed that God was
involved in the struggle they had when this nation was formed. They
learned that not a single one of the Founding Fathers was an atheist[66]
including Thomas Paine.

They read for themselves the First Amendment and the circumstances
of the "separation of church and state" misnomer being perpetrated on
the unsuspecting population today. This amendment prohibited the
government from interfering with the free exercise of religion. It couldn't
establish Christianity because it was already established everywhere in our
country. Without it, this country wouldn't have the freedoms it provided.
Christianity was so pervasive in their minds that they used religion as
a synonym for denominations within Christianity. It permeated the
nation and was purposely kept prominent as witnessed by the memorials
of Moses and the Ten Commandments on the wall and doors of the
Supreme Court and of Moses at the top of the gable of the Court. "In
God We Trust" was intentionally put on our money. The oath of public
office and the oath of a juror included the hand on the Holy Bible and
"so help me God." So dominant was Christianity in the nation that
originally every office in the country required the swearing of faith in
Almighty God, Jesus Christ as his Son, and the acknowledgement of

---

[66]   Quoted by Ben Franklin

the Old and New Testaments as God's Word before they were even eligible to run for office![67]

The Founding fathers already had influence from various Christian denominations such as Anglicans, Puritans, Separatists, Congregationalists, Presbyterians, Mennonites, Baptists, Lutherans, Methodists, Quakers, and others. Some of these had already been promoted to positions as the recognized church of their colonies. These state churches were all removed from that position, while Christianity remained the religion of the nation. Religious diversity was the law of life in this new country and pluralism was an irrepressible reality. The people understood it to be a divine right.

Later in a press conference, reporters were free to question the President.

"Will non-Christian religions be discriminated against in this 'new' government agenda?" one reporter asked in a threatening tone. He represented the numerous Americans who actually agree with the Constitution and believed in God, but who were so careful to protect the smallest snail, bird and fish, along with the "potentially hurt feelings"

---

[67] "I do believe in one God the Creator and Governor of the universe, the Rewarder of the good, and the Punisher of the wicked; and I acknowledge the Scriptures of the Old and New Testaments to be given by inspiration."—Constitution of Pennsylvania. [Every person] "chosen governor, lieutenant-governor, or representative, and accepting the trust, shall subscribe a solemn profession that he believes in the Christian religion, and has a firm persuasion of its truth."—Constitution of Massachusetts, 1780. All states required similar oaths. "Besides, the Constitution of the United States contemplates, and is fitted for; such a state of society as Christianity alone can form."—George Washington "In perusing the[first] thirty-four [state] Constitutions of the United Sates we find all of them recognizing Christianity as the well-known and well-established religion of the communities whose legal, civil, and political foundations they are."—Reverend Benjamin Franklin Morris (1810-1867), son of Honorable Thomas Morris, pioneer opponent of slavery, U.S. Senator from Ohio.

of every wicked enemy of the Cross who resisted and fought against God, that they willingly gave up the freedoms Almighty God provided to all, and allowed the Christ-rejecters a special room at the table! They innocently were ignorant of the fact that these fierce children of the devil would twist their position into the face of all opposition and destroy every liberty they possibly could.

"We plan to follow the wise teachings of our Founding Fathers," the President replied. "It's not new and it's not an agenda. It's what we began with and what has brought blessings to everyone."

"What about tolerance, acceptance and freedom to disagree with Christianity?" asked another reporter, obviously provoked by the previous answer.

"Christianity has never experienced a time when it wasn't disagreed with," the President replied. "The reason it has and always will triumph over criticism is because of its superior truth. And true Christians are taught to practice the love of Jesus for others." Then, looking directly at the reporters in front of him, he said, "We will do our best to avoid profane and vain squabbling and oppositions which some couch and disguise as knowledge."[68]

The President announced to the public his confidence in what the early colonies did when they laid the very basis of their institutions upon Christianity.[69] "Today those meeting in Washington have the privilege

---

[68]   1 Timothy 6:20

[69]   "Our laws and our institutions must necessarily be based upon and embody the teachings of The Redeemer of mankind. It is impossible that it should be otherwise; and in this sense and to this extent our civilization and our institutions are emphatically Christian...This is a religious people. This is historically true. From the discovery of this continent to the present hour, there is a single voice making this affirmation...we find everywhere a clear recognition of the same truth...These, and many other matters which might be noticed, add a volume of unofficial declarations to the mass of organic utterances that this is a Christian nation"—Supreme Court Decision, 1892; Church of the Holy Trinity v. United

of doing exactly what the Founding Fathers had to do—figure out how to best please God, whose presence is right above in the New Jerusalem or Cube. And it'll have to be done through His revealed Word."

Meanwhile, as Jim Waltham was concluding his portion of the seminar, he said, "And ladies and gentlemen, at the time that the New Jerusalem, or Cube, arrived, we were living in those dangerous days our forefathers feared. Days when all religions were promoted as equal in value, all opinions equal in importance, all teachings pertinent, people demanding that others accept their doctrines while being hostile toward anyone who disagreed with them. Educators were refusing God a place in the classroom, substituting for him, atheism, evolution, materialism, socialism, Communism, and foolish theology, willing to allow this nation to suffer the inevitable consequences of these concepts. It's no wonder that Ben Franklin announced to the people after the ratification of the Constitution, 'You have a Republic . . . if you can keep it.' The vast majority of Americans still believe in the God of the Bible, and America still intends to keep it a Republic!"

When the three-day session was completed, the President and the vast majority of those attending were so enlightened that they were begging for more. Leaders of the sessions reminded the attendees that the New Jerusalem was a wake-up call for the world. It reminded them of their accountability to Almighty God and their need of Christ. Salvation assured them of participating in the coming future Kingdom.

States. "The moral principles and precepts contained in the Scriptures ought to form the basis of all our civil constitutions and laws. All the miseries and evils which men suffer from vice, crime, ambition, injustice, oppression, slavery, and war, proceed from their despising or neglecting the precepts contained in the Bible."—Noah Webster.

The President called for a sixty-day moratorium of everything that could be neglected in order for all servants of the government of the American people to complete the longer course. The presence of the Cube had given a "breather" to so much of the business of government that this would literally fill in the gap. The Vice President, cabinet officers, senators, congressmen, justices, and governors were urged to attend. They would be enlightened by a history lesson that they likely missed in school!

The excitement of those that attended the sessions didn't stop when they left the classroom. Facts about America's origin were received with surprise and with joy. The President announced future teaching sessions to follow with three more rounds.

The first round required five-and-a-half days for one week. Each session was designed to last a little longer. The second round, would last two weeks; and the third round, three weeks. Various teams would lead these sessions from the large group of Cubicles. After the third round, the material would be developed into an on-going seminar by DVD and online. Eventually, the essence of the conference could reach multiplied millions here and abroad.

There were uproars against the scheduling of these seminars. Marcus noted it was amazing that those to whom the Constitution was originally handed and which had been purchased through tears, sweat, and blood still had to fight the liberal ungodly resistance to what was best for all. "And the descendants of those who oppose freedom are still around fighting against patriots today. This government belongs to the people and they're determined to keep while pleasing God," he said.

Americans Against Religious Governments (AARG) was the first to raise its voice. "It's unconstitutional for these groups to meet, much less to be sponsored and paid for by the government!" Emily Pendingdorf, attorney for the AARG, complained.

"I wish those who oppose what is taking place were familiar with those who actually wrote the Constitution before they try to use it to suit themselves." Marcus responded. "She probably doesn't know that during a period of about fifty years, four different churches met in the United States Capitol building. The Founding Fathers worshipped with them, so it wasn't against the Constitution then. The United States government bought thousands of Bibles at the approval of Congress. The government was committed to do what was best for the nation," replied Robert Hackney, attorney and attendee of the conference. "Tax money was to be used for the general welfare of the United States. There's not a better use of it than by these educational seminars for the improvement of government and the good of the people."

Americans United Against Church and State (AUACS) filed a suit with the Supreme Court attempting to at least halt the beginning of other conferences. "It ought to be studied and determined whether the conferences are constitutional or not," a representative asserted. They were certain they could find a judge somewhere who could be bribed to uphold their complaints. Obviously, such groups only used the word "constitution" when it would advance their cause.

The U.S. Government, Jim, and the Space Telescope Science Association were sued individually by the American Civil Liberties Union. This hung a cloud over Jim as to the unknown future of these actions. And the usual atheistic and humanistic organizations followed the seminar howling their disfavor and seeking publicity. Philosophers from various universities rallied students to protest.

Marcus Loshan responded that the defiant obstructionists were somehow oblivious to the nature of true liberty, the enormous responsibility that freedom brought, and the cost of preserving it. "Apparently there are only a few that can handle it," he stated.

Billionaire Alfred Dunstan, a militant atheistic humanist, vowed to pour as much money as needed to squash anything that had to do with God, the Church, Christianity, or religion. His basic target was blaming Jews and Christians for anything he didn't like. His network of favors to politicians, and his business leverage that strengthened his support, and his humanitarian involvement in various charities caused those without a strong foundation for truth and righteousness to be reluctant to oppose anything he suggested.

Dr. Amelang reminded the public that in spite of opposition and past failures, God still had a plan for His world and He was going to bring it to completion. From Adam to Noah, to Moses, to the generation who saw and heard Jesus Christ Himself, people had failed to understand and appreciate true freedom. The Founding Fathers, too, were opposed by many influential citizens every step of the way. Today's intelligentsia, elite, and power brokers, were still rebelling against the Truth. But the common, God-fearing righteous followers of Christ would push the will of God to the front, and His divine providence would continue to prevail against all odds. Those contending against Christ would come to ruin. This current generation was facing danger because of their lack of understanding and appreciation. "Every generation inevitably tends to take the valuable freedom they enjoy for granted, feeling everything ought to be easy and uncomplicated because they deserve it!" he said.

Meanwhile the Walthams had to examine their future.

∞

27

ASTOUNDING!

Jim and Laura had a discussion about their finances since the Cube had come on the scene. Jim was out of his job at Quad, but still had income from STSA. It was these two incomes that had allowed them to move out into the country with several acres around them. Surprisingly, six months later they were still doing okay, and he was receiving pay for his tenure from Quad. They realized that prices had been lowered on practically all merchandise. Food was so plentiful that Jim wondered if the grocery stores would still be open. But they were actually expanding to provide unbelievable selections of food and other products. Though prices were low, volume was up. Local individuals were bringing their produce to the stores and truckers expanded their cargo to include more than one source with smiles on their faces. It was quite an adjustment to make so quickly. The US government had backed off their iron-fisted control—manipulated as only chameleon politics and pressure could do—of land and dictatorship as to what can and can't be done with it, so that free enterprise had flourished. Gas was already at $1.59 per gallon and America would be totally free from dependence upon foreign oil before the end of the following year.

Jim hadn't taught school in six months and missed it. He decided to explore the options of teaching again. Laura agreed he should do it part-time. With Scott in excellent health, her time was freed up greatly. She had become a "sports mom"—meaning she ran from one sporting event to the next with her two sons participating in them all. Keith would be entering college this fall, and they could use more income.

Within a couple of days of this decision, Jim received a call from the president of Southwest Astronomy University located in Albuquerque, New Mexico. He explained to Jim that the university had purchased five hundred acres of land near Alpine, Texas, where the school was being relocated.

Jim could hardly believe his ears! *Another university coming to a location near home? What did he say his name was?*

Streets had already been paved, several buildings had been erected and temporary buildings were being constructed. Some classes were to begin in four months. The move and extensive layout of the campus had been kept quiet until all legal and architectural work had been approved and it took longer than anticipated. That's why the president hadn't contacted Jim before now. He explained that Jim's position on the faculty would not only give a boost to the identity of the school, but would send notice to prospective students of the kind of school it would be. Jim's brain was working overtime trying to absorb this information. It was a shocker!

Then the president said, "In case you're wondering about my name—yes, it's Archie Fain. Thomas Fain, chairman of the trustees at Quad University, is my father."

Jim's mental alarm buttons went off in every direction, shouting, "What?"

"However," Mr. Fain continued, "this university has a different base from that of Quad. We're committed to the Word of God, the literal

Creation account of Genesis, and the Bible is an automatic textbook in every classroom. Jesus said, *I came not to send peace but a sword.*[70] That sword separated my father from me. I chose Christ and he chose atheistic humanism. The message of the Gospel of Christ always separates believers from unbelievers. I still love my father and pray for him daily, though he doesn't have a kind word to speak to me. But my marching orders come from above as I serve the Lord Jesus Christ, the one whose Cube dominates the attention of the world today. This university will be a powerful competitor to Quad, which is a headquarters for so much superficial science."

Jim remained speechless for a while.

"Dr. Waltham, I apologize for dropping all this upon you at once, but because of legal procedures, we have just now cleared the way for the new location to be publicized and new professors to be hired. Funding has only now become available and will allow the university to expand into the next decade. I'd appreciate your serious consideration to become a faculty member, and we want to use your name in some of the publicity. You can see on our website our mission statement, the soundness of our doctrines, and the commitment to train scientists to bring glory to the God of Creation."

"Mr. Fain, I'm so shocked I hardly know what to say. Of course I'll give this my full attention and let you know as soon as possible. But I want you to know that my time is so limited that I'm only interested in teaching part-time. I'm still involved with five observatories and a loving family."

"I know, Dr. Waltham. Your strategic position is perfect for us both. Your scholarship and rapport with students is excellent. I know you love your work and it shows in your accomplishments. And we're

---

[70]   Matthew 10:34

not deterred by the 'blackballing' you've received from Quad. The administration evidently sent a negative evaluation of you to all the observatories in the country, as well as to all the universities with an astronomy curriculum."

Jim was astonished! The president left his phone number, and Jim went directly to the school's website and read everything. It was so well done, he was speechless. The school had been in operation for twenty-five years with endorsements from well-known Christian leaders. He and Laura were astounded at the whole situation and considered it a direct answer to prayer. The next day Jim and Laura toured the new site and were surprised to see that basic plans were already set up for the future. Several buildings were already complete and prefab buildings were being installed.

"I remember now," Jim said, "seeing construction in this area some time ago, but thought it was a new community with shopping centers around it. They certainly did keep it quiet for me not to hear anything about it! I'm sure there would have been political opposition from Quad otherwise." The following day, Jim discussed with the president the details of his responsibilities, classes, salary, and other matters, and he accepted the position.

Work on the new campus near Alpine exploded with full force. Advertisements appeared in all the local papers and were announced on the airwaves. As expected, certain media persons picked up on Jim's position on the faculty and had sarcastic comments about his exit from Quad and noted he was to teach in this "fundamental" school that defied modern science. Trustees and faculty members of Quad were fuming about the university locating so near, and Jim Waltham's faculty position was poison poured on their cake! They sought every opportunity to criticize Jim and the school. It was amazing that they knew so much about what they didn't believe. The Waltham family took everything in stride. They were used to being fried, baked, and hashed every day by someone. The Astronomical Club, a group of "scientists" which evidently existed to give admiration to each other and criticism to those they didn't like, wasted no time spilling their gossip and condemnation upon Jim, disclaiming his findings concerning the Cube and his lack of qualification for a faculty position teaching astronomy.

The closer it got to opening day of the new university the worse the criticism became. While driving on the way to the LT one morning, Jim heard a loud bang in the vehicle and noticed a hole in the windshield of his pickup. The shot had penetrated the seat next to him and went through the floor of the back seat. Jim was so scared he ducked and floor-boarded the gas pedal. He was too shaken to use his cell phone until he pulled into the parking lot at the LT, and called the police as soon as he arrived. An investigation got underway immediately. The shooter had to have been on the side of a mountain where Jim was on the highway and the weapon, a high-powered rifle. It was an attempted murder. If a passenger had been riding with Jim, he would have been killed instantly.

The news reported the incident with lots of coverage, connecting it with the possibility of the new university being re-located so close to Quad. Trustees of Quad were incensed and protested that anyone would dare indicate that someone from their university would be accused of attempted murder over the trivial matter of another school being located in the area. They let it be known that their school was far superior to the fledgling southwest school and weren't afraid of losing students to it. However, the FBI figured the trustees and faculty were the best place to start—especially when they learned about the suspicious auto in Jim's driveway a few months ago. They lined up Jim's vehicle at the place where the shooting took place and connected the angle of the holes with a spot on the mountainside. No bullet casing was found at the suspected area, so the shooter may have been careful not to leave that evidence.

Jim, Laura, and the boys were put under special protection for the time being. Their travel was approved and cleared day by day. They encouraged each other by their closeness and prayer. God had been good, and they were certain he had a plan for the future.

The two suspects who were chased off by Keith were interrogated thoroughly and admitted they joked about eliminating Jim, but had no intention of carrying out such a thing. They were also asked if anyone else heard them voicing their "joke," and they picked up three other names. With a search warrant, the homes of these three were explored with a fine-comb and one of them owned a 3006 rifle that had recently been fired. Russell Salisbury, a Quad faculty member was arrested under suspicion and interrogated until he broke, admitting that he didn't intend to kill Jim, just scare him. But scaring him wouldn't have prevented him from teaching, competing with Quad or airing his religious views, which violently irritated Salisbury. He was tried, eventually found guilty and sent to prison.

During the months it took to prosecute Salisbury, the Walthams had a somber relationship that dampened the otherwise fantastic paradise they were enjoying. It was sad to see someone with such hatred in his heart that he would do such a thing. But they were relieved that it was finally over.

There were multitudes of awakened souls with questions.

∞

28

Adventurous Experiment

Pleas for help from foreign nations seeking advice on how to govern accurately within the will of the God of the Cube generally were addressed to the U.S. Congress, who funneled them to the Cubicles since they'd been a significant resource for America's adjustment after the coming of the New Jerusalem. Various Cubicles had handled the questions and issues to individual nations, but more problems kept coming up. Eventually it seemed best that a general convocation be conducted to thoroughly cover the broad subject matter. Such a meeting was widely discussed among the Cubicles with the pros and cons of the possible outcome of such a meeting. Finally, after much discussion, it was the consensus that God had chosen the Cubicles for the purpose of giving guidance to the U.S. government and others as well. He had already used them to bring about major changes in America. They proceeded to schedule a group of foreign presidents, leaders, and dictators who would come to America seeking principles that could be implemented that would assure the blessings of God upon their countries. America's ability to conform to biblical teachings obviously distanced it immediately ahead of others. The assembly would come from several African and Asian nations, from Spain to Norway, South America, the Eastern block of what was formerly Russia, as well as Mexico and Canada. Time and location eventually came down to Jim, Marcus and Rex Fleming. The five day event was set and an excellent meeting hall was rented in Midland, Texas.

Jim, Rex, Marcus, and Dr. Stone were meeting at Faith Church On The Rock as they finalized the details for the luxurious hall and scheduling the others who would lead in the presentations. "Thank God there won't be a language problem," said Rex. He leaned back in his chair with one arm over the back, obviously relaxed at last. "Can you imagine what it would require if that weren't the case?"

"The Lord knows what he's doing, doesn't he?" Jim smiled across the table and leaned back in his chair as Rex had done. "It's astounding that I'm even taking part in such an elaborate meeting! Who'd ever thought that we'd be planning and leading a group of nations concerning the purpose and principles of good government? The responsibility's pretty scary. But praise God, at least we have all the information and topics we used for the seminar in Washington D.C. and it's all available on CDs for everyone's guidance. I just can't feature the results of such a meeting because of the power and money dictators accumulate. It'll be difficult for them to relinquish those, and the corruption that comes with power is astounding. Even if the leaders want to implement godly government, they'll have to get it past the multitude of others who'll balk at surrendering authority and greed. It'll absolutely take God to achieve the impossible in this gathering!"

"Not only that," Marcus added as he leaned forward in his chair with serious concern, "but sometimes it's the army and police force—those with guns, who are the greatest fear to citizens. On the other hand, I believe the timing's right for the Lord to put more pressure on each government to remove corruption and unfair business practices and to implement safe working conditions. We have the opportunity to call for these leaders to become virtuous and committed to the good of society and to be bold in abolishing arbitrary laws that are trivial and unevenly practiced. Justice can become harsh and not balanced with mercy when needed. They must see that the pursuit of happiness is a God-given right to all."

Jim was making the rounds with fresh coffee, and Dr. Stone reminded him that he only took black. As Jim poured more coffee into his mug, Stone concurred, "Think of the freedom that's controlled by all governments. To our advantage, America began with a sweeping knowledge of the Word of God, the work ethic of getting the job done the best you can, and the expectation of an honest reward for every pound of sweat. Of course, if there's ever going to be a change in the nations, it'll likely come at such a time as this when the holiness of God is felt throughout the world, and we hold the highest standard before these nations. We mustn't compromise about what God wants from His governments. He doesn't state that they have to be democracies, or dictatorships, or monarchies—but He does make it clear what the government's job description is and what it's to achieve. It all begins with the moral character of the leaders."

"Well, I hope they're up to it—they're coming a long way to learn, and we can't let them down," Jim responded.

"This seems like an astounding and impossible undertaking," said Dr. Stone, scratching his head and removing his glasses. "I wouldn't even give it consideration if it weren't for the Cube's presence! I'm even laughing at the idea while participating in it! Just think of how difficult it was for our Founding Fathers to accomplish what they did. And do these other nations have a George Washington? A Thomas Jefferson? A James Madison? A John Adams? These men along with many others made a great sacrifice to bring this nation into being, and it didn't happen in a day or a year. It was a long road! We'll have to give these leaders a history lesson about the cost of following the Holy Spirit. I'm dumbfounded about it as well as excited about the possibilities!"

"I couldn't agree more," Rex stated. "It will take a miracle. And that's what we're expecting! The results won't be up to us, but up to the Lord. It's sort of like a revival meeting. The people come, but we don't know the hearts of those who attend. The results will depend upon the people and the Holy Spirit of God."

The group of men structured the convocation by dividing it into four groups to facilitate better interaction and questions. They agreed that the way to begin the first session was to give foundational facts to each nation, showing how America's government was developed and the necessity of following the teachings and principles of the Holy Bible. Each attendee was to receive an accurate American history lesson, beginning with how this nation began with a search for freedom to practice their true religion. Many were Christians fleeing from other "Christians"! That fact should open their eyes. The original Christian immigrants to America came from countries where many who claimed to be Christians didn't practice true Christianity. They were retreating from those who wrongfully used Christianity to promote their own agenda and exalt themselves. There was an absence of uniform love and rights. So this country was founded upon the belief that all persons were created by God and had equal value. Everyone had the same right to life, the right to be free from oppression of all kinds, free to pursue happiness, and free to worship God the way they believed He would have them to, as long as it didn't encroach upon the common freedom and unalienable rights of others. Even those who had slaves were motivated to set them free, and eventually did.

They wanted the attendees to understand that America's freedom was resisted and persecuted by others and had to be won through war for independence. Americans cherished their freedom believing it was the highest form of life that could be enjoyed. It was still hated, fought against, and threatened by others who were jealous, who'd never learned the principles of the New Testament and who were prejudiced toward anything different from the customs handed to them by their ancestors or indoctrinated through miseducation. The test of what pleased God was found in His blessing. Surely no nation had enjoyed the blessings of God as had America for the past two hundred and thirty-six years.

But these leaders should understand also that America had fallen away from the God who offered eternal salvation and earthly freedom. America had used its freedom to sin against Him, disobey His laws, and failed to return His love and give Him glory for what He had lovingly done for it.

As a result, they experienced chastisement, suffering, and loss just as other nations. But since the coming of the Cube, America had returned to his Word and become committed to following His principles. He was pleased with their efforts as they applied His truth in every area of society. He had a purpose and plan for all governments, and it was from His Word that America gained knowledge of that plan. Attendees would be alerted to the fact that God's will could be distorted by those who sought only selfish objectives. It would take wisdom, humility, and trust in God to learn and apply His teachings to any nation. They were to be challenged to meet the difficulties though it might call for suffering on their part. Their motivation must be to please God.

> So now the Lord says, "Stop right where you are! Look for the old, godly way, and walk in it. Travel its path, and you will find rest for your souls. But you reply, 'No, that's not the road we want!'
>
> (Jeremiah 6:16 NLT)

The convocation would emphasize the unalienable rights upon which America's Constitution was based, and point out that these rights actually supersede the authority of the Constitution itself because they were inherent rights endowed by God Himself. It was in order for people to secure these rights that the government was instituted and derived its just powers from the consent of the governed. Therefore whenever any form of government became destructive of these ends, it was the right of the people to alter or to abolish it and to institute new government. The Bill of Rights and amendments would be provided for all participants and emphasized, along with all of founding Constitutional documents.

"Who authorized this group of religious fanatics to determine how other nations should govern their countries?" the Organization Against Free Enterprise asked in a paid advertisement over television and in newspapers. "This is another springboard for them to push Christianity off on other nations who already have their religions. Every nation and individual should be free to choose their own religion and run their own government," the anti-freedom organization ranted.

When asked for a response by the media, Marcus Loshan stated, "No one's choosing anything for others. The nations of the world have come to the citizens of this great country asking for help from those who have answers that work. Attacks against the truth of God are hardly worth a reply to those who evidently are covetous for attention and bankrupt of solutions for the problems of their neighbors."

The "noise" raised by a few critics and media attacks concerning the international gathering of the heads of nations helped promote the convocation, and it caught the attention of the entire United States. There had never before been such an event. Unexpected publicity caused the occasion to mushroom out of proportion. Multitudes of individuals wanted to attend, but were turned away for lack of space. There even had to be a special pass printed and a check in at the doors for those who came from foreign countries. Even the media had to be limited to an available room with television projection screens. Jim was flabbergasted over the size of the crowd wanting to attend and how to handle them. Though it created extra work and planning, the facilities were excellent for accommodating most of the unexpected hazards that came up, and the planners were pleased for the cooperation of lots of helpers!

* * *

The Waltham family needed a break from all the heavy schedules and activities. They were glad it became necessary earlier to purchase an additional four wheeler for Scott when he was capable of driving one. He'd already learned to master most of the drainage ditch in the back acreage with Keith's help and encouragement. The family had an excursion over the entire parcel of land with a picnic lunch to boot. Scott said, "Boy, this is great. I've never had so much fun!" as he parked his cycle and took a seat on the logs that surrounded a fire pit. He anticipated the hot dog wiener he was roasting on the end of his coat hanger.

"It's hard to beat a loving family outing," Laura said with a big smile.

"I'll second that motion," Keith chimed in.

"I'll bet this is the first cookout and picnic that a group has ever had with the critters who've also been invited." He pointed to a rattlesnake lying by a rock a few feet away, two jack rabbits that stood on their hind legs nearby observing the get-together, and walking toward them a short distance away was a buck with eight horns. "It's hilarious to think that these wild things are so friendly and actually like to be petted by humans," Jim chuckled. "There's even a skunk behind the shrubbery over there," he pointed off to his right. "But I guess they don't spray and stink anymore!"

"I hope not, Dad!" Keith hesitantly stated.

Scott rose and met the buck, offering him a wiener but he wouldn't eat it. He just wanted to lick Scott's cheek. It was paradise and an especially welcomed rest for Jim.

*   *   *

Jim Waltham began the first day's convocation of nations welcoming everyone and sharing the humbling and inadequate feeling he and the others had for the task before them. Then he brought up a very important matter for their primary consideration. The Cube, the New Jerusalem, the dwelling place of God's presence stationed above them, was the cause of all the blessings they'd received thus far. Almighty God, the Creator of Earth and Heaven was making known His love and plans for humanity after this life. He wanted everyone to enter His family and live in His Kingdom forever. He'd brought about the restoration of nature and tamed the wild beasts. He'd caused the radical changes in health, climate, language, and peace throughout the world. But these things were temporary just as the life of Jesus Christ, God's Son, was temporary upon the Earth. Jesus taught the same things they would hear today. He healed the sick, raised the dead, and fed the multitudes to show His power and purpose for humanity. He wanted everyone to enjoy the new Heaven and the new Earth that He would create in the future. Only those who recognized Him, worshipped Him and followed Him from their hearts would be able to enjoy those forever plans. He was coming first to judge the world for all its sin and wickedness and hateful treatment of Him and His creation. The Cube was actually postponing that judgment, giving the world a little more time to repent and receive Christ as Savior and Lord. He wanted everyone to be saved, but most people wouldn't come to Him.

Jim continued as seriously as he knew how, "The changes you decide to make this week will bring the best peace and blessings to your people that they'll ever have. But you must take advantage of the opportunity now. We don't know how long the Cube will stay with us. It could leave at any time, and things will return to the way they were before. No one wants that to happen, but it will someday. The nations that respond with submission to the Word of God, the Holy Bible, and especially the New Testament, will receive the greatest blessings now and in the future when the judgment of God comes. You must implement as many of the principles you learn about this week as quickly as possible. Put them into action. Overcome all resistance with bold love. You'll be opposed by many people, but those who oppose you are the ones who don't want the best for your countries, they only want what's best for themselves. It'll be difficult to apply some of these principles. But you must do the best you can. Honestly look into your heart and see if you are willing to pay the cost of loving your country. Freedom is not easy to obtain, and it's even harder to keep. We give glory to God for what He has done for us. May God bless you as you listen, ask questions, be patient, use your head and heart as you see what happened in America and what can happen in your country. We love you and are here to help you in any way we can."

This challenge was likely the most radical that the attendees had ever considered. It was against their culture, political persuasion, and practices of their citizens. But the truth had to be faced. The Lord God was calling to their hearts to take a giant step forward and leave the results of their decisions to Him. These were not usual days.

Surprisingly, most of those who attended the convocation were desperate to understand and receive help from the Lord and America. They were open to advice, instruction, and even religious information about Christianity and the Bible. Sure, there were some who wanted the facts laid before them so they could consider their options. But since God was at work it was rare that these leaders chose the options rather than accepting the challenge. It would be exciting to bring about a change, and they knew that without supernatural help it would be impossible.

They were open for others to come to their countries and take charge of making it work! They wanted classes taught so the people would grasp what could be theirs. They rejoiced in experienced leadership that could save them time and prevent failure. Jim and the others were astounded at how God had moved in these nations preparing them to hear his Word. It was even humorous to see and speak to persons from other countries who spoke such perfect English!

At the end of the five days, the group felt like a family. The power of God had done its work and it would resound to the ends of the Earth. The populations of these countries were anticipating the return of their leaders and expected blessings from their journey. It was evident that all was well—at least better—everywhere.

Praise the Lord.
Praise, O servants of the Lord,
    praise the name of the Lord.
Let the name of the Lord be praised,
    both now and forevermore.
From the rising of the sun to the place where it sets,
    the name of the Lord is to be praised.
The Lord is exalted over all the nations,
    his glory above the heavens.
Who is like the Lord our God,
    the One who sits enthroned on high,
who stoops down to look
    on the heavens and the earth?
He raises the poor from the dust

and lifts the needy from the ash heap;
he seats them with princes,
with the princes of their people.
He settles the barren woman in her home
as a happy mother of children.
Praise the Lord.[71]

And there was more . . . other deliberations and excitement was happening all over the world.

∞

---

71   Psalm 113 (NIV84)

29

BENEFITS CLOSE AND PERSONAL

C hange permeated the whole world. People took advantage of the realities around them. They made phone calls to distant parts of the world and clearly understood anyone who answered. It was fun to make a call just to enjoy getting acquainted with others in faraway places. People of all nations began to travel not only to see the beauty of the Earth in other countries, but to meet those who lived there. They were no longer reluctant to go to parts of the Earth that were previously considered dangerous.

Eventually, the whole world became aware of the influence of the Cube in partial fulfillment of Isaiah's prophecy ". . . the Earth will be full of the knowledge of the Lord as the waters cover the sea."[72] Multitudes, the world over, experienced prosperity while others suffered loss. Businesses and organizations that were unneeded or couldn't deceive anymore were unable to function. Evil was restricted by the effect of holiness emanating from the Cube.

---

[72] Isaiah 11:9

The Cubicles emailed their ideas and potential conclusions about the purpose of the Cube to the entire group. The main idea added to what had already been compiled was that God wanted governments to enforce security and provide justice and peace to all nations. Other suggestions were still waiting for further revelation or confirmation from the Lord Himself.

Laura read of the astounding changes that had been made all around the world and shared with Jim and the two boys, "I feel like I've been dropped down in Heaven! As I read the reports of these changes, I heard beautiful music like you'd expect to hear when something good and wonderful is happening in a movie, only infinitely more astounding! The Heavens were applauding and singing glory to God's goodness and grace to all humanity."

United Nations' President, Duran Koyambounou, declared starvation would cease to exist if the current bounty continued worldwide. He feared the organization would be without salaries because there appeared to be no problems for them to solve. Africa, India, and China confirmed that crop growth was astounding. The curse of Genesis 3 had been removed and agriculture was running wide open. Unemployment was without excuse. Anyone who wanted to work could start today. Animosity and the rule of the jungle no longer existed as all sorts of animals were friendly with each other again.

Nations that had bitterness against each other found it impossible to carry out war with each other. "I'm afraid to continue our plan to terrorize Israel," Hamas leader, Sayyed Abdulla, declared to his band of followers. "Something's wrong with all our weapons. We must be getting defective shipments from Russia." He was meeting in his secret headquarters where they usually formed their plots.

"It's the same everywhere," one of his captains complained with a scowl on his face. "In Iraq, Syria, Egypt, Lebanon, Iran, and Jordan, the word is that nothing works. Our intelligence has gathered reports that say it may be a powerful magnet from a Cube in space."

"It's the New Jerusalem," another interjected. "Israel has hired the United States to join them in this trickery, and they have all the technology. Every time we try to carry out our plans, they fall flat."

Dictators found it useless to fund great armies and weaponry, but they quickly wanted to get the credit for the bountiful crops and turned to humanitarian improvement. They claimed the gods were smiling upon them because they'd been so good. Quality of life advanced more every day. Free enterprise became a real option, as poorer national government leaders promoted ways to make their political positions deserving and secure. Leaders surprised themselves, but couldn't help smiling at the attention and praise they were receiving. They put their plans of evil and war away in a drawer.

More requests came from other nations for teams to come and give additional help with how to implement the principles they'd received in America. They faced a difficult task—clashing with so many religious traditions, customs, and prejudices that prevented liberty. The application of the life of Jesus and the New Testament would be the only powerful force that could bring about the improvements desired. There was a growing demand for teachers who could communicate what was good and godly throughout all the nations. America also needed the same lesson. Serious turmoil existed over what was really right and wrong. Organizations sent out a call for those who could properly teach moral absolutes. Honesty was a trait few knew anything about! The Benefits of Obedience was a new course in demand.

Nations also pled for help in applying their skills at more advanced challenges. Third World countries now had the means to improve themselves but didn't know how to build, to drill, to mine, to compute, to construct, to invent, to discover, and to enjoy the resources around them. Instead of financial aid, they desperately needed information and instruction—the "how to" for every undertaking. The demand for instructors in every field was high, and the gifted were of great value. Volunteers with a servant's heart had more than their hands full.

New jobs were available to thousands in the tourist trade. Guides, senior citizens who had knowledge of their homelands, those with boats, vehicles, and every means of travel became potential for the pool of employment and development.

Dr. Jeffrey Maxwell, a scientist in the medical profession, confessed that he had changed his mind about the light from the Cube. At first, he was certain that it would be harmful to the skin, but experiments had convinced him that there were actually healing qualities in it. Skin blemishes and cancers had greatly improved and even disappeared along with numerous other diseases.

Wicked acts brought immediate shame to those who took advantage of others. Criminals learned it was much better to go to work when released from prison or jail. They found out crime did pay—and the wages weren't worth their trouble. Prison employees saw their jobs being cut back. But some inmates eligible for parole wanted to stay in. They lacked job skills to make a living and were fearful of failing. They hadn't been rehabilitated and trained for the free world. There was a need for instructors to meet this situation. One governor said, "Well, that's a worthy problem for good people and good government to solve, isn't it?"

Armed forces, police forces, and court systems came to a constant "at ease," though they were still on duty for emergencies. Courts cleared their dockets and recessed. Grand Juries had little to consider. The same thing was true about many professions. Medical doctors who had to study and train for years to gain their specialized skills didn't appreciate that suddenly their skills weren't needed. However, they discovered the discipline of study aided them in becoming proficient in other fields that were just as fulfilling. A Pentagon spokesman reported that nations seem to be beating their swords into plowshares. Peace permeated the Earth as it never had before.

Employment in various industries was changing. With raw materials available and governmental restrictions greatly removed, free enterprise was flourishing. Many union members lost interest in their mundane employment and sought fulfillment in personal hobbies and more creative fields. Union dues were falling and benefits hard to sustain. International Unions complained, writing petitions, rallying protests, and using every means they could imagine to keep things going as they had been, but many union members were indifferent. As one of them said when it was time for him to pay his dues, "I don't care what you do. I want to get in on all this abundance of food. Besides, there're plenty of people calling on me to use my skills in other fields, and life is too exciting not to get in on all the fun. I'm no longer working for benefits, money or positions." Numerous new job opportunities never before dreamed of came into existence faster than the old ones disappeared. Worldwide economic cooperation threw open doors in every category. Prices for merchandise and services reached an all-time low, but people were happy to work for less to produce products beneficial to others. No one lacked any necessity.

The AFL-CIO lobbied Congress to pass legislature assuring that their millions of members who were still working would receive on-going pay, benefits, and retirement. Other professional employee unions sought relief for their members. But the government members who studied the Constitution backed away from such involvement, stating it had no authority to interfere with free enterprise and its results unless it restricted individual freedom. Tax money and laws had nothing to with these matters. Personal initiative and planning was up to the workers. Those leaving their jobs were well able to find work elsewhere because new opportunities were opening up like never before.

Certain professions such as the Internal Revenue Service personnel were in little demand. Many liberal university professors resigned because they couldn't figure out what to teach. Their philosophies were contradicted by their own daily experience. There were lots of complaints, protests, and embarrassments. Those losing jobs grumbled, "All this 'good' is destroying our world!" The American Civil Liberties Union had entered a suit against the U.S. Government for "allowing the Cube to be positioned overhead. It's keeping people from exercising their civil rights."

A church member asked Rev. Rex Fleming why there was so much commotion in the business world. He told his congregation the shift of supply and demand had caused all occupations to evaluate their existence and justify their place living under the Rule of God. It was the best time to be alive in all the history of the world! Rex went on to say, "It reminds me of what the Lord said, 'When a man's ways please the Lord, He makes even his enemies to be at peace with him.'[73] I believe that's true with a nation as well."

Deserts blossomed like roses. Ants, mosquitoes, chiggers, and red bugs no longer posed a problem or danger. People could lay down

---

[73]   Proverbs 16:7

anywhere on Earth without pests or irritations. Even stuffy noses and hay fever had disappeared. The physical world had become a Paradise!

Animal and pet extremists wanted all animals protected from being bought, sold, or eaten since they were "creatures like us." They asked for legislation to protect animals. It was up to those who knew the Creation account to correct such foolishness reminding Americans that only humans were created in the image of God, and the instructions from God to Noah to eat meat was still in effect, unchanged by Him.

Weather stations, Doppler radar, and emergency warning systems were not needed. Pristine weather was being enjoyed everywhere! Expected weather patterns for each time of the year were non-existent. The whole world had come to a rest. No hurricanes, typhoons, tornadoes, floods, forest fires, volcanic eruptions or earthquakes had occurred in over eight months. Places on the Earth that normally saw extremes of twenty feet between high and low tides reported that the ebb and flow of the tides were mild and serving a beneficial difference. A change in the atmosphere brought a balance to the Earth's new conditions.

That wasn't good enough for some. Environmentalists claimed the ebb and flow of tides were essential for marsh lands and even protected acreage was jeopardized by the sameness of the climate. Mother earth needed something to be done to help her prevent the loss of special wet lands and national forests from the potential lack of rain and snow. But the government and majority of citizens shrugged and said it was probably best to leave the world in the hands of its true Maker.

A woman in Paris, Texas, who was fond of cactus plants, was amazed to see her collection looking so different. Instead of thorns, the plants had all produced something as soft as fox fur.

Religious cults and "isms" were still around, but less vocal since Satan, the arch-deceiver had been removed. It was easier for Christians, as well as non-believers to spot error than before. People could still choose to worship gods other than the One True Father, Son, and Holy Spirit, but they had to do so in spite of their better knowledge.

Christian churches were growing larger than they had ever been. Some were having worship, Bible studies, prayer meetings, evangelistic training, and praise sessions early and late every day. Others met around the clock. Some churches had standing room only, while still others were using sports stadiums and similar facilities where thousands of people could meet together. Great numbers of people in all nations were turning to the Lord.

American troops and agents in Colombia and other tropical countries fighting drug traffic and drug cartels were shocked to learn that extractions from cocaine plants had lost its punch. The leaves no longer contained the chemicals used to produce the white powder! Narcotics had completely disappeared. A fix, if it could be found, was cost prohibitive. Farmers were happy to grow new crops for their fields and didn't have to pay for protection from drug dealers.

The Department of Public Health declared every sort of illness had been affected. Troubled patients filled with hate, discord, belligerence, and animosity had become amazingly tranquil and were even showing love to others! It appeared that before long there wouldn't be any sickness on Earth! However, the need for doctors

> *No one living in Zion will say, "I am ill;" and the sins of those who dwell there will be forgiven.*
>
> *(Isaiah 33:24 NIV)*

and professionals was still there to treat those who had accidents and who became victims of foul-play. Casualties still happened even by out-of-control skateboard enthusiasts, and the innocent still suffered because of the careless. Psychologists, psychiatrists, and counselors were doing little business. Pharmaceutical companies lost money as drug sales were at rock bottom. Fertilizers and certain other chemicals were unnecessary because the Earth was producing at full capacity. Physicians everywhere reported miracles taking place. Terminally ill patients had improved to the point of actually disconnecting themselves from life support equipment, walking out of the hospital and dancing in the streets. Obviously, every disease had been weakened, and all immune systems were improved. Retirement centers and nursing homes saw patients recover enough to be dismissed. Some were able to live alone and others even went back to work out of desire. Better alertness in day-to-day living reduced accidents. Pregnant women were having their babies before they could reach the hospital or doctor. They kept waiting for labor pains to tell them when to go, and there were none.

Presidents, rulers, and politicians had a totally different job description. They still had the biblical assignment of protecting the people under their authority and administering justice to those who abused the law. But they found that when a nation follows the will of God, that nation experienced the peace He wanted them to have and enjoyed His blessings. He would provide for their needs, rather than having to punish them for their disobedience through taxation, threat of war, and acts of God through weather, earthquakes, and other fits of nature.

Forty-three members of Congress resigned their positions, being unable to get a grip on what they were supposed to do. They were confused and lost interest because most of the endless issues they used to handle no longer existed.

Government defense programs were reduced. The national debt was being paid off. Taxation was greatly lowered. The blessing of God made prosperity available to everyone. Congress had a new job—that of eliminating the numerous, frivolous laws that had plagued man more than they had protected him. Lawyers were only needed for serious cases.

High profile cases of murder, rape, and other atrocities were handled easily without flamboyant flair and trickery. The guilty couldn't stand to face the righteous court system and officials. They confessed their crimes or were clearly exposed. Swift judgment brought peace and relief. Death sentences were carried out quickly. There was little possibility of appeal because cases were treated with absolute justice and fairness. Life was simplified. Common sense, fairness, and justice ruled.

Headstrong, prideful politicians found no place in leadership. Foolish wrangling and lying were easy to detect and to reject. Public servants who loved God and righteousness were easily elected to all positions.

Laws were already on the books against adultery, child molestation, pornography, nudity, occult practices, or any sort of theft, violence or drugs. These matters were simply being eradicated from public view as if the law were already hunting them down. Vices continued to be practiced in hiding, but when it appeared in public, it was instantly judged and removed.

"It's hard to believe," said a widow in Sri Lanka, as she sat down in her chair on her shaded porch and commented to a visitor. "Factions that have gone on here during twenty years of civil war have come to an end. I've heard people asking for forgiveness and forgiving each other. They've finally realized they were fighting in vain."

News from Khartoum, Sudan, brought similar relief to its population. Several elements involved in the "solution" were the inability to figure out how to fight now that weapons of violence were no longer reliable. Crops were growing with such prolific results that everyone wanted to get in on the plenteous supply. The many changes in nature reduced the confusion as to where their priorities should lie. Contentment appeared to be within grasp if one would only set aside his differences and participate in such a wonderful world.

A lady preparing for bed walked toward the door—then turned back and smiled, leaving it unlocked! She was not afraid anymore. There was literally "peace on Earth."

Satan, the great deceiver and accuser had obviously been placed into the Bottomless Pit. Without his powerful deception and demonic invasion, mankind was relieved, though still sinful. His false accusations were no longer a force to contend with. Sin was still seething beneath the surface in the hearts of mankind. Individual choice was still a gift of God. But righteousness ruled from the New Jerusalem like a rod of iron. Yet, within the hearts of a number of unbelievers, there was resentment against the changes, and a secret desire to be able to plot evil and carry it out.

The heavenly City could be seen by the unaided eye by most people on Earth even in the daytime, but it was more delightful to view through a telescope. Because the Earth was revolving, and the Cube was stationary, it was only visible at certain times of the day and night. At night, all its glory seemed to unleash to the viewer. As New Jerusalem made its journey along with the Earth at evening, a new phenomenon in the Heavens could be seen. Light from the City made its way through the many precious stones, pearls and diamonds, creating the most dazzling sight ever witnessed in all creation. Non-believers, still spiritually in the dark, couldn't understand why Christians stopped and stared so long every evening as the world turned exposing its glory to that side of the Earth. It called out of them that which pleases the Lord most—worship.

The Lord looks down from heaven;
He observes everyone.
He gazes on all the inhabitants
of the earth from His dwelling place.

He alone crafts their hearts;

He considers all their works.

A king is not saved by a large army;

a warrior will not be delivered

by great strength.

The horse is a false hope for safety;

it provides no escape by its great power.

Now the eye of the Lord is on those

who fear Him—

those who depend on His faithful love

to deliver them from death

and to keep them alive in famine.[74]

God, be exalted above the heavens,

let Your glory be over the whole earth.[75]

∞

---

[74] Psalm 33:13-19 (HCSB)
[75] Psalm 57:11 (HCSB)

30

EFFECTIVE ACTIONS

The suit filed by the ACLU over the seminars taught in Washington came up and Jim had to seek counsel to represent him. It seemed impossible that during this time of unprecedented peace and safety he would have to be plagued by something like this! The case came to court and each side was given opportunity to lay out their charges and rebuttals. At the end, the judge fined the ACLU for taking the time and expense to pursue their frivolous and prejudiced claims. Their attempt to squash liberty in America was a serious mistake. All attorneys participating in the case were barred from practicing law in America and the money was given to Jim. The suits against the Space Telescope Science Association and the U.S. Government met with similar actions. Legal actions attacking freedom guaranteed by the Constitution and twisting the law that prevented justice met with powerful force. Also, prosecutors and those who testified falsely to condemn the innocent faced the treatment they tried to inflict upon the righteous.

Most of the Supreme Court Justices were removed from office.[76] They were given a simple test of their understanding of the Constitution and common sense. Most couldn't tell the difference between right and wrong; art from porn; free speech from profanity; purity from obscenity; absolutes from lies; innocence from defilement; a family from phony substitutes; or dignity from humiliation. They couldn't define liberty as used in the Constitution and were ignorant of the history of freedom in America. They couldn't define any unalienable rights. They were unquestionably unqualified for the highest office of justice in the United States.

Other law suits throughout the country caught the attention of the multitudes and legal authorities. A man was tried and found guilty for auto theft and fined. He was responsible for paying for all damages to the vehicle. The attorney for the thief stated that the car was insured. But the judge said, "Why should anyone be able to wreck a car and damage other property and only serve time in jail? He must learn the value of property." If property was stolen and then sold or lost, the

---

[76] The U.S. Constitution clearly states that all judges are answerable to the people and may be impeached—including federal judges and Supreme Court Judges. Being appointed for life doesn't remove them from accountability. The Constitution defines the causes: treason, bribery, or other high crimes and misdemeanors.—Article II, Section 4, ¶ 1. The House of Representatives … shall have the sole power of impeachment.—Article I, Section 2, ¶ 5. The Senate shall have the sole power to try all impeachments. Art. I Sec. 3, ¶ 6-7. To date, Sixty-one federal judges or Supreme Court Justices have been investigated for impeachment, of which thirteen were impeached, plus three others impeached for non-judicial causes. The process is initiated when *the people* believe a judge behaves in a manner that disqualifies him from further public service and they put pressure upon the House of Representatives to pursue the cause. The people's superior power "is put into operation to protect their rights and to rescue their liberties from violation."—Justice Joseph Story, Founder of Harvard Law School, called the "foremost of American legal writers," and nominated to the Supreme Court my President James Madison.

thief was accountable to restore the value of the property or do work equivalent to it. Having to pay for things stolen quickly became a panic to thieves. One of them faced his frustration by saying, "Well then, I'm not going to steal anything again." What an interesting statement! Another principle levied upon mischief was that what people attempted to do against others was done to them.[77] The intent to deprive someone else of something of value was to lose that value themselves.

A judge said explained, "We don't want people in jail. We want them working for their living and making their own way. With the world full of freedom and opportunities, anyone who wants to work, can. Criminals will be given work if they don't have a job. They'll be penalized and they'll pay back what they have stolen or destroyed." Courts enforced the law that removed licenses from dishonest lawyers who practiced deceitful tactics favorable to criminals nullifying justice. Judges who accepted bribes were fined and barred from the practice of law. America was enforcing the Constitution, preserving the liberty of the people whose government belonged to them.[78]

With new elected officers in Washington D.C., the government got out of the business of education. Schools became a matter of free enterprise and were to compete with others through motivated parents

---

[77] Deuteronomy 19:16-20

[78] "We the People," found not only in the opening line and preamble of the federal Constitution, but in almost all early State Constitutions, made clear that "[T]he fundamental principle of our Constitution ...enjoins [requires] that the will of the majority shall prevail.—George Washington. Judges who set aside election results are subject to impeachment. Examples are numerous today: One judge ordered a tax increase after the people had voted it down; the will of the people through legislation expressed their will concerning the American Flag. But a court ruled that the American flag could not in **any** circumstance—be protected from desecration. Judges have overruled the will of the people who voted on the definition of marriage being between one man and one woman. The vast majority of Americans believe that life begins at conception and abortion is wrong. Yet the Supreme Court decision still stands after over fifty million abortions.

and citizens. Education was basically intended to meet practical needs. Every school immediately had to determine the best basis of its foundation for their curriculum. Many turned quickly to the Bible as the early schools in America had done. Others took the liberal "we know best" trail. Within a year it was evident that Christian educated students were far superior in knowledge and people skills.

The government got out of the welfare business. Their efforts were sputtering from lack of backing and dismal failure. Congress found it was unconstitutional. When unusual cases occurred and need existed, it was handled by to citizens, churches, and volunteer organizations who were face to face with the unfortunate and who provided hands-on help to restore them to productive dignity. Otherwise, there were no handicapped or poor, for God had restored all people with a one-time healing.

                              *   *   *

Jim received a call from George Riddle thanking him for leading him to Christ. His health had improved and even amazed the doctors. Dark spots on his lungs had totally disappeared and his cough and chest pain were gone. He was breathing better than he could even remember, and he gave praise to God for it all.

Jim rejoiced with him, pointing out that with the New Jerusalem in place wonderful things were happening everywhere, and anything good was possible. He shared with George about Scott's healing. He was walking normal for the first time in fourteen years. He'd be talking perfectly as soon as his vocabulary and inflection caught up with his ability to enunciate. Down syndrome had been completely removed. Jim and George celebrated the fact that their families were well and prosperous. They were all growing in knowledge and understanding of the Lord daily, and living the Christian life was exciting and fun!

When Jim arrived home one evening, Laura turned with a smile, tilted her head back a little, and said, "There is a surprise on the way."

"A surprise huh? What sort of surprise?" He gave her a hug and kiss. "And 'on the way' when . . . in the mail or on the way from your parents, or . . . ?"

Laura took him by the hand and said, "Relax and drink your iced tea while I tell you about it."

Jim obediently did as she said, tried to act relaxed, and looked up into her beautiful face. Smiling, Laura sat next to him and said, "Cousin Zeke is on the way and will be here in a few minutes."

"On the way? You mean driving himself, or someone's bringing him?" Jim said jokingly.

"He's driving himself," she confidently stated.

Jim was so shocked his jaw dropped, his face lit up, pushing away his unbelief of her statement. Suddenly it all sank in. The healing presence of the New Jerusalem had "fixed" the slowness of Zeke's mind. He'd already conquered the art of driving and evidently even had a driver's license!

"Now that really is a surprise, Honey! What do you know about that! God's been busy all over the world, but he hasn't forgotten the folks back home." They both embraced and danced around the room.

Laura and Jim commented on other blessings they had received and marveled in the newness of the entire world. "God is so good!" they agreed.

Soon Zeke arrived and wanted to show off his newly acquired automobile. He was wearing a different outfit—dress pants and an ironed, long sleeved shirt. His hair had grown longer and was combed, parted, and classy. Of course, his smile was bigger than ever because of the excitement of breaking this surprise to Jim and Laura. "Come look at it Jim."

It was a six year old shiny black Ford that had obviously been fixed up or someone had taken mighty good care of it since it was new. "It looks great, Zeke! I like it." Then Jim sort of frowned and bent his head to the side saying, "Now, you've been keeping something from me for many months, haven't you? You got this car, learned to drive, and probably have your license, haven't you?"

Zeke couldn't hold in the laughter. "Yep. I knowed you wouldn't a' believed it 'less I drived over here and showed it to you," Zeke happily announced.

Jim was seriously thrilled and full of laughter too, and agreed, "I couldn't be any prouder of you, Zeke," Jim responded. "Now tell me what else you have been up to. I have a hunch that you have some other things on your mind too."

Zeke looked up with that sly smile on his face, "Yep," he said. "I wanna go to school. You know I didn't get much learnin' before. But now I hear they have a GED program fer fellers like me, and they can make you learn all them years 'ya missed before."

"Yes, Zeke, that's right," said Jim as he took Zeke by the arm and led him to a soft chair in the living room. "You can start right where you are, pick up at your own pace, and take your time at it. You can get a diploma showing that you've learned everything that a regular graduate from high school has learned. That's a great idea, Zeke. I hope you'll do that. You obviously have a desire for education, and that's the main thing."

"Yep, I do, Jim. I've learnt more thangs in the past few months than I ever thought I would. And Jim, when I get thu' with all 'lat, I wanna know more 'bout them stars you scientists know 'bout."

Jim was blown away at Zeke's desire and goals. They spent the evening discussing the future and how Jim could help along the way. After Zeke left, all Jim could do was shake his head in astonishment. God's power and love truly were amazing.

Eleven months had gone by since the Cube stopped its descent and began to travel alongside the Earth. Jim and Laura were enjoying a relaxing evening in their backyard with their sweetened tea, looking at the self-starting fruit trees in the field, and all the changes that were on their minds. The evening sun was relinquishing the last of its light, leaving the shadows to grow together. Peace permeated the homesite like no one had ever known since Adam was shut out of Eden.

"It's hard to believe isn't it honey," Jim spoke slowly, as he looked around the acreage behind the house and then took a seat in the outside lounge chair, "There isn't a single thing that God's overlooked: government, nature, health, politics, education, occupations, human needs . . ."

". . . I know . . . and it's all personalized," Laura interjected, taking her place next to him on the patio. "Right down to our own little Scottie! I almost cry just thinking about it."

"Ten months ago I was facing the 'firing squad' at Quad U, a close encounter with STSA, didn't even know Dr. Fleming. and the Cubicles group didn't exist. Never in my wildest dreams, did I think the President of the United States would call me to come give him advice. I never thought I would be teaching classes in another university down the street from us, and I didn't know much about how Christianity related to our government and our founding documents. I never conceived that I would be teaching other nations about how to govern in a way that pleases God. I didn't know that God's earthly related Throne was in the North, and the New Jerusalem was a faint recollection in my mind from somewhere in Revelation. Whew! I'm almost tired just thinking about it all."

"It's hard to believe that it happened so fast," she said, reaching for her glass of tea. "But it didn't seem fast at the time, did it sweetheart?" she said.

"It sure didn't. It was agonizingly slow," Jim said shaking his head. "It was a pressure cooker! But God was right there all along, wasn't He?"

"We know He was," Laura turned facing her husband with a loving smile.

"You know, Laura, I've been seriously thinking about my life before I got saved. Though I claimed I was an atheist, I always thought that someday I'd take the time to study the Bible and consider the reality of God. But you know what? It's likely that I never would've done so! It took that revival at the church to reach my heart and expose my soul to the choice of faith. And even then, I fought it for several weeks! Otherwise, I believe I would've gone on with my full schedule of activities and stayed lost all these years! So I never would've had the privilege of going through the 'fire' at Quad U and learning the power and ability of God to bring me assurance in times of strain. I would've missed the joy of being at least a little persecuted for my faith. I would've missed out on the Cube event entirely except from the position of an unbeliever! Imagine me taking my place along with other skeptics and blind scientists against the New Jerusalem—the very presence of God! And worst of all, I would've missed immortal happiness and would've been eternally condemned by my own procrastination and self-centered interests."

"Oh, sweetheart, that's scary. But it's quite a description of God's intervention in your life for His glory isn't it?"

"You bet it is! And the pain, torment, agony and bewilderment aren't worthy to compare with the personal involvement of Jesus in my life."

"Of course, I was always the 'believer,' but didn't truly have Christ in my life either. I'm so glad we were saved at the same time. It gave us a new start at the same place." After a long pause, Laura continued, "Where do we go from here, honey? I wonder what's out there in the future."

"I'm afraid to venture a guess. A life of obedience, that's for sure. Whatever He wants for us is what we want too. My daily existence has been so blurred, I haven't had time to express what's on my mind, and I know yours has been, too, sweetheart. In fact, it's amazing that we are sitting here having a casual, restful, loving evening together. How'd that work out?"

"Well, someone planned it. It didn't just happen. Someone knew we needed it."

"And that someone was you, you sweet little angel."

"You bet. And we're going to enjoy it, unhurriedly, for as long as we want," she said turning to him with a big smile.

"I'll say amen to that!" Jim said. "And another thing, you know what's been on my mind is how long will the New Jerusalem stay here? I've been too busy enjoying the changes to give it any meditation, but now, I wonder if we can know."

"Well, what do you think?" said Laura.

"I don't think we can know. We didn't even know it was coming. We know it can't stay here forever, 'cause it has to come again after the millennium—when it will be forever present."

"Would God want us to know?" Laura wondered.

"That's just it. He wouldn't. The unknown is better for mankind. There're plenty of numbers in the Bible that are significant—one, three, seven, twelve, forty, and so on. But I'm sure there's no way we can know. And then we have to think of what life would be like if the Cube leaves during our lifetime."

"Wow, that's frightening! I can just imagine—no, I don't even want to imagine what the world would be like."

"Actually, we need to make plans for that possibility—but not now! I'm not ready for that. Later on, we can give that some attention." Jim gave a big sigh of relief, shaking his head.

"I agree," Laura said.

"Meanwhile . . . ," Jim said reaching out to Laura and looking at her in the face, "while we are living in a literal paradise, all the bills are paid, there's food in the kitchen, the children are spending the night at their grandparents . . ."

"Let's have a party!!" they both said together.

∞

31

APPLICATION

After a good day's work, Jim came into Keith's room to say, "Hi." Scott was also in the room. They began talking about the things that had changed over the past few months and how they were doing in school. Jim sat on the edge of the bed while Keith was seated at his computer chair. Scott was looking through picture albums at himself before he was healed. He was astounded at what he didn't know during those years. The room was accented with a football on the desk, walls with sporting events and achievements awarded to Keith.

Keith looked at his dad and said, "One of the guys in school criticized the government for allowing manger scenes and Christmas trees on property owned by the government. He said it was being prejudice against other religions. What about that, Dad? I told him I was a Christian and didn't have any prejudice against other religions. But I didn't know what else to say."

"Well, Keith, I think everyone in the world is prejudiced in some ways, we just don't see it in ourselves. But this is a very important matter to understand," as he shifted his weight on the bed. Scott turned and gave full attention to his dad. "Let's see if I can explain it by reviewing a few facts about America. You know that this country was based upon Christian teachings, right?"

"Sure. That's evident everywhere in our history," Keith said.

"Our Founding Fathers were familiar with every kind of government and modeled ours from the best, using the Word of God as their main source," Jim said.

"Freedom to practice religion in America is one of the fundamental guarantees of our Constitution. We want all people to believe in Jesus and go to Heaven. But they are free to not believe and to even oppose that belief if they want to—in a peaceful way."

"Yeah."

"Something like eighty-five percent of Americans profess to believe in God—that's the God who created the world and redeemed us from sin through Christ's death on the Cross. They may not be able to explain in detail what they believe, but they've been exposed to what's called the Judeo-Christian, or Jewish-Christian, morality of the Bible. Christianity was overwhelmingly the dominate religion of early America, and it was declared to be a Christian nation. The Founding Fathers believed it was, said it was, wrote that it was, and intended for it to remain a Christian nation. And the people gladly accepted it as such. Without that basis of morality and the superior laws of our Republic, America would've soon become warped, weak as any other country, and even extinct. In fact, we've fallen far short of the strength of our beginnings."

"I know that's true!"

"Our Founders also looked into the future and saw what might happen if the following generations failed to remember and pass on the truth of Christianity and its essential influence in the security and continuance of this nation."

"What did they do?" Scott asked.

"Let's see if you guys can answer that question yourself." Jim could see that he needed to have a talk with his sons that every family should have. His father didn't have that talk with him, and he wondered how few in the entire country had! What an opportunity this was. He would try to think it through carefully with them. He continued, "Think about it. Why do you suppose there's so much opposition to Christian religious monuments, crosses, Christmas displays, the Ten Commandments, the Pledge of Allegiance with the phrase, 'under God,' and so on?"

"I don't know. People say it is prejudice against them," said Keith.

"Keith, always remember that clashes, arguments, resentments, fights, wars, violence, and so on are really more spiritual than physical or just differences of opinions.[79] Our wise Founding Fathers knew there was a need to keep the truth before the general public for their own future's sake. So they searched the Scripture for ways to keep America from doing what the Israelites did. Israel forgot their glorious deliverance from slavery and began conforming to other religions and governments! So these men did something similar to what God told the Israelites to do."

"What was that, Dad?" asked Scott.

"God told them first to put his commandments into their hearts, impress them upon their children, talk about them when they sat around at home and when they walked along together. He even told them to tie reminders of them around their hands and wear them on their foreheads and write them on the door-frames of their homes and upon their gates.[80] Pretty far out huh?"

"Yeah," they both chimed.

---

[79] Ephesians 6:12
[80] Deuteronomy 6:4-9

"In other words," Jim went on, "people are so prone to forget the most important things in life that they needed a blatant reminder of the truth. Can you imagine how it would be to take the Lord's Name in vain while wearing a commandment not to do so on their forehead?"

Keith and Scott both laughed at the very idea.

". . . Or to steal something while having a 'thou shalt not steal' written in a box and wrapped around the hand that stole?"

Surprised laughter followed again.

"Well, that's the purpose of the reminders that our Founders put into place throughout our society. They inscribed the Ten Commandments on the doors of the Supreme Court and put them on the walls inside the Court. They instituted the practice of each government official taking an oath of office swearing with their hand on the Bible to uphold the Constitution. They later printed 'In God We Trust' on our money to help prevent covetousness. They erected monuments all around the country with reminders printed upon them from the Word of God. So, who is it that works so hard to have these things removed and hidden from view?"

"The devil and his followers," said Keith.

"You're correct. In the past seventy-five years or so, people have removed the Ten Commandments from court houses and city—owned property. They've tried their best to have 'In God We Trust' removed from our money and 'under God' from our Pledge of Allegiance. They're even cases where our founding documents have been kept out of public classrooms—afraid that students might notice the words like "Laws of Nature and of Nature's God," "Created equal . . . endowed by their Creator," "Divine Providence," and other references to the Lord. Students might realize the liberties they have were given by the true God—not the government. It's too bad that so many common people in America don't know that Almighty God, Christianity, and the Bible had everything to do with the outstanding freedoms we've enjoyed for the past about two hundred thirty-six years! Some serious efforts have been taken to keep these things from public attention while speaking out against Christianity. Why would they want to do that?"

"Because they do not know God or his Son Jesus Christ," Keith responded.

"Beautiful, Keith! You're exactly right. They resent His Holy Presence and constraint upon their fleshly appetites. They want freedom to do whatever they please without the godly responsibility that comes with it. They mistakenly think that a person can be good, or 'godly' without God! They'd siphon off every form of the basis of our liberty so that the people would forget where they came from and why they're in such trouble. Then the enemies of the Lord would present their propositions with the usual yokes of a new 'deliverer'—like socialism, Communism, or evolution, and make slaves of the people again. Just as the Israelites did—wanting to be like other nations when they already had the best nation with God as their King!"

"So Christmas scenes and things like that are important as reminders of our heritage?" Keith perceived.

"I can understand that, Dad," said Scott.

"Yes. But be aware of where the 'rub' comes in. Our Christian heritage belongs to all Americans, not just to Christians in America. Not all Israelites were 'saved' either. But they all enjoyed what God provided the nation. Failure to educate all new Americans, who are born here or immigrate here about their heritage, has created a cancer of ignorance. Critics of Christianity attack the very heritage that belongs to them. They can't appreciate what they don't know. Some are evidently envious of the spirit of joy and celebration we have in Christ. They want to have the same thing. So instead of understanding their own heritage as Americans and appreciating the liberty that Christianity has supplied to them, they compete with Christianity through their different religions or biased opinions by trying to remove these remembrances and replace them, or include their own in that heritage!"

"Yeah, I've seen and heard of others wanting to put their religious displays next to ours. I guess they feel slighted if they can't," Keith said.

"Yes, they do, Keith. Because they haven't been educated about *their own American* heritage! Now, why isn't every American taught the truth about America's history so that everyone would be proud to recognize the providential events, persons, and benefits that came about and which have been preserved for everyone to enjoy? Even if they had another religion, they could still give recognition to what God did by those who believed in and fought for liberty so much that they were willing to die to provide it for all.

"The United States was the first country to recognize individual rights and produce a place where all races and religions could live in harmony. Everyone has the freedom to pursue happiness and his own personal interests. That's how it's possible for so many to become wealthy. The freedom that comes with American citizenship provides individuals the opportunity to make discoveries, cure diseases, invent technology, TVs, produce more and better food, and thousands of other desirable, helpful things. It also builds character when they have to work hard to overcome obstacles and opposition. We have the freedom to *think* for ourselves! All these unique privileges are the result of our relationship with God.

"Special days like Christmas and Easter can be celebrated with all other Americans for this reason. Using government property to do it is no different than having God's name on our money and in our founding documents. It only demonstrates the truth of His Providence to us."

"Don't we teach Americans and immigrants about our heritage?" Scott asked.

"Yes, but it's not being put into practice. You've had studies in school about the Constitution, but you are weak in its application because you're inexperienced. The more the population grows, the more time people tend to put into learning a vocation, and less time concentrating upon these finer details. They assume the previous generations are managing the balance of power for them. But the flaw of Americans is the same one that the Israelites had after the Lord gave them the Promised Land. They were too busy enjoying their freedoms, and didn't keep a jealous eye on instructing each generation and enforcing the Law. They turned away from Him and began to copy-cat other beliefs, philosophies, and traditions. After all, Satan was waiting for them to let down their defenses.

"It's difficult for new Americans to appreciate and defend our history if they don't know it. People still come to America because they want what we have. But they don't know where it came from and why we have it. Some immigrants and American born citizens fail to realize the powerful dynamic that brought about the liberty that's freely offered to them, but they must, if they want that liberty to last. Infusing other religious teachings and cultures into Christian holidays is to disregard their significance. America is solidly permeated with the God of the Bible and those who trusted Him for the liberty we enjoy. It's easy to see that if some other religion is mixed with Christianity or supplants it, that liberty would soon erode away. We've already lost much of it by compromising with opinions, objections and false assertions. After all, why don't other countries where other religions are dominant, have this liberty we enjoy where other religions are dominant? It's because it's impossible if they don't know and reverence the true and living God."

"Yeah, they're in poverty and hurting because the government's stealing the money, isn't it?" Keith interjected.

"Exactly right. And by the way, the same theft is happening by our elected officials because of the same negligence and rejection of their heritage. Their oaths of office are meaningless to them. For people of other religions to expect equal recognition and respect is understandable. But America's religious holidays are mostly and signally Christian. Christianity is the reason why everyone can freely practice what they believe without persecution. It can't be supplanted by any other. All other religions bring potential trappings of fear, despotism, and slavery—physically or spiritually. We even had to deal with the slavery issue, and had the knowledge of the New Testament to rid ourselves of it."

"What about holidays?" Keith asked. "What should they do during those days?"

"There is plenty of room for other religions to celebrate *their* holidays as long as we enforce our Constitution, but they must not be mingled with the truth and heritage that became theirs when they became Americans. It's absolutely fine for all religions to celebrate special holidays if they chose to. But it was not the events they celebrate that brought about the freedoms they enjoy here in America. If people of other religions want their employers to give special holidays for their beliefs, the employers could consider that in exchange for the Christian ones. No one should be forced to worship on a Christian holiday. But each employer will have to determine what's best for his particular business. You see, many of our holidays have their origin in Christianity and its contribution to America's lifestyle. Labor Day is another example of appreciation and recognition of the common working man. Give him another day off! That's the Christian motive. Even Sunday is specifically the Christian's day of worship. What a heritage *all* Americans have! It must be understood, appreciated, and recognized before differing religious views can take their place in the free society Christianity has provided. The Jewish day of worship is Saturday, the Sabbath, but they've been able to assimilate their practices into American society and the work schedules."

"I can understand that," Keith said.

"Me too," said Scott.

"It's the presence of the Cube that has brought about the reality of where we began. Thank God He did it. Otherwise, we'd still be running away from Him and freedom. You can see the necessity of honest and accurate education. When someone is born in or immigrates to this country, they should pledge their allegiance to America and to its Republic—the rule of law. And by doing so, they'll claim the heritage that's common to us all. Then they wouldn't try to remove it, or push it aside, or bring other customs into it. They would appreciate it and celebrate it with us. It's foolish to allow the basic truths of our Constitution to be treated as merely equal to other religious beliefs or laws. The eventual outcome of that intention would be the institution of unequal laws based upon another religion. Imagine the impossibility of mingling many religions together! It would be a colossal failure. It's already been tried and has failed many times throughout the world. This isn't a matter of prejudice, but a sacred commitment to truth that's offered free to all people. The past two centuries prove that what takes place here in America, effects the entire world."

"I guess it can get pretty complicated, huh dad?" said Keith.

"Actually it's very basic and simple. America exists because of Christianity. Therefore let's celebrate Christ. To get involved deeper than that will require information and examples in our history. It's not a matter of arguments or opinions. There are many religions and denominations, beliefs, and isms. But there is only one Savior!"

"Right!" said Keith and Scott.

"And anyone in public office who doesn't understand this plain truth is unqualified to properly serve the people who elected them."

"Boy! That's a truth that needs to be publicized!" Keith said.

"It sounds like there's a fight going on, Dad. What can we do about it?" asked Scott.

"Yes, Scott. Those who deny and try to destroy these truths stand at the foundation of this country with sledge hammers and wrecking balls trying to tear down what George Washington called 'the experiment of Freedom' that has blessed the whole world. They want to substitute their own self-serving systems which always include chains for every citizen. So we must walk with God in this real spiritual warfare, knowing that He is ultimately in control. We do our best trusting Him for victory. And either way we're on the winning side."

Then, looking over at Keith's desk, Jim asked, "What's that on your computer?"

"Oh, just a drawing."

"What? Looks like a Cube . . . and the Earth."

"Yeah, I guess an 'Earth-Cube.'"

"Well, now, . . . how 'bout let's call it a . . . Cube-o-sphere!"

Keith laughed, "I like that. It sounds more space-like. I'm putting it together for Grandma Waltham for Christmas. She seems to have a problem perceiving where it is in space. So I want to get the Cube about the right distance, size, and position next to Earth."

"Yep, right next to where earthly Jerusalem passes! Great idea, Keith. But how'd you do such a beautiful job on the computer?"

"I used a graphics program I've been learning in school."

"It's excellent! I'm proud of you. You've got a creative talent."

"Thanks, Dad. It's surprising to me about how the Earth compares with the New Jerusalem. I used to think of the New Jerusalem as being sort of flat, but when I take in the fact of its height—wow, it's huge. "

"Yes, the Earth is only a little over five times the size of the Cube, Jim said. "It has a special shape, doesn't it? And the startling description with many mansions[81] cause us to think of it being even larger, but, remember God said, Heaven is my throne and the Earth my footstool.[82] And also God will create a new Heaven and a new Earth. Today's space actually appears to be confused, chaotic, and dangerous. But in the recreation it will be totally practical and habitable for our pleasure. And the Earth will have a different terrain—probably rolling hills—and there'll be no more sea—three times the land area we have now. And there'll be no more night! It'll be perfect for an everlasting habitation and all the saints will inherit everything God ever made!"

"Yep. Everything God created is magnificent, microscopically perfect, and detailed," Keith said.

"Yes. And as for the size of the Cube, just think of the Tabernacle of Moses and Solomon's Temple. They were very small compared to the millions of Israelites and the City of Jerusalem. But what were they? The physical manifestation of the presence of God among his people. And that's exactly what the New Jerusalem is."

"Man! There's a lot to understand, huh, Dad?" said Scott.

Laughing, Jim replied, "You think so huh? Well, just add this to your 'thinking cap.' The New Jerusalem is both physical and spiritual. Just as Jesus' resurrection body was physical—He ate fish and honey, and it was spiritual—He walked through walls."

"I just can't wait to get there!" Keith said.

"Me too," Scott agreed.

---

[81] John 14:2
[82] Isaiah 66:1; Matthew 5:34-35; Acts 7:48-49

*   *   *

"How could there be a more blessed Christmas than this?" Laura said to her extended family and friends after their sumptuous meal, as they sat around the table, still piled with more food than anyone could eat. They were rising to move into the living room, as Laura continued, "There's truly peace on Earth, just as the angels announced at the birth of Christ."

"The Christmas tree is the biggest and the best we've ever had," chimed Keith.

"Yes, and as a matter of fact," said Jim, "there's even peace in Jerusalem and the nations surrounding Israel, and that's an astounding miracle!"

"Who'd ever thought these things could happen?" Jim's father inquired. "This Cube's made a believer out of me! There's simply no other explanation for such radical benefits around the entire world."

Laura stood, smiling at all the guests and announced, "Before our neighbor, Bev Bradley, begins playing the piano and we all sing Christmas carols, her husband, Andrew, is going to let us hear the new song he's written for this first Christmas-with-the-Cube celebration."

∞

32

THE PLAN OF GOD

Jim discovered people recognized him wherever he went, and some wanted to enroll in his classes even without receiving university credit, just to hear him. They were thirsting and hungering for the atmosphere of freedom where truth and error could be discussed in an agreeable setting.

On a special day, Jim had invited his pastor, Dr. Samuel Stone, to visit his class at the new Southwest Astronomy University and answer some theological questions students had about the Cube's visit. The atmosphere was one of relaxed fellowship. Religious themes and biblical insights were common and welcomed in this academic setting. While they enjoyed snacks and drinks, Dr. Stone took the opportunity to share with them some breaking news. Snow had been melting all over the North and South Poles and the high mountains.

"That includes the mountains of Ararat where Noah's Ark has finally been exposed," he announced. Every student quickly became interested in the find, since numerous expeditions had been made in pursuit of the famous Ark. "It's been examined from one end to the other," he continued. "It was broken in two pieces, one part sliding down the mountain a little way. But the long freezing temperature had preserved the remains of some food, and the dung at the bottom of the Ark! So, apparently God's releasing some things He's had stored up until now to be examined by the world, showing them the veracity of His infallible Word."

The class broke out into applause and shouts of glory to God.

After things settled down again, a student stood and addressed a matter that had been on his mind for many months.

"Since God can do all this and give us such an almost perfect society," asked the student, "why did He wait so long to do it? He's allowed mankind to be enemies of each other all these years."

Jim passed this question on, "Dr. Stone, would you answer this one please?"

"Good question. Let's recall how He began the world," said Stone. He gave Adam and Eve a perfect world—no death, no fierce animals, ideal weather, and governed by their loving God who visited them every evening at the cool of the day. And what did they do?"

"They believed the devil's lie and sinned," answered another student.

"Correct. Then, He was so kind as to allow them and their descendants the 'freedom' to demonstrate their love of personal liberty without giving them *any rules or laws* to get in their way. They could enjoy life and 'give it their best shot,' so to speak. Of course, they still sinned in the eyes of God, but they couldn't break any laws that didn't exist. And where there is no law, there is no transgression of the law.[83] And how well did they do?"

---

[83]   Romans 4:14-15

"They became so wicked and violent that God had to destroy the entire world by the Flood, saving only righteous Noah and his family," was the answer by another student.

"Yes. And death, the consequence of sin, has been in effect from Adam 'till now. And Noah's three sons and their wives moved out into the world, scattering widely, losing touch with their patriarch father, and failing to practice the truths they had received from Adam, Seth, Enoch, Methuselah, and Noah, giving no respect to their heritage and becoming ungodly.

"So God began with righteous Abraham, and offered Israel, his descendants, the rare opportunity to have that near perfect society again by giving them the Mosaic Law. He said, 'If you will keep my laws, I'll be your King. I'll bless you in every way—with long and peaceful lives, no diseases, no enemies threatening your borders, abundant livelihoods, numerous children, and other nations will learn of me through you. But if you don't keep My laws, I'll punish you for your ungratefulness. I'll send pestilence, withhold the rain, bring enemies into your territory to kill you and enslave you. I'll put fear in your hearts in place of peace.'[84] And what did they do?"

"They turned away and wanted to be like other lawless, godless, idolatrous nations!" was the answer summarized by several students.

"Yes. So it wasn't that God didn't want the world to experience the 'good life.' He tried to give it to them repeatedly. Why did he send his Son, Jesus? Of course, to die on the Cross for our sins, but what else? Jesus demonstrated the kind of world God wanted for humanity. He went about doing good, healing the sick, raising the dead, casting out demons, teaching them wisdom, kindness, and love like they'd never heard or seen before. And what was their response?"

---

[84] Deuteronomy 11:13-31

Someone spoke out from the back of the room, "We don't want this man to be our Messiah. Crucify him!"

"Exactly. They turned down Jesus and the Kingdom of God which He offered them. And now, after two thousand years, God has done it again. Not by sending a prophet, not by legislating laws, not by picking out only one individual or one nation to bless, but by bringing in the utopia the whole world has longed for. He did it in an unthinkable fashion, so unique that some still don't even believe it's real. And we're literally experiencing the blessedness of Eden's paradise upon the whole Earth right now. With the spectacular New Jerusalem, He has demonstrated His power to bring about world-wide peace and safety that all the nations together couldn't begin to even conceive of. And what are we doing about it? Those who refuse His Lordship simply enjoy the material blessings and die without Him. Those who choose to love Him enter the Kingdom and appreciate his magnanimous grace, giving Him the glory.

"I hope this answers your question as to why has God waited so long to bless the world. His Word tells us that He's been offering the world something better all along. Sin and Satan have blinded the minds of those who believe not, and they simply cannot see, just as they can't see the New Jerusalem because of their disbelief."

After a pause, the original questioner asked, "I guess my next question is, 'What will the world do this time?'"

"I think you know," Stone replied. "Like always, most of the world will reject, mock and miss eternal life, focusing upon the cares of this life, the deceitfulness of riches, and the excessive desires of their hearts,[85] while the fullness of God's blessings here and forever is available only to

---

[85]   Mark 4:19

those who believe in Him. And theirs is an eternity of perfection beyond our capacity to conceive."

"What an answer!" said a Cubicle.

"That was superb," added another.

"I feel so happy and unworthy," agreed a student.

Jim asked if others had questions or things to share with the class.

Another student voiced his determination to raise his children to be champions in Christ. The reality of the Lord was fresh on his mind every day and made them look forward to the time when everyone would be out of these bodies and into their new ones and be completely unable to sin. What a wonderful future God must have in store for them that would last forever!

A visitor to the class that day had another question. He was a middle aged man who admired Jim's work and had attended a few

> *Whoever comes to Me I will never cast out.*
>
> *(John 6:37)*

classes to get the feel of how this astronomer taught—especially the Word of God. He asked, "How can God bring all these wonderful changes in the world and still most of the world still hasn't been saved? It looks like they would all run to Him, accept Him and worship Him."

Dr. Stone smiled, held up his hand before him and looked up, as he was so used to doing, and said, "It's always a mystery to some that people keep on resisting, fighting God, and even persecuting those who love God when they can't find anything against Him. The automatic opposition to Him simply points out the truth of the enmity of the human flesh nature. Everyone still needs the Gospel to change lives and attitudes.

"During this time of the Cube's visitation, the saints are learning that the unseen sovereignty of God still controls national leaders and turns the hearts of kings like water turns on the banks of rivers."[86] He moved his arm back and forth like a river bending on its run.

"God causes peace to come to the Earth by His sovereign holy influence like a magnetic pull, like the wind blowing back evil, and a spiritual restraint for His own purposes. But when He does these great things, it doesn't overly persuade a man to choose Christ as his Lord. It merely presents an opportunity. Think of all the miracles Jesus worked and even the religious leaders still rejected Him. But this power is evident today just as it was in days of old when 'the terror of God fell upon the cities around Jacob, because he thought he might be destroyed by them.[87] His sons had wiped out the city of Shechem for the rape of their sister, and Jacob was afraid of repercussions. Also, the 'fear of Isaac' kept Jacob safe from the vengeance of his uncle Laban when he discovered his homemade gods had been stolen and he falsely accused Jacob.[88] This same power kept the Nation of Israel safe when all the men were called to Jerusalem to observe the three feasts of Passover, Pentecost, and Tabernacles. That would've been a perfect time for their enemies to attack their cities. But God said, '. . . Neither will any man desire your land, when you shall go up to appear before the Lord your God three times in the year.'[89]

"And He does it without negating the liberty of volition or forcing a choice in any individual. Choice is still God's very special gift to all persons. He doesn't interfere with it. He delights in those who make decisions that are right and to His glory. It's worth everything for someone to deliberately trust Him and return His love through obedience. Even when He hardened Pharaoh's heart—it wasn't to *prevent* him from

---

[86]   Proverbs 21:1
[87]   Genesis 35:5
[88]   Genesis 31:42
[89]   Exodus 34:24

choosing Israel's God for his own, or to stop him from letting Israel go. But by twisting and squeezing out the hardness that was already there, God could use it to demonstrate His greatness and glory over the false gods of Egypt. God's sovereign foreknowledge enabled Him to bring about what He wanted to happen without overriding human will. He literally made the wrath of man to bring about praise to Him, as we see again in the Cross of Christ.[90]

"You'll find that hostilities will always be around even when good and mighty things take place that common sense wouldn't deny. People will especially express their enmity toward those in authority who follow the Lord's will, from a president to the simplest local believer. The thirst for power on the part of God's enemies turns them against the godly. They want to have dominion over the Earth, but not while being in submission to the God that gives that dominion. Sinful man can't have it. God took it away from Adam the day he disobeyed him. But men today still strive against God and one other to be in charge. That's what ruined Lucifer and the same attitude persists toward the Church and even the Cube. Not even today's near perfect environment can solve that problem. Only the Gospel of Christ can change hearts."[91]

At the end of the class time, Jim gave thanks for the time of sharing together and the sacred privilege of being alive in the present time. The Lord was giving everyone in the world a long occasion to rejoice. He was showing them the kind of world and life he wanted them to have. It offered them an incentive to believe. "And remember judgment is coming, too," he said. "Isn't God wonderful to give us a taste of the future? Let's not take it for granted, but give it to others so they can walk in the same light we have!"

---

[90] Psalm 76:10
[91] Ephesians 4:18

Jim's family lingered in the den before going to bed one evening to discuss the conditions of the world since the Cube had come. Keith wondered if people in other countries long ago wished they could live in times like these. Jim assured him that they did.

"Without doubt even before the Flood, people wondered what it must've been like in the Garden of Eden. Haven't you?"

"Yeah, I try to imagine Adam and Eve sleeping on the ground with all those animals around," Keith said. "I wonder if they built a little place under a shade tree or something."

"I don't think so," Jim replied with a smile. "You see, they didn't know any danger or ever conceive of any problem. They could simply lay down anywhere and sleep. There were no hot or cold nights, the wind didn't blow against them, and it never rained."

"Wow," said Scott. "I'd like to be there."

"You're too late, Scott. They blew it, so God has planned something even better for us!" Jim stated. "The conditions we enjoy today are similar to what it will be like someday, only it'll be so much better it's hard to compare! But at least in the Millennium, there will be most of the same conditions we have now.

"Then after the Flood, the only people on Earth were Noah and his family of eight. And the world wasn't much to look at! Remember it had all been underwater for over a year! It must've looked wrecked and bent, destroyed and dried out like a desert. Nothing looked familiar. They must have desired a more beautiful place to live."

"Yeow, I didn't think of that," said Keith. "And the only animals in the world were those that got off the Ark! They had the whole world to live in, and it was a mess!"

"That's correct, Son," said Jim. "And while Israel was in Egypt as slaves for four hundred years, I'm sure they imagined how nice it must have been in Eden, too! Then Moses came along and described Canaan as a land flowing with milk and honey, a place where every man would have his own fig tree and vineyard, and that God was going to give it to them! Think of how excited they must have been."

"From slavery to paradise, I'm sure," said Laura. "Like suddenly becoming millionaires!"

Jim went on, "Then after living in Canaan more than five hundred years, Isaiah, Zechariah and other prophets pricked their imagination with promises of future generations enjoying the kind of life we have now with the Cube above us."

"We're getting in on the very best of conditions since the Garden of Eden, then, aren't we Dad?" asked Scott.

"Right. But these wonderful things we see now had died out in the minds of certain Bible scholars. Because as time dragged on, the very idea of a world-wide peace among animals and people was too good to be true and became labeled by doubters and skeptics as myths and wishful thinking. Now the New Jerusalem has changed all that and brought a fulfillment as near as it could be without Jesus, the Prince of Peace, ruling from earthly Jerusalem. Everywhere people look, their hearts can only smile."

∞

33

AMERICA, THE MODEL

D uring the next two years more facts and reports about the worldwide consequences of the New Jerusalem were collected by the Cubicles. The benefits were so numerous it was staggering. Of special interest was the function of governments around the world. The Cubicles realized that one purpose for the Cube's coming was to bring about change in governments and cause them to serve the good of the people in each country. They wanted to know how the nations had responded to that purpose. They believed that America was chosen to become the pattern for all nations to follow and that all Christians—and especially the Cubicles—were personally chosen by the Lord to help America achieve that pattern. Jim reminded his students that they were part of that plan as well.

Holy God was using His miraculous powers to reveal Himself to His world, driving nations to the Word of God for instruction. He loved the world and without violating their freedom of choice, He contrasted His love with the wicked practices of nations toward their citizens. Conviction reminded them of their failure. The moral teachings of Jesus formed the essential base necessary to infuse righteousness into governmental policies. As Israel of old, though, people and leaders, alike, had rationalized, thinking *they deserved* the blessings they enjoyed.

America's government had clearly taken a giant step in submitting to the will of God as best it knew how from his Word. The seminars held in Washington and the distribution of their content on DVDs had caused Congress to reign in much of their gross waste and the interference of government into the liberty and affairs of private citizens. Security became primary to all else, and righteousness had now become the goal of the justice system. Proper respect for the true God of all Creation had basically been restored. Only the presence of the Cube could have made these matters a reality. Without it, the country would've surely been ruined. It was doubtful that any other nation in the world could match America's serious endeavor to please the Father. It was astounding that God had brought about such a reversal of the path the nation was on before the Cube's arrival.

Because of the sins and disrespect of God and His Word, the United States had become trillions of dollars in debt, and Christian America was borrowing money from atheistic China![92] America was being infiltrated, threatened, and terrorized by confessed enemies, who worshiped a false god.[93] Other nations were providing arms to North Korea and Iran who declared themselves aggressors and America had many adversaries. Rather than praying and working for the peace of Jerusalem,[94]America's administration was pulling away from and jeopardizing Israel, one of its closest allies. It had long neglected its own God-given resources and purchased oil from countries which had made gold their god, funding their way of life while at the same time reducing its own liberty. Its educational institutions had removed God

[92]   Deuteronomy 15:6; 28:12
[93]   1 Kings 11:14-16; 23-26
[94]   Psalm 122:6-8

from their premises and curriculum, replacing it with empty, godless philosophies. Its government was convinced that more money and taxes would fix every problem—leaving God out of the solution. The majority of its manufacturers were closing down because its people preferred purchasing almost everything from other countries even if it were inferior in quality, at a lower cost—thus pricing itself out of liberty and becoming dependent of those who knew not God.

Morality was at an all-time low, shocking even the heathen, making it a mockery to those who rejected America's God.[95] America was founded upon the Word of the true God of Creation by its Founding Fathers, but this generation had refused to give Him credit,[96] being ashamed to use His name, because it might offend someone. Thus it had joined those who turned their backs upon the only Savior and Redeemer of mankind. It had refused to populate and replenish[97] the Earth as God commanded, choosing rather to destroy unborn babies and practice parenthood prevention, so He sent immigrants who would populate it, but whose loyalty was not to America or to America's God. Rather than have children, love them, and trust God to take care of them, it claimed it couldn't afford them. And the poor continued to increase because America was ignorant of its cause—the failure to obey the Lord's commandments as a nation.[98]

America had existed long enough to see excuses for every form of disobedience to the revealed will of God. His removal of the devil and his demons accounted for the elimination of much of the abominations on Earth. For America to turn away from its sinful practices and mindset of rebellion against God was absolutely miraculous.

---

95   Deuteronomy 29:24-25
96   John 12:43
97   Genesis 1:28; 9:1
98   Deut. 15:4-5

The Cube was definitely God's last opportunity for America to repent and receive His blessings again. He restored to leadership those who hate bribery and were committed to fight against every encroachment against the Constitution, and the right to life, liberty, and the pursuit of happiness. Elected officials were now making laws for the good of the people without respect of persons. God had spared the nation from being scattered as Israel had been, chastised, enslaved, ridiculed, and destitute.

It was fortunate that America rejected those false leaders who felt they were smarter than the wisdom of God, more humble than the Founding Fathers, and who shunned the clear freedoms secured by the Founding Documents. America's present leadership saw clearly beyond the radical environmentalists who were attached to their god, "mother earth." They knew the Earth was to be used with the best of common sense as well as the divine wisdom. They also knew that this Earth was destined to be destroyed with fire by the Creator, followed by the creation of a new Heaven and a new Earth.[99]

Of course, the early New Testament churches didn't change nations through their governments, but by individual conversions and living the life of true believers. But the United States was unique—being founded on the Bible. So by living out His bountiful blessings of liberty as Christians this nation would again impact the world to the glory of God, just as it had done it in the past with their freedoms, prosperity, and advances in all areas of endeavor. It would no longer be ashamed of Christ.

Israel's failure, predicted by the Lord through Moses[100] and played out in their history, captivity, and eventual scattering throughout the world, was America's 'example' *not* to follow.[101] Yet America had been

---

[99]   2 Peter 3:10-13
[100]   Deuteronomy 28:15-29:28
[101]   1 Corinthians 10:11

hard on their heels without looking back. It awakened and returned to
its assignment—to be the salt that preserves the nation and a light to
the world of Jews and Gentiles through the Gospel of Christ, to enforce
the Constitution, and to be an example of New Testament teachings in
all political affairs. The end was near, but not so near that God wouldn't
send the Cube to give America and the rest of the world one more season
to repent. He still wanted more souls to be saved before Judgment Day.

Muslim nations had adjusted their positions dramatically because of
the overwhelming freedom through prosperity everyone was experiencing.
The removal of the Curse from the Earth had resulted in such peace,
travel, and interpersonal contact with other nations, they could tell who
God was blessing and who was lagging behind. Rigid Islamic social laws
required such undesirable limitations upon the masses that the people
put pressure on their leaders. And since all governments were ordained
by God, they were subject to his scrutiny. It was clear that God held
all political leadership to a close account in every country. Where there
was abuse of power, the divine discipline that followed was always too
conspicuous and ironic for them to miss. In Iran, North Korea, and
Saudi Arabia, there had been numerous accounts where unjust laws
were carried out and those in charge met with quick misfortune, if not
supernatural disaster. The fear of the Lord had taken up residence in all
systems of authority. Some were asking for Bibles so they could learn the
ways of the Lord.

Communist nations, such as China, North Korea, Cuba, and other
dictatorships learned that human life, created in God's image, couldn't
be treated as things. Policies such as limiting families to one child had
been overturned. There was plenty of food, shelter, and necessities for
all. The false ideology of socialism was covered up and replaced with a
freedom unknown before. Though many municipal policies were clearly
the result of "conformity and convenience," it was still a fact that liberty

was experienced in those nations, and a large number of their citizens were coming to Christ for salvation.

Nigeria was a country known largely for its bribery, but leaders had been continually rebuked by their own people for not giving God his rightful place in everyday business. They learned that honesty paid off best. Instead of looking at others as an opportunity for scams, they faced the fact that working for their wages and wholesome morality made more sense than stealing, threats, and deceit. God didn't require a specific kind of government—but He did insist on the just treatment of the unfortunate, righteous laws, honest business practices, and mercy.

Pride continued to cloud out the truth. And what Jesus said was still true about the end—only a few would find the Way of life.[102]

India's government, as well as other Hindu and Buddhist countries, had merely adjusted to the demands of their people. Some had become believers in Christ, but the bulk of the people had only added Almighty God to their list of other gods. They felt they deserved the blessings God had given and were only giving Him a little of the glory He deserved.

While political leaders in some nations had embraced the Gospel and Christianity, most appeared to only endure the changes they felt were required by society and the world in general. It was remindful of the Philistines, who captured the Ark of the Covenant from Israel.[103] God's Ark overpowered their own idol god, and he sent rats and tumors throughout their territories. What did they do? Did they exchange their defeated god for the real One? No! They just returned the Ark to Israel and went on worshiping the same false god they had—knowing better. The same thing happened in Egypt when the Lord sent ten plagues that defeated all the idols and false gods of Egypt. So what did they do after

---

[102]   Matthew 7:13-14
[103]   1 Samuel 5-6

Israel was gone? Change their hearts and embrace the true God? No. They let Israel go and returned to their idolatry—without excuse. There were many examples of these things happening in other countries where governments merely placated God with words, while despising Him in their hearts.[104]

There was a renewed interest in the Nation of Israel, the Jews, their place in the world now, and what it would be later. The Cube was, after all, the one Abraham looked for, ". . . He looked for a city that had foundations, whose architect and builder was God."[105] The Old Testament saints with Abraham's faith had to view these invisible things from afar, but today Christians were seeing them through their telescopes! And eventually, they will enjoy the Kingdom together forever.[106]

The Lord called Israel, instructed her, and used her. The Church began with Jews, and after all, Jesus was still a Jew. They were God's chosen nation. But they'd been temporarily cut off from their Olive Tree. During the present time, the Temple had been destroyed. The place of sacrifices couldn't be used. The one central place of worship couldn't be totally under their control. They were truly without a king, a prince, a sacrifice, an image, an Ephod, and teraphim.[107] The Lord prevented them from possessing the Temple site. But there was a great future for those who survived the Tribulation when they would see him whom they had pierced.[108]

During the international conference held in Midland, Texas, national administrators were told to get godly leaders. Early in its history, Israel

---

[104]   Matthew 15:8; Isaiah 29:13
[105]   Hebrews 11:10-16
[106]   Hebrews 11:39-40
[107]   Hosea 3:4 Images in human form
[108]   Revelation 1:7

was given strict instructions concerning the kings they would choose.[109] America's Founding Fathers used the same requirements as a pattern, and said that the people should always choose Christians for their leaders.[110] In time, God charged Israel with the crime of choosing kings and princes against his will.[111] God's priorities were obvious in his Word. For example, instead of voting on someone with primarily a 'save the environment' theme or other issue, they should examine the moral fiber of each candidate in the light of righteous living. It would be difficult for some foreign nations to insist on godly character, but there was no better time than now to begin bringing it to the attention of both people and their potential officials.

∞

---

[109] Deuteronomy 17:14-20

[110] "Providence has given to our people the choice of their rulers, and it is the duty, as well as the privilege and interest, of a Christian nation to select and prefer Christians for their rulers."—John Jay, Attorney, public official, diplomat, member of the Continental Congress and president of Congress, Chief-Justice of New York, and appointed first Chief-Justice of the US. Supreme Court by President George Washington.

[111] Hosea 8:4

34

And Now . . .

I
t was late as Jim worked overtime at the observatory and Laura had just laid down to go to sleep. An unusual feeling came upon her suddenly—as if something strange was going to happen. Words began to roll through her mind. They were familiar words; they sounded like Scripture. She allowed them to flow for a while, then, thought, *I'd better get up and write this down or I'll not be able to remember it.*

Be not afraid; do not be dismayed; the things that happen will be for your good; I will rescue you.

The hands that reach out and touch you will be My hands. The eye that will guide you will be My eye. Never fear, you are greatly loved.

There seemed to be more words than this. *But were they different words or was there a repetition of the same ones?* She couldn't tell, nor remember any others. She asked herself, *What's this mean? What's going to happen?* She should have been frightened, but He had told her not to be afraid. Finally she was able to fall asleep. Jim was bewildered about it when she told him. At first he was extremely upset, wondering if something terrible might happen like losing Laura or one of the children. They prayed for safety, but couldn't actually feel fear. The Lord would have to show them what it was all about later. He had promised to deliver them.

Three and a half years after the coming of the Cube, the world had adjusted to the changes that were mandated upon them. Every country had become a paradise of peace and safety. Incredible influence from the Holy Cube had affected behavior and society in a powerful and positive way. Jim and his family were on the patio taking it easy, talking about issues of life and how God was controlling His world. The boys were sharing their experiences and knowledge, too.

"It's nothing but miraculous that God has brought about all these thorough changes throughout the world so quickly," said Laura. "Even though He hasn't forced anyone on Earth to believe in Him, they can't escape the truth of His presence and power."

"You're so right honey," replied Jim. "It's surprising that the Lord would do something so astounding as to send the New Jerusalem to Earth and bring about all these fantastic changes to benefit the whole world. He's truly blessed the world."

"He's *the* good God. That's what He wanted them to know," Laura replied.

"Well, he's done an astounding job of it! Of course, he doesn't know how to do anything but the best." Jim laughed. "Everyone should know something about what eternity will be like when this life is over!"

"What a lesson of power. Just think of how he overcame evil, war, disease, and cured everything in nature!" Laura remarked.

"And He did it without even having to come to Earth and be a human king or anything. And He didn't even fire a shot!" said Scott.

"Yeah, He did it by camping out about 21,500 miles away in His glorious home and puttin' the influence of holiness on it!" Keith asserted.

Everyone smiled and entered into the fray. "He didn't even have to pass any laws," said Jim.

"He didn't hold court in any country," said Scott.

"He didn't even consult the Supreme Court to see if it would be all right," said Jim.

"He didn't raise an army to overthrow any government," said Laura.

"He didn't even send twelve thousand angels to enforce or supervise the change," Keith blabbed.

"He hasn't even *said* anything," Jim reminded them as he rolled his eyes.

The whole family was laughing and throwing new thoughts at each other about the blessedness of their Lord, Savior, and reigning King.

"How long will it last?" asked Scott.

"Ouch" Jim winched. "That sort of brings us down to a very good inquiry," as he kept smiling. "That's the unknown, my precious boy. Surely not a thousand years. That will come later when Jesus physically comes to the Earth and sits on the Throne of David in Jerusalem and actually does rule the world with His rod of iron. I don't know how long the Cube will remain. But long enough to get His truth across to the nations. Long enough to let the message stick in the ears of the world that He loves them and can save even the worst of sinners, if they will come to Jesus and trust Him."

"Then what, Dad?" asked Keith.

"Well, then, the Cube will go back to Heaven and wait on the time when Jesus returns to Earth for a thousand years. After that, He'll create new Heavens and a new Earth, and the City of God will come again to remain in its chosen place forever. And *weee*," pointing to each of them, "will be exploring it, walking the street of gold, and eating the fruit of the Tree of Life that grows by the River of Life. Best of all, we'll all be there together with our blessed Lord Jesus."

"Meanwhile, let's grab some dessert and get that game of croquet going," Laura smiled. "What a time to be alive!"

"I want the blue set," Scott declared.

*   *   *

It was an especially dark night with no moonlight in the sky, three and a half years after the Cube arrived. Marcus had been working late and taking one last look at the New Jerusalem before he left for home. The heavenly City was so spectacular that it was always difficult to stop looking at it. He felt he could just live with his eyes fixed on the beauty of the Cube and his imagination running wild with spiritual thoughts and a longing to see the Light of the City, Jesus.

But this time, he noticed that the telescope wasn't adjusted at the same spot it was when he last looked. He checked the computer to see if someone had interrupted the tracking mechanism. It was still working. He looked again, and was jarred to realize that the City had moved! A rush of adrenalin raced through his body, preparing him for total emergency! His eyes were wide with fear. His mind was pressing to assimilate the information and make sense out of it. *No, it couldn't be!* he thought. *It's moving! Is it leaving?*

His next thought was to quickly call Jim and let him know something was happening. But then, he was afraid if he left the telescope the City might take off, and he wouldn't get to see it depart. "Would it disappear all at once? Would it slowly lift off and let us watch?" he thought. He kept his eyes glued on it for a few minutes. Then with panic, decided to call Jim.

He shouted to the co-workers at the observatory, "Harry, Don, Doris, come quickly. The Cube is leaving! Look and keep watching it while I call Jim!"

It was three o'clock in the morning when the phone awakened the Walthams. "Jim, the New Jerusalem is moving. I believe it's departing. I don't know how long it'll be 'til it disappears."

The news hit Jim like a ton of bricks in the middle of the night. He was able to utter, "Keep an eye on it. I'll be there as fast as I can!"

Jim hastily dressed, blazed a hot trail to the LT, and noted that Marcus and the other workers had been weeping. He was so frustrated and determined to get there before it went out of sight that he hadn't had time to give in to his emotions. Sure enough, they were all able to watch it for the next two hours before dawn became mixed with distance, and it was no more. After a few minutes, Jim was finally able to relax. He'd been so tense that his arms and legs didn't want to work properly. The staff had to just sit there for a while and *think* before anyone even wanted to speak.

"Prepare an announcement," Jim said quietly. "Word it any way you can, and let me read it before sending it. This is something we all knew and expected would come someday. It just happened before we were ready. But I'm sure we never would've been ready, humanly speaking."

The staff at the LT took their time and worded the announcement as carefully as possible before submitting it for Jim's approval. It was sent as a memo by email to news sources as well as to the Cubicles. Others were notified by phone and fax. Jim wasn't looking forward to the response he knew there would be. The discouraging day dragged on as he spoke to several friends and fellow workers. He was ready for home long before the time came.

But the repercussions were more enormous than he anticipated.

The believing world was saddened to know that the Cube had left. But there were others who felt relieved. Publications followed the notification, along with many mocking headlines: "Square Disappears," "Time Runs Out For Cube," "No More Mr. Nice Guy," "Heavenly Phenomenon Heads Back North," "Earth Relieved of Invasion," "Let's Get Back to Normal," and "The Heat Is Off."

Channel 43 TV newscaster, Bernard Tovey, was speaking: "This is a great day for all of us. The confusion has been removed. We no longer have to guess about who's in charge. We have our elected officials and we can change them if we so desire. And we're so glad to have in our studios today, Reverend Doctor Theodore Lanier, Dean at Mt. Clemens Seminary. What's your take on the situation Reverend?"

As I've said all along, all these changes that have taken place over the past three years—they've been beneficial—but they've limited the personal freedoms and rights which all of us have as humans. It's about time we were able to exercise our civil rights like we used to. It took us many years to attain the position of true equality in America, and now it's time for the whole country to take full advantage of it."

"They say the Cube will return someday and that a reckoning will be faced," Tovey commented.

"Not on my watch!" Lanier arrogantly replied.

Angry, wicked, selfish crowds waved their fists and said, "Good riddance, get out of here, and don't come back!" "We don't want you telling us what to do."[112] Then they smiled at each other saying, "Let's get back to living our way."

While some reveled in the removal of the City of Gold, a large part of the world was confused about it, and the world-wide community of believers was saddened. Jim Waltham said, "The powerful influence

---

[112] Luke 19:14

of holiness was seriously felt by us while the Cube was here, but we've not lost the Holy Spirit who lives in our human spirits. He's still God. He's still revealing Christ to us. He'll still be the source of all that we need for the days ahead. Godly followers of the Lamb shouldn't be discouraged."

Evil rulers pulled out their files that contained old plans and plots against their own people as well as other nations, with a twinkle in their eyes. Slowly but surely, wickedness began to raise its ugly head. The flesh nature felt bold enough to drag people back down to the dregs of life they were in before the Cube came along. Crime came back in spurts. Ethnic groups retreated back to their former prejudices. Families, schools, local organizations, and even nations began to bicker and criticize each other. Pride climbed back on its throne. Covetousness and greed took another grip on souls, and sooner than anyone would've expected the peaceful world became a war zone. Communication became a barrier too, as all languages returned to their former state at Babel.

Even Margaret Thames announced, "Most likely the asteroid that paused over the Earth for a while went on about its business, as Christians capitalized upon its unusual behavior to brainwash multitudes with their own fundamental, judgmental, demands upon others, and now want to impose their own mental conclusions about the Cube and its departure."

Three months later, a woman named Marjorie Owens was diagnosed with cancer—the first such case since the day the Cube left.

Jim was surprised to receive a phone call from Yeats Roberts, trustee at Quad University. "Dr. Waltham, I know you've been vocal in praise concerning the Cube while it was here. But I have a question I'd like to ask you. If God is real and so good, why would he take the Cube away and allow the world to suffer the way it did in the past and likely repeat the evils we know again, such as cancer and other diseases, violence and war, injustice and hatred?"

"Well, Mr. Roberts, "I'm almost reluctant to answer such an obvious question with the bald truth, but don't you think it's because the world is full of people who don't appreciate Him and what He has done? Hasn't He given you and the world a taste of what He wants for everyone to enjoy forever? And it will be given again forever to those who love Him and want to return their gratitude for all His blessings—especially for the love He had for us all when He suffered and died on the Cross for the sins of the world. Strange as it may seem, He has blessed the entire world for three and a half years, while at the same time he was angry with the wicked every day.[113] And our wonderful God will continue to allow people to live—giving them the opportunity to turn away from selfishness and trust themselves to His care. But then, final judgment will come and the entire world will give account of their lives and rejection of His authority. So these blessings won't be for those who don't need Him or honor Him, don't want Him or believe in Him. Is that simple enough, Mr. Roberts?"

"Well, I just think He ought to be good to all of us, if He created us."

"Isn't He good to you, Mr. Roberts? Is there something that you need that you don't have? You know—food, water, housing, clothing, transportation, education, affluent lifestyle, prestige?"

"Yes, I have those, but what about the others who don't have all these?"

"Mr. Roberts, you won't be answering for them at the final judgment. You'll only have to answer for the way you personally have treated Him and them in this life. They'll have to give account for the blessings God gave them too, and what they did about it. As you have confessed that

---

[113]   Psalm 7:11

God has given you quite a number of benefits, are you going to show that you understand they came from Him and that you are a good steward of what you have received—whether much or little? And will you tell that to others and worship Him?"

"You're getting a little ahead or away from my first question, Dr. Waltham."

"Am I? You asked why. Now you know. Is that a satisfying answer? In other words, *if* God weren't good, why would He have provided these blessings for the whole world when they don't deserve them or even acknowledge Him or even care about Him? If He weren't good, would He die for people who don't even give Him recognition for such a sacrifice? Would He offer forgiveness and Heaven for them if He weren't good?"

"Well, you are looking at it from a different point of view."

"Mr. Roberts, you are exactly right. But now you see it from God's point of view, don't you?" Jim said.

"Uh, it's been nice talking to you Dr. Waltham. Thank you and have a good day."

"And may God bless you too, Mr. Roberts," Jim replied.

*   *   *

The Walthams had invited several guests to their home for a time of fellowship and encouragement now that the Cube was gone. Around the outside table and chairs near the barbeque pit, it was easy to sit back and talk casually about what was on everyone's mind.

"I hate to think of what the world will come to," said a guest. "Remember what it was like before the Cube came? That was unbearable!"

"Yes," another said, "I just wonder how long it'll take for it to get that bad again."

Rex replied, "Probably happen sooner than we think. After all the flesh nature never changes. It can be 'unplugged' by faith, and restrained by the law, but when it's in control again, it takes up right where it left off."

"I guess the Curse placed on the Earth after Adam's sin has already been reinstated?" Jim commented to Rex.

"No doubt. So we can expect everything to be affected just as it was before—illnesses, thorns and thistles, earthquakes, storms, and other catastrophes of nature, wars, and so forth. I wouldn't be surprised if the dictators of the world are already talking against their neighbors and taking their war weapons out of mothballs. He took a deep sigh. Good night! I hadn't thought about the return to the past. This means the devil and his demons will be at it again!"

"Oh, no! That's not good," said Marcus.

"Well, what are we going to do?" said Rex. "We're simply going to put on the whole armor of God, be strong, and resist the devil.[114] We're going to love the lost and give them the opportunity to be saved. Evil will still be around to test our loyalty, love, and gratitude when it's so easy to simply enjoy selfish pursuits. We'll need each other for encouragement and support. And we'll need to rest in the peace God's given and fight the good fight of faith."

"You know," said Jim, "there's another thing that's surprising. Dr. Harris and some of the faculty members at Quad U have managed to hold on to their positions and still haven't been saved. They just sort of melted into the woodwork and still teach the same old lies as before."

---

[114] Ephesians 6:11

"Yes," Rex stated, "Unbelievers don't just drop off the Earth. God keeps giving them many years of peace and plenty. They'll have nothing to blame God for at their final judgment."

"It's that old saying, 'some things never change,'" said Marcus.

"Dad, will the animals get wild again like they were?" asked Keith.

"That's a good question, Keith. I'm sure they will in due time. It'll probably happen little by little as it did after Noah's Flood, and the food becomes scarce."

Laura spoke up, "Jim, do you think . . ."

"What?"

She looked at Scottie with her eyes wide.

"Not a chance! Whatever God does He does forever. His healing is a gift just like salvation. No, darling, don't you worry about that! Praise God!"

Cindy said, "People all over the world have always wondered what it would take to make things right. Now we know . . . God!"

"Oh, now I know!" said Laura.

"Know what?" Jim said.

"That dream. The one I had a few months ago, when the Lord said not to fear! It was to prepare us for the departure of the Cube! He wanted to comfort us for this very time. I have it memorized.

Be not afraid, don't be dismayed, the things that happen will be for your good. I'll rescue you.

The hands that reach out and touch you will be My hands. The eye that will guide you will be My eye. Never fear, you are greatly loved.

"Amazing," said Marcus.

"What a blessing," remarked a Cubicle.

"That's so precious," agreed another Cubicle.

"It's all going to be all right," Laura affirmed. "The future will turn out for our good and God will rescue us from evil. He'll direct us. One day his will shall be done perfectly on Earth as it is in Heaven. Until then, we have to live in an imperfect world where people are wronged every day, where lives are lost over selfish ambition, where pride is leading souls to an eternal fire. As believers we have the job of living by faith without being perfect at it! It'll be a bumpy ride until God's time arrives. Meanwhile, He's with us and wants our companionship. And we are absolutely loved!"

The whole crowd seemed to need a time of silence after that.

"I'm just thinking out loud," said Rex. "It's clear to me that the Cube definitely accomplished its mission. God's holiness has been exalted, nations have adjusted their purpose and agenda accordingly, and America has rebounded to what God wanted her to be. The whole world has experienced a taste of what the loving God desires for all mankind. And when you consider the Cube, it seems to parallel Jesus' first coming to the Earth. His ministry lasted three and a half years, just like the duration of the Cube here. We saw it. We know about it. We're eyewitnesses and can testify to it. And like Christ, it's going to come again. Jesus came to preach the Kingdom of God, and we're sent by God to tell the world about Christ and His Kingdom. The past three and a half years were like His ministry among His disciples all over again. Only instead of Jesus being here in a physical body, we've searched the entire Scriptures for His teachings and His will. After He ascended His disciples were to tell the story. Now, we know firsthand what the Kingdom is like, physically as well as spiritually. Isn't that an amazing likeness?"

"Wow, that's too good to be accidental. The Lord had to have planned it that way," said Marcus. "We're in the same kind of situation the early disciples were in after the resurrection and ascension!"

"It's His love story again," said Laura. "I just remembered a prayer that my neighbor, Phyllis, prayed after she got saved. It was so beautiful for a new Christian to say that I couldn't get it out of my mind. It went something like this,

'God, I'm so at peace. I feel like a tired person who's been placed in a soft bed. I wish the whole world could be this way. How will the people out there ever know? I wish you'd do something so that everyone could get to know how good you are. Amen.'

"Isn't that something? God answered her prayer when He came down in the New Jerusalem and blessed everyone. The entire world has received something so special they're without excuse if they think God's not good to them."

"To connect the Cube with the Resurrection and Great Commission to go into all the world and spread the Gospel is the most penetrating news I've ever thought about," said Cindy. "We are so blessed!"

"And there's one more final thing we can look forward to," Rex added. "Jesus made a promise to the church at Philadelphia, as well as to all overcomers, that He would write upon us the name of God "and the name of the City of God, which is the New Jerusalem!"[115] Evidently, that blessed City will be *our identity*, our 'home base,' or *address* as we serve the Lord throughout the universe forever. Even all future created beings will know we're part of those who've been redeemed by the blood of the Lamb. And until then, everything's going to be all right. After all, as Jim says, 'We're built for trouble.'"

The End

---

[115] Revelation 3:12

ADDENDUM

---

a. CUBE Time Line

Jim, & Laura both graduate	22 yrs. old, from college, marry
Both become Christians	24 yrs. old
Laura has a job + 3 yrs.	25 ""
	25 Keith born
Jim graduates Ph.D + 2 yrs.	27 Scott born
Jim Joins faculty of Lyle U	27 yrs. old
Jim teaches at Lyle U + 6 yrs.	31 Keith 6, Scott 4
Jim takes two new jobs + 2 yrs.	33 Keith 8, Scott 6
Jim has been working at new jobs	41 for 8 yrs.
Coming of CUBE	41 Keith 17, Scott 15
CUBE present 3 ½ yrs.	44 Keith 20, Scott 18

b. All Characters as they appear in the story:

Marcus Loshan—associate to Jim; American history buff
Jim Waltham—astronomer
Rex Fleming—Pastor, Skyview Church, Odessa, TX
Brother Shannon—member of Skyview Church

Cubicles—large group of scholars, Bible students, and prayer warriors

Judy Carter—secretary at the Lippershey Observatory Telescope

Laura (Drake) Waltham—Jim's wife, mother of Keith & Scott

Keith—son of Jim and Laura

Scott—son of Jim and Laura

Martha—Jim's mother-in-law

Joseph Markle—American Atheistic Society

Emma Van Dosler—Head of Psychology, Berkley University

David Harris—Head of Dept. of Astronomy at Quad State Univ.

Thomas Fain—Chairman of Quad U. Trustees

Carl Eckert—Quad trustee

Oscar Huckelby—Quad trustee

Yeats Roberts—Quad trustee

Cindy—wife of Marcus Loshan

Doug Ingram—Quad U. Trustee—on Jim's side

Brian Sanders—ABC anchor man

Richard Millikan—physicist, scientist, Univ. of TX

Wesley Lansbury—author, psychologist, Univ. of Richmond, VA.

Victor Malory—philosophy professor at Quad Univ.

Gary Blankenship—student

Helen Goodrich—Senator from NY

Dr. Philip Emmett—of St. Stephens Theological Seminary

Dr. Bridget McMillan,—journalist, Public Broadcasting Association

Aunt Clara—Jim's aunt

Zeke—Jim's cousin, son of Uncle Tue

Anthony Cagney—staff member at STSA who doubted the reality of the Cube

Samuel Stone—Pastor, Faith Church on the Rock

Ralph—student

Lawrence Taylor—Secretary of Defense

Alvin Lawndale, Chairman of Joint Chiefs of Staff, at the Pentagon

Jeanine Huntington—Congress woman

Phyllis Coe—neighbor to the Walthams

Trudy Walker—secretary of the President of the USA

Kenneth Snow—President of the United States of America

Jesse Wheeler—Vice President of the USA

Herman Jennings—congressman

Asa—four year old son of Marcus & Cindy

Kristin—nine year old daughter of Marcus and Cindy

Earl Wilson—CEO of Objects In Space

Claude Moriau—Pastor of Ohio's largest mega church

George Riddle—acquaintance in hospital—amateur astronomer

Margaret Thames—TV reporter at enmity with Jim

Jeremy Green—amateur astronomer—Calif. Explained lost people couldn't see the Cube

Claudia Webster—writer and photographer for National Geographic Society

Charlie—comment on bad content of movies

Mr. Branson—owner of Maxim Computer Corporation.

Mary & Bill—changed their bad language habits

Leonard Sims—board member of STSA

Molly Sims—wife of Leonard

Bruce Coulter—STSA board member

Larry Atwood—board Chairman of STSA

Nathan Amelang—expert on American History, author of *Christianity and the Civil Institutions of Government*

Roland Mayfield—noted Bible scholar, author of *God Is Ready, Israel*

Emile Pendingdorf—attorney for ACLU

Robert Hackney—attorney and attendee of President's conference

Alfred Dunstan—billionaire atheist

Archie Fain—President of Southwest Astronomy University

Russell Salisbury—Faculty member of Quad U, attempted murderer of Jim

Duran Koyambounou—United Nations President

Sayyed Abdulla—Hamas leader

Dr. Jeffery Maxwell—medical scientist

Bernard Tovey—Channel 43 TV newscaster

Theodore Lanier—of Mt. Clemens Seminary

Other Characters—name only, who have no speaking part

Jay Smith—first to site and report the location of the Cube

Sammy Whitfield—Los Alamos Natl. Lab, New Mexico

William Parker—Head of NASA

Dr. Davenport—advised Jim & Laura to abort Scott

Pope Johan Martin—religious leader

William Grahamson—religious leader

Jennifer—wife of the President of the U.S.A.

Gene Rollins—photo asst.

James Davis—Jeep driver

Bev & Andrew Bradley—piano player and husband, Christmas song

Harry, Don, Doris—observatory workers when Cube departed

Marjorie Owens—first cancer patient after Cube leaves

CPSIA information can be obtained at www.ICGtesting.com
Printed in the USA
LVOW121947240912

300156LV00001B/4/P